A DICTIONARY OF CANTONESE COLLOQUIALISMS IN ENGLISH

關傑才 著

英譯廣東口語詞典

U0116538

商務印書館

英譯廣東口語詞典
A Dictionary of Cantonese Colloquialisms in English

作　　者：關傑才

責任編輯：劉秀英　黃家麗

封面設計：張　毅

出　　版：商務印書館（香港）有限公司
　　　　　香港筲箕灣耀興道 3 號東滙廣場 8 樓
　　　　　http://www.commercialpress.com.hk

發　　行：香港聯合書刊物流有限公司
　　　　　香港新界荃灣德士古道 220-248 號荃灣工業中心 16 樓

印　　刷：美雅印刷製本有限公司
　　　　　九龍觀塘榮業街 6 號海濱工業大廈 4 樓 A 室

版　　次：2024 年 4 月第 1 版第 7 次印刷
　　　　　© 2010 商務印書館（香港）有限公司
　　　　　ISBN 978 962 07 0293 8
　　　　　Printed in Hong Kong

目　錄
Contents

Reprint Note 再版説明

　　本詞典為常用廣東口頭俚語及歇後語約 2,500 條提供字面義及對照義的英語翻譯。

　　廣東俚語詞彙豐富，生動傳神，不容易用英語表達它們的意義，比如“作狀”，英語是 put on an act；“迷頭迷腦”英語是 indulge oneself in。同時，因應上下文及語氣，同一俚語的意義會有延伸變化，比如“烏卒卒”有時譯為 be entirely ignorant，有時應譯為 as black as night。也有近義的俚語，如“望天打卦”和“摩囉差拜神”，英譯都是 be left to the mercy of God。

　　由於實用性強，本書曾重印多次。由於原版出版時間較早，採用當時慣用的注音方案。為使本詞典更合今日使用，現將原版的注音系統，改為“粵語拼音方案”系統。香港語言學學會研製的“粵拼”方案易學易用，也是目前較為普及的粵語注音方案。全書經過重新排版，更方便閱讀及檢索。

商務印書館編輯部

PREFACE

It is comparatively easy to study a foreign language but it is not so to study a local dialect. This is because local dialects have their own local colours, their own traditional habits and their own pronunciations and these problems are outstanding in Cantonese dialect.

There is no doubt that Cantonese dialect derived from ancient Chinese language and so it still reserves more or less some old sayings and archaic expressions, which we can see in our famous writings, poetries, stories and legends or even fictions. In addition to this, as Canton has become one of the main passages to and from foreign countries for hundreds of years, it is natural that some loanwords have come into the dialect and thus made it rather complicate and rich with words, phrases and glossaries.

Although I am sometimes taken for a northerner or even Japanese, I am a hundred percent Cantonese born at Fatshan (Fushan) in Kwongtung province and brought up in Canton, and have taken interest in 'my mother tongue', especially the colloquial expressions each of which can convey a whole complicated thought in only a simple phrase or sentence.

I can now remember that when I worked as dean of studies for Canton YMCA Middle School, I used to have a chat with some of the foreigners who came to study Cantonese and they also used to ask me the meanings of the colloquial expressions which they occasionally heard about and which they hadn't been taught in their lessons. This kind of slangs, I daresay, still puzzle most of the younger Cantonese people of today, not to speak of foreigners.

In view of this, I began to sort out and rectify the materials I had collected for years and set my hand to the work to translate them into English in 1983. I did my best to match as many as possible with homologous English expressions. I, however, sincerely hope that your advices will be given should there be mistakes.

Kwan Kit Choi

原版序言

　　學習一種外國語較易，但學習一種地方方言則難。因地方方言有地方色彩、傳統習慣等語音問題，此等問題，在廣州話，更為顯著。

　　廣州話是由古代漢語蛻變而來，因此在日常口語中，仍保留古詞古語，所異者為音變而已。此外，廣州又為歷代對外交通通道和貿易商埠，在交接之間，滲入外來語，亦屬自然。這是廣州話詞彙複雜及豐富的原因。

　　余為廣東人，雖南人北相，但確生於禪而長於穗，且對我廣東俚語，知之不少。猶記於四十年代末，常為數來穗習粵語之外邦人士解答他們偶有所聞而從未有所學之俗諺。他們更促余擇其常要者，編成講義，藉助他們學之未逮。余對此提議，唯莞爾而卻，蓋為避嫌，免使他們教師誤會。

　　由於內地推行普通話，年青廣東人皆能講普通話，反而對於粵語俗諺，多不理解，遑論泰西外人乎。有見於粵語有其本身歷史因素，且在內在外的溝通上仍不失其效用，遂亦邯鄲學步，進行編寫。況環視書肆中，缺粵諺英譯者。乃於癸亥（一九八三年）因眼疾息景後，着手整理多年所積素材，除英譯外，並盡所知，加以普通話相應詞，使成為普通話，廣東話，英語三位一體。三年獨耕，卒底於成。

丙寅重九

關傑才序於蓼莪書齋

Usage Guide

❶ This title covers common Cantonese colloquial expressions, slangs and xiehouyu. Each entry is followed by Chinese explanation, background or origin of the slang.

❷ Each entry is provided with transliteration and literalization. The transliteration is based on "Linguistic Society of Hong Kong Cantonese Romanization Scheme" or "Jyutping". The number on the top right hand corner of the transliteration stands for the tone marks. (1,2,3,4,5,6) in Cantonese.

❸ The word-for-word translation is given after the literalization. Often more than one English equivalents and paraphrases are given in order to help learners understand the meaning of the colloquial expressions better by comparison. If no English equivalent is available for a particular expression, a phrase of similar meaning is given instead.

❹ In Cantonese, a number of words merely have sounds but no written forms. Or sometimes the standard written form is no longer in use and only the non-standard form survives. Therefore, a number of entries are given non-standard forms or words which sound alike. If the standard form is commonly used, the non-standard form is followed by 〈 〉, indicating the word within the brackets is a standard form. Take 鬼鼠 as an example, the 鼠 sounds like the word 祟. If there were two sounds for one word, the slash is used to indicate the alternative. Take 眼大睇過籠 as an example, an alternative for籠 is界 and thus this expression is presented as眼大睇過籠/界.

❺ This title is organized according to the number of strokes. To look up a word or an expression, find out the number of strokes of the first character and then the starting stroke: " 一 " (Examples are 木、扭、去、平)，" 丶 " (Examples are 江、羊、安、放、高)，" 丿 " (Examples are 手、

今、年、多)，" 丨 "(Examples are 睇、喑、口、量、臨、過)，
" 𠃌 "(Examples are 陪、蛋、也、門、發)" ㄴ "(Examples are 將、嫌、縮、收). Take 冤 as an example, look up the total number of strokes in the Index, which is ten strokes, and then find out the starting stroke, which is " 、 ". Thus, the reference number of 冤 is 1195.

❻ There are no standard written forms for some Cantonese slangs. For example, in 刁眼角, 刁 is sometimes replaced with 丟. The number of strokes and the starting stroke of 刁 and 丟 are different. But this title provides the reader with a pinyin index. The reader can look up "diu" where both 刁 and 丟 can be found.

The symbols used in this title:

Symbols	Meaning of symbols
/	The characters or expressions before the slash can be used as alternatives.
〈 〉	The character within 〈 〉 is the standard form.
[ ]	The character within [ ] can be done without.
「 」	The character within " 「 」 "has the same sound with the captioned.
( )	The character within ( ) adds supplementary information.
〔 〕	The content within 〔 〕 is explanation.
____	The words after —— is the second part of the colloquial expression or xiehouyu.

使用説明

❶ 本書只收廣東人日常口頭俚語及歇後語。每條條目有中文解釋，有時補充該俚語的來源或背景，並有互相參照。

❷ 每條條目均用音譯、直譯及對譯。音譯以 translit.（transliteration）標明，直譯以 lit.（literalization）標明。粵語拼音是根據"香港語言學學會粵語拼音方案"或簡稱"粵拼"。在拼音右上角的數字為調號（1，2，3，4，5，6）。1 代表高平（包括高入）；2 代表高上；3 代表高去（包括中入）；4 代表低平；5代表低上；6 代表低去（包括低入）。

❸ 在音譯之後附直譯，直譯按字面義譯出，後跟英語對應詞或同義詞。為讓讀者從比較之中掌握俚語，一般給出兩個或以上英語對應詞。若在英語中沒有恰當的對應詞，則盡量貼近原意譯出。

❹ 廣東話不少是有音無字，或有字有音而該字早已廢棄。因此，每條條目所用的字，皆為俗字或近音字。如果有正字，則在俗字後以〈 〉符號一併列出，表示〈 〉內的字為正字。如鬼鼠的鼠字，實為祟字的粵音，故條目寫成鬼鼠〈祟〉。又如遇一音兩字時，則以 / 符號表示"或者"的意思，如眼大睇過籠 / 界。

❺ 本書有兩種查閱方法。筆畫查閱是先根據條目的首字的筆畫數目，然後再根據該首字的起筆在索引中按次翻查。起筆次序為"一"起（如木、扭、去、平）、"、"起（如江、羊、安、放、高）、"丿"起（如手、今、年、多）、"丨"起（如睇、嗌、口、量、臨、過）"㇆"起（如陪、蛋、也、門、發）、"乚"起（如將、嫌、縮、收）。

❻ 不少廣東俚語沒有正統寫法，如"刁眼角"的"刁"字，有人寫"刁"或"丟"，兩字不但筆畫不同，起筆也不同。因此，本書又提供首字拼音索引（一般用英文拼音）。例如"刁"和"丟"的拼音都是 diu，按字母次序翻查，即可查出。

本書所用符號：

符號	符號含義
/	表示或者。即 / 前後的字或句子都可以替換使用。
〈 〉	表示該符號內的字為正字。
[ ]	表示該符號內的字可有可無。
「 」	表示該符號內的字為諧音字。
( )	表示該符號內的字為解釋或補充。
〔 〕	表示注釋
——	表示該符號後面的字或句為前句的歇後語。

Cantonese Romanization Scheme
粵語拼音方案簡介

1. On sets 聲母

b（巴）	p（怕）	m（媽）	f（花）	
d（打）	t（他）	n（那）		l（啦）
g（家）	k（卡）	ng（牙）	h（蝦）	
gw（瓜）	kw（誇）			w（蛙）
z（渣）	c（叉）		s（沙）	j（也）

2. Nuclei 韻腹

aa（沙）	i（詩／星／識）	u（夫／風／福）	e（些／四）	o（疏／蘇）
a（新）	yu（書）	oe（鋸）	eo（詢）	

3. Codas 韻尾

p（濕）	t（失）	k（塞）
m（心）	n（新）	ng（生）
i（西／需）	u（收）	

4. Syllabic nasals 鼻音單獨成韻

m（唔）	ng（吳）

5. Tones 字調

Tone marks 調號：

1（夫／福）	2（虎）	3（副／霍）	4（扶）	5（婦）	6（父／服）

Position of tone marks 標調位置：at the end of the syllable 放在音節後。Examples 舉例：fu¹（夫），fu²（虎），fu³（副）fu⁴（扶），fu⁵（婦），fu⁶（父）。

Credit 出處：http://www.lshk.org

一畫

0001 一人計短，二人計長

jat¹ jan⁴ gai³ dyun² , ji⁶ jan⁴ gai³ coeng⁴ *(translit.)*

One man's device is short, two men's is long. (lit.)

Two heads are better than one.

Four eyes see more than one.

📘相當 "三個臭皮匠合成一個諸葛亮"。

0002 一人做事一人當

jat¹ jan⁴ zou⁶ si⁶ jat¹ jan⁴ dong¹ *(translit.)*

A man does, a man undertakes.(lit.)

One must bear the consequences of one's own act.

0003 一人得道，雞犬升天

jat¹ jan⁴ dak¹ dou⁶, gai¹ hyun² sing¹ tin¹ *(translit.)*

When a man becomes immortal, all his hens and dogs ascend to heaven. (lit.)

When a man gets to the top, all his friends and relatives get there with him.

0004 一了百了

jat¹ liu⁵ baak³ liu⁵ *(translit.)*

One finished and a hundred also finished. (lit.)

Death pays all debts.

Do away with the main trouble and the others will end with it.

0005 一刀兩斷

jat¹ dou¹ loeng⁵ dyun⁶ *(translit.)*

One knife cuts it into two. (lit.)

Make a clean break with somebody.

Cut the connection with somebody.

Have done with somebody.

0006 一口咬定 / 實

jat¹ hau² ngaau⁵ ding⁶ / sat⁶ *(translit.)*

One bite, it is fixed. (lit.)

Speak in an assertive tone.

To insist on saying.

0007 一山不能藏二虎

jat¹ saan¹ bat¹ nang⁴ cong⁴ ji⁶ fu² *(translit.)*

A mountain cannot hide two tigers. (lit.)

At daggers drawn.

Have an exclusive attitude.

0008 一弓射兩箭

jat¹ gung¹ se⁶ loeng⁵ zin³ *(translit.)*

A bow shoots two arrows. (lit.)

Kill two birds with one stone.

📘相當於 "一箭雙雕"。

0009 一子錯，滿盤皆落索

jat¹ zi² co³, mun⁵ pun⁴ gaai¹ lok⁶ sok³ *(translit.)*

One careless move makes the whole game of chess get confused. (lit.)

One careless move loses the whole game.

A wrong step causes a masty tumble.

📘相當於 "一着不慎，滿盤皆輸"。

0010 一天光晒

jat¹ tin¹ gwong¹ saai³ *(translit.)*

The sky becomes bright. (lit.)

Be happy to see the clouds roll by.

Be happy to see the silver lining of the cloud.

注形容霧霾盡散,重見光明。參閱"守得雲開見月明"(0802)條。

0011　一五一十

jat¹ ng⁵ jat¹ sap⁶ *(translit.)*

One five and one ten. (lit.)

Go into details.

Spill one's guts.

In full detail.

注詳盡地或把自己所知的原原本本地説出來。

0012　一不做,二不休

jat¹ bat¹ zou⁶, ji⁶ bat¹ jau¹ *(translit.)*

The first doesn't do it, the second doesn't stop it. (lit.)

In for a penny, in for a pound.

As well be hanged for a sheep as for a lamb.

0013　一手一腳

jat¹ sau² jat¹ goek³ *(translit.)*

One hand and one foot. (lit.)

Go on with something all by oneself.

0014　一本萬利

jat¹ bun² maan⁶ lei⁶ *(translit.)*

One capital earns ten thousand profits. (lit.)

Gain big profits with a small capital.

注以小本獲取大利。

0015　一生兒女債,半世老婆奴

jat¹ saang¹ (sang¹) ji⁴ neoi⁵ zaai³, bun³ sai³ lou⁵ po⁴ nou⁴ *(translit.)*

The whole life is full of sons' and daughters' debts; half a life is a slave for wife. (lit.)

A man husbands his family.

A wife and children are a man's burdens.

注指男子要負起家庭重擔。

0016　一死了之

jat¹ sei² liu⁵ zi¹ *(translit.)*

A death finishes all. (lit.)

Death pays all debts.

Death quits all scores.

0017　一竹篙打死一船人

jat¹ zuk¹ gou¹ daa² sei² jat¹ syun⁴ jan⁴ *(translit.)*

Beat a whole boat's people to death with a bamboo pole. (lit.)

Take one for all.

Completely negate all with a word.

Knock all down at one stroke.

注表示"一棍子統統打死"或"以一概全"的意思,但通常用作否定語式來表示不能輕率推論或不可以以一概全,又作"一竹篙捅沉一船人"。

One swallow does not make a summer.

Can't take a bad one for all.

0018　一件還一件

jat¹ gin⁶ waan⁴ jat¹ gin⁶ *(translit.)*

One piece is still one piece. (lit.)

This is this and that is that.

These two cases should be handled respectively.

注指事情不能混淆,應分別處理。參閱"一筆還一筆"(0063)條。

0019　一向

jat¹ hoeng³ *(translit.)*

Always. (lit.)

Consistently.

All along.

注一貫,始終或向來。

0020　一次生，兩次熟

jat¹ ci³ saang¹, loeng⁵ ci³ suk⁶
(translit.)

Strangers the first time, but friends the second time. (lit.)

Soon get to know each other.

Strangers at first, friends later on.

Be clumsy at first but skilful later on.

0021　一次過

jat¹ ci³ gwo³ *(translit.)*

One time past. (lit.)

At one go.

In one breath.

Without a break.

Once for all.

Once and away.

No more than once.

㊟表示"一氣"或限於這一次的意思。
參閱該條（0041）。

0022　一字咁淺

jat¹ zi⁶ gam³ cin² *(translit.)*

As simple as the character '一 (one)'. (lit.)

Be as easy as ABC.

㊟形容事情非常簡單。

0023　一把火

jat¹ baa² fo² *(translit.)*

A column of fire. (lit.)

Be filled with rage.

Be hot with rage.

㊟滿肚子怒氣或冒火的意思。

0024　一身蟻

jat¹ san¹ ngai⁵ *(translit.)*

The whole body is covered with ants. (lit.)

Subject oneself to annoyance.

Get into trouble.

㊟形容招惹了不少麻煩。

0025　一言為定

jat¹ jin⁴ wai⁴ ding⁶ *(translit.)*

One word fixes it. (lit.)

A bargain is a bargain.

That's a deal.

You've got a deal.

0026　一言難盡

jat¹ jin⁴ naan⁴ zeon⁶ *(translit.)*

One word can't say all. (lit.)

It's a long story.

Can't put all in a word.

0027　一言驚醒夢中人

jat¹ jin⁴ ging¹ sing² mung⁶ zung¹ jan⁴
(translit.)

One word wakes up a dreaming person. (lit.)

Put one wise.

Give a wise word to a fool.

0028　一沉百踩

jat¹ cam⁴ baak³ caai² *(translit.)*

One man sinks and a hundred men will trample him. (lit.)

Everyone hits a man who is down.

Once one meets with a crushing defeat, everybody joins to condemn him.

㊟比喻一個人一旦失敗便受歧視。相當
於"牆倒眾人推"。

0029　一坺迾

jat¹ pek⁶ lek⁶ *(translit.)*

Be muddled up. (lit.)

Be as thick as paste.

Make a mess of something.

Be all muddled up.

㊟本意為稠得像糊狀，但又表示把事情
弄糟得不可收拾的意思。

一
畫

0030　一枝公

jat¹ zi¹ gung¹ *(translit.)*

Only one man. (lit.)

Be all alone.

By oneself.

㊟一個人（詼諧說法，指男性），相當於
"光棍兒一個"。

0031　一物治一物，糯米治木蝨

jat¹ mat⁶ zi⁶ jat¹ mat⁶, no⁶ mai⁵ zi⁶
muk⁶ sat¹ *(translit.)*

*One thing controls another thing;
glutinous rice controls bed-
bugs. (lit.)*

Everything has its vanquisher.

㊟相當於"一物降一物"。

0032　一波三折

jat¹ bo¹ saam¹ zit³ *(translit.)*

One wave with three curves. (lit.)

**Meet with difficulties one after
the other.**

Strike one snag after another.

0033　一波未平，一波又起

jat¹ bo¹ mei⁶ ping⁴, jat¹ bo¹ jau⁶ hei²
(translit.)

*Before a wave comes down,
another arises. (lit.)*

Troubles come one after another.

0034　一面之詞

jat¹ min⁶ zi¹ ci⁴ *(translit.)*

One-faced remarks. (lit.)

One-sided statement.

0035　一面屁

jat¹ min⁶ pei³ *(translit.)*

A faceful of wind from bowels. (lit.)

**Feel ashamed of (having been
abused).**

㊟表示碰一鼻子灰或被人罵得滿面羞慚
的意思。

0036　一哥

jat¹ go¹ *(translit.)*

Elder brother the first. (lit.)

A man of men.

The leader.

A man of mark.

**A man who seeks to do others
down.**

㊟指男性的第一把手或爭強好勝的人。

0037　一戙都冇

jat¹ dung⁶ dou¹ mou⁵ *(translit.)*

Have not even a pile. (lit.)

Have no cards to play.

Be at one's wit's end.

Be not a penny worth.

㊟表示沒有辦法或一文不值。

0038　一時一樣

jat¹ si⁴ jat¹ joeng⁶ *(translit.)*

One time one shape. (lit.)

**Change one's mind as time goes
on.**

Have an unstable temperament.

Be unsteady in mind.

㊟參閱"五時花六時變"條（0280）。

0039　一時時

jat¹ si² si⁴ *(translit.)*

Sometimes. (lit.)

Sometimes for a single moment.

㊟不經常，只有時一次，參閱"一陣陣"
條（0051）。

0040　一時唔偷雞做父老 / 保長

jat¹ si⁴ m⁴ tau¹ gai¹ zou⁶ fu⁶ lou⁵ / bou²
zoeng² *(translit.)*

*When a hen-stealer doesn't steal
for only once, he becomes an
elder of a country / the head of a
hundred households. (lit.)*

一畫

A rogue goes so far as to moralize to another rogue.

注 比喻一時不做壞事便假裝正人君子。

0041 一氣
jat¹ hei³ *(translit.)*
One breath. (lit.)
At one go.
Without a break.
In one breath.
注 一口氣，一直或沒稍停的意思。

0042 一個做好，一個做醜
jat¹ go³ zou⁶ hou², jat¹ go³ zou⁶ cau² *(translit.)*
One does good and another does bad. (lit.)
One puts out an iron hand and another, a velet glove.
注 相當於“一個唱紅臉，一個唱白臉”。

0043 一個夠本，兩個有利
jat¹ go³ gau³ bun², loeng⁵ go³ jau⁵ lei⁶ *(translit.)*
One is enough for the capital and two make profit. (lit.)
Sell one's life dearly.

0044 一個餅印噉
jat¹ go³ beng² jan³ gam² *(translit.)*
Be out of the same cake-mould. (lit.)
Be as like as two peas.
Be the spitting image of...
注 形容兩個人或物十分相像。

0045 一隻乙噉
jat¹ zek³ jyut⁶ gam² *(translit.)*
Be like a duckling. (lit.)
Be tired like a dog.
Be out of spirits.
注 形容人在工作後累得很的樣子。

0046 一隻手掌拍唔響
jat¹ zek³ sau² zoeng² paak³ m⁴ hoeng² *(translit.)*
One palm cannot clap a sound. (lit.)
It needs two to make a quarrel.
注 相當於“一個巴掌拍不響”。

0047 一隻屐噉
jat¹ zek³ kek⁶ gam² *(translit.)*
Be like one of clogs. (lit.)
Be crestfallen.
注 形容人垂頭喪氣的樣子。

0048 一息間
jat¹ sik¹ gaan¹ *(translit.)*
One minute. (lit.)
A little while.
In a moment.
One moment.
注 和“一陣間”同，參閱該條（0052）。

0049 一家便宜，兩家着數
jat¹ gaa¹ pin⁴ ji⁴, loeng⁵ gaa¹ zoek⁶ sou³ *(translit.)*
Advantage to one family and to two families as well. (lit.)
Not only does it profit oneself but both sides.
注 形容做一件事對兩方面都有好處。

0050 一家唔知一家事
jat¹ gaa¹ m⁴ zi¹ jat¹ gaa¹ si⁶ *(translit.)*
Our family does not know another family's affairs. (lit.)
No one knows what the other side of the world looks like.
注 即一家不知一家事。參閱“唔同牀唔知被爛”條（1373）。

0051 一陣陣
jat¹ zan² zan⁶ *(translit.)*
Sometimes. (lit.)

一
畫

Sometimes for a single moment.

📖 指次數而言，和 "一時時" 同，參閱該條（0039）。

0052　一陣間

jat¹ zan⁶ gaan¹ *(translit.)*

A moment. (lit.)

A little while.

In a moment.

One moment.

📖 即一會兒。

0053　一理通，百理明

jat¹ lei⁵ tung¹, baak³ lei⁵ ming⁴ *(translit.)*

One reason is understood and a hundred reasons are also understood. (lit.)

Have a profound grasp of the basic principle and everything is within one's grasp.

0054　一眼關七

jat¹ ngaan⁵ gwaan¹ cat¹ *(translit.)*

An eye watches seven. (lit.)

Be all eyes.

Keep one's eyes open.

Keep one's eyes polished.

📖 相當於 "眼觀六路"。

0055　一啖砂糖一啖屎

jat¹ daam⁶ saa¹ tong⁴ jat¹ daam⁶ si² *(translit.)*

A swallow of sugar and a swallow of dung. (lit.)

With an iron hand in velvet, glove.

Temper justice with mercy.

📖 形容 "恩威並施" 的態度。

0056　一動不如一靜

jat¹ dung⁶ bat¹ jyu⁴ jat¹ zing⁶ *(translit.)*

A movement is not so good as a repose. (lit.)

You may go farther and fare worse.

It would be better not to move about.

📖 表示寧願按兵不動。

0057　一條鎖匙唔聞聲，兩條鎖匙冷冷響

jat¹ tiu⁴ so² si⁴ m⁴ man⁴ seng¹, loeng⁵ tiu⁴ so² si⁴ laang¹ laang¹ hoeng² *(translit.)*

One key makes no sound, but two keys sound loudly. (lit.)

A bell without striker never rings by itself.

Two women mating with a man are great quarrellers.

📖 比喻夫婦之間不容第三者，否則難免齟齬頻生了。

0058　一部通書睇到老

jat¹ bou⁶ tung¹ syu¹ tai² dou³ lou⁵ *(translit.)*

Read only an almanac through life. (lit.)

Follow the beaten track.

Go on in the same old rut.

Stick in the mud.

📖 指做人不識變通。

0059　一清二楚

jat¹ cing¹ ji⁶ co² *(translit.)*

One cleaning and two distictions. (lit.)

Be as plain as noonday.

Be as clear as day.

📖 表示非常清晰明白。

0060　一場歡喜一場空

jat¹ coeng⁴ fun¹ hei² jat¹ coeng⁴ hung¹ *(translit.)*

Once of happiness and once of

emptiness. (lit.)

Draw water with a sieve.

0061　一朝天子一朝臣

jat¹ ciu⁴ tin¹ zi² jat¹ ciu⁴ san⁴ *(translit.)*

Every new emperor has his own new courtiers. (lit.)

A new chief brings in his own trusted followers.

A new nail drives out another.

0062　一筆勾銷

jat¹ bat¹ ngau¹ siu¹ *(translit.)*

One stroke of the pen cancels all. (lit.)

Write off at a stroke.

Annul all.

0063　一筆還一筆

jat¹ bat¹ waan⁴ jat¹ bat¹ *(translit.)*

One pen is still one pen. (lit.)

This is this and that is that; both should not get tangled.

These two sums / terms should be managed respectively.

🈯 基本上和"一件還一件"相同，但這較着重於金錢方面，而"一件還一件"則着重於事情方面。參閱該條（0018）。

0064　一就一，二就二

jat¹ zau⁶ jat¹, ji⁶ zau⁶ ji⁶ *(translit.)*

One is one and two is two. (lit.)

It should be unequivocal.

It should be perfectly clear. / as clear as noonday.

🈯 不容模棱兩可或應要清清楚楚的意思。

0065　一傳十，十傳百

jat¹ cyun⁴ sap⁶, sap⁶ cyun⁴ baak³ *(translit.)*

One person spreads to ten and ten persons spread to a hundred. (lit.)

Spread from mouth to mouth.

0066　一腳牛屎

jat¹ goek³ ngau⁴ si² *(translit.)*

One foot is full of cow's dung. (lit.)

Be country-born.

A country cousin.

🈯 諷刺別人土氣。

0067　一腳踢

jat¹ goek³ tek³ *(translit.)*

Kick with one foot. (lit.)

Do everything alone.

Do all jobs without an assistant.

🈯 指獨自做某事，或"全包了"的意思。

0068　一腳踏兩船

jat¹ goek³ daap⁶ loeng⁵ syun⁴ *(translit.)*

One foot stands on two boats. (lit.)

Play both ends against the middle.

Seek favour with opposing parties.

Attempt to make profit in two ways.

0069　一箸夾中

jat¹ zyu⁶ gaap³ zung³ *(translit.)*

Pick up the right food with chopsticks. (lit.)

Hit the right nail on the head.

Make a right guess.

🈯 表示一語道破或一猜便中。

0070　一網打盡

jat¹ mong⁵ daa² zeon⁶ *(translit.)*

One net gets all. (lit.)

Sweep everything into one's net.

Make a clean sweep.

0071　一模一樣

jat¹ mou⁴ jat¹ joeng⁶ *(translit.)*

One mould and one shape. (lit.)

Be as like as two peas.

Be exactly alike.

注 參閱 "一個餅印噉" 條（0044）。

0072　一樣米養百樣人

jat¹ joeng⁶ mai⁵ joeng⁵ baak³ joeng⁶ jan⁴ *(translit.)*

One kind of rice feeds hundred kinds of men. (lit.)

Brothers born of the same mother differ from each other in characters.

Many men, many minds.

0073　一輪嘴

jat¹ leon²˙ zeoi² *(translit.)*

A wheel of mouths. (lit.)

Wag one's tongue.

注 形容人説話滔滔不絕。

0074　一擔擔

jat¹ daam³ daam¹ *(translit.)*

A carrying pole with two loads on it. (lit.)

Two of a kind come together.

There is not much to choose between the two.

Six of one and half-a-dozen of the other.

注 表示同一類，半斤八兩，或臭味相投的意思，多含貶義。

0075　一頭霧水

jat¹ tau⁴ mou⁶ seoi² *(translit.)*

A headful of dews. (lit.)

Make neither head nor tail of something.

Be lost in a fog.

Be buried at sea.

Smile in a mist of tears.

注 "糊裏糊塗" 或 "摸不着頭腦"。

0076　一磚豆腐想升仙

jat¹ zyun¹ dau⁶ fu⁶ soeng² sing¹ sin¹ *(translit.)*

After eating a cake of bean-curd, one wants to ascend to heaven to become a supernatural being. (lit.)

Be eager to attain the highest position in one step.

Be anxious to accomplish one's purpose in one move.

注 指某些人妄想成功捷徑，相當於 "妄想一步登天"。

0077　一龍去，二龍追

jat¹ lung⁴ heoi³, ji⁶ lung⁴ zeoi¹ *(translit.)*

One dragon goes and two dragons pursue. (lit.)

While one (A) goes to fetch / look for somebody (B) along one route, he (B) comes back along the other.

注 指當甲從這處去接或找乙時，乙從別路回來。

0078　一講曹操，曹操就到

jat¹ gong² cou⁴ cou¹, cou⁴ cou¹ zau⁶ dou³ *(translit.)*

At the mention of Cou Cou*, Cou Cou arrives. (lit.)

(*Cou Cou was the Prime Minister of the state of Wei(魏) in the period of Three Kingdoms 220 – 265 A.D)

Talk of the devil and he will appear.

注 參閱 "日頭唔好講人，夜晚唔好講神" 條（0355）。

0079 一轆木噉

jat¹ luk¹ muk⁶ gam² *(translit.)*

Be like a log. (lit.)

Be awkward in one's movement.

📌 比喻呆板，不靈活，木頭人似的。

0080 一雞死，一雞鳴

jat¹ gai¹ sei², jat¹ gai¹ ming⁴ *(translit.)*

When one cock dies, another cook crows. (lit.)

Qualified successors come forth one after another.

Persons of a kind come forth in succession.

Waves urge waves.

There is always a successor regime.

📌 後繼有人，同類者一個接替一個，後浪推前浪或常有人接着上台的政權。

0081 一蟹不如一蟹

jat¹ haai⁵ bat¹ jyu⁴ jat¹ haai⁵ *(translit.)*

Each crab is worse than the one before. (lit.)

Go from bad to worse.

From the smoke into the smother.

Each one is worse than the last.

📌 相當於 "每況愈下"。

0082 一嚿飯噉

jat¹ gau⁶ faan⁶ gam² *(translit.)*

Be like a clump of cooked-rice. (lit.)

Be as stupid as an owl.

Be fat witted.

📌 形容人笨拙無能或不機靈。相當於 "飯桶"。

0083 一鑊泡

jat¹ wok⁶ pou⁵ *(translit.)*

A frying-pan of foam. (lit.)

Be irremediable.

Be unmanageable.

📌 比喻事情糟到不可收拾。

0084 一鑊熟

jat¹ wok⁶ suk⁶ *(translit.)*

Be well-done in one frying-pan. (lit.)

Not a single one survives.

Be destroyed lock, stock and barrel.

Make a clean sweep of...

📌 形容一夥人中無一倖免。

0085 一鑊撟起

jat¹ wok⁶ kiu⁵ hei² *(translit.)*

Scratch up with a frying-pan. (lit.)

Fall to the ground.

Be forced to declare bankcruptcy.

📌 表示徹底失敗或被迫破產。

二 畫

0086 二一添作五

ji⁶ jat¹ tim¹ zok³ ng⁵ *(translit.)*

Divide ten by two to get five. (lit.)

Go fifty-fifty.

Go halves with somebody.

📌 表示均分兩份的意思。

0087 二口六面

ji⁶ hau² luk⁶ min⁶ *(translit.)*

Two mouths and six faces. (lit.)

Talk face to face.

Have a face-to-face talk.

📌 指面對面地談。也有人説 "三口六面"。

0088 二打六

ji⁶ daa² luk⁶ *(translit.)*

Two beats six. (lit.)

Be inferior.

二畫

Be low-graded.

Be of poor quality.

A junior member of the staff.

Be low-levelled.

注 形容東西質量低劣或低檔，形容人為低級職員或水平低。

0089　二世祖

ji⁶ sai³ zou² *(translit.)*

An ancestral inheritor of the second generation. (lit.)

A fop.

注 指不務正業，揮霍祖業的敗家子。

0090　二四六八單 —— 冇得變

ji⁶ sei³ luk⁶ baat³ daan¹ — mou⁵ dak¹ bin³ *(translit.)*

Two, four, six, eight and single — they have no change. (lit.)

It is unchangeable.

Be decided / fixed / settled.

Reach a final decision.

It is a foregone conclusion.

注 比喻已成定局或事情已定難以改變。這是以天九牌作 "鬥牛" 賭博的術語，賭法為每人手上有五隻牌，三隻作 "牛蟸"，其餘兩隻作 "牛幾"，最大為 "牛冚"，最小為 "牛釘"，十一點是 "牛釘"，十二點或二十點為 "牛冚"。如果手上的牌為地二（二點），板樻四（四點），長衫六（六點），人八（八點）及七點則無法變為 "牛蟸" 了。

0091　二仔底 —— 死跟

ji⁶ zai² dai² — sei² gan¹ *(translit.)*

The bottom card is '2', — following to die. (lit.)

Stick like a limpet.

注 "二仔底" 原指人沒有甚麼真本領，所以別人做甚麼，他也做甚麼。

0092　二叔公割禾 —— 望下撅

ji⁶ suk¹ gung¹ got³ wo⁴ — mong⁶ haa⁶ kyut⁶ *(translit.)*

Great Uncle II cuts paddies. — He hopes for the second half part. (lit.)

Hope for the future.

Hope for the coming profit.

注 意即希望將來。

0093　丁文食件

ding¹ man¹ sik⁶ gin⁶ *(translit.)*

Buy one and eat one. (lit.)

Pay for one first and then another.

Pay by the piece.

注 表示論件付值或付酬的意思。

0094　十人生九品

sap⁶ jan⁴ saang¹ gau² ban² *(translit.)*

Ten men have nine characters. (lit.)

Brothers born of the same mother differ from each other in characters.

Many men, many minds.

注 形容每個人的性格和想法都不一樣。參閱 "一樣米養百樣人" 條（0072）。

0095　十三點

sap⁶ saam¹ dim² *(translit.)*

Thirteen o'clock. (lit.)

Be more deranged than normal.

注 形容一個人的性格 "神經質"。

0096　十五十六

sap⁶ ng⁵ sap⁶ luk⁶ *(translit.)*

Fifteen and sixteen. (lit.)

Be of two minds.

Feel some hesitation in doing something.

注 參閱 "十五個銅錢分兩份"（0097）及 "三心兩意"（0164）各條。

0097　十五個銅錢分兩份 —— 七又唔係，八又唔係

sap⁶ ng⁵ go³ tung⁴ cin⁴ fan¹ loeng⁵ fan⁶ — cat¹ jau⁶ m⁴ hai⁶, baat³ jau⁶ m⁴ hai⁶ *(translit.)*

Divide fifteen copper cashes into two equal parts, — it is neither seven nor eight. (lit.)

Cannot make up one's mind.

One's mind goes pit-a-pat.

Be greatly upset.

注 指"拿不定主意"。參閱"三心兩意"（0164）、"心多多"（0418）及"寡母婆咁多心"（2130）各條。

0098　十月芥菜 —— 起心

sap⁶ jyut⁶ gaai³ coi³ — hei² sam¹ *(translit.)*

Tenth month's mustard plant — the heart grows. (lit.)

Begin to be fond of love affairs.

Hope to get married in haste.

Begin to know love affair.

注 相當於"臘月的白菜 —— 凍（動）了心"，意指少男少女已懂男女間的事。

0099　十年唔耕，九年唔種

sap⁶ nin⁴ m⁴ gaang¹, gau² nin⁴ m⁴ zung³ *(translit.)*

Have neither ploughed for ten years nor planted for nine years. (lit.)

Be out of practice [on something].

Seldom or never make a practice [of something].

注 指久不練習或"荒疏"。參閱"丟生晒"（0767）及"丟疏咗"（0769）各條。

0100　十年唔逢一閏

sap⁶ nin⁴ m⁴ fung⁴ jat¹ jeon⁶ *(translit.)*

Not to meet a leap year in ten years. (lit.)

Once in a blue moon.

It is a chance of lifetime.

注 形容稀有或罕見。

0101　十指孖埋

sap⁶ zi² maa¹ maai⁴ *(translit.)*

Ten fingers stick together.

One's fingers are all thumbs.

注 形容笨手笨腳的樣子。

0102　十個甕缸九個蓋

sap⁶ go³ ung³ gong¹ gau² go³ goi³ *(translit.)*

Ten big earthen water-jars with nine lids. (lit.)

Fail to make both ends meet.

Run into debt to repay debts.

注 比喻收支無法相抵或過着借債還債的生活。相當於"挖東牆補西牆"。

0103　十隻手指有長短

sap⁶ zek³ sau² zi² jau⁵ coeng⁴ dyun² *(translit.)*

Among ten fingers, there are long ones and short ones. (lit.)

Every bean has its black.

No rose without a thorn.

Not all roses.

注 形容人或物難免有缺點。

0104　十拿九穩

sap⁶ naa⁴ gau² wan² *(translit.)*

Grasp ten and assure nine. (lit.)

With an ace of success.

Hold the cards in one's hand.

Only one out of ten would be missed.

Safe bind, safe found.

It's dollars to buttons.

二畫

0105　十畫都未有一撇

sap⁶ waak⁶ dou¹ mei⁶ jau⁵ jat¹ pit³ *(translit.)*

There is not a left-falling stroke in ten strokes yet. (lit.)

Even the slightest sign of the commencement of something is still unseen.

注 相當於 "八字還沒一撇"。

0106　七七八八

cat¹ cat¹ baat³ baat³ *(translit.)*

Seventy and eighty percent. (lit.)

The great majority of something.

0107　七老八十

cat¹ lou⁵ baat³ sap⁶ *(translit.)*

Seventy or eighty years old. (lit.)

Live to a great age.

注 指人上了年紀。

0108　七國咁亂

cat¹ gwok³ gam³ lyun⁶ *(translit.)*

Be as disorderly as the seven warring states. (lit.)

Be in a disorderly situation.

注 形容地方亂得一塌糊塗。

0109　七零八落

cat¹ ling⁴ baat³ lok⁶ *(translit.)*

Seven pieces and eight drops. (lit.)

Go to rack and manger.
Scattered here and there.
In disorder.

0110　七嘴八舌

cat¹ zeoi² baat³ sit⁶ *(translit.)*

Seven mouths and eight tongues. (lit.)

All are talking at once.
Cause a hot discussion with each other at the same time.

0111　七竅生煙

cat¹ hiu³ (kiu³) saang¹ jin¹ *(translit.)*

The seven cavitiess are spurting smoke. (lit.)

Fly into a rage.
Bluster oneself into anger.
See red.

0112　人一世，物一世

jan⁴ jat¹ sai³, mat⁶ jat¹ sai³ *(translit.)*

The whole life of a man and the whole life of a thing. (lit.)

Seldom or never in life is it to exist with such a thing.
Can hardly meet with such a wonderwork in life.

注 形容遇上人生難見的事物或難得一見的奇觀等等時，須抓緊時機去看，去嘗試。

0113　人山人海

jan⁴ saan¹ jan⁴ hoi² *(translit.)*

People mountain people sea. (lit.)

A sea of faces.
Huge crowd of people.

0114　人比人，比死人

jan⁴ bei² jan⁴, bei² sei² jan⁴ *(translit.)*

When a man compares himself with another person, the comparision will cause death. (lit.)

Comparisions are odious.

注 表示不能拿自己較劣處境跟別人的較優境遇相比。

0115　人心不足蛇吞象

jan⁴ sam¹ bat¹ zuk¹ se⁴ tan¹ zoeng⁶ *(translit.)*

A man with a discontented heart is like the snake which wants to swallow up an elephant. (lit.)

No man is contented with his own possessions.

Man is greedy for gains.

Millionaires always think they ought to be billionaires.

🈯 即貪得無饜。

0116　人心肉做

jan⁴ sam¹ juk⁶ zou⁶ (translit.)

A man's heart is made of flesh. (lit.)

Have a good conscience.

Be conscientious.

🈯 表示憑着良心的意思。

0117　人心隔肚皮

jan⁴ sam¹ gaak³ tou⁵ pei⁴ (translit.)

A person's heart is separated by the skin of belly. (lit.)

No one can read the mind of another person.

🈯 即人心難測。

0118　人生路不熟

jan⁴ saang¹ lou⁶ bat¹ suk⁶ (translit.)

The man is new and the road is unknown. (lit.)

Be a complete stranger.

🈯 相當於 "人地生疏"。

0119　人老心不老

jan⁴ lou⁵ sam¹ bat¹ lou⁵ (translit.)

Old but young in the heart. (lit.)

Be young in spirit for one's old age.

An old demon of lust.

🈯 形容人不因上了年紀而感衰老。

0120　人老精，鬼老靈

jan⁴ lou⁵ zeng¹, gwai² lou⁵ leng⁴ (translit.)

An old man is wise and an old ghost is efficacious. (lit.)

Experience teaches.

Old birds are not so easily caught with chaff.

A fall into the pit, a gain in your wit.

🈯 相當於 "薑是老的辣"。參閱 "大一歲，長一智" 條（0184）。

0121　人在人情在

jan⁴ zoi⁶ jan⁴ cing⁴ zoi⁶ (translit.)

While a man exists, his sensibilities also exist. (lit.)

While a man lives, his favours are remembered.

0122　人有三急

jan⁴ jau⁵ saam¹ gap¹ (translit.)

A man has three emergencies. (lit.)

Have one's needs to do.

🈯 這是表示要上廁所去的委婉語。

0123　人有三衰六旺

jan⁴ jau⁵ saam¹ seoi¹ luk⁶ wong⁶ (translit.)

A man has three declining fortunes and six prosperities. (lit.)

Man sometimes suffers misfortunes and sometimes has strokes of good fortune.

🈯 表示人生有不如意之時，也有得意的日子。

0124　人有失手，馬有失蹄

jan⁴ jau⁵ sat¹ sau², maa⁵ jau⁵ sat¹ tai⁴ (translit.)

A man may have a slip of hand, a horse may have a slip of hoof.

Even a sharp shooter may miss the target.

There is always many a slip-up in a man's job.

0125　人同此心，心同此理

jan⁴ tung⁴ c² sam¹, sam¹ tung⁴ ci² lei⁵ *(translit.)*

Every man has the same mind and every mind has the same reason. (lit.)

Everybody feels the same.

0126　人多手腳亂

jan⁴ do¹ sau² goek³ lyun⁶ *(translit.)*

More men make hands and feet confused. (lit.)

Too many cooks spoil the broth.

0127　人多好做作

jan⁴ do¹ hou² zou⁶ zok³ *(translit.)*

More men can do better. (lit.)

Many hands make light work.

0128　人多熠狗唔焾

jan⁴ do¹ saap⁶ gau² m⁴ nam⁴ *(translit.)*

Too many persons cannot cook dog's meat soft. (lit.)

Too many cooks spoil the broth.

注 參閱 "人多手腳亂" 條（0126），兩者意義相同。

0129　人爭一口氣，佛爭一爐香

jan⁴ zang¹ jat¹ hau² hei³, fat⁶ zang¹ jat¹ lou⁴ hoeng¹ *(translit.)*

A man strives for a mouthful of air; Buddha strives for a pot of incense-sticks. (lit.)

Make a good show of oneself.

Try to win credit for...

Try to bring credit to...

0130　人怕出名豬怕壯

jan⁴ paa³ ceot¹ meng⁴ zyu¹ paa³ zong³ *(translit.)*

Man is afraid to be well-known and pigs are afraid to become fat. (lit.)

Fame brings trouble.

0131　人要衣裝，佛要金裝

jan⁴ jiu³ ji¹ zong¹, fat⁶ jiu³ gam¹ zong¹ *(translit.)*

A man needs clothes to look nicer; Buddha needs gold-foil to look more magnificent. (lit.)

Fine feathers make fine birds.

The tailor makes the man.

0132　人面獸心

jan⁴ min⁶ sau³ sam¹ *(translit.)*

A man's face with a beast heart. (lit.)

A wolf in lamb's skin.

0133　人急智生

jan⁴ gap¹ zi³ saang¹ *(translit.)*

The wisdom comes out when a man worries. (lit.)

Have quick wits in an emergency.

0134　人望高處，水往低流

jan⁴ mong⁶ gou¹ cyu³, seoi² wong⁵ dai¹ lau⁴ *(translit.)*

Men hope for the heights; water flows downwards. (lit.)

Everybody hopes to climax himself.

No priestling, small thought he may be, but wishes someday Pope to be.

It is everybody's hope to be promoted.

注 比喻人總要往上爬。

0135　人情世故

jan⁴ cing⁴ sai³ gu³ *(translit.)*

Human feelings and the world affairs. (lit.)

The ways of the world.

Worldly wisdom.

注 泛指做人的道理。

0136　人情物理
jan⁴ cing⁴ mat⁶ lei⁵ *(translit.)*
Human feelings and the reasons of things. (lit.)
Gifts in general.
注 指禮物。

0137　人細鬼大
jan⁴ sai³ gwai² daai⁶ *(translit.)*
A small boy has the nature of a big ghost. (lit.)
Be young but tricky.
Be young but mature.
注 比喻小孩子年紀雖輕但已成熟或詭計多端。

0138　人無千日好
jan⁴ mou⁴ cin¹ jat⁶ hou² *(translit.)*
A man has not a thousand good days. (lit.)
No man is fortunate forever and ever.
A man cannot tempt his own fate.
No man can always have fortune on his side.

0139　人渣
jan⁴ zaa¹ *(translit.)*
Dregs of men. (lit.)
A scum of a community.
A black sheep.
One of the dregs of society.
注 指社會渣滓，敗類。

0140　人算不如天算
jan⁴ syun³ bat¹ jyu⁴ tin¹ syun³ *(translit.)*
A man's calculation is not so good as that of heaven. (lit.)
Man proposes, God disposes.
An ounce of luck is better than a pound of wisdom.
The Fates decide all.

0141　人窮志不窮
jan⁴ kung⁴ ji³ bat¹ kung⁴ *(translit.)*
The man is poor but his aspiration is high. (lit.)
Be poor but ambitious.

0142　人窮志短
jan⁴ kung⁴ ji³ dyun² *(translit.)*
The man is poor and so his ambition is short. (lit.)
Humble oneself for being poor.

0143　人講你又講
jan⁴ gong² nei⁵ jau⁶ gong² *(translit.)*
You say what other people have said. (lit.)
Echo the statement of others.
You are a parrot.

0144　入埋……（某人）嘅數
jap⁶ maai⁴ ... ge³ sou³ *(translit.)*
Enter into somebody's account. (lit.)
Charge it to somebody's account.
Lay the blame on somebody.
Attribute the guilt / fault / success etc. to somebody.
Impute the guilt / responsibility...to somebody.
注 表示記入某人的賬（這是本意），或把事情歸咎某人所為。

0145　入鄉隨俗，出水隨灣
jap⁶ hoeng¹ ceoi⁴ zuk⁶; ceot¹ seoi² ceoi⁴ waan¹ *(translit.)*
Entering a village, one should follow the traditional habits of the village; coming out of the

*river, one should follow the
curves of the bay. (lit.)*

Do in Rome as The Romans do.

0146　入境問禁

jap⁶ ging² man⁶ gam³ *(translit.)*

*Entering a country, one has to ask
the prohibitions of the country.
(lit.)*

Do in Rome as the Romans do.

0147　八十歲番頭嫁——攞路行

baat³ sap⁶ seoi³ faan¹ tau⁴ gaa³ — lo²
lou⁶ haang⁴ *(translit.)*

*Remarry at the age of eighty — look
for roads to walk. (lit.)*

Make a rod for one's own back.

🈟比喻自尋煩惱。

0148　八仙過海——各顯神通

baat³ sin¹ gwo³ hoi² — gok³ hin² san⁴
tung¹ *(translit.)*

*Eight Immorals cross the
sea — each shows his magical
powers. (lit.)*

Each has his merits.

Each dispays his special powers.

**Each shows his strong
points / abilities.**

🈟各出奇謀，各有千秋或各顯所長的意
思。

0149　八卦

baat³ gwaa³ *(translit.)*

The eight diagrams. (lit.)

Put one's finger in another's pie.

Have an oar in every man's boat.

Make fetishes ahd superstition.

🈟形容人愛管閒事或某些迷信的人的舉
動。

0150　八婆

baat³ po⁴ *(translit.)*

An eight diagrams woman. (lit.)

A Nosy Parker.

A shrewish woman.

**A woman with superstitious
disposition.**

🈟指好管閒事的女人，潑婦或迷信婦女。

0151　刁 / 丟眼角

diu¹ ngaan⁵ gok³ *(translit.)*

Cast eye corners. (lit.)

Cast sheep's eyes at somebody.

Make eyes at somebody.

🈟表示送秋波或使眼色的意思。

0152　刁 / 丟僑扭擰

diu¹ kiu⁴ nau² ning⁶ *(translit.)*

*Create difficulties and be bashful.
(lit.)*

Strike attitudes.

Put on affected manners.

🈟形容女孩子麻煩，難以對付。

0153　刁 / 丟蠻

diu¹ maan⁴ *(translit.)*

Be rude and unreasonable. (lit.)

Be impervious to reason.

🈟表示蠻不講理。

0154　又姣又怕痛，見人生仔又
眼紅

jau⁶ haau⁴ jau⁶ paa³ tung³, gin³ jan⁴
saang¹ zai² jau⁶ ngaan⁵ hung⁴
(translit.)

*Be both coquettish and afraid of
aching, but jealous of seeing
someone give birth to a baby.
(lit.)*

**Be not ambitious but jealous of
other's achievement.**

🈟含貶義，指自己不肯做，卻嫉妒別人
的成就。

0155　又試

jau⁶ si³ *(translit.)*

Again. (lit.)

Once again.

注 即再次。

0156　乜都〔係〕假

mat¹ dou¹ [hai⁶] gaa² *(translit.)*

All is false. (lit.)

Pledge not to give up.

It can't be helped.

注 常表示 "誓不罷休" 的意思，但亦表示 "無能為力" 之意。

三　畫

0157　三十六度板斧都出齊 / 埋

saam¹ sap⁶ luk⁶ dou⁶ baan² fu² dou¹ ceot¹ cai⁴ / maai⁴ *(translit.)*

Exercise up all one's thirty-six movements of the broad axe. (lit.)

Be at the end of one's wits.

注 表示想盡辦法或智窮才盡。

0158　三十六着，走為上着

saam¹ sap⁶ luk⁶ zoek⁶, zau² wai⁴ soeng⁶ zoek⁶ *(translit.)*

Of thirty-six ways, running away is the best. (lit.)

It is best to seek safety in flight.

It is best to take to one's heels.

The best thing to do is to run away as fast as one's legs could carry one.

0159　三九兩丁七

saam¹ gau² loeng⁵ ding¹ cat¹ *(translit.)*

Three nines become two persons and seven-tenths. (lit.)

Only a few people.

There are only ones and twos.

注 指人數不多，只有兩三人而已。

0160　三口兩脷

saam¹ hau² loeng⁵ lei⁶ *(translit.)*

Three mouths and two tongues. (lit.)

Show an unstable temperament.

Play fast and loose.

Eat one's words.

注 比喻言而無信。

0161　三不管

saam¹ bat¹ gun² *(translit.)*

Three sides do not administer. (lit.)

Be under nobody's jurisdiction.

Be nobody's business.

0162　三水佬睇走馬燈 —— 陸續有來

saam¹ seoi² lou² tai² zau² maa⁵ dang¹ — luk⁶ zuk⁶ jau⁵ loi⁴ *(translit.)*

A native of Sam Sæy watches a lantern with paper horse running around and around, — they come one after another. (lit.)

Come in succession.

Come one after another.

注 表示人或事接踵而來。

0163　三分顏色當大紅

saam¹ fan¹ ngaan⁴ sik¹ dong³ daai⁶ hung⁴ *(translit.)*

Hope for big red (scarlet) after gaining three Chinese grams of colour. (lit.)

Get an inch and then an ell.

Be a little favoured and then hope for much more.

注 形容人稍獲別人青睞，便囂張起來。亦有得寸進尺的意思。參閱該條(1657)。

三畫

0164　三心兩意

saam¹ sam¹ loeng⁵ ji³ *(translit.)*

Three minds and two ideas. (lit.)

Cannot make up one's mind.

Shilly-shally.

Be in two minds about...

Show a manner of instability.

Be in minds about...

注 參閱 "心多多"（0418）, "十五個
銅錢分兩份"（0097）及 "寡母婆咁
多心"（2130）各條。

0165　三扒兩撥

saam¹ paa⁴ loeng⁵ but⁶ *(translit.)*

Rake thrice and poke twice. (lit.)

Hurriedly.

Promptly.

Hurry through.

With the utmost promptitude.

注 表示急急忙忙的意思。

0166　三句不離本行

saam¹ geoi³ bat¹ lei⁴ bun² hong⁴
　　(translit.)

*Three sentences are not beyond
one's own business. (lit.)*

Talk shop.

**Can hardly speak without a shop
talk.**

0167　三更窮，四更富

saam¹ gaang¹ kung⁴, sei³ gaang¹ fu³
　　(translit.)

*Be poor at the third beating of the
watchman's drum, but rich at
the fourth beating. (lit.)*

**One's poverty or wealth is
inconstant.**

注 形容一個人貧富不定。

0168　三長兩短

saam¹ coeng⁴ loeng⁵ dyun² *(translit.)*

*Three lengths and two
shortnesses. (lit.)*

An unexpected misfortune.

**Something unfortunate,
especially death.**

注 常指不幸事故，尤指死。

0169　三枝桅

saam¹ zi¹ wai⁴ *(translit.)*

A fishing junk with three masts. (lit.)

A re-married widow.

注 含貶義，指再婚婦女。

0170　三姑六婆

saam¹ gu¹ luk⁶ po⁴ *(translit.)*

*Three maidens and six old women.
(lit.)*

A bevy of shrewish women.

注 Three maidens（三姑）: 1. Buddhist
nun（尼姑）2. Taoist nun（道姑）
3. Fortune telling woman（卦姑）。

Six old women（六婆）: 1. Procuress（牙
婆）2. Marriage go-between（媒婆）3.
Medium（師婆，巫婆）4. Villianess（虔
婆，鴇母）5. Female quack（藥婆）6.
Midwife（穩婆）。

0171　三〔九〕唔識七

saam¹ [gau²] m⁴ sik¹ cat¹ *(translit.)*

*Know not seven out of three [and
nine] men. (lit.)*

Be strange to each other.

Nobody knows one another.

注 表示誰也不認識誰。

0172　三隻手

saam¹ zek³ sau² *(translit.)*

Three-handed. (lit.)

A pickpocket.

0173　三歲定八十

saam¹ seoi³ ding⁶ baat³ sap⁶ *(translit.)*

Age of three decides on the age of eighty. (lit.)

The child is father of the man.

注 相當於 "三歲看大，七歲看老"。

0174　三腳凳

saam¹ goek³ dang³ *(translit.)*

Three-legged stool. (lit.)

An unreliable person or thing.
Be unreliable.

注 比喻不可靠的人或靠不住的東西。

0175　三羣五隊

saam¹ kwan⁴ ng⁵ deoi⁶ *(translit.)*

Three crowds and five teams. (lit.)

In groups.
In small parties.

0176　三頭六臂

saam¹ tau⁴ luk⁶ bei³ *(translit.)*

Three heads and six arms. (lit.)

Be superman-like.
An extraordinarily able person.

0177　工多藝熟

gung¹ do¹ ngai⁶ suk⁶ *(translit.)*

More practice makes craftsmanship become mature. (lit.)

Practice makes perfect.

0178　土鯪魚

tou² leng⁴ jyu⁴ *(translit.)*

Local dace. (lit.)

A small freshwater fish.

注 土鯪魚是一種廣東特有的人工養殖淡水魚。

0179　士（事）急馬行田

si⁶ gap¹ maa⁵ haang⁴ tin⁴ *(translit.)*

When a soldier is in emergency, he lets the horse walk across the field. (lit.)

By hook or crook.
By fair means or foul.
Act according to the circumstances.

注 中國象棋有士、馬及象等。馬走 "日" 字形的對角線，而象則走 "田" 字的對角線，兩者不能混亂。"士" 和 "事" 同音。這句話的意思是説當 "士"（暗喻 "事情"）告急時，便要不擇手段或隨機應變了。

0180　下扒輕輕

haa⁶ paa⁴ heng¹ heng¹ *(translit.)*

The chin is light. (lit.)

Talk at random.
Only cackle without laying an egg.
Talk through one's hat.
With one's tongue in one's cheek.

注 比喻人説得出，做不到或不顧後果，胡説八道。

0181　下馬威

haa⁶ maa⁵ wai¹ *(translit.)*

Show power while getting down from a horse. (lit.)

Display one's authority soon after one comes into power.
Deal somebody a head-on blow at first sight.

0182　下氣

haa⁶ hei³ *(translit.)*

Lower the air. (lit.)

Humble oneself.
Humble one's own pride.
Be out of rage.

注 表示低聲下氣，把自己的氣焰壓下去或怒氣全消的意思。（和中醫的術語 "下氣" 或抽薪止沸的 "下氣" 完全無關）。

三畫

0183　下欄

haa⁶ laan⁴ *(translit.)*

Inferior income. (lit.)

Tips.

Additional income.

Service charge.

注 指外快或小賬。

0184　大一歲，長一智

daai⁶ jat¹ seoi³, zoeng² jat¹ zi³ *(translit.)*

Being one more year older, one gets one more wit. (lit.)

Experience teaches.

A fall into the pit, a gain in one's wit.

注 參閱 "人老精，鬼老靈" 條（0120）。

0185　大人大姐

daai⁶ jan⁴ daai⁶ ze² *(translit.)*

A big man and a big girl. (lit.)

An adult.

Grown-up.

注 成年人的意思。

0186　大人物

daai⁶ jan⁴ mat²ᐟ⁶ *(translit.)*

A big man. (lit.)

A somebody.

A great man.

0187　大丈夫能屈能伸

daai⁶ zoeng⁶ fu¹ nang⁴ wat¹ nang⁴ san¹ *(translit.)*

A real man can both bow and stand up. (lit.)

Stretch one's leg according to one's own blanket.

Be ready to accept either a higher or a lower post.

Be ready to give one's head for the washing or hold one's head high.

注 形容人能隨機應變，能任高職或低職或既可俯首受辱復可趾高氣揚的意思。

0188　大大話話

daai⁶ daai⁶ waa⁶ waa²ᐟ⁶ *(translit.)*

Tell a big lie. (lit.)

Estimate approximately.

Inflatedly speaking.

注 表示粗略估計或誇張地說的意思。

0189　大小通吃

daai⁶ siu² tung¹ hek³ *(translit.)*

Big and small ones are all eaten. (lit.)

Sweep everything into one's net.

Sweep all before one.

0190　大王眼

daai⁶ wong⁴ ngaan⁵ *(translit.)*

Big ruler's eyes. (lit.)

A glutton for gains.

注 比喻人貪心，胃口很大。

0191　大方

daai⁶ fong¹ *(translit.)*

Be generous. (lit.)

Be liberal.

Be generous with one's money.

Have a dignified bearing.

Be graceful and poised.

0192　大石責死蟹

daai⁶ sek⁶ zaak³ sei² haai⁵ *(translit.)*

A big rock suppresses a crab to death. (lit.)

Bring pressure to bear on somebody.

Pressure somebody into doing something.

注 比喻用強硬手段來壓服別人。

0193　大耳窿

daai⁶ ji⁵ lung¹ *(translit.)*

A big aperture of ear. (lit.)

A loan-shark.

注 即放高利貸者。

0194　大光燈

daai⁶ gwong¹ dang¹ *(translit.)*

Gasificational lamp. (lit.)

A person panting with rage.

A person who has a big mouth.

A loud mouth.

注 原指汽燈，煤氣燈（打氣煤油燈）。
這種燈燃點時，發出很大的"嘘嘘
聲"。後來有人用此語比喻怒氣沖沖
或大聲説話的人。

0195　大行其道

daai⁶ hang⁴ kei⁴ dou⁶ *(translit.)*

Be popular. (lit.)

Be in the trend.

Prevail throughout.

0196　大好沉香當爛柴

daai⁶ hou² cam⁴ hoeng¹ dong³ laan⁶
caai⁴ *(translit.)*

*The best lign aloe is regarded as
decayed firewood. (lit.)*

Pure gold is regarded as copper.

Waste one's talent on a petty job.

**Be unable to tell good and bad
apart.**

Be sold like refuse.

注 比喻不知人善用或把高檔貨作低檔貨
賤價出售等。

0197　大好鮮花插在牛屎裏

daai⁶ hou² sin¹ faa¹ caap³ zoi⁶ ngau⁴
si² leoi⁵ *(translit.)*

*Transplant a very good fresh flower
in a lump of cow's manure. (lit.)*

Cast pearls before a swine.

Come into bloom under night.

注 即"一朵鮮花插在牛糞上"。

0198　大把

daai⁶ baa² *(translit.)*

A big grasp. (lit.)

A great deal of.

A good / great many.

注 有的是；很多。

0199　大花面揰眼淚——離行離捺

daai⁶ faa¹ min² giu² ngaan⁵
leoi⁶ — lei⁴ hong⁴ lei⁴ laat⁶ *(translit.)*

*An actor with painted face wipes
tears — separate by a space.
(lit.)*

Be out of the place.

Go beyond what is proper.

Have no relation with...

注 表示不合規格或距離甚遠的意思，也
可轉喻指和某人（物）扯不上關係。

0200　大花筒

daai⁶ faa¹ tung⁴ *(translit.)*

A big kaleidoscope. (lit.)

An extravagant spender.

注 比喻亂花錢的人。

0201　大枝嘢

daai⁶ zi¹ je⁵ *(translit.)*

A big piece. (lit.)

Be as proud as Punch.

Be puffed up with pride.

注 表示驕傲，傲慢的意思。

0202　大事化小，小事化無

daai⁶ si⁶ faa³ siu², siu² si⁶ faa³ mou⁴
(translit.)

*Turn big affairs into small ones and
small ones into none. (lit.)*

Bring the problem to naught.

三畫

0203　大命

daai[6] meng[6] *(translit.)*

Big life. (lit.)

Escape with bare life.

Turn all ill luck into a good one.

📝 亦即"命大",表示死裏逃生,僅以身免或逢凶化吉的意思。

0204　大泡和

daai[6] paau[1] wo[4] *(translit.)*

Daai Paau Wo. (a nickname of a certain man) (lit.)

Be muddleheaded.

📝 從前有人渾名為"大泡和"的,做事糊裏糊塗。後人便以此名比喻人糊塗或無能,笨拙。

0205　大食有指擬

daai[6] sik[6] jau[5] zi[2] ji[5] *(translit.)*

Have dependence to gluttonize. (lit.)

Have a firm backing to do such a deed / for one's extravagance.

📝 比喻一個人敢於去幹一種行為或敢去花錢,當有其背後支持或背景。

0206　大食唔窮倒算窮

daai[6] sik[6] m[4] kung[4] dou[2/3] syun[3] kung[4] *(translit.)*

Big eater will not become poor but reverse calculation causes poverty. (lit.)

Lose a ship for a halfpenny worth of tar.

Go for wool and come home shorn.

📝 比喻因小失大。

0207　大食細

daai[6] sik[6] sai[3] *(translit.)*

The big eat the small. (lit.)

Small fish are always the best food of big ones.

0208　大炮友

daai[6] paau[3] jau[2] *(translit.)*

A cannon-friend. (lit.)

A teller of tall stories.

A man who fonds of talk big.

📝 指愛吹牛的人。

0209　大限難逃

daai[6] haan[6] naan[4] tou[4] *(translit.)*

Be unable to run away from the big limitation. (lit.)

Meet one's fate.

Pay one's debt to Nature.

What is worried about is sure to occur.

0210　大隻騾騾

daai[6] zek[3] leoi[4] leoi[4] *(translit.)*

A man of strong build. (lit.)

As big as a mule.

Be as stout as a horse.

📝 形容人個子高大,含貶義。

0211　大拿拿

daai[6] naa[4] naa[4] *(translit.)*

A big sum. (lit.)

A considerable sum of money.

📝 表示大大的一份或可觀的金額的意思。

0212　大海撈針

daai[6] hoi[2] laau[4] zam[1] *(translit.)*

Dredge a needle in a big sea. (lit.)

Look for a needle in a bottle of hay.

Fish a needle out of the ocean.

0213　大家心照

daai[6] gaa[1] sam[1] ziu[3] *(translit.)*

Understand each other without saying. (lit.)

Have a tacit understanding.

注 表示不言而喻的意思。

0214 大陣仗

daai[6] zan[6] zoeng[6] *(translit.)*

A big formation. (lit.)

Go in for an ostentation.

Break a butterfly on the wheel.

注 表示排場大或小題大做的意思。

0215 大粒佬

daai[6] lap[1] lou[2] *(translit.)*

A big cubic one. (lit.)

A man of mark.

A man of men.

注 大人物的謔稱。

0216 大喊十

daai[6] haam[3] sap[6] *(translit.)*

A big shouter. (lit.)

A person who shouts out for trifles.

A loud mouth.

注 比喻嗓門大，常為小事便大喊大叫的人。

0217 大喉腩

daai[6] hau[4] naam[5] *(translit.)*

Have a big throat and a big belly. (lit.)

A rapacious person.

A person who has a very good appetite.

注 形容人胃口大，貪多，貪心。

0218 大番薯

daai[6] faan[1] syu[4/2] *(translit.)*

A big sweet potato. (lit.)

A fool.

注 比喻愚笨的人。

0219 大搖大擺

daai[6] jiu[4] daai[6] baai[2] *(translit.)*

Big shake and big display. (lit.)

Swagger about.

0220 大碌藕

daai[6] luk[1] ngau[5] *(translit.)*

Big lotus root. (Daai Luk Ngau was a nickname of a certain person) (lit.)

An extravagant spender.

A debauchee.

注 比喻亂花錢的人。"大碌藕"是一個人的渾名。往昔佛山每年均有"秋色"舉行，而且需要很多人抬"色"。該名"大碌藕"的人年年均往抬"色"。他抬"色"時姿態別具一格，把"色"左搖右擺。這種動作廣東人稱為"抍"(fing[6]音)。而"抍"中又有亂花錢的意思。所以借"大碌藕"抬色──亂抍來比喻"亂花錢的人"。

0221 大話夾好彩

daai[6] waa[6] gaap[3] hou[2] coi[2] *(translit.)*

Big lies with good luck. (lit.)

All by good luck.

注 表示幸虧或僥倖的意思。

0222 大禍臨頭

daai[6] wo[6] lam[4] tau[4] *(translit.)*

Big calamity comes onto the head. (lit.)

The black ox has trod on one's foot.

0223 大種乞兒

daai[6] zung[2] hat[1] ji[1/4] *(translit.)*

A big-raced beggar. (lit.)

A person who refuses to accept a handout in contempt.

A person who disregards small gains.

注 比喻不願接受嗟來之食的人或不屑小利的人。

三畫

0224　大模屍樣

daai⁶ mou⁴ si¹ joeng⁶ *(translit.)*

A big mould like a corpse. (lit.)

Be haughty.

Be in ostentatious manner.

🈂️比喻人神氣十足的樣子，含貶義。

0225　大諗頭

daai⁶ lam² tau⁴ *(translit.)*

A big thought. (lit.)

Be too ambitious for...

Hot oneself up with ambition

Hitch one's waggon to a star.

🈂️形容人抱負過高的意思。

0226　大雞唔食細米

daai⁶ gai¹ m⁴ sik⁶ sai³ mai⁵ *(translit.)*

A big hen does not eat small rice.
(lit.)

Care naught for trifles.

🈂️比喻不屑於幹小事或做賺錢少的生意。

0227　大懶友

daai⁶ laan⁵ jau² *(translit.)*

A big lazy guy. (lit.)

An idler.

A lotus-eater.

A gluttonous lazybones.

🈂️指遊手好閒的人，貪圖安逸者或好吃懶做的人。

0228　大懵

daai⁶ mung² *(translit.)*

A big muddler. (lit.)

A blunder head.

Be muddle-headed.

🈂️指頭腦糊塗。

0229　大覺瞓

daai⁶ gaau³ fan³ *(translit.)*

Have a big sleep. (lit.)

Sleep on both ears.

Be carefree.

Not to care a pin.

🈂️比喻睡大覺，安心，或無憂無慮。

0230　大驚小怪

daai⁶ ging¹ siu² gwaai³ *(translit.)*

Great terror and small pecularity.
(lit.)

A storm in the tea cup.

Make a fuss.

0231　大癲大廢

daai⁶ din¹ daai⁶ fai³ *(translit.)*

Big insaneness and big rubbish.
(lit.)

Be playsome.

Be casual.

Be too optimistic to care anything.

🈂️形容人大大咧咧，漫不經心，好玩或樂觀。

0232　大纜絞唔埋

daai⁶ laam⁶ gaau² m⁴ maai⁴ *(translit.)*

Cannot twist together with a rope.
(lit.)

Make a world of difference.

It is far from the argument each sticks to.

There is some difference to something.

Cannot meet somebody halfway.

🈂️指人們各持己見，不能互相遷就。

0233　上天無路，入地無門

soeng⁵ tin¹ mou⁴ lou⁶, jap⁶ dei⁶ mou⁴ mun⁴ *(translit.)*

There is neither a road to heaven nor a door to hell. (lit.)

Be in desperate straits.

Be in a quandary.

Be in a devil of a hole.

0234　上咗岸

soeng⁵ zo² ngon⁶ *(translit.)*

Have gone ashore. (lit.)

Have earned more than enough.

Have struck oil.

Have made one's fortune.

注 賺夠了或發了大財。

0235　上氣唔接下氣

soeng⁶ hei³ m⁴ zip³ haa⁶ hei³ *(translit.)*

The upper air cannot connect with the lower air. (lit.)

Be out of breath.

Be panting.

注 形容人呼吸急促，氣喘吁吁。

0236　上得山多終遇虎

soeng⁵ dak¹ saan¹ do¹ zung¹ jyu⁶ fu² *(translit.)*

The one who goes up mountains too often will one day meet a tiger. (lit.)

The fish which nibbles at every bait will be caught.

0237　上當

soeng⁵ dong³ *(translit.)*

Be taken in. (lit.)

Be fooled.

Be caught with chaff.

Be duped.

Can be put in pledge.

Have a hocking value.

注 意為受騙，但有時又用於表示東西有典當的價值。

0238　上樑唔正下樑歪

soeng⁶ loeng⁴ m⁴ zeng³ haa⁶ loeng⁴ me² *(translit.)*

If the upper beam is crooked, the lower one will be out of plumb. (lit.)

(lit.)

Those below will follow the bad example set by those above.

注 即 "上樑不正下樑歪"。

0239　小心駛／使得萬年船

siu² sam¹ sai² dak¹ maan⁶ nin⁴ syun⁴ *(translit.)*

Care can drive a ship for ten thousand years. (lit.)

Take care and care will prevail.

0240　小財唔出，大財唔入

siu² coi⁴ m⁴ ceot¹, daai⁶ coi⁴ m⁴ jap⁶ *(translit.)*

If no small money is given out, no big money will come in. (lit.)

An empty hand is no lure for a hawk.

A hook without a small fish makes no big fish jump at the bait.

注 形容在商業上，如果不花少量的錢去做廣告或搞其他足以吸引顧客的活動，則無法賺到大錢。

0241　小氣

siu² hei³ *(translit.)*

Small air. (lit.)

Be narrow-minded.

Be small-minded.

注 表示心胸狹窄或小心眼的意思。

0242　小鬼唔見得大神

siu² gwai² m⁴ gin³ dak¹ daai⁶ san⁴ *(translit.)*

A small ghost does not dare to see a big god. (lit.)

Be not natural and liberal enough.

Humble oneself too much to rub elbows with upper-crusts.

注 形容人不夠自然大方，或指人過分自

三畫

卑而不敢和上流社會交往。

0243　小家種

siu² gaa¹ zung² *(translit.)*

The clan of mean persons. (lit.)

Act in a mean-spirited manner.

A mean-spirited person.

注指卑鄙而吝嗇的人。

0244　小意思

siu² ji³ si¹ *(translit.)*

A little meaning. (lit.)

A slight token of regard.

Nothing important.

注常用於對自己所送出的禮物的謙稱，但亦指事情並不嚴重。

0245　口不對心

hau² bat¹ deoi³ sam¹ *(translit.)*

The mouth is not compatible with the heart. (lit.)

Carry fire in one hand and water in the other.

Speak with one's tongue in one's cheek.

注參閱 "口是心非" 條（0250）。

0246　口水多過茶

hau² seoi² do¹ gwo³ caa⁴ *(translit.)*

Mouth water is more than tea. (lit.)

Talk the hind leg off a dog.

Have a loose tongue.

Wag one's tongue.

Shoot off one's mouth.

注形容人說話太多，含貶義。

0247　口多多

hau² do¹ do¹ *(translit.)*

Many-mouthed. (lit.)

Be loose-tongued.

Shoot off one's mouth.

注形容人多嘴多舌。

0248　口花花

hau² faa¹ faa¹ *(translit.)*

Have a flowery mouth. (lit.)

Talk frivolously.

Speak frivolity.

注形容人輕浮，能說會道（尤指男人對女人）。

0249　口垃濕

hau² lap⁶ sap¹ *(translit.)*

The odds and ends for the mouth. (lit.)

Between-meal nibbles.

Snacks.

注指零食。

0250　口是心非

hau² si⁶ sam¹ fei¹ *(translit.)*

The mouth says 'yes', but the heart says 'no'. (lit.)

Carry fire in one hand and water in the other.

Speak with one's tongue in one's cheek.

注參閱 "口不對心" 條（0245）。

0251　口爽荷包垃

hau² song² ho⁴ baau¹ lap⁶ *(translit.)*

Mouth is brisk but purse is stickly. (lit.)

Words pay no debts.

Words come out fast, money goes out slow.

注比喻表面慷慨，實則吝嗇。亦即所謂 "口惠而實不至"。

0252　口甜舌滑

hau² tim⁴ sit⁶ waat⁶ *(translit.)*

The mouth is sweet and the tongue is smooth. (lit.)

Be honey tipped.

Oil one's tongue.

0253 口窒窒

hau² zat⁶ zat⁶ *(translit.)*

The mouth obstructs. (lit.)

Stammer out.

Stutter out.

Hum and ha.

注 表示結結巴巴地説話或欲言又止。

0254 口疏疏

hau² so¹ so¹ *(translit.)*

The mouth slips. (lit.)

Make no secret of anything.

Be loose-lipped.

注 形容人嘴快，沒法保守秘密。

0255 口輕輕

hau² heng¹ heng¹ *(translit.)*

The mouth is light. (lit.)

Make easy promises.

注 表示輕諾的意思。參閱 "下扒輕輕"
（0180）及 "托塔都應承" 條（0630）。

0256 山人自有妙計

saan¹ jan⁴ zi⁶ jau⁵ miu⁶ gai³ *(translit.)*

A mountain dweller naturally has a good plan. (lit.)

I have hit an idea.

I have had an inspiration.

0257 山大斬埋有柴

saan¹ daai⁶ zaam² maai⁴ jau⁵ caai⁴
(translit.)

One can gather a lot of firewood to cut sticks in a big mountain. (lit.)

Many a pickle makes a mickle.

Drip-drops become a river.

0258 山水有相逢

saan¹ seoi² jau⁵ soeng¹ fung⁴ *(translit.)*

Mountains and waters have chance to meet each other. (lit.)

It is likely for somebody to meet each other again in travels one day.

注 比喻總有一天會再相逢或彼此總會有
機會再相見。

0259 山高水低

saan¹ gou¹ seoi² dai¹ *(translit.)*

The mountain is high and the river is low. (lit.)

An unexpected misfortune.

Something unfortunate.

注 比喻不幸事情或意外，參閱 "有乜冬
瓜豆腐" 條（0660）。

0260 山窮水盡

saan¹ kung⁴ seoi² zeon⁶ *(translit.)*

The mountain impoverishes and the river ends. (lit.)

Beat the end of one's rope.

Be up the creek.

Live with one's bottom dollar.

注 比喻身處絕境或走投無路。

0261 千年道行一朝喪

cin¹ nin⁴ dou⁶ hang⁶ jat¹ ziu¹ song³
(translit.)

A thousand years' high moral attainment losee in one morning. (lit.)

All the good deeds are spoilt by only an ill doing.

0262 千里送鵝毛，物輕情意重

cin¹ lei⁵ sung³ ngo⁴ mou⁴, mat⁶ hing¹
cing⁴ ji⁶ zung⁶ *(translit.)*

The goose feather is sent from a thousand li away; it is light, but it is full of affection. (lit.)

The trifling gift sent from afar conveys deep affection.

三
畫

0263　千金小姐當作丫鬟賣

cin¹ gam¹ siu² ze² dong³ zok³ aa¹ waan⁴ maai⁶ *(translit.)*

A young lady of high birth is sold as a slave girl. (lit.)

Pure gold is regarded as copper.

Waste one's talent on a petty job.

Be unable to tell good and bad apart.

Be sold like refuse.

注 參閱 "大好沉香當爛柴" 條（0196）。

0264　千真萬確

cin¹ zan¹ maan⁶ kok³ *(translit.)*

One thousand of truth and ten thousand of accuracy. (lit.)

Be as sure as fate.

The truth, the whole truth, and nothing but the truth.

0265　千揀萬揀，揀着個爛燈盞

cin¹ gaan² maan⁶ gaan², gaan² zoek⁶ go³ laan⁶ dang¹ zaan² *(translit.)*

Having made a thousand and even ten thousand choices, one eventually chose a broken shallow cup for oil. (lit.)

The most careful choice is often the worst choice.

注 表示儘管精挑細選，仍然有可能選擇錯誤。

0266　也文也武

jaa⁶ man⁴ jaa⁶ mou⁵ *(translit.)*

Be well-versed in polite letters and martial arts. (lit.)

Make a show of power.

Swagger about.

注 形容人耀武揚威，橫行霸道。

0267　女人纏腳布——又長又臭

neoi⁵ jan² zin⁶ goek³ bou³ — jau⁶ coeng⁴ jau⁶ cau³ *(translit.)*

A woman's foot-binding cloth-tapes — they are both long and stinking. (lit.)

Be long and tiresome. (of lecture/speech or composition)

注 諷喻人的演講或文章長而使人厭煩。

四畫

0268　天下烏鴉一樣黑

tin¹ haa⁶ wu¹ aa¹ jat¹ joeng⁶ hak¹ *(translit.)*

All crows in the world are equally black. (lit.)

Devils everywhere are devils of the same kind.

There is nothing different under the sun.

0269　天堂有路你不走，地獄無門闖進來

tin¹ tong⁴ jau⁵ lou⁶ nei⁵ bat¹ zau², dei⁶ juk⁶ mou⁴ mun⁴ cong² zeon³ loi⁴ *(translit.)*

You do not take the road to heaven, but push yourself to hell where there is not a door. (lit.)

You cut your own throat.

You go to your doom.

You bring yourself to ruin.

0270　天跌落嚟當被冚

tin¹ dit³ lok⁶ lai⁴ dong³ pei⁵ kam² *(translit.)*

If the sky falls down, use it as a quilt. (lit.)

Take it easy.

Be unconcerned with one's present situation.

表示對目前處境處之泰然。

0271　天無絕人之路
tin¹ mou⁴ zyut⁶ jan⁴ zi¹ lou⁶ *(translit.)*

Heaven never puts a man in a dead end. (lit.)

It is a long lane that has no turning.

God always tempers the wind to the shorn lamb.

0272　天網恢恢，疏而不漏
tin¹ mong⁵ fui¹ fui¹, so¹ ji⁴ bat¹ lau⁶ *(translit.)*

The heaven's net is vast; it never leaks though it is thin. (lit.)

Justice has long arms.

Heaven's vengeance is slow but sure.

0273　扎扎跳
zaat³ zaat³ tiu³ *(translit.)*

Jump about. (lit.)

Be all at sea.

Be like an ant on a hot griddle.

Be on the rack.

Jump the traces.

Kick over the traces.

Be in a rage.

Be hot with rage.

表示感到極度不安，無定性且不受拘束及憤怒的意思。

0274　扎炮
zaat³ paau³ *(translit.)*

Tie up firecrackers. (lit.)

Suffer from hunger.

Have nothing to eat.

餓肚子。參閱"吊砂煲"條（0742）。

0275　扎實
zaat³ sat⁶ *(translit.)*

Be sound enough. (lit.)

Be sturdy enough.

Be firm enough.

Be strong enough.

形容物品堅固或人身材健碩。

0276　木口木面
muk⁶ hau² muk⁶ min⁶ *(translit.)*

Wooden mouth and wooden face. (lit.)

Be wooden-faced.

Be slow in reacting.

Be wooden-headed.

無表情；遲鈍，比較"木獨"條（0278）。

0277　木匠擔枷 —— 自作自受
muk⁶ zoeng⁶ daam¹ gaa¹ — zi⁶ zok³ zi⁶ sau⁶ *(translit.)*

A carpenter carries a woodencollar — suffering from his own work. (lit.)

As one brews, so one must drink.

Fry in one's own grease.

0278　木獨
muk⁶ duk⁶ *(translit.)*

Wooden-faced. (lit.)

Be as wooden as a dummy.

Be unsocial.

Not to have a social nature.

形容人不大好講話或不善交際。比較"木口木面"（0276）。

0279　五行欠金
ng⁵ hang⁴ him³ gam¹ *(translit.)*

There lacks gold in the five primary elements. (lit.)*

Be in low water.

Be penniless.

Be broke.

比喻沒有錢的意思。

The five primary elements are:

四畫

gold （金）, wood （木）,
water （水）, fire （火） and
earth （土）.

0280　五時花六時變

ng⁵ si⁴ faa¹ luk⁶ si⁴ bin³ *(translit.)*

*The flower comes into bloom at 5
o'clock and changes at 6. (lit.)*

Have an unstable temperament.

**Change one's mind as time goes
on.**

Be unsteady in mind.

🈔表示拿不定主意的意思。參閱"一時
一樣"條（0038）。

0281　支質

zi¹ zat¹ *(translit.)*

Variety. (lit.)

Item.

Be long-winded.

Be too wordy.

Push and pull.

🈔作名詞用時，意為"名堂"或"項
目"。作形容詞用時，意為"囉唆"。
作動詞用時，意為"把禮物推來推
去"，亦有人說"支支質質"。

0282　支整

zi¹ zing² *(translit.)*

Dress up. (lit.)

**Be fond of making / dressing
oneself up like a peacock.**

Care much about dresses.

Like to be affected.

🈔形容人過分講究打扮。

0283　不了了之

bat¹ liu⁵ liu⁵ zi¹ *(translit.)*

*Let the unfinished thing finish
itself. (lit.)*

Let it take its own course.

End up with nothing definite.

0284　不打不相識

bat¹ daa² bat¹ soeng¹ sik¹ *(translit.)*

*No fighting, no friends are made.
(lit.)*

No discord, no concord.

**Build up friendship after an
exchange of blows.**

0285　不打自招

bat¹ daa² zi⁶ ziu¹ *(translit.)*

*Self confess without being beaten.
(lit.)*

Make a confession without duress.

0286　不至於

bat¹ zi³ jyu¹ *(translit.)*

Not as to... (lit.)

Be unlikely...

It is unlikely that...

It is not likely that...

🈔表示不可能會的意思。

0287　不到黃河心不死

bat¹ dou³ wong⁴ ho⁴ sam¹ bat¹
si² / sei² *(translit.)*

*The heart will not die until reaching
the Yellow River. (lit.)*

Go to all lengths to do something.

Hang on.

**Refuse to give up until all hope is
gone.**

0288　不是冤家不聚頭

bat¹ si⁶ jyun¹ gaa¹ bat¹ zeoi⁶ tau⁴
(translit.)

*If they were not opponents, they
would not meet together. (lit.)*

Dogs and cats are sure to meet.

**Enemies are bound to meet in
the same place.**

0289　不留

bat¹ lau¹ *(translit.)*

Regularly. (lit.)
Often.
Constantly.
Frequently.

注 經常，一直的意思。

0290 不理三七二十一

bat¹ lei⁵ saam¹ cat¹ ji⁶ sap⁶ jat¹
(translit.)

Not to care if three times seven is twenty-one. (lit.)

Rain or shine.
Fling caution to the winds.
Be regardless of the consequences.
Chance the duck.

注 即不顧一切，無論如何或不管怎樣的意思。

0291 冇一定

mou⁵ jat¹ ding⁶ *(translit.)*
Have no fixture. (lit.)

It is unfixable.
It is irregular.

注 表示不固定的意思。

0292 冇口齒

mou⁵ hau² ci² *(translit.)*
Have no mouth and teeth. (lit.)

Break one's promise.
Break one's words.

注 形容人不講信用。

0293 冇天裝

mou⁵ tin¹ zong¹ *(translit.)*
No place in the sky to hold. (lit.)

An evil-doer.

注 指連上天也不容的作惡分子。

0294 冇牙老虎

mou⁵ ngaa⁴ lou⁵ fu² *(translit.)*
A toothless tiger. (lit.)

Fire.

注 比喻火災。

0295 冇手尾

mou⁵ sau² mei⁵ *(translit.)*
No hands and tails. (lit.)

Leave things about.

注 形容人做事有頭無尾，或者做完一件事，不收拾東西。

0296 冇心肝

mou⁵ sam¹ gon¹ *(translit.)*
Have no heart and liver. (lit.)

Pay no attention to...
Be inattentive.
Be unconcerned with...

注 形容人對甚麼事情都不在意。

0297 冇心機

mou⁵ sam¹ gei¹ *(translit.)*
Have no heart. (lit.)

Be in no mood.
Be impatient.

注 指沒有心情或沒有耐性。

0298 冇出息

mou⁵ ceot¹ sik¹ *(translit.)*
Have no interest to let out. (lit.)

Be futureless.
Be good for nothing.

注 表示沒有前途或飯桶似的。

0299 冇耳性

mou⁵ ji⁵ sing³ *(translit.)*
Without nature of ears. (lit.)

Have a memory like a sieve.
Have bad memory.
Be forgetful.

注 表示健忘的意思，含貶義。

0300 冇行

mou⁵ hong⁴ *(translit.)*

四畫

Have no hope. *(lit.)*

There is no hope.

It is hopeless.

🈁表示沒有希望。

0301　冇衣食

mou⁵ ji¹ sik⁶ *(translit.)*

Have neither clothes to wear nor food to eat. *(lit.)*

Disregard one's morality and righteousness.

Be guilty of bad faith.

Break faith with somebody.

🈁指背信棄義。語出粵劇伶人輩，但已成為一般人的口語了。

0302　冇收（修）

mou⁵ sau¹ *(translit.)*

Have no close. *(lit.)*

Be at loose ends.

Fail to make an end of the trouble.

Be unable to bring things to a satisfactory conclusion.

Be at one's wit's end.

🈁表示難以收拾或毫無辦法的意思。

0303　冇走盞

mou⁵ zau² zaan² *(translit.)*

Without any extent. *(lit.)*

Leave no margin of...（time／space／money）

Leave no space for something.

Be in the bag.

🈁指沒有餘地，但也表示有把握，十拿九穩的意思。參閱“冇走雞”（0304）條。

0304　冇走雞

mou⁵ zau² gai¹ *(translit.)*

No hens to run away. *(lit.)*

Be in the bag.

Be well in hand.

🈁相當於“十拿九穩”。參閱該條（0104）。

0305　冇尾飛鉈

mou⁵ mei⁵ fei¹ to⁴ *(translit.)*

A flying plummet without tail. *(lit.)*

A person without any trace.

🈁相當於“斷線風箏”，指難以尋找他蹤跡的人。

0306　冇兩句

mou⁵ loeng⁵ geoi³ *(translit.)*

Without two sentences. *(lit.)*

Be too intimate with somebody to have anything to argue.

🈁形容與人相處融洽，沒有爭執。

0307　冇咁大個頭就唔好戴咁大頂帽

mou⁵ gam³ daai⁶ go³ tau⁴ zau⁶ m⁴ hou² daai³ gam³ daai⁶ deng² mou² *(translit.)*

If one has not such a big head, one should not put on such a big hat. *(lit.)*

🈁同“冇咁大隻鴿就唔好喊咁大聲”（0310）。

0308　冇咁大個頭就唔會戴咁大頂帽

mou⁵ gam³ daai⁶ go³ tau⁴ zau⁶ m⁴ wui⁵ daai³ gam³ daai⁶ deng² mou² *(translit.)*

If one had not such a big head, one would not put on such a big hat. *(lit.)*

🈁同“冇咁大隻鴿，就唔會喊咁大聲”（0311）。

0309　冇咁大隻蛤乸隨街跳

mou⁵ gam³ daai⁶ zek³ gap³ naa² ceoi⁴ gaai¹ tiu³ *(translit.)*

There is no such a big frog hopping about in the street. (lit.)

Greed often causes loss.

Go for wool and come back shorn.

注 告誡別人貪心反招損失。

0310 冇咁大隻鴿就唔好喊咁大聲

mou⁵ gam³ daai⁶ zek³ gap³ zau⁶ m⁴ hou² haam³ gam³ daai⁶ seng¹ *(translit.)*

If the pigeon is not so big, it should not cry so loudly. (lit.)

Do not throw straws against the wind.

One should not swim beyond one's depth.

Cut one's coat according to one's cloth.

Spend no more than one can afford.

Undertake what one can do.

注 比喻做事應量力而為。

0311 冇咁大隻鴿，就唔會喊咁大聲

mou⁵ gam³ daai⁶ zek³ gap³, zau⁶ m⁴ wui⁵ haam³ gam³ daai⁶ seng¹ *(translit.)*

If the pigeon were not so big, it would not cry so loudly. (lit.)

Within one's power.

Be fully competent for...

Be fully able to...

One can spend as much as one can afford.

注 暗示有這麼的勢力或財力才能夠⋯⋯。

0312 冇咁衰講到咁衰

mou⁵ gam³ seoi¹ gong² dou³ gam³ seoi¹ *(translit.)*

Be not so bad but be said to be so bad. (lit.)

Paint somebody / something in dark colour.

Put false colour upon somebody / something.

注 表示把人或物描得更黑。

0313 冇呢枝歌仔唱

mou⁵ ni¹ (nei¹) zi¹ go¹ zai² coeng³ *(translit.)*

There is no such a song to sing. (lit.)

The times are different.

Such an opportunity is no longer seen.

Sing another song.

注 相當於"過了這村，沒有這個店"。暗示時代不同了或再沒有這個機會了。

0314 冇相干

mou⁵ soeng¹ gon¹ *(translit.)*

Have no concern. (lit.)

Nothing serious.

It doesn't matter.

Never mind.

It's nothing.

It's all right.

注 即沒關係，不要緊。

0315 冇根兜

mou⁵ gan¹ dau¹ *(translit.)*

Have no roots. (lit.)

Have no sense of propriety.

Do not act on principle.

Be careless and casual.

注 同"冇紋路"（0322）。

0316 冇晒符

mou⁵ saai³ fu⁴ *(translit.)*

Have not any Taosit magic

四畫

incantations. *(lit.)*

Be at one's wit's end.

Be at the end of one's tether.

注 表示智窮才盡，完全沒了辦法。

0317　冇晒符弗〈法〉

mou⁵ saai³ fu⁴ fit¹ *(translit.)*

None of charms and amulets can do. *(lit.)*

注 同"冇晒符"（0316）。

0318　冇哪更

mou⁵ naa¹ gaang¹ *(translit.)*

Have no connection. *(lit.)*

Not to the point.

Be wide of the mark.

Have not a bit relation with...

注 即完全沒有關係。參閱"冇哪哽"條（0319）。

0319　冇哪哽

mou⁵ naa¹ nang³ *(translit.)*

Be not related to. *(lit.)*

Have nothing to do with...

Do not get entangled with...

Establish no relations with...

注 表示沒聯繫或沒關係的意思。參閱"冇哪更"條（0318）。

0320　冇料

mou⁵ liu² *(translit.)*

Have no materials. *(lit.)*

Be ill-educated.

Be low-level in knowledge / technique.

注 形容人沒有學問或知識，技術水平低。

0321　冇家教

mou⁵ gaa¹ gaau³ *(translit.)*

Have no family teaching. *(lit.)*

Lack home education.

Be not cultured.

注 泛指缺乏家庭教育，尤指小孩不懂禮貌。參閱"有爺生冇乸教"（0693）條。

0322　冇紋路

mou⁵ man⁴ lou⁶ *(translit.)*

Be like the wood without any grain. *(lit.)*

Have no sense of propriety.

Do not act on principle.

Be careless and casual.

注 形容人做事沒分寸，無原則，或漫不經心。

0323　冇掩雞籠——自出自入

mou⁵ jim² gai¹ lung⁴ — zi⁶ ceot¹ zi⁶ jap⁶ *(translit.)*

A chicks' bamboo — cage without door — everyone goes out and comes in freely. *(lit.)*

The place where everybody can cine and go at random.

注 指可以隨意來去的地方。

0324　冇眼屎乾淨盲

mou⁵ ngaan⁵ si² gon¹ zeng⁶ maang⁴ *(translit.)*

Become cleanly blind without any gum in the eyes. *(lit.)*

Out of sight, out of mind.

Let the loss be loss.

Cut the loss.

注 表示眼不見，心不煩或趕緊脱手，免多受損失等意思。

0325　冇眼睇

mou⁵ ngaan⁵ tai² *(translit.)*

Have no eyes to see. *(lit.)*

Turn a blind eye to...

Throw in one's hand.

注 表示撒手不管的意思。

0326 冇得斟

mou[5] dak[1] zam[1] *(translit.)*

Have no more discussion. (lit.)

Leave something out of consideration.

Make no concession to...

Be at one's wit's end.

🈯表示沒商量，不加考慮或不作讓步等意思。

0327 冇得諗

mou[5] dak[1] nam[2] *(translit.)*

Be not worth thinking. (lit.)

Leave something out of consideration.

🈯表示無法加以考慮的意思。

0328 冇揸拿

mou[5] zaa[1] naa[4] *(translit.)*

Have nothing to get hold of. (lit.)

Gain no guarantee against loss.

🈯即沒有保證的意思。

0329 冇幾何

mou[5] gei[2] ho[2] *(translit.)*

Not many times. (lit.)

Not...so often.

Seldom.

Seldom or never.

🈯表示不經常；不常的意思。

0330 冇腰骨

mou[5] jiu[1] gwat[1] *(translit.)*

Have no spinebone. (lit.)

Be not reliable.

Be untrustworthy.

Be undependable.

🈯指人沒骨氣；靠不住。

0331 冇解

mou[5] gaai[2] *(translit.)*

Have no explanation. (lit.)

It is unreasonable （that...）

🈯意為"不像話"，多作引語。

0332 冇話好講

mou[5] waa[6] hou[2] gong[2] *(translit.)*

Have not any words to say. (lit.)

Can find nothing to say.

Be stuck for an answer.

🈯即無話可説。

0333 冇趟雙

mou[5] tong[3] soeng[1] *(translit.)*

There is not another row. (lit.)

Not to double-cross somebody at all.

It is not a fish story.

There is no...more than this.

Be absolutely genuine.

Be as true as a die.

🈯表示不騙人，確實如此的意思。

0334 冇樣叻

mou[5] joeng[6] lek[1] *(translit.)*

Nothing good. (lit.)

Be good for nothing.

Be good for naught.

🈯形容人一無所長。

0335 冇頭烏蠅

mou[5] tau[4] wu[1] jing[1] *(translit.)*

A headless fly. (lit.)

Act / Run helter-skelter.

Do not act in a planned way.

🈯形容人亂闖亂撞或做事無計劃。

0336 冇聲氣

mou[5] seng[1] hei[3] *(translit.)*

Have no sound and air. (lit.)

Have got no information.

Beyond hope.

🈯表示沒有消息或沒有希望的意思。

四畫

0337　冇釐正經

mou⁵ lei⁴ zing³ ging¹ *(translit.)*

Have not a bit of seriousness. (lit.)

Be not so decent as one should be.

注 表示不夠嚴肅或不夠正派的意思。

0338　冇釐搭霎

mou⁵ lei⁴ daap³ saap³ *(translit.)*

Have not a bit of care. (lit.)

注 同"冇紋路"（0322）。

0339　冇檳榔唔嚼得出汁

mou⁵ ban¹ long⁴ m⁴ ziu⁶ dak¹ ceot¹ zap¹ *(translit.)*

Without betel-nuts, no juice can be chewed out. (lit.)

Every why has its wherefore.

There is no smoke without fire.

Nothing is stolen without hands.

注 表示事出有因的意思。參閱"無風不起浪"條（1839）。

0340　冇譜

mou⁵ pou² *(translit.)*

Have no musical notes. (lit.)

Be incoherent.

Be unreasonable.

Break the routine.

注 即"離譜"。也指某些狀態達到令人不能忍受的程度。

0341　冇彎轉

mou⁵ waan¹ zyun³ *(translit.)*

There is no bend to turn. (lit.)

There is no leeway to save the situation.

There is no way to break a deadlock.

Reach an impasse.

Have no room for manoeuvre.

注 沒有轉彎的餘地，沒有補救的辦法或

陷入僵局的意思。

0342　冇癮

mou⁵ jan⁵ *(translit.)*

No addiction. (lit.)

Bored.

Senseless.

Feel no interest in something.

注 無聊，沒意思，沒趣或對（某事）不感興趣。

0343　牙尖嘴利

ngaa⁴ zim¹ zeoi² lei⁶ *(translit.)*

The teeth are pointed and the mouth is sharp. (lit.)

Be flannel-mouthed.

Be eloquent.

0344　牙斬斬

ngaa⁴ zaam² zaam² *(translit.)*

The teeth are chopping and chopping. (lit.)

Chop in.

Shoot one's mouth.

Wag one's tongue.

Tend to speak about oneself.

Be talky.

注 形容人好滔滔不絕地講話來表現自己。

0345　牙煙

ngaa⁴ jin¹ *(translit.)*

The teeth are smoky. (lit.)

Be dangerous.

Be unsteady.

Be horrible.

注 表示危險的，不穩固的，恐怖的，難看的。

0346　牙齒痕

ngaa⁴ ci² han²ᐟ⁴ *(translit.)*

The scar caused by teeth. (lit.)

四
畫

The offence given to somebody.
An old score.

🈯 指對別人的冒犯或宿怨。

0347　牙齒當金使

ngaa⁴ ci² dong³ gam¹ sai² *(translit.)*

Teeth are used as gold. (lit.)

Be as good as one's words.
Keep one's promise.
Keep one's words.

🈯 表示一諾千金或説話算數的意思。

0348　牙擦擦

ngaa⁴ caat³ caat³ *(translit.)*

The teeth keep on brushing. (lit.)

Be talky.
Wag one's tongue.
Boast too much of oneself.

🈯 形容人誇誇其談,驕傲自大。

0349　比上不足比下有餘

bei² soeng⁶ bat¹ zuk¹ bei² haa⁶ jau⁵ jyu⁴ *(translit.)*

It is insufficient when one is compared to the uppermost but it is more than enough when one is compared to the lowest. (lit.)

Be worse as compared with the best but better as compared with the worst.

0350　切肉不離皮

cit³ juk⁶ bat¹ lei⁴ pei⁴ *(translit.)*

The flesh cut still sticks to the skin. (lit.)

Blood is thicker than water.
Nothing is as affectionate as flesh and blood.

🈯 表示親情難捨的意思。

0351　少件膶

siu² gin⁶ jeon² *(translit.)*

Lack of a piece of liver. (lit.)

Be flighty.
Be more abnormal than normal.

🈯 形容人心理不正常。廣東人稱"肝"為"膶"。

0352　少數怕長計

siu² sou³ paa³ coeng⁴ gai³ *(translit.)*

A little quantity fears to be counted for long. (lit.)

Many a little makes a mickle.

🈯 指儘管每次算起來都微不足道,但長期計算也就很可觀了。

0353　日久見人心

jat⁶ gau² gin³ jan⁴ sam¹ *(translit.)*

A person's heart can be seen in long course of time. (lit.)

Time makes one understand a person.
It takes a long time to understand a person's heart.

🈯 指時間是檢驗人心的最好方法。

0354　日慳夜慳,唔夠老公一鋪攤

jat⁶ haan¹ je⁶ haan¹, m⁴ gou³ lou⁵ gung¹ jat¹ pou¹ taan¹ *(translit.)*

What is spared day and night is not enough for a husband to gamble 'Fantan' for once. ('Fantan' is a form of gambling) (lit.)

All is lost on an occasion.
All goes down the drain at once.
Penny wise and pound foolish.

🈯 比喻小處精明,大處浪費。

0355　日頭唔好講人,夜晚唔好講神

jat⁶ tau² m⁴ hou² gong² jan⁴, je⁶ maan⁵ m⁴ hou² gong² san⁴ *(translit.)*

四畫

Don't speak of men by day and of gods by night. (lit.)

Talk of the devil and he will appear.

🈲 相當於一説曹操，曹操就到。

0356　水上扒龍船，岸上人有眼

seoi² soeng⁶ paa⁴ lung⁴ syun⁴, ngon⁶ soeng⁶ jan⁴ jau⁵ ngaan⁵ *(translit.)*

Row dragon boats on the water, the people on both banks have eyes. (lit.)

Lookers-on see better.

Lookers-on see more than the players.

On-lookers see most of the game.

🈲 比喻旁觀者清。

0357　水上扒龍船，岸上夾死仔

seoi² soeng⁶ paa⁴ lung⁴ syun⁴, ngon⁶ soeng⁶ gaap³ sei² zai² *(translit.)*

Others row dragon boats on the water but people on the bank squeeze child to death. (lit.)

Key oneself up over other's business.

Feel both anxious and nervous at other's business.

🈲 原義指在龍舟競渡中，岸上人看得緊張時，連小孩也夾死。因此轉喻指替別人着急。

0358　水瓜打狗——唔見咗一撅

seoi² gwaa¹ daa² gau² — m⁴ gin³ zo² jat¹ kyut⁶ *(translit.)*

Beat a dog with a cucumber — one half of it is lost. (lit.)

Half of something is lost.

🈲 表示失去一半的意思。

0359　水汪汪

seoi² wong¹ wong¹ *(translit.)*

Be watery. (lit.)

Have only a forlorn hope.

Come to nothing.

Be below the standard.

🈲 表示希望不大，渺茫，及不上要求等。

0360　水鬼升城隍

seoi² gwai² sing¹ sing⁴ wong⁴ *(translit.)*

A water ghost is promoted to being City God. (lit.)

Set a beggar on horse back and he will ride to the devil.

🈲 現多含貶義，表示小人得志的意思。

0361　水浸眼眉

seoi² zam³ ngaan⁵ mei⁴ *(translit.)*

The water floods eyebrows. (lit.)

The black ox has trod on one's foot.

Be at death's door.

🈲 指災害已降臨到頭上。

0362　水落石出

seoi² lok⁶ sek⁶ ceot¹ *(translit.)*

When the water goes down, the rock comes out.

Come out in the wash.

0363　水過鴨背

seoi² gwo³ aap³ bui³ *(translit.)*

The water flows over the back of a duck. (lit.)

Be like water off duck's back.

Be forgetful of...

🈲 比喻聽説話，唸書等不在意，轉眼便忘得一乾二淨。

0364　水溝油

seoi² kau¹ jau⁴ *(translit.)*

Mix water with oil. (lit.)

Cannot get along with each other.

Feel hostility towards each other.

注 "溝"即"混合",水與油是無法混合的,故此語表示合不來的意思。

0365 水靜河飛

seoi² zing³ ho⁴ fei¹ *(translit.)*

The water is still and the river is flying. (lit.)

There is nobody everywhere.

There is not anybody here and there.

Silence reigns in the place.

The market is dull.

注 表示到處無人或市場清淡。(按"水靜河飛"實為"水靜(淨)鵝飛"的音誤,而且和本意也不同。)

0366 牛一

ngau⁴ jat¹ *(translit.)*

Cow and one. (lit.)

Birthday.

注 這是拆字式的俚語。"牛"字下加"一"字便成"生"字,因此便藉以比喻生日。

0367 牛皮燈籠——點極都唔明

ngau⁴ pei⁴ dang¹ lung⁴ – dim² gik⁶ dou¹ m⁴ ming⁴ *(translit.)*

A lantern mounted with hide — not transparent — no matter how it is lit. (lit.)

Not understand what one is taught.

Be poor at understanding what somebody says.

Be thick-headed.

注 歇後語,"點"(燃點,指點)和"明"(光明,明白)都是雙關詞。

0368 牛死送牛喪

ngau⁴ sei² sung³ ngau⁴ song¹ *(translit.)*

Attend a funeral procession of a cow when it is dead. (lit.)

Flog a dead horse.

Feed a dead horse with nice hay.

Work for a dead horse.

Throw good money after bad.

Throw helve after the hatchet.

注 比喻明知絕望還花功夫去幹或想補償損失,反而損失更大。

0369 牛唔飲水,唔撳得牛頭低

ngau⁴ m⁴ jam² seoi², m⁴ gam⁶ dak¹ ngau⁴ tau⁴ dai¹ *(translit.)*

If a cow does not want to drink water, no one can push its head down. (lit.)

You may take a horse to the water, but you cannot make him drink.

Of one's own will.

Of one's own accord.

注 指任何事不能強迫人去做,一切必須自願。

0370 牛高馬大

ngau⁴ gou¹ maa⁵ daai⁶ *(translit.)*

As tall as an ox and big as a horse. (lit.)

Stand like a giant.

注 形容人生得高大,但常用於貶義句子中。

0371 牛頭唔對馬嘴

ngau⁴ tau⁴ m⁴ deoi³ maa⁵ zeoi² *(translit.)*

A cow's head does not match with a horse's mouth. (lit.)

The answer is incongruous with the question.

Fly off at a tangent.

Lose the thread of one's discourse.

Beside the point.

四畫

Be irrelevent to...

注 即"牛頭不對馬嘴"。

0372　牛嚼牡丹——唔知花定草

ngau⁴ ziu⁶ maau⁵ daan¹ — m⁴ zi¹ faa¹ ding⁶ cou² *(translit.)*

An ox chews peony.—It does not know whether it is flower or grass. (lit.)

Not know chalk from cheese.
Cast pearls before swine.

注 比喻不識好歹。

0373　手瓜硬

sau² gwaa¹ ngaang⁶ *(translit.)*

The muscle of arms is hard. (lit.)

Have real power.
Be in a position of strength.

注 比喻有實力或有勢力。

0374　手多多

sau² do¹ do¹ *(translit.)*

Have many hands. (lit.)

Touch anything that one sees.

注 形容多手多腳,愛亂摸亂弄。

0375　手忙腳亂

sau² mong⁴ goek³ lyun⁶ *(translit.)*

Hands busy and feet confused. (lit.)

Be all in a hustle of excitements.

0376　手作仔

sau² zok³ zai² *(translit.)*

Hand-working guy. (lit.)

Craftsman.

注 手藝人,工匠。

0377　手尾長

sau² mei⁵ coeng⁴ *(translit.)*

The hand and tail is long. (lit.)

The trouble lasts long.
The trouble is endless for the future.

注 後患無窮的意思。

0378　手板係肉;手背又係肉

sau² baan² hai⁶ juk⁶; sau² bui³ jau⁶ hai⁶ juk⁶ *(translit.)*

The palms of hands are flesh and the backs of them are also flesh. (lit.)

Have friendly relation with both parties.
Cannot treat either side with partiality.

注 表示和雙方都有友情關係故很難偏袒哪一方的意思。

0379　手指拗出唔拗入

sau² zi² aau² ceot¹ m⁴ aau² jap⁶ *(translit.)*

Fingers are bent out but not bent in. (lit.)

Help and protect outsiders.

注 指自己人不幫自己人卻去幫助外人的行為。

0380　手指罅疏

sau² zi² laa³ so¹ *(translit.)*

The gaps between fingers are estranged. (lit.)

Money burns a hole in one's pocket.
Spend money like water.
Can hardly save any money.

注 表示有錢便花光或揮金如土沒有甚麼積蓄的意思。

0381　手急眼快

sau² gap¹ ngaan⁵ faai³ *(translit.)*

Deft hands and quick eyes. (lit.)

Save the tide.
Seize the right time.
Be quick of eye and deft of hand.

0382　手氣
sau² hei³ *(translit.)*
The air of hands. (lit.)
Luck at gambling.

0383　手痕痕
sau² han⁴ han⁴ *(translit.)*
The hand itches. (lit.)
Be eager to try.
注 即手癢；躍躍欲試的意思。

0384　手搵口食
sau² wan² hau² sik⁶ *(translit.)*
Hands gain and mouth eats. (lit.)
Live from hand to mouth.
注 形容收入不多，沒積蓄，僅能糊口。

0385　手緊
sau² gan² *(translit.)*
The hand is tight. (lit.)
Be short of cash.
Be in low water.
One's money is tight.
Be out at elbows.
注 表示缺乏現金或拮据。

0386　片面之詞
pin³ min⁶ zi¹ ci⁴ *(translit.)*
One-faced remarks. (lit.)
One-sided statement.
注 指單方面的意見或說法。

0387　反口咬一啖
faan² hau² ngaau⁵ jat¹ daam⁶ *(translit.)*
Turn around the mouth and give a bite. (lit.)
Trump up a countercharge against somebody.
Turn around and hit back.
注 表示反咬一口或反戈一擊的意思。

0388　反口覆舌
faan² hau² fuk¹ sit⁶ *(translit.)*
Turn over the mouth and tongue. (lit.)
Not to keep one's words.
Break one's promise.
Deny one's words.
注 即不履行諾言，言而無信。

0389　反斗
faan² dau² *(translit.)*
Overturn a peck of trouble. (lit.)
Be naughty/mischievous.
注 形容小孩子坐不住，淘氣調皮。

0390　反面
faan² min² *(translit.)*
Turn over the face. (lit.)
Suddenly turn out to be hostile to one's...
注 即翻臉。

0391　反骨
faan² gwat¹ *(translit.)*
Over-turned bones. (lit.)
Have a rebellious disposition.
注 形容人忘恩負義，翻臉無情。

0392　反骨仔
faan² gwat¹ zai² *(translit.)*
A person with over-turned bones. (lit.)
A betrayer.
A rebel.
注 參閱 "反骨" （0391）。

0393　反轉豬肚就係屎
faan² zyun³ zyu¹ tou⁵ zau⁶ hai⁶ si² *(translit.)*
Turn a pig's stomach inside out and there manure appears. (lit.)
Turn friendship into hostility.
Change friendship into anger.
Suddenly turn out to be hostile to

四畫

one's friend.

注 即瞬即翻臉無情。

0394　今時唔同往日，一個酸梅兩個核

gam¹ si⁴ m⁴ tung⁴ wong⁵ jat⁶, jat¹ go³ syun¹ mui⁴ loeng⁵ go³ wat⁶ *(translit.)*

The present time is different from the past days, a sour plum has two stones. (lit.)

The two cannot be mentioned in the same breath.

There have been the vicissitudes of life.

One's present situation is different from the past one.

注 即今非昔比。

0395　分甘同味

fan¹ gam¹ tung⁴ mei⁶ *(translit.)*

Share the sweet to have the same taste. (lit.)

Enjoy the diet together.

Share and share alike.

0396　公死有肉食，婆死有肉食

gung¹ sei² jau⁵ juk⁶ sik⁶, po⁴ sei² jau⁵ juk⁶ sik⁶ *(translit.)*

There is flesh to eat no matter whether the husband or the wife dies. (lit.)

Effortlessly gain profit / cash in on others' efforts / conflict.

Take advantage of a conflicting situation to profit oneself.

注 表示坐收漁人之利的意思。

0397　公說公有理；婆說婆有理

gung¹ syut³ gung¹ jau⁵ lei⁵; po⁴ syut³ po⁴ jau⁵ lei⁵ *(translit.)*

Husband says he has reason; wife says she also has reason. (lit.)

There is much to be said on both sides.

Everything has two sides.

Each clings to his own view.

Both parties claim to be in the right.

0398　勿歇

mat⁶ hit³ *(translit.)*

Without a pause. (lit.)

Unceasingly.

Continuously.

Without a pause.

注 表示不停地或不斷地。

0399　欠債還錢

him³ zaai³ waan⁴ cin⁴ *(translit.)*

Repay the debt. (lit.)

Promise a debt.

注 借了錢便該還。

0400　六耳不同謀

luk⁶ ji⁵ bat¹ tung⁴ mau⁴ *(translit.)*

Six ears cannot plot together. (lit.)

Two's company, three's none.

注 表示三人共同做事，意見多，難於一致的意思。

0401　六神無主

luk⁶ san⁴ mou⁴ zyu² *(translit.)*

The six vital organs lose their function. (lit.)

Be covered with confusion.

Be thrown into confusion.

0402　六親不認

luk⁶ can¹ bat¹ jing⁶ *(translit.)*

Not to recognize six relations. (lit.)

Turn one's back upon all one's relations.

0403　文雀

man⁴ zoek³ *(translit.)*

Gentle bird. (lit.)

Pickpocket.

🈲指扒手。

0404　火上加油

fo² soeng⁶ gaa¹ jau⁴ *(translit.)*

Add oil on the fire. (lit.)

Pour oil on fire.

0405　火腿繩

fo² teoi² sing⁴ *(translit.)*

The rope used to tie a ham. (lit.)

The person who puts himself under the patronage of somebody.

The person who depends on somebody's status for his position.

🈲諷刺倚仗有權勢的人抬高自己的身價或攀龍附鳳的人。中國火腿價格昂貴，奸商取巧，綁以粗大麻繩上秤，如此則麻繩的重量和價值，便和火腿相等。

0406　火遮眼

fo² ze¹ ngaan⁵ *(translit.)*

The fire covers the eyes. (lit.)

Be too angry to see anything / anybody.

🈲形容人極度憤怒的樣子。

0407　火頸

fo² geng² *(translit.)*

Firy neck. (lit.)

Be irritable.

Be irascible.

🈲指脾氣暴躁或容易激動。

0408　火燒棺材 —— 大炭（歎）

fo² siu¹ gun¹ coi⁴ — daai⁶ taan³
(translit.)

The fire burns a coffin — big charcoal (enjoyment). (lit.)

Live high.

Live like pigs in clover.

Lie on a bed of flowers.

🈲比喻過着享受的生活，養尊處優。

0409　火燒旗杆 —— 長炭（歎）

fo² siu¹ kei⁴ gon¹ — coeng⁴ taan³
(translit.)

The fire burns the flag staff-long charcoal (enjoyment). (lit.)

Live in clover as long as life lasts.

🈲比喻人一生能養尊處優。

0410　火燒燈芯 —— 冇炭（歎）

fo² siu¹ dang¹ sam¹ — mou⁵ taan³
(translit.)

The fire burns a wick — on charcoal (enjoyment). (lit.)

Lead a dog's life.

Bear hardship.

🈲比喻過着貧困的生活或境況堪悲。

0411　火麒麟 —— 周身引（癮）

fo² kei⁴ leon²ᐟ⁴ — zau¹ san¹ jan⁵
(translit.)

A firy Chinese unicorn (Kylin) — the whole body is full of fuses (addiction). (lit.)

The person who is addicted to all kinds of lusts.

🈲比喻嗜好多的人。

0412　心大心細

sam¹ daai⁶ sam¹ sai³ *(translit.)*

The heart is either big or small. (lit.)

Feel come hesitation in doing something.

Hesitate to do something.

🈲形容猶疑不決，拿不定主意。

0413　心不在焉

sam¹ bat¹ zoi⁶ jin⁴ *(translit.)*

The heart is out. (lit.)

Be absent-minded.

Listen inattentively.

0414　心中有屎

sam¹ zung¹ jau⁵ si² *(translit.)*

There is manure in the heart. (lit.)

Have a guilty conscience.

注 相當於作賊心虛或心中有鬼。

0415　心中有數

sam¹ zung¹ jau⁵ sou³ *(translit.)*

There is a sum in the heart. (lit.)

Know what is what.

Know fairly well.

Have a pretty good idea of...

0416　心甘命抵

sam¹ gam¹ meng⁶ dai² *(translit.)*

The heart is will and the fate deserves it. (lit.)

On a voluntary basis.

Of one's own accord.

On one's own initiative.

注 表示自願或主動的意思。

0417　心灰意冷

sam¹ fui¹ ji³ laang⁵ *(translit.)*

The heart is ashy and the will is cold. (lit.)

Feel disheartened.

Be downhearted.

Lose interest in...

0418　心多多

sam¹ do¹ do¹ *(translit.)*

Have many minds. (lit.)

Cannot make up one's mind.

Shilly-shally.

Be in two minds about...

Show a manner of instability.

Be in minds about...

注 表示三心兩意，拿不定主意。參閱 "十五個銅錢分兩份"（0097），"三心兩意"（0164）及 "寡母婆咁多心"（2130）各條。

0419　心安理得

sam¹ on¹ lei⁵ dak¹ *(translit.)*

The heart is void of offence. (lit.)

Feel at ease and justified.

Have a clear conscience.

0420　心足

sam¹ zuk¹ *(translit.)*

The heart contents itself. (lit.)

To one's heart's content.

Express one's satisfaction.

0421　心肝椗

sam¹ gon¹ ding³ *(translit.)*

The footstalk of heart and liver. (lit.)

One's darling.

One's dear heart.

Hold somebody/something dear.

Somebody/something nearest one's heart.

注 即心肝寶貝。

0422　心抱

sam¹ pou⁵ *(translit.)*

Hearted embrace. (lit.)

Daughter-in-law.

注 即兒媳婦。廣東人叫 "兒媳婦" 為 "心抱"，為 "新抱" 的變音。

0423　心服口服

sam¹ fuk⁶ hau² fuk⁶ *(translit.)*

Both the heart and the mouth are subordinate to. (lit.)

Be sincerely convinced.

0424　心郁郁

sam¹ juk¹ juk¹ *(translit.)*

The heart moves about. (lit.)

Find it in one's heart to do something.

Would like very much to do something.

注 表示動了心想做⋯⋯的意思。

0425　心思思

sam¹ si¹ si¹ *(translit.)*

With a thought in the mind. (lit.)

Have a mind to do something.

Ponder over...

Be spoiling for...

注 即老是想着或惦記着的意思。

0426　心急

sam¹ gap¹ *(translit.)*

The heart hurries up. (lit.)

Be short-tempered.

Be impatient.

In a hurry.

0427　心神恍惚

sam¹ san⁴ fong² fat¹ *(translit.)*

The heart becomes blurred and indistinct. (lit.)

Lose one's presence of mind.

Have a bee in one's bonnet.

Suffer from fidgets.

0428　心都涼晒

sam¹ dou¹ loeng⁴ saai³ *(translit.)*

The heart feels cool. (lit.)

Gloat over one's enemy's misfortune.

注 表示幸災樂禍的心態。

0429　心都實

sam¹ dou¹ sat⁶ *(translit.)*

The heart becomes solid. (lit.)

Be downhearted.

Be depressed.

Be melancholic.

Mope oneself.

注 表示鬱鬱不樂或悶悶不樂的意思。

0430　心淡

sam¹ taam⁵ *(translit.)*

The heart becomes insipid. (lit.)

Be discouraged.

Show indifference towards...

Lose heart.

Lose confidence in...

注 表示心灰意冷，失去信心或不感興趣。參閱 "心灰意冷"（0417）。

0431　心照不宣

sam¹ ziu³ bat¹ syun¹ *(translit.)*

The heart understands without mentioning. (lit.)

Have a tacit understanding.

0432　心噏句，口噏句

sam¹ go² geoi³, hau² go² geoi³ *(translit.)*

The heart says so and the mouth also says so. (lit.)

Say what one thinks about.

The tongue speaks what the heart thinks.

Say from the bottom of one's heart.

Be outspoken in the expression of one's opinions.

注 即心中想甚麼，嘴上説甚麼。

0433　心亂如麻

sam¹ lyun⁶ jyu⁴ maa⁴ *(translit.)*

The heart is as confused as tangled hemp. (lit.)

One's mind is in a tangle.

Be utterly confused and

四畫

disconcerted.

Be completely upset.

0434　心煩

sam¹ faan⁴ *(translit.)*

The heart is troubled. (lit.)

Vex oneself.

Be vexed.

注 表示獨自煩惱的意思，參閱 "腌悶" 條（1866）。

0435　心酸

sam¹ syun¹ *(translit.)*

The heart feel sour. (lit.)

Be deeply grieved.

Nurse a grievance.

Feel sad.

0436　心領

sam¹ ling⁵ *(translit.)*

The heart accepts it. (lit.)

No, thank you.

I appreciate your kindness but I must decline the offer.

注 用於婉言謝絕對方禮物或好意的客氣話。

0437　引狼入屋拉雞仔

jan⁵ long⁴ jap⁶ uk¹ laai¹ gai¹ zai² *(translit.)*

Invite a wolf into the house to drag chickens. (lit.)

Bring disaster upon oneself.

Invite loss for oneself.

Invite a wolf to watch chickens.

注 即 "引狼入室"。

0438　巴閉

baa¹ bai³ *(translit.)*

Noisy. (lit.)

Make a noise about something.

Be bustling with noise and excitement.

Be in a bustle.

Speak in excitement.

Make a noise in the world.

Be great in strength and impetus.

Of great celebrity.

Win popularity.

A great occasion.

注 形容人做事緊張忙亂，喧囂，或者形容人在社會上了不起，勢力大，亦可以形容場面隆重，排場大。

0439　巴渣

baa¹ zaa¹ *(translit.)*

Make a noise. (lit.)

Long-tongued.

Gossipy.

Nosy.

注 形容人多嘴，好管閒事。

0440　巴結

baa¹ git³ *(translit.)*

Flatter. (lit.)

Play up to somebody.

Fawn upon somebody.

Toady somebody.

Tickle somebody's ears.

0441　巴結有錢佬好過拜靈菩薩

baa¹ git³ jau⁵ cin⁴ lou² hou² gwo³ baai³ leng⁴ pou⁴ saat³ *(translit.)*

It is better to toady rich men than it is to worship efficacious gods. (lit.)

It is much more advantageous to rub elbows with the rich.

注 "佬" 即人，"好過" 即勝過。

四畫

五 畫

0442 未有來

mei[6] jau[5] loi[1/2] *(translit.)*

Not yet. (lit.)

It is still a long time before...

It is quite a while before...

📌表示要很久才會……或離……還早的意思。參閱"有排"條（0685）。

0443 未見其利先見其害

mei[6] gin[3] kei[4] lei[6] sin[1] gin[3] kei[4] hoi[6] *(translit.)*

See the injury before seeing the profit. (lit.)

Visible disadvantage comes before the invible advantage.

Suffer a loss before an uncertain gain.

📌同"未見官先打三十大板"。

0444 未見官先打三十大板

mei[6] gin[3] gun[1] sin[1] daa[2] saam[1] sap[6] daai[6] baan[2] *(translit.)*

Be put to torture with a plank for thirty times before seeing the county Magistrate. (lit.)

Suffer a loss before the gain.

Visible disadvantage comes before the invisible advantage.

📌相當於"未見其利，先見其害"。

0445 未知心腹事，先聽口中言

mei[6] zi[1] sam[1] fuk[1] si[6], sin[1] ting[3] hau[2] zung[1] jin[4] *(translit.)*

Listen to the words by mouth before knowing the affairs in the heart. (lit.)

Words out of the mouth are the words indeed.

A straw shows which way the wind blows.

0446 未登天子位，先置殺人刀

mei[6] dang[1] tin[1] zi[2] wai[6], sin[1] zi[3] saat[3] jan[4] dou[1] *(translit.)*

Buy a knife to kill people before coming to the throne. (lit.)

Exercise one's power before filling the position.

Be puffed up with pride before becoming rich.

Begin to do something that one is incompetent to do before one is qualified to do it.

0447 未學行先學走

mei[6] hok[6] haang[4] sin[1] hok[6] zau[2] *(translit.)*

Begin to run before learning to walk. (lit.)

Learn to run before learning to walk.

📌即不會走就想跑。

0448 未觀其人，先觀其友

mei[6] gun[1] kei[4] jan[4], sin[1] gun[1] kei[4] jau[5] *(translit.)*

See his friends before seeing the man. (lit.)

You can judge a man by the friends he keeps.

0449 打牙祭

daa[2] ngaa[4] zai[3] *(translit.)*

Beat teeth ceremony. (lit.)

Eat one's fill.

Gorge oneself with a tuck-in.

📌即大吃一頓。

0450 打牙骹

daa[2] ngaa[4] gaau[3] *(translit.)*

Beat the jawbones. (lit.)

Have a chat with somebody.

注 表示和人閒談，閒聊。

0451　打地鋪

daa² dei⁶ pou¹ *(translit.)*

Sleep on the ground. (lit.)

Make up a bed on the ground.

注 把被褥等鋪在地上睡覺。

0452　打死不離親兄弟

daa² sei² bat¹ lei⁴ can¹ hing¹ dai⁶ *(translit.)*

It is full brothers who can fight to death together to defend each other. (lit.)

Blood is thicker than water.

0453　打死狗講價

daa² sei² gau² gong² gaa³ *(translit.)*

Drive a hard bargain over the dog which was beaten to death. (lit.)

Fish in trouble water.

Take advantage of somebody's fault to practice an extortion.

注 指既成事實後再談條件或講價錢，一方可漫天要價，另一方處於不利地位。

0454　打尖

daa² zim¹ *(translit.)*

Jump into the middle of a queue. (lit.)

Push oneself into a queue out of the turn.

Jump the queue.

注 即插隊。

0455　打同通

daa² tung⁴ tung¹ *(translit.)*

Have a mutual communication. (lit.)

Act in collusion with each other.

Be in collaboration with each other.

注 即串通，互相勾結。

0456　打如意算盤

daa² jyu⁴ ji³ syun³ pun⁴ *(translit.)*

Reckon on the abacus of wishful thinking. (lit.)

Wish to have one's own will.

Work out a plan advantageous to oneself.

Have one's smug calculations.

0457　打〔大〕赤肋

daa² [daai⁶] cik³ / cek³ lak⁶ *(translit.)*

Bare oneself. (lit.)

Strip oneself to the waist.

注 打赤膊的意思。

0458　打劫紅毛鬼，進貢佛蘭西

daa² gip³ hung⁴ mou⁴ gwai², zeon³ gung³ fat⁶ laan¹ sai¹ *(translit.)*

Rob red-haired ghost of something and offer it to France. (Red-haired ghost a nickname standing for Englishman) (lit.)

Rob Peter to pay Paul.

注 比喻取之於甲而予之於乙。

0459　打完齋唔要和尚

daa² jyun⁴ zaai¹ m⁴ jiu³ wo⁴ soeng² *(translit.)*

After the Buddhist fasts, Buddhist monks are no longer needed. (lit.)

Kick down the ladder.

Once on shore, pray no more.

注 相當於 "過河拆橋"。參閱 "過橋抽板" 條（2004）。

0460　打到褪

daa² dou³ tan³ *(translit.)*

Go backward. (lit.)

五畫

Be retrogressive.

Be out of luck.

Be down on one's luck.

注 表示後退或倒運的意思。如意為"倒運"時，廣東人又説成"行路打倒退"。

0461　打斧頭

daa² fu² tau⁴ *(translit.)*

Beat the head of an axe. (lit.)

Cook up an expence account to line one's pockets.

Do not give the whole story.

注 即揩油（常指代買東西或代辦事從中佔點小便宜），亦轉喻表示講述一件事時作了些隱瞞。

0462　打店

daa² dim³ *(translit.)*

Beat a shop. (lit.)

Put up for the night in an inn or a hotel.

注 表示在旅館或酒店投宿的意思。

0463　打底

daa² dai² *(translit.)*

Beat the bottom. (lit.)

Give somebody a hint beforehand.

注 表示先給人一個暗示或露些口風的意思。

Put something under something.

注 墊底，先在某些東西下放些另外的東西的意思。

Eat something before having wine.

注 有些不慣喝酒的人很易醉酒，據説先吃些東西然後喝酒，便不易飲醉，這又説是"墊底"。

0464　打法功夫還鬼願

daa² faat³ gung¹ fu¹ waan⁴ gwai²

jyun⁶ *(translit.)*

The work to expound the teachings of Buddhism is to fulfil the vow of ghosts. (lit.)

Work in a perfunctory manner.

Lie down on the job.

注 指敷衍塞責。

0465　打草驚蛇

daa² cou² ging¹ se⁴ *(translit.)*

Beat the grass and frighten the snake. (lit.)

Wake a sleeping dog.

Cause undesired agitation.

0466　打真軍

daa² zan¹ gwan¹ *(translit.)*

Fight with real weapons. (lit.)

Work in real earnest.

Do the business with special capital.

注 即認真地幹或以實際資本做生意。

0467　打特

daa² dak⁶ *(translit.)*

Be stunned. (lit.)

Be astounded.

Be startled.

注 表示事情來得很突然，使自己暗暗吃驚的意思。又作"打突兀"。

0468　打個白鴿轉

daa² go³ baak⁶ gap³ zyun³/⁶ *(translit.)*

Make a pigeon round. (lit.)

Turn around.

Walk around.

注 表示打一個轉或到附近走走的意思。

0469　打退堂鼓

daa² teoi³ tong⁴ gu² *(translit.)*

Beat the drum to dismiss the court. (lit.)

五畫

Back out one's promise.

Beat a retreat.

注 指人收回承諾的意思。

0470　打理

daa² lei⁵ *(translit.)*

Take care of. (lit.)

Manage.

Run.

注 料理，管理。

0471　打荷包

daa² ho⁴ baau¹ *(translit.)*

Beat the purse. (lit.)

Pick a pocket.

注 小偷或扒手掏錢包。

0472　打敗仗

daa² baai⁶ zoeng³ *(translit.)*

Be defeated. (lit.)

Fall sick.

Take sick.

Be taken ill.

注 即"病倒了"，在口語上和戰爭沒有甚麼關係。

0473　打蛇隨棍上

daa² se⁴ ceoi⁴ gwan³ soeng⁵ *(translit.)*

Beat a snake and it creeps up along the stick. (lit.)

Take advantage of the tide.

Seize occasion by the forelock.

At the bare idea of...

注 表示順着情勢，乘機提出自己的想法或要求。

0474　打得更多夜又長

daa² dak¹ gaang¹ do¹ je²ᐟ⁶ jau⁶ coeng⁴ *(translit.)*

The more the night-watching drum is beaten, the longer the night becomes. (lit.)

It wastes time only to talk.

Fine words butter no parsnips.

Actions speak louder than words.

注 表示空言無益，行動勝於空言的意思。

0475　打掂

daa² dim⁶ *(translit.)*

Beat uprightness. (lit.)

Set / Put something upright.

Set / Put something with one end upward and the other downward.

With the head / one end northward and the feet / the other end southward.

注 表示把東西垂直或直立放或一端向北另一端向南平放的意思。

0476　打單

daa² daan¹ *(translit.)*

Type an invoice. (lit.)

Blackmail somebody.

Practise extortion.

Extort money from somebody.

注 匪徒給人寫恐嚇信，勒索錢財。

0477　打單泡

daa² daan¹ paau¹ *(translit.)*

Do business single-handed. (lit.)

A travelling trader working all by himself.

Take independent action.

注 跑單幫的人或表示單獨行動的意思。

0478　打腳骨

daa² goek³ gwat¹ *(translit.)*

Beat the bone of the leg. (lit.)

Fleece somebody of his money.

Hold up.

注 表示攔路搶劫或敲竹槓。

0479　打橫嚟

daa² waang⁴ lai⁴ *(translit.)*

Lay crosswise. (lit.)

Be impervious to all reasons.

注 即不講道理。

0480　打輸數

daa² syu¹ sou³ *(translit.)*

Be thought as a loss. (lit.)

Give up for loss.

注 表示已作為損失計。

0481　打頭陣

daa² tau⁴ zan⁶ *(translit.)*

Fight in the van. (lit.)

Take the lead.

注 表示領頭的意思。

0482　打醒十二個精神

daa² sing² sap⁶ ji⁶ go³ zing¹ san⁴
　　(translit.)

Wake twelve spirits. (lit.)

Raise one's spirits.

Arouse one's spirits.

Cheer up.

Prick up one's ears.

注 表示提起精神，當心，"提高警惕"
　的意思。

0483　打錯主意

daa² co³ zyu² ji³ *(translit.)*

Beat out a wrong idea. (lit.)

Get a wrong idea into one's head.

**Get down from the wrong side of
the wall.**

0484　打錯算盤

daa² co³ syun³ pun⁴ *(translit.)*

Wrongly reckon on the abacus. (lit.)

Form a wrong estimation.

Make a wrong decision.

Be out in one's reckoning.

0485　打齋鶴

daa² zaai¹ hok⁶ *(translit.)*

*The crane which does penace for
the crime of the dead. (lit.)*

A steerer.

**A person who seduces somebody
to live the life of Riley.**

**A person who leads somebody
astray.**

注 引誘人墮落的人。

0486　打雜

daa² zaap⁶ *(translit.)*

Do all jobs. (lit.)

Do odd jobs.

A person of all work.

注 即雜工。

0487　打瀉茶

daa² se² caa⁴ *(translit.)*

Over-turned tea. (lit.)

**A widowed maiden. (a maiden
whose fiancé died before
wedding.)**

注 指訂了婚而未出嫁便喪未婚夫的女
　人。

0488　打邊爐同打屎窟

daa² bin¹ lou⁴ tung⁴ daa² si² fat¹
　　(translit.)

*Beat chafing dish and beat the
buttocks. (lit.)*

Out of all comparison.

Cannot be in comparison with...

**As different as chalk from
cheese.**

注 比喻兩者不能相比。

0489　打鐵趁熱

daa² tit³ can³ jit⁶ *(translit.)*

Strike the iron while it is hot. (lit.)

Strike the iron while it is hot.

五畫

Take advantage of the
   opportunity.
At the first opportunity.

0490　打爛砂盆問到篤

daa² laan⁶ saa¹ pun⁴ man⁶ dou³ duk¹
(translit.)

*Breaking an earthen rice-washing
basin, one asks to the bottom.*
(lit.)

Get to the bottom of the matter.
Search into a matter.
Seek after truth.

🈯即"打破沙鍋問到底"。

0491　打爛齋鉢

daa² laan⁶ zaai¹ but³ *(translit.)*
*Break the bowl for holding
vegetarian diet. (lit.)*

Break one's fast.
Break abstinence.
Break oneself of a habit.
Return to laity.

🈯比喻破戒或還俗。

0492　打響頭炮

daa² hoeng² tau⁴ paau³ *(translit.)*
Fire the first cannon. (lit.)

Meet with a first success.

🈯表示旗開得勝的意思。

0493　正一陳顯南

zing³ jat¹ can⁴ hin² naam²ᐟ⁴ *(translit.)*
*Be really the man by the name of
Can Hin Naam. (lit.)*

Be verbose.
Make repetition to a tiresome
   extent.

🈯指喜歡反反覆覆地説同一件事的人。

0494　正斗 / 正嘢

zeng³ dau² / zeng³ je⁵ *(translit.)*

Be legitimated. (lit.)
Certified product.
Be genuine.
Be excellent.

🈯表示好貨色或真貨色的意思。

0495　正話

zing³ waa⁶ *(translit.)*
Just. (lit.)

Just now.
A moment ago.
Just.
Happen to...
As it happens.

🈯表示正要,剛才或剛剛的意思。

0496　扒灰

paa⁴ fui¹ *(translit.)*
Rake ashes. (lit.)

Incest with one's daughter-in-
   law.

🈯指公公和媳婦有亂倫關係。

0497　扒逆水

paa⁴ ngaak⁶ seoi² *(translit.)*
Row against the current. (lit.)

Deal with something in contrary
   manner.

🈯相當於"反其道而行"。

0498　瓦風領 —— 包頂頸

ngaa⁵ fung¹ leng⁵ — baau¹ ding²
geng² *(translit.)*
*An earthen wind-collar — be sure
to support the neck. (lit.)*

Be sure to argue to the contrary.
The person who likes to bicker.

🈯指專和人抬槓的人。

0499　去搵周公

heoi³ wan² zau¹ gung¹ *(translit.)*
Go to look for Duke Zau. (lit.)

Go to bed.

Go to sleep.

注 這是把孔子說過 "久矣乎不夢見周公" 的話來比喻去睡覺。

0500　甘心咯！

gam[1] sam[1] lok[3] *(translit.)*

How sweet my heart is! (lit.)

How pleased I am to see it!

注 在幸災樂禍的時候所說的話，即 "我的心很涼啊！"。

0501　世界仔

sai[3] gaai[3] zai[2] *(translit.)*

The guy of the world. (lit.)

A lickspittle.

A worldly-wise person.

A person who knows the ways of the world.

注 指善於逢迎拍馬，八面玲瓏的人。

0502　世界輪流轉

sai[3] gaai[3] leon[4] lau[4] zyun[2] *(translit.)*

The world goes around and around. (lit.)

Everybody has the turn of the wheel.

Everybody meets with the Fortune's wheel.

By turns does the Fortune's wheel go around.

注 表示人的命運如車輪般轉動（變）。參閱 "風水輪流轉"（1257）條。

0503　古老石山

gu[2] lou[5] sek[6] saan[1] *(translit.)*

Ancient potted rocky mountain. (lit.)

An old fogy.

注 指頑固保守的人。

0504　古老當時興

gu[2] lou[5] dong[3] si[4] hing[1] *(translit.)*

Old fashion is thought as a new trend. (lit.)

Take an old style as the vogue of the day.

0505　古／蠱惑

gu[2] waak[6] *(translit.)*

Be sly. (lit.)

Be tricky.

Be as crafty as a fox.

Know a trick or two.

注 表示詭計多端或狡猾的意思。

0506　古縮

gu[2] suk[1] *(translit.)*

Old and shrinkable. (lit.)

Be quiet and unsocial.

Shrink into oneself.

注 形容人沉默寡言，性情不合羣，不愛交際。

0507　本地薑唔辣

bun[2] dei[6] goeng[1] m[4] laat[6] *(translit.)*

Local gingers are never hot. (lit.)

Grass is always greener on the other side of the fence.

注 指本地培養的人材不及外來者，含貶義。

0508　本事

bun[2] si[6] *(translit.)*

The originality. (lit.)

Be capable.

Ability.

0509　可大可小

ho[2] daai[6] ho[2] siu[2] *(translit.)*

It may be either big or small. (lit.)

It may be either serious or unimportant.

注 表示事情可能嚴重，也可能不重要的意思。

五畫

0510　左手嚟，右手去

zo² sau² lai⁴, jau⁶ sau² heoi³ *(translit.)*

Come to the left hand and go from the right. (lit.)

In at one hand and out at the other.

注 比喻金錢來的容易去的快。

0511　左右做人難

zo² jau⁶ zou⁶ jan⁴ naan⁴ *(translit.)*

It is difficult to be a human on either the left or the right. (lit.)

Be in a quandary about...

Be between Scylla and Charybdis.

Be a friend with a saint and a devil.

0512　左耳入，右耳出

zo² ji⁵ jap⁶, jau⁶ ji⁵ ceot¹ *(translit.)*

Come into the left ear and out of the right ear. (lit.)

In at one ear and out at the other.

0513　石地堂鐵掃把 —— 硬打硬

sek⁶ dei⁶ tong⁴ tit³ sou³ baa² — ngaang⁶ daa² ngaang⁶ *(translit.)*

Stone threshing floor and iron broom — hardness against hardness. (lit.)

A Roland for an Oliver.

Nip and tuck.

When Greek meets Greek, then comes the tug of war.

注 即 "勢均力敵"。參閱 "半斤八兩"（0584）條。

0514　石灰籮

sek⁶ fui¹ lo⁴ *(translit.)*

A bamboo basket used for holding lime. (lit.)

A person who is hated wherever he goes.

注 比喻到處幹壞事，到處留有污點穢跡的人，到處都不受歡迎的人。

0515　石沉大海

sek⁶ cam⁴ daai⁶ hoi² *(translit.)*

A rock sinks into a big sea. (lit.)

Disappear forever.

Be obliterated from one's memory.

0516　石罅米 —— 雞啄

sek⁶ laa³ mai⁵ — gai¹ doeng¹ *(translit.)*

The rice in the cleft of the rock — to be picked by hens. (lit.)

A man who is generous only in giving money to ladies.

注 諷刺只肯在女人身上花錢的男人，在廣東話裏，"雞" 常指妓女。

0517　平生不作虧心事，半夜敲門也不驚

ping⁴ saang¹ bat¹ zok³ kwai¹ sam¹ si⁶, bun³ je⁶ haau¹ mun⁴ jaa⁵ bat¹ ging¹ *(translit.)*

Nothing against the conscience is done in the ordinary life, there is no fear to knock on the door at midnight. (lit.)

A long roll of thunder frightens no man with a clear conscience.

0518　卡罅

kaa³ laa² *(translit.)*

A gap. (lit.)

The crevice between two things.

Either this or that.

Be equivocal.

注 表示兩物之間的縫隙（這是本意）或

兩可之間。

0519 田雞東

tin⁴ gai¹ dung¹ *(translit.)*

Frog hosts. (lit.)

Each pays his share for a meal.

Go Dutch.

Club together.

注 指幾個人湊錢或分攤費用吃東西的意思。

0520 田雞過河——各有各蹄

tin⁴ gai¹ gwo³ ho⁴ — gok³ jau⁵ gok³ jaang³ *(translit.)*

Frogs swim across the river — each stretches its legs for its own way. (lit.)

Need makes the old wife trot.

Make the best of one's own way.

Everyone puts his best leg forward.

Each takes to his legs.

注 即各走各路。

0521 四方木——踢一踢,郁一郁

sei³ fong¹ muk⁶ — tek³ jat¹ tek³, juk¹ jat¹ juk¹ *(translit.)*

A square log — kick it once and it moves once. (lit.)

A slow coach.

A lazybones.

注 形容遲鈍的人。又指懶人。

0522 四方辮頂

sei³ fong¹ bin¹ deng² *(translit.)*

Square head with a pigtail. (lit.)

A person who spends money on the lady who doesn't really love him.

注 指把金錢花在不是真心愛自己的女人身上的人。

0523 四正

si³ / sei³ zeng³ / zing³ *(translit.)*

Square-shaped. (lit.)

Regular-featured (of appearance).

注 表示端正不差(指外型)。

0524 生人勿近

saang¹ jan⁴ mat⁶ gan⁶ *(translit.)*

A person no living man can get near. (lit.)

A person whom one finds it hard to get along with.

注 形容一個難以相處的人。

0525 生人唔生膽

saang¹ jan⁴ m⁴ saang¹ daam² *(translit.)*

Born without a gall. (lit.)

Be as timid as a hare.

注 比喻膽小。

0526 生人霸死定

saang¹ jan⁴ baa³ sei² deng⁶ *(translit.)*

A living man occupies the place for his death. (lit.)

Act like a dog in the manger.

注 相當於"佔着茅坑不拉屎"。

0527 生水芋頭

saang¹ seoi² wu⁶ tau²/⁴ *(translit.)*

Water-bearing taro. (such a taro is not soft and floury even it is well-cooked) (lit.)

Be foolish-looking.

Be block-headed.

A simpleton.

A blockhead.

注 芋頭在煮熟後,應該是綿軟而粉的,但"生水芋頭"則否,雖然煮得很熟,仍是"腎"(讀高上聲san²)的,所謂"腎"san²意即不夠綿軟

五畫

而粉的，後以一音之轉，把"腎"讀
作san⁵音（低上聲），同時san⁵又喻
作傻氣的或傻氣的人。此語比喻傻裏
傻氣，不機靈或神經不大正常的人。

0528　生勾勾

saang¹ ngau¹ ngau¹ *(translit.)*

Be raw. (lit.)

Be undone.

Be still alive.

注 指未煮熟的或仍然活着的。

0529　生白果——腥夾悶

saang¹ baak⁶ gwo² — seng¹ gaap³
mun⁶ *(translit.)*

Raw ginkoes — they smell evil frowsy and sulky. (lit.)

Be fastidious.

Be hypercritical.

注 形容人難以討好的性格或好吹毛求疵。

0530　生仔唔知仔心肝

saang¹ zai² m⁴ zi¹ zai² sam¹ gon¹
(translit.)

Give birth to a son but know nothing about his heart and liver. (lit.)

It is hard to know people's hidden intention.

注 相當於"人心難測"。

0531　生死有定

saang¹ si² (sei²) jau⁵ ding⁶ *(translit.)*

Life and death are destined. (lit.)

Every bullet has its billet.

0532　生色

saang¹ sik¹ *(translit.)*

Bear colours. (lit.)

Add lustre to...

Add colour to...

注 增添光彩的意思。

0533　生安白造

saang¹ on¹ baak⁶ zou⁶ *(translit.)*

Make believe. (lit.)

Tell the tale.

Invent a story.

Make up an out-and-out fabrication.

注 表示虛構，編造的意思。

0534　生步

saang¹ bou² *(translit.)*

Unfamiliar space. (lit.)

New to somebody.

Strange.

Unfamiliar.

注 陌生的意思。

0535　生晒

saang¹ saai³ *(translit.)*

Come to life. (lit.)

Recover one's health / energy.

Rehabilitate oneself.

Resume one's spirits.

注 恢復健康或體力，恢復自己的地位或名譽或重新振作起來的意思。

0536　……生晒

... saang¹ saai³ *(translit.)*

Continuously. (lit.)

Keep on...

Without a pause.

Continuously.

注 放在動詞後；表示老是……或不斷……的意思，例如"嘈生晒"（老是吵鬧）或"催生晒"（不斷地催促）等。

0537　生骨大頭菜——種"縱"壞

saang¹ gwat¹ daai⁶ tau⁴ coi³ — zung³
waai⁶ *(translit.)*

Bony turnips — ill planted (spoiled). (lit.)

Be ill spoiled.

五畫

注 "種" 和 "縱" 同音，借諧音來喻 "被寵壞" 的意思。

0538 生息

saang¹ sik¹ *(translit.)*

Bear interest. (lit.)

Bear interest.

Build up one's own.

注 表示金錢存放銀行或貸給別人收取利息或樹立自己勢力的意思。

0539 生鬼

saang¹ gwai² *(translit.)*

Of living ghost. (lit.)

Jocular.

Comical.

注 詼諧或滑稽。

0540 生猛

saang¹ maang⁵ *(translit.)*

Living and fierce. (lit.)

Vigorous.

Lively.

Energetic.

Living.

注 表示精力充沛，生龍活虎或活生生的意思。

0541 生番晒

saang¹ faan¹ saai³ *(translit.)*

Come to life again. (lit.)

Recover one's health/energy.

Rehabilitate oneself.

Resume one's spirits.

注 同 "生晒" （0535），不過意義較強一些。

0542 生蝦咁跳

saang¹ haa¹ gam³ tiu³ *(translit.)*

Hop like a living shrimp. (lit.)

Be hot under the collar.

Be like a cat on hot bricks.

Have ants in one's pants.

注 表示因氣憤而坐立不安。

0543 生蟝貓入眼

saang¹ zi¹ maau¹ jap⁶ ngaan⁵ *(translit.)*

A cat with ringworms coming into its eyes. (lit.)

Feast one's eyes on somebody/something.

Love at first sight.

Take to somebody/something at sight.

注 比喻一見便喜歡而瞇着眼睛盯着的神態，即 "一見鍾情" 的意思。

0544 生蟲枴杖

saang¹ cung⁴ gwaai² zoeng² *(translit.)*

A worm-eaten walking stick. (lit.)

A person lacking responsibility.

A person who can't be relied upon for help.

A broken reed.

注 比喻不可靠的人。

0545 生雞精

saang¹ gai¹ zing¹ *(translit.)*

The spirit of a cock. (lit.)

A luster.

注 比喻好色的人。

0546 生曬

saang¹ saai³ *(translit.)*

Be dried while living. (lit.)

Be dried in the sun while something is living/alive/raw.

注 這 "生曬" 和 "生晒" 音同異義，"生曬" 的意思是當一種動物或其肉未經煮熟或仍是活生生的便在太陽下曬乾，多作表語或形容詞用，例如 "這片豬肉是生曬的" 或 "生曬的豬肉" 等。

五畫

0547　失失慌

sat[1] sat[1] fong[1] *(translit.)*

Get frightened. (lit.)

Be all in a fluster.

Be in a flurried manner.

注 慌慌張張。參閱 " 慌失失 " 條（2048）。

0548　失威

sat[1] wai[1] *(translit.)*

Lose power. (lit.)

Lose face. / Humiliate oneself.

Be thrown into the shade. / Commit a breach of etiquette.

Be completely discredited.

注 指丟臉或出醜。

0549　失匙夾萬

sat[1] si[4] gaap[3] maan[6] *(translit.)*

The safe without key. (lit.)

A guy who can hardly obtain money from his rich father.

注 指無法從父親處要到錢的富家子。

0550　失魂

sat[1] wan[4] *(translit.)*

Lose soul. (lit.)

Be in a trance.

Be absent-minded.

Be all in a fluster.

Be scared out of one's wits.

注 表示精神恍惚，魂飛魄散或慌張。

0551　失魂魚

sat[1] wan[4] jyu[2] *(translit.)*

The fish losing its soul. (lit.)

An absent-minded person.

A rash person.

A person who is scared out of his wits.

注 泛指心不在焉，莽撞，或驚慌失措的人。

0552　失魂落魄

sat[1] wan[4] lok[6] paak[3] *(translit.)*

Lose one's soul and drop one's spirit. (lit.)

Stand aghast.

Be like a duck in a thunderstorm.

Have a bee in one's head.

Suffer from the fidgets.

注 形容人精神恍惚，驚慌失措，坐立不安或受驚的樣子。

0553　失驚無神

sat[1] ging[1] / geng[1] mou[4] san[4] *(translit.)*

Suddenly get frightened. (lit.)

Be seized with a panic.

Be caught unawares.

Be taken by surprise.

注 形容人受驚嚇以後神色變異的樣子。

0554　禾稈冚珍珠

wo[4] gon[2] kam[2] zan[1] zyu[1] *(translit.)*

Rice-straws cover pearls. (lit.)

Put on rags over glad rags.

Feign oneself to live in poverty.

注 比喻裝窮相。又指把珍貴的東西用平凡的東西掩蓋着。

0555　白手興家

baak[6] sau[2] hing[1] gaa[1] *(translit.)*

Start a family with empty hands. (lit.)

Start from scratch.

0556　白食

baak[6] sik[6] *(translit.)*

Eat without paying. (lit.)

Have a free meal.

Have the run of one's teeth.

注 即免費吃一頓。

0557　白斬雞

baak[6] zaam[2] gai[1] *(translit.)*

A steamed hen chopped into pieces. (lit.)

A steamed hen.

注 即 "白切雞" ，為粵菜之一。

0558　白鼻哥

baak[6] bei[6] go[1] *(translit.)*

A white nose. (lit.)

A failure as a candidate.

注 常指考試落第的人。

0559　白撞

baak[6] zong[6] *(translit.)*

Seek after a chance. (lit.)

Pass oneself off as somebody's friend to deceive.

Be on the loaf, inventing a lame excuse to cheat somebody.

注 形容人藉詞或藉着關係來騙人。

0560　白撞雨 —— 濽 "讚" 壞

baak[6] zong[6] jyu[5] — zaan[3] waai[6]
(translit.)

Shower — be badly spatted (praised). (lit.)

Be spoiled by being praised.

Spoil somebody by praising too much.

注 "白撞雨" 即 "驟雨" ， "濽" 即 "濺落" 。 "濽" 和 "讚" 同音，因此借指 "被人讚壞了" 。

0561　白霍

baak[1] fok[3] *(translit.)*

Have a look at nobody. (lit.)

With colours flying and band playing.

Faint oneself in bright colours.

Make a boast of oneself.

Take pride in oneself.

注 形容人態度輕浮。常和 "沙塵" 連用，組成 "沙塵白霍" 一語。參閱 "沙塵" （0953） 條。

0562　白鴿眼

baak[6] gap[3] ngaan[5] *(translit.)*

White pigeon's eyes. (lit.)

Be snobbish.

Look upon somebody with disdain.

注 即 "勢利眼" 。

0563　白蟮上沙灘 —— 唔死一身潺

baak[6] sin[5] soeng[5] saa[1] taan[1] — m[4]
sei[2] jat[1] san[1] saan[4] *(translit.)*

A white eel gets on to the sand — thoug it may not be dead, its body gets full of synovia. (lit.)

Get out of disatress but into trouble.

When fatality goes out of the door, trouble comes in at the rear window.

注 表示縱能逃過死亡，但也麻煩很多的意思。

0564　仔大仔世界

zai[2] daai[6] zai[2] sai[3] gaai[3] *(translit.)*

It is the son's world since he is grown up. (lit.)

Let one's adult son take the responsibility for a decision.

注 表示兒子大了，由他自己作主的意思。

0565　他他條條

taa[1] taa[1] tiu[4] tiu[4] *(translit.)*

Have a comfortable life. (lit.)

Go easy.

Lead a happy-go-lucky life.

Be as snug as a bug in a rug.

Calmly.

五畫

注 表示生活舒適，工作清閒的意思。但
當作副詞用時，則有穩重，沉着之意。

0566　瓜老襯

gwaa¹ lou⁵ can³ *(translit.)*

Old enough to collapse while it is time. (lit.)

Meet with one's death.

Meet one's fate.

Die a death.

注 死亡的俗稱。

0567　瓜直

gwaa¹ zik⁶ *(translit.)*

Collapse straight. (lit.)

Fall flat.

Meet with one's death.

Meet one's fate.

注 表示完全失敗或死亡的意思。
參閱"瓜老襯"（0566）及"瓜得"
（0569）條。

0568　瓜柴

gwaa¹ caai⁴ *(translit.)*

Collapse like a piece of firewood. (lit.)

注 同"瓜老襯"（0566）。

0569　瓜得

gwaa¹ dak¹ *(translit.)*

Collapse. (lit.)

Be done for.

Meet with one's death.

Meet one's fate.

Fall flat.

注 "瓜老襯"和"瓜柴"着重死亡的意
思。但"瓜直"及"瓜得"則着重於
"一切完蛋"這方面的意義。

0570　甩身

lat¹ san¹ *(translit.)*

Get off the body. (lit.)

Get away from...

Extricate oneself from...

Slip one's pursuer.

Lay down one's responsibility.

Put the blame on others.

注 表示脫身或把責任或過失委於他人的
意思。

0571　甩拖

lat¹ to¹ *(translit.)*

Separate the trailer. (lit.)

Break off friendly relation with one's lover.

Break one's appointment.

注 常指和愛人分手。參閱"掟煲"
（1578）條。但亦表示失約。參閱"甩
底"（0572）條。

0572　甩底

lat¹ dai² *(translit.)*

The bottom comes off. (lit.)

Break one's appointment.

注 表示失約的意思。

0573　甩繩馬騮

lat¹ sing⁴ maa⁵ lau¹ *(translit.)*

A monkey on the loose. (lit.)

Be on the loose.

A person who kicks over the trace.

Be like a dog on the loose.

注 比喻難駕馭，難以約束的人。

0574　甩鬚

lat¹ sou¹ *(translit.)*

Whiskers come off. (lit.)

Be unbecoming.

Lose face.

Make a fool of oneself.

Bring disgrace upon oneself.

注 即丟臉或出醜。

0575 包尾大番

baau[1] mei[5] daai[6] faan[1] *(translit.)*

The band at the end of a procession. (lit.)

Close the rear.

Come out last.

The last of the successful candidates.

注 廣東各地每有酬神巡遊時，例有一隊樂隊殿後，這樂隊稱為＂大番＂。現轉喻指壓尾或壓尾的人。

0576 包拗頸

baau[1] aau[3] geng[2] *(translit.)*

Be sure to band a neck. (lit.)

Be sure to argue to the contrary.

Ram an argument home.

注 表示專門跟人抬槓的意思。

0577 包撞板

baau[1] zong[6] baan[2] *(translit.)*

Be sure to knock against the board. (lit.)

Always make a mistake.

Be sure to go wrong.

Be sure to make trouble.

注 表示專出岔子的意思。

0578 市橋蠟燭 —— 假細芯＂心＂

si[5] kiu[4] laap[6] zuk[1] — gaa[2] sai[3] sam[1] *(translit.)*

The candle-sticks made in Si Kiu (the name of a small town near Canton) — they pretend to be small wick (heart). (lit.)

With one's tongue in one's cheek.

Show hypocritic loving concern for somebody.

Make a false display of affection.

注 借＂芯＂字的諧音作＂心＂用，意指＂假情假義＂。市橋為廣州附近的一小市鎮。過去當地的製蠟燭商人，為了減低成本，增加利潤，把燭芯做得特別粗大，但露出燭外的燃點部分則特細，使人錯覺以為燭芯也一樣細。

0579 立心不良

laap[6] sam[1] bat[1] loeng[4] *(translit.)*

Set a wicked heart. (lit.)

Be ill-disposed.

0580 立立亂

laap[6/4] laap[6/2] lyun[6] *(translit.)*

Disordered. (lit.)

Be all in a muddle.

Be topsy-turvy.

Be at sixes and sevens.

Be in a mess.

Be terribly upset.

Be in a turmoil.

注 表示亂七八糟，心煩意亂，或處於混亂之中。

0581 立實心腸

laap[6] sat[6] sam[1] coeng[4] *(translit.)*

Fix the heart and intestines firmly. (lit.)

Make up one's mind.

Make a definite decision.

注 即下定決心。

0582 立糯

lap[6] no[6] *(translit.)*

Sticky and slow. (lit.)

Slow-motioned.

Be slow in action.

Be snail-paced.

注 表示慢吞吞的意思。

0583 半天吊

bun[3] tin[1] diu[3] *(translit.)*

Hang half way to the sky. (lit.)

Be neither willing to stoop to

五畫

conquer nor able to stand on tiptoe to obtain.

Hang in the balance.

注 比喻高不成，低不就或安危或成敗未定。參閱"高不成，低不就"條（1502）。

0584　半斤八兩

bun³ gan¹ baat³ loeng² *(translit.)*

Half a catty and eight taels. (16 taels=a catty) (lit.)

Six of one and half a dozen of the other.

Draw level with...

When Greek meets Greek, then comes the tug of war.

Tweedledum and tweedledee.

Be even with...

Break even.

There is not much to choose between the two.

注 參閱"石地堂，鐵掃把"（0513）和"你有張良計，我有過牆梯"（0924）。

0585　半吞半吐

bun³ tan¹ bun³ tou³ *(translit.)*

Half swallow and half vomit. (lit.)

Hums and ha's.

Hesitate in speaking.

0586　半夜三更

bun³ je⁶ saam¹ gaang¹ *(translit.)*

Half night and the third beating of a watchman's drum. (lit.)

In the depth of night.

Late at night.

0587　半夜食黃瓜 —— 不知頭定尾

bun³ je⁶ sik⁶ wong⁴ gwaa¹ — bat¹ zi¹ tau⁴ ding⁶ mei⁵ *(translit.)*

Eat cucumber at midnight — not knowing if it is head or tail. (lit.)

Not know the whole story.

Be ignorant of the beginning and the end of...

Make neither head nor tail of...

注 比喻對事情摸不着頭腦。

0588　半信半疑

bun³ seon³ bun³ ji⁴ *(translit.)*

Half believe; half doubt. (lit.)

Be not quite convinced.

Be somewhat suspicious of...

0589　半桶水

bun³ tung² seoi² *(translit.)*

Half a pail of water. (lit.)

A smatterer.

注 相當於"半瓶醋"。比喻知識膚淺，對事物一知半解的人。

0590　半途出家

bun³ tou⁴ ceot¹ gaa¹ *(translit.)*

Become a Buddhist monk or nun late in life. (lit.)

Switch to a job one hasn's been trained before.

0591　冚到密／實

kam² dou³ mat⁶／sat⁶ *(translit.)*

Cover tight. (lit.)

Block the passage of information.

Keep one's mouth shut.

Not to breathe a word about...

注 表示封鎖消息，秘而不宣或對……一言不發／隻字不提的意思。

0592　冚唪唥（借音字）

ham⁶ baang⁶ laang⁶ *(translit.)*

All. (lit.)

All...

The whole of...
In all.
One and all.
All told.
Altogether.
注 表示全部，一共或總額共……的意思。

0593　冚蓆瞓石
kam² zek⁶ fan³ sek⁶ *(translit.)*
Cover the body with a mat and sleep on the rock. (lit.)
Lead a beggar's life.
Sleep in the open.
注 比喻過着乞丐般的生活。但有時作露宿街頭的詼諧語。

0594　冚檔
kam² dong³ *(translit.)*
Cover the stall. (lit.)
Close down.
Mop up the den (of illegal business).
注 表示倒閉或掃蕩非法經營的地方的意思。

0595　出人頭地
ceot¹ jan⁴ tau⁴ dei⁶ *(translit.)*
Above other's heads. (lit.)
Come out first.
Be beyond all others.
Be out of the ordinary.

0596　出口成文／章
ceot¹ hau² sing⁴ man⁴／zoeng¹ *(translit.)*
What is out of the mouth becomes a composition. (lit.)
Keep a civil tongue in one's head.
Words out of the mouth are like those written by the pen of a writer.

注 誇獎別人説話措詞謹慎或文謅謅的。

0597　出山
ceot¹ saan¹ *(translit.)*
Go out of the mountain. (lit.)
Hold a funeral procession.
注 即出殯。

0598　出手
ceot¹ sau² *(translit.)*
Show out of the hand. (lit.)
Raise a hand to blow.
Hit out.
注 即動手打架。

0599　出手低
ceot¹ sau² dai¹ *(translit.)*
Put out the hand low. (lit.)
Be not so generous with one's money.
Be mean over money matters.
Be too mean to loosen one's purse strings a little longer.
Offer as low as possible.

0600　出年
ceot¹ nin²′⁴ *(translit.)*
Go beyond the year. (lit.)
Next year.
注 即明年。

0601　出名
ceot¹ meng² *(translit.)*
The name is well-known. (lit.)
Come to fame.
Be famous.

0602　出色
ceot¹ sik¹ *(translit.)*
Let the colour out. (lit.)
Acquit oneself well.
Make oneself remarkable.
Outstanding.

五畫

注 表示使自己表現良好，顯出光芒或突出的意思。"出息"為音同異義的另一句俚語，參閱（0611 條）。

0603　出車

ceot[1] ce[1] *(translit.)*

Take out the car. (lit.)

Work as a streetwalker.

Make easy money. (a lady)

注 即當妓女。

0604　出身

ceot[1] san[1] *(translit.)*

Come out of the body. (lit.)

One's family background.

Begin the world.

Start earning one's living.

注 指家庭背景，或表示開始謀生。

0605　出門

ceot[1] mun[4] *(translit.)*

Go out of the door. (lit.)

Be away from home.

Be married out.

Marry to a man.

Marry off.

注 表示離家遠去；姑娘出門子或出嫁。

0606　出面

ceot[1] min[2] *(translit.)*

Show off face. (lit.)

Act as a mediator.

注 即為別人挺身而出解決問題。

0607　出便

ceot[1] bin[6] *(translit.)*

Out of somewhere. (lit.)

Outside.

注 即外面。

0608　出風頭

ceot[1] fung[1] tau[4] *(translit.)*

Let the wind head come out. (lit.)

Cut a dash.

Make a fine figure of oneself.

Be fond of the limelight.

Be in the limelight.

注 即炫耀自己的特長，以博得眾人的讚譽。

0609　出馬

ceot[1] maa[5] *(translit.)*

Take out the horse. (lit.)

Take the field.

Deal with.

注 開戰，開始打鬥，應付或處理的意思。

0610　出氣

ceot[1] hei[3] *(translit.)*

Let out the air. (lit.)

Vent one's disgust on somebody / something.

注 即將一己不快發洩在別人身上。

0611　出息

ceot[1] sik[1] *(translit.)*

Get the interest out. (lit.)

Promising / Be promising.

High-spirited / Be above the average.

High-minded.

High-toned.

注 作形容詞用，意為有前途的，品格高尚的或優秀的。和"出色"有別，參閱 0602 該條。

0612　出處不如聚處

ceot[1] cyu[3] bat[1] jyu[4] zeoi[6] cyu[3] *(translit.)*

The original place is not like the gathering place. (lit.)

Exported articles are better and more than they are in the place where they are produced.

五畫

注 指產品在產地不如在外地市場質量好，數量多。

0613　出符弗〈法〉

ceot[1] fu[4] fit[1] *(translit.)*

Let out incantations. (lit.)

Plot a conspiracy.

注 即打鬼主意。參閱"出鷯哥"條（0621）。

0614　出術

ceot[1] seot[6] *(translit.)*

Make a trick. (lit.)

Work out a practical scheme.

Device means.

注 表示打鬼主意的意思。

0615　出爾反爾

ceot[1] ji[5] faan[2] ji[5] *(translit.)*

Come out of you and go back to you. (lit.)

Go back on one's words.

Go back on one's promise.

注 指說了又翻悔，或說了不照着做，表示言行前後自相矛盾。

0616　出頭

ceot[1] tau[4] *(translit.)*

Show up the head. (lit.)

Take the lead.

Bear responsibility.

Show one's talent and the talent shows itself.

注 指為別人出面解決問題或者比喻脫離困境顯露才華。

0617　出貓

ceot[1] maau[1] *(translit.)*

Take out a cat. (lit.)

Exercise fraud in an examination.

Take a written examination by

unfair means.

注 指考試時作弊。

0618　出醜

ceot[1] cau[2] *(translit.)*

Show off ugliness. (lit.)

Be in disgrace.

Incur disgrace.

注 表示出洋相，失體面。

0619　出嚟搵食

ceot[1] lai[4] wan[2] sik[6] *(translit.)*

Come out to find something to eat. (lit.)

Come into the world to earn a living. (of both male and female)

Prostitute oneself (of female only).

Make easy money.

注 表示在社會上掙錢（正當職業）；當娼妓或掙不正當的錢。

0620　出嚟撈

ceot[1] lai[4] lou[1] *(translit.)*

Come out to scoop up. (lit.)

1. of male

Drift about in the world to engage in dishonest work.

注 指男人時，意為從事不正當的勾當，混飯吃。

2. of female Prostitute oneself.

Earn one's living by becoming a social butterfly.

注 指女人時，意為當娼妓或當交際花謀生。

0621　出鷯哥

ceot[1] liu[1] go[1] *(translit.)*

Let out a mynah. (lit.)

Plot a conspiracy.

注 即打鬼主意。參閱"出符弗"條（0613）。

五畫

0622　奶媽湊／抱仔——人家物

naai⁵ maa¹ cau³／pou⁵ zai² — jan⁴ gaa¹ mat⁶ *(translit.)*

A wet-nurse carries a baby in her arms, — It belongs to the others. (lit.)

Belong to another person.

🈷 形容東西是人家的。

0623　加埋……

gaa¹ maai⁴... *(translit.)*

Add into... (lit.)

Include.

Add up to...

🈷 包括或總共計起來的意思。

0624　加料

gaa¹ liu² *(translit.)*

Add more material. (lit.)

Feed more raw material(s) to something.

Add one／some more.

Reinforce something with...

Be reinforced with something.

Make a greater effort.

Put one's back into something.

Add some more (to the meal).

🈷 意即增加原料，加倍努力，加勁或在吃飯時加菜。

0625　加鹽加醋

gaa¹ jim⁴ gaa¹ cou³ *(translit.)*

Add both salt and vinegar. (lit.)

Lay on thicker colours.

Pain somebody／something with thicker colours.

Lend colour to...

Give an exaggerated report.

0626　皮鞋筋——一扯到口

pei⁴ haai⁴ gan¹ — jat¹ ce² dou³ hau² *(translit.)*

The string used to make shoes, — one pull reaches the mouth. (lit.)

Be impatient of waiting for...

Be short-tempered.

An impetuous person.

Be impetuous.

🈷 指性急的人。

六 畫

0627　托大腳

tok³ daai⁶ goek³ *(translit.)*

Support a big leg on one's shoulder. (lit.)

Lick the boots of somebody.

Eat somebody's toads.

Butter up somebody with fine words.

🈷 相當於 "拍馬屁" 或 "抱粗腿"。

0628　托水龍

tok³ seoi² lung⁴ *(translit.)*

Support a water dragon. (lit.)

Embezzle somebody's money.

🈷 表示盜用別人的款項的意思。

0629　托手踭

tok³ sau² zaang¹ *(translit.)*

Support an elbow. (lit.)

Give somebody a flat refusal.

Refuse somebody's request.

🈷 表示拒絕的意思。

0630　托塔都應承

tok³ taap³ dou¹ jing¹ sing⁴ *(translit.)*

Promise even to hold a pagoda on the palm of a hand. (lit.)

Give promise easily.

🈷 相當於 "上刀山也答應"，但實在指

輕諾而已。

0631 老人成嫩仔

lou[5] jan[4] sing[4] nyun[6] zai[2] *(translit.)*

An old person becomes a child.
(lit.)

Once a man and twice a child.

0632 老人院都唔收

lou[5] jan[4] jyun[2] dou[1] m[4] sau[1] *(translit.)*

Shelters for the old do not accept.
(lit.)

One's remarks are too superfluous.

Be long-winded.

Be garrulous.

Repeat to a tiresome extent.

注 喋喋不休或長氣，參閱"滲氣"條
（2127）。

0633 老人精

lou[5] jan[4] zing[1] *(translit.)*

The spirit of an old man. (lit.)

A young child of prudence.

An old head on young shoulders.

注 形容小孩子年紀雖小，但行為老練，
參看"年少老成"（0756）及"老積"
（0647）條。

0634 老友記

lou[5] jau[5] gei[3] *(translit.)*

Old friend. (lit.)

An old acquaintance.

An old friend.

注 老相識；老朋友。

0635 老行（音肯）

lou[5] hang[2] *(translit.)*

Old popular man. (lit.)

A person in luck.

A person who is winning popularity.

A man of the moment.

A man of mark.

注 指當紅的人或走運的人。

0636 老行尊

lou[5] hong[4] zyun[1] *(translit.)*

An old hand in the trade. (lit.)

An old timer in the line.

注 指本行的老手或老行家。

0637 老奸巨猾

lou[5] gaan[1] geoi[6] waat[6] *(translit.)*

Old cunningness and big hypocrite. (lit.)

Be as cunning as an old fox.

0638 老虎乸

lou[5] fu[2] naa[2] *(translit.)*

A tigress. (lit.)

One's shrewish wife.

One's wife.

注 謔稱悍妻或自己的妻子。

0639 老虎唔發威當病貓

lou[5] fu[2] m[4] faat[3] wai[1] dong[3] beng[6] maau[1] *(translit.)*

A tiger exercising no power is thought as sick cat. (lit.)

Take / Mistake a sleeping wolf for a dead dog.

Regard a warrior with gentle looks as a coward.

注 這口語用以警告對方，不可以為自己
可欺。

0640 老虎頭上釘虱（蝨）乸

lou[5] fu[2] tau[4] soeng[6] deng[1] sat[1] ngaa[2] *(translit.)*

Spike lice on a tiger's head. (lit.)

Beard the lion in his den.

Dare to pull the tail of a fierce dog.

六
畫

注"耗子舔貓鼻子──找死"或"太歲頭上動土"。

0641　老定

lou⁵ ding⁶ *(translit.)*

Be calm. (lit.)

Not stir an eyelid.

Calm oneself.

Remain calm in face of...

Keep one's head.

注即鎮定；冷靜。

0642　老契

lou⁵ kai³ *(translit.)*

Close friend. (lit.)

A blossom friend.

A swearing friend.

An adulterer / adulteress.

A paramour.

注本指結誼關係的互稱。由於廣東人稱情夫為"契家佬"及情婦為"契家婆"的緣故，又轉為情夫或情婦的謔稱。

0643　老番睇榜

lou⁵ faan¹ tai² bong² *(translit.)*

A foreigner has a look at the list of successful candidates. (lit.)

Bring up the rear.

The first from the bottom.

注為名列榜尾的幽默説法。

0644　老鼠拉龜──冇埞埋手

lou⁵ syu² laai¹ gwai¹ — mou⁵ deng⁶ maai⁴ sau² *(translit.)*

A rat drags a tortoise, —no place to put a hand on. (lit.)

Get no access to...

Be at one's wit's end.

注相當於"狗咬刺蝟──下不得嘴"。

0645　老鼠貨

lou⁵ syu² fo³ *(translit.)*

Mouse goods. (lit.)

The stolen good sold at a bargain price.

注指以低價出售的賊臟。

0646　老鼠跌落天平──自己秤自己

lou⁵ syu² dit³ lok⁶ tin¹ ping⁴ — zi⁶ gei² cing³ zi⁶ gei² *(translit.)*

A rat falls down on to the scales — it weighs (praises) itself. (lit.)

Sing one's own praise.

Plume oneself on...

注借"秤"字的諧音來挖苦別人自己稱讚自己。

0647　老積

lou⁵ zik¹ *(translit.)*

Old-aged accumulation. (lit.)

Be young but steady.

Have an old head on young shoulders.

注年少老成的意思，參閱"年少老成"（0756）條。

0648　老貓燒鬚

lou⁵ maau¹ siu¹ sou¹ *(translit.)*

An old cat burns its beard. (lit.)

An experienced marker misses the target.

注相當於"老馬失蹄"。

0649　老糠榨出油

lou⁵ hong¹ zaa³ ceot¹ jau⁴ *(translit.)*

Squeeze oil out of old chaffs. (lit.)

Get oil out of rocks.

Put a squeeze on poor people.

注即在窮人身上壓榨的意思。

0650　老竇 / 豆都要多

lou⁵ dau⁶ dou¹ jiu³ do¹ *(translit.)*

Have a desire for more fathers. (lit.)

Be greedy for gains.

Be covetous to grasp all.

🈲 形容一個人貪得無厭。

0651 老襯

lou⁵ can³ *(translit.)*

An old fool. (lit.)

A sucker.

A relation by marriage.

🈲 指容易被騙的人。後來因姻親的"親"字廣東人讀成"襯"音，所以又謔稱"親家"為老襯。

0652 地膽／地頭蟲

dei⁶ daam²／dei⁶ tau⁴ cung⁴ *(translit.)*

The gall of land. (lit.)

A cock on his own dunghill.

Local villain／bully.

The man on the spot.

🈲 指土生土長的人或地痞的頭子，後者相當於"地頭蛇"。

0653 耳邊風

ji⁵ bin¹ fung¹ *(translit.)*

A puff of wind at the ear. (lit.)

An unheeded advice.

🈲 指不被人接受的忠告。

0654 朽榜

naau² gaau⁶ *(translit.)*

Be tangled. (lit.)

At sixes and sevens.

Be in a mess.

Have a tangled relation with one another.

Build up a carnal relationship.

🈲 形容亂七八糟，又指不正常的男女關係。

0655 西南二伯父

sai¹ naam⁴ ji⁶ baak³ fu² *(translit.)*

Second uncle of Sai Naam. (lit.)

An indulgent senior.

🈲 從前西南（沿廣三鐵路的一小市鎮）有醬園東主，人尊稱之為二伯父。他對懶散伙計，從不嚴加管束，反而任其所為，甚至給予錢財揮霍，及至不可救藥時，才把他解僱，使他在醬園行業中無法立足。比喻：指見到青少年幹壞事，採取袖手旁觀，縱容甚至慫恿的老年人。

0656 在意

zoi⁶ ji³ *(translit.)*

Lay an idea on. (lit.)

Pay attention to...

Take notice of...

Use caution.

🈲 表示留心，注意或謹慎的意思。（同義的有"為意"一語，參閱 1284 條。）

0657 有一利必有一害

jau⁵ jat¹ lei⁶ bit¹ jau⁵ jat¹ hoi⁶ *(translit.)*

Where is an advantage, there is a disadvantage. (lit.)

No rose without a thorn.

Fire can make our houses warm but it can also burn them down.

There is no fire without smoke.

🈲 按事物規律，有其利必有其害。

0658 有人做咗手腳

jau⁵ jan⁴ zou⁶ zo² sau² goek³ *(translit.)*

There is a man having done hands and feet. (lit.)

Somebody has secretly got up to little tricks.

Somebody has secretly done damage to something.

🈲 表示別人暗中做了些小動作或背地破壞的意思。

六畫

0659　有人辭官歸故里，有人漏夜趕科場

jau⁵ jan⁴ ci⁴ gun¹ gwai¹ gu³ lei⁵,
jau⁵ jan⁴ lau⁶ je⁶ gon² fo¹ coeng⁴
(translit.)

Some resign from their official posts and return to their own native places, but others rush to the Examination Hall at night. (lit.)

Some go up the steps but others come down.

Some people are willing to take over what others give up.

注 表示人對功名有不同看法，有人辭官因看到社會黑暗，有人趕科場，急於求取功名。

0660　有乜冬瓜豆腐

jau⁵ mat¹ dung¹ gwaa¹ dau⁶ fu⁶
(translit.)

In case of hard-skinned cucumber and bean curd. (lit.)

If worst comes to worst.

In case of misfortune.

注 表示萬一不幸的意思。

0661　有口無心

jau⁵ hau² mou⁴ sam¹ *(translit.)*

Having mouth but having no heart. (lit.)

Not really mean what one says.

Be sharp-tongued but not malicious.

注 表示心直口快或隨口説説，毫不放在心上。

0662　有口難言

jau⁵ hau² naan⁴ jin⁴ *(translit.)*

Having mouth but hard to say. (lit.)

Find it hard or embarrasing to say.

注 指不敢説出口或難以啟齒。

0663　有毛有翼

jau⁵ mou⁴ jau⁵ jik⁶ *(translit.)*

Have feathers and wings. (lit.)

Be tameless.

Be uncontrollable.

注 比喻孩子長大不順從父母或難以駕御的意思。相當於＂翅膀硬了＂。

0664　有仇不報非君子

jau⁵ cau⁴ bat¹ bou³ fei¹ gwan¹ zi²
(translit.)

He who does not revenge himself on enmity is not a gentleman. (lit.)

Demand blood for blood.

注 表示以牙還牙。

0665　有分有寸

jau⁵ fan¹ jau⁵ cyun³ *(translit.)*

Have fractions and inches. (lit.)

Know one's distance.

Know what to do.

注 即能把握説話或做事的標準或限度。

0666　有分數

jau⁵ fan¹ sou³ *(translit.)*

Have graduation. (lit.)

Know what to do and what not to do.

Have a good sense of propriety.

注 即有主意；心中有數。

0667　有心唔怕遲，十月都係拜年時

jau⁵ sam¹ m⁴ paa³ ci⁴, sap⁶ jyut⁶ dou¹
hai⁶ baai³ nin⁴ si⁴ *(translit.)*

An intention is never late; the tenth month is also the time to pay a lunar new year call. (lit.)

Better late than never.

注 表示只要有心、用心就不怕遲。

六畫

0668 有心無力

jau⁵ sam¹ mou⁴ lik⁶ *(translit.)*

Have heart but have no strength. (lit.)

Have a good mind but lack ability to...

Be unable to do what one wants very much to...

🈯即雖然有意幫忙，卻無力解決問題。

0669 有心裝冇心人

jau⁵ sam¹ zong¹ mou⁵ sam¹ jan⁴ *(translit.)*

Deliberately watch somebody that does something unintentionally. (lit.)

Find fault with somebody with cherished desire.

Have intention to seek fault done without intention.

Set a trap for somebody.

🈯指故意找無心之失或設圈套陷害人。

0670 有奶便是娘

jau⁵ naai⁵ bin⁶ si⁶ noeng⁴ *(translit.)*

Any woman that can give the breast is mother. (lit.)

He that serves God for money will serve the devil for better wages.

🈯即誰給好處就為誰辦事。

0671 有自唔在，攞苦嚟辛

jau⁵ zi⁶ m⁴ zoi⁶, lo² fu² lai⁴ san¹ *(translit.)*

Not to get free and easy but endure hardship and toil. (lit.)

Make a rod for one's own back.

🈯表示自找麻煩的意思。

0672 有行

jau⁵ hong⁴ *(translit.)*

Have hope. (lit.)

There is hope.

It is hopeful.

Be in the money.

🈯表示有希望，有辦法或有錢的意思。

0673 有名無實

jau⁵ ming⁴ mou⁴ sat⁶ *(translit.)*

Have name but no reality. (lit.)

In name but not in deed.

Exist in name only.

Not worthy of the name.

🈯即虛有其名而無實際內容。

0674 有屁就放

jau⁵ pei³ zau⁶ fong³ *(translit.)*

Break your wind! (lit.)

Say away!

Say it out!

🈯即有話便說。

0675 有尾學人跳，冇尾又學人跳

jau⁵ mei⁵ hok⁶ jan⁴ tiu³, mou⁵ mei⁵ jau⁶ hok⁶ jan⁴ tiu³ *(translit.)*

Learn to jump with a tail and also do the same even without a tail. (lit.)

Blindly imitate somebody.

Act like a copycat.

Imitate somebody without measuring one's own capability.

🈯指人盲目仿效或不自量力去仿效別人。

0676 有招架之功，無還手之力

jau⁵ ziu¹ gaa³ zi¹ gung¹, mou⁴ waan⁴ sau² zi¹ lik⁶ *(translit.)*

Can resist but cannot return a blow. (lit.)

Can only ward off blows.

Fail to return a like for like.

注 指勉強抵擋，無還擊之力。

0677　有其父必有其子

jau⁵ kei⁴ fu⁶ bit¹ jau⁵ kei⁴ zi² *(translit.)*

Such a father has such a son. (lit.)

Like father, like son.

Like begets like.

注 含褒貶兩義。褒義參閱〝虎父無犬子〞條（1057）。貶義表示其父不仁，其子亦不仁的意思。

0678　有事鍾無艷，無事夏迎春

jau⁵ si⁶ zung¹ mou⁴ jim⁶, mou⁴ si⁶ haa⁶ jing⁴ ceon¹ *(translit.)*

Call for Zung Mou Jim when there is trouble, but as soon as the trouble has gone, go on the spree with Haa Jing Ceon. (lit.)

Zung Mou Jim — the lawful wife of Emperor Syn of Cai（齊）.

Haa Jing Ceon — Emperor Syn's royal concubine.

Pray God for help while drowning, but once go on shore, pray no more.

Once out of danger, cast the deliverer behind one's back.

注 參閱〝打完齋唔要和尚〞（0459）及〝過橋抽板〞（2004）條。

0679　有兩下散手

jau⁵ loeng⁵ haa⁵ saan² sau² *(translit.)*

Having two tactics. (lit.)

Have real skill.

Know one's stuff.

注 即確有一手。

0680　有咁啱得咁蹺

jau⁵ gam³ ngaam¹ dak¹ gam³ kiu² *(translit.)*

Things happen at the same time. (lit.)

By a curious coincidence.

What a happy coincidence!

As luck would have it.

注 表示巧合的意思。

0681　有咗

jau⁵ zo² *(translit.)*

Have had it. (lit.)

Be heavy with child.

Conceive a child.

Be pregnant.

注 （指女人）有喜或懷孕。

0682　有便宜唔使使頸

jau⁵ pin⁴ ji⁴ m⁴ sai² sai² geng² *(translit.)*

Whenever there are small gains, there is no need to make use of the neck. (lit.)

Be all out for small advantages in spite of reluctance.

注 表示有便宜便要做的意思。

0683　有風駛盡𢃇

jau⁵ fung¹ sai² zeon⁶ lei⁵ *(translit.)*

When there is wind, set up all sails. (lit.)

Pack all sails before the wind.

Take advantage of opportunity to the full extent.

注 表示盡量利用機會的意思。

0684　有酒有肉多兄弟

jau⁵ zau² jau⁵ juk⁶ do¹ hing¹ dai⁶ *(translit.)*

When one has wine and meat, many friends come together. (lit.)

A heavy purse makes friends come.

The one that holds the purse holds friends.

注 指當人有錢吃喝玩樂時，就有很多酒肉朋友。

六畫

0685　有排

jau²ᐟ⁵ paai²ᐟ⁴ *(translit.)*

For a long time. (lit.)

It is long before...

🈯表示還有很長時間才⋯⋯的意思，參閱"未有來"條（0442）。

0686　有眼不識泰山

jau⁵ ngaan⁵ bat¹ sik¹ taai³ saan¹ *(translit.)*

Having eyes but not knowing Taai Saan. (lit.)

Be too blind to recognize the sun.

🈯比喻不知禮敬或認不出權貴的人。

0687　有眼無珠

jau⁵ ngaan⁵ mou⁴ zyu¹ *(translit.)*

Having eyes without pupils. (lit.)

Be as blind as a bat.

Wrongly exercise one's judgement.

Misvalue somebody.

🈯參閱"走眼"（0851）、"睇差一皮"（1804）及"跌眼鏡"（1811）各條。

0688　有得震冇得瞓

jau⁵ dak¹ zan³ mou⁵ dak¹ fan³ *(translit.)*

Tremble without sleep. (lit.)

Tremble with fear.

Be terror-stricken.

Strike terror into one's heart.

🈯暗喻膽戰心驚的心態。

0689　有得諗

jau⁵ dak¹ nam² *(translit.)*

Have something to think about. (lit.)

Be worth a consideration.

🈯表示值得考慮的意思。

0690　有景轟

jau⁵ ging² gwang² *(translit.)*

Have something behind. (lit.)

There must be an inside story.

There must be a sinister design.

🈯即"內有乾坤"。

0691　有幾何呀？

jau⁵ gei² ho² aa¹ *(translit.)*

How many times? (lit.)

Seldom or never.

Seldom, if never.

Not so often.

🈯和"冇幾何"意同。見該條（0329），"有幾何"用於反詰式的疑問句而"冇幾何"則用於否定式的陳述句，其實都是表達"不經常"的意思。

0692　有碗話碗，有碟話碟

jau⁵ wun² waa⁶ wun², jau⁵ dip⁶ waa⁶ dip⁶ *(translit.)*

Say bowls when there are bowls; say dishes when there are dishes. (lit.)

Tell the whole story.

Tell it as it is.

Tell the truth, the whole truth, and nothing but the truth.

🈯指老老實實地説。

0693　有爺生冇乸教

jau⁵ je⁴ saang¹ mou⁵ naa² gaau³ *(translit.)*

Have father to breed but have no mother to teach. (lit.)

Be not cultured at home.

Lack home education.

🈯參閱"冇家教"（0321）條。

0694　有意栽花花不發，無心插柳柳成蔭

jau⁵ ji³ zoi¹ faa¹ faa¹ bat¹ faat³, mou⁴ sam¹ caap³ lau⁵ lau⁵ sing⁴ jam¹ *(translit.)*

六畫

*Plant flowers intentionally,
but they never come into
bloom; transplant willow slips
unintentionally, but they grow to
be a shade. (lit.)*

**Deliberation causes failure but
incuriosity brings forth success.**

注 同 "無心插柳"。

0695　有福同享，有禍同當

jau⁵ fuk¹ tung⁴ hoeng², jau⁵ wo⁶ tung⁴
dong¹ *(translit.)*

*Have bliss to share and calamity to
face together. (lit.)*

Cast in one's lot with somebody.

**Stand together through thick and
thin.**

**For better or worse, friendship
exists.**

注 指無論是禍是福都願意共同承擔。

0696　有頭毛冇人想生鬎鬁

jau⁵ tau⁴ mou⁴ mou⁵ jan⁴ soeng²
saang¹ laat³ lei¹ *(translit.)*

*If the head were full of hair, no one
would prefer to have favus of
the scalp on it. (lit.)*

**Have no alternative but to make
such an unwise decision.**

Be driven to such a stupid move.

注 隱喻迫於無奈，才出此下策。

0697　有頭有面

jau⁵ tau⁴ jau⁵ min⁶ *(translit.)*
Have head and face. (lit.)

Be famed for one's post.

Be well-known and titled.

注 表示在社會上有地位的意思。

0698　有頭威，冇尾陣

jau⁵ tau⁴ wai¹ , mou⁵ mei⁵ zan⁶
(translit.)

*Having heading power and
influence but no ending
formation. (lit.)*

**A brave beginning but a poor
ending.**

Fine start, poor finish.

Do something by halves.

Leave one's work half done.

注 參閱 "虎頭蛇尾" （1059）。

0699　有錢佬話事

jau⁵ cin² lou² waa⁶ si⁶ *(translit.)*
Rich men master all. (lit.)

Money talks.

注 即有錢人有權勢左右大局。

0700　有錢使得鬼推磨

jau⁵ cin² sai² dak¹ gwai² teoi¹ mo⁶
(translit.)

*Money can make a ghost push a
grinder. (lit.)*

**Where there are wages, there are
pages.**

Money makes the mare go.

注 參閱 "財可通神" 條 （1364）。

0701　有錢就身痕

jau⁵ cin² zau⁶ san¹ han⁴ *(translit.)*
*Whenever one has money, his
body feels itching. (lit.)*

**Money burns a hole in one's
pocket.**

注 表示一有錢便要花光的意思。

0702　有聲氣

jau⁵ seng¹ hei³ *(translit.)*
Have sound and air. (lit.)

There is hope.

It is hopeful.

Be in the money.

注 和 "有行" 意同，參閱該條 （0672）。

0703 有雞仔唔管管麻鷹

jau⁵ gai¹ zai² m⁴ gun² gun² maa⁴ jing¹ *(translit.)*

Not to restrain one's own chicks, but restrain eagles. (lit.)

Lay the blame on the wrong shoulder.

Put the shoe on the wrong foot.

📝 表示責備不該責備的人的意思。

0704 有蹺蹊

jau⁵ kiu¹ kei¹ *(translit.)*

There is a trick. (lit.)

There are some tricks.

There is something secret about...

There are some clever devices.

Have other fish to fry.

There is something fishing about...

📝 內有乾坤，內有巧妙，另有他圖或裏面有鬼的意思。

0705 有麝自然香

jau⁵ se⁶ zi⁶ jin⁴ hoeng¹ *(translit.)*

Musk has its natural fragrance. (lit.)

Good wine needs no bush.

📝 相當於＂好酒客自來，不必自我吹噓＂。

0706 百足咁多爪

baak³ zuk¹ gam³ do¹ zaau² *(translit.)*

Have as many legs as a centipede. (lit.)

Cover up one's track.

Put nobody on one's track.

Go everywhere one likes.

📝 比喻行蹤飄忽。

0707 百忍成金

baak³ jan² sing⁴ gam¹ *(translit.)*

A hundred pieces of patience will become gold. (lit.)

Patience is a plaster for all sores.

0708 而依哦哦

ji⁴ ji¹ ngo⁴ ngo⁴ *(translit.)*

Hesitate to say. (lit.)

Feel some hesitation in doing / saying something.

Be shilly-shally.

Hum and haw.

📝 形容猶豫不決或支吾其詞。

0709 死人尋舊路

sei² jan⁴ cam⁴ gau⁶ lou⁶ *(translit.)*

A dead man looks for his old way. (lit.)

Follow one's own old tracks.

Do something in the usual way.

📝 原指依照行過的路徑走，但引伸喻按老方法做。

0710 死人燈籠——報大數

sei² jan⁴ dang¹ lung⁴—bou³ daai⁶ sou³ *(translit.)*

A dead man's lentern, — reporting a bigger sum. (lit.)

Make a mountain out of a molehill.

Pull the long bow.

Cook up an exaggerative report.

📝 比喻小題大做，吹牛或虛構誇大報告等。俗例在成年人死後，家人例在門外懸掛燈籠。籠上用藍色寫上死者年歲，但必按死者實際年齡加多三歲。

0711 死口咬實

sei² hau² ngaau⁵ sat⁶ *(translit.)*

Dead mouth bites firmly. (lit.)

Stand by one's guns.

Stick to what one says.

📝 表示堅持所說的意思。

六畫

0712　死牛一便頸

sei² ngau⁴ jat¹ bin⁶ geng² *(translit.)*

A dead cow turns its head on one side. (lit.)

Take the laws into one's own hand.

Insist on going one's own way.

Be hell-bent on having one's own way.

Be as stubborn as a mule.

Be stiff-necked.

Stick to one's guns.

注 比喻形容人固執，堅持己見，不聽勸告。

0713　死心不息

sei² sam¹ bat¹ sik¹ *(translit.)*

Death would make no stop. (lit.)

Insist on not giving up.

Have a one-track mind.

Be as obstinate as a mule.

注 相當於"死心眼"。

0714　死心塌地

sei² sam¹ taap³ dei⁶ *(translit.)*

The heart is bent to. (lit.)

Be hell-bent on somebody.

0715　死有餘辜

sei² jau⁵ jyu⁴ gu¹ *(translit.)*

Death would be too good. (lit.)

Death would not expiate all one's crimes.

注 表示雖死亦不足蔽其罪的意思。

0716　死死地氣

sei² sei² dei⁶ hei³ *(translit.)*

Do with dead air. (lit.)

Be reluctant but have no alternative but to...

注 指無可奈何地幹。

0717　死估估

sei² gu⁶ gu⁶ *(translit.)*

Quite dead. (lit.)

Be dull.

Be poor-witted.

Be inactive.

Be inflexible.

注 表示呆板不識變通或不夠活躍的意思。

0718　死咗條心

sei² zo² tiu⁴ sam¹ *(translit.)*

The heart dies. (lit.)

Better give up the idea altogether.

Drop the idea foever.

Have no more illusions about the matter.

注 表示不再作幻想。

0719　死性不改

sei² sing³ bat¹ goi² *(translit.)*

The dead nature does not change. (lit.)

Be as stubborn as a mule.

All ill nature never turns.

0720　死唔眼閉

sei² m⁴ ngaan⁵ bai³ *(translit.)*

Died with eyes open. / Not close one's eyes when one dies. (lit.)

Nurse a grievance even when one dies.

Die with an everlasting regret.

0721　死冤

sei² jyun¹ *(translit.)*

Tangle to death. (lit.)

Stick like a limpet.

Pester somebody endlessly for something.

注 參閱"二仔底"（0091），"吊靴鬼"（0744）及"死纏爛打"（0725）各條。

0722　死蛇爛蟮

sei² se⁴ laan⁶ sin⁵ *(translit.)*

A dead snake and rotten eel. (lit.)

Be too lazy to stir a finger.

Be too tired to move.

💡形容人懶得不想動或疲倦得動也不想
動。

0723　死慳死抵

sei² haan¹ sei² dai² *(translit.)*

Deadly save and deadly sustain.
(lit.)

Pinch and screw.

Tighten one's belt.

0724　死雞撐飯蓋

sei² gai¹ caang³ faan⁶ goi³ *(translit.)*

A dead hen still props up the lid of
a rice-cooker. (lit.)

Be the devil's advocate.

Show reluctance to eat crow.

Be shabby-genteel.

💡暗喻理虧也嘴硬，仍要強辯，或擺窮
架子。

0725　死纏爛打

sei² cin⁴ laan⁶ daa² *(translit.)*

Annoy with death and beat badly.
(lit.)

Pester somebody endlessly for
something.

💡相當於"死氣白賴"或"胡纏"。參閱
"二仔底"（0091），"死冤"（0721）
及"吊靴鬼"（0744）各條。

0726　成日

seng⁴ jat⁶ *(translit.)*

A whole day. (lit.)

All day long.

All the day.

Nearly a whole day.

Always.

💡表示"整天"或"老是"的意思。

0727　成數

sing⁴ sou³ *(translit.)*

Percent. (lit.)

Percent / Percentage.

It is likely that / whether...

There is possibility that...

By any possibility...

💡表示百分率或有……可能的意思。

0728　光棍佬教仔──便宜莫貪

gwong¹ gwan³ lou² gaau³ zai² ─ pin⁴
ji⁴ mok⁶ taam¹ *(translit.)*

A swindler teaches his son ─ not
to be covetous of any
advantage. (lit.)

Do not jump at any easy baits.

Don't try to get things on the
cheap.

💡勸人不要貪便宜。

0729　光棍遇着冇皮柴

gwong¹ gwan³ jyu⁶ zoek⁶ mou⁵ pei⁴
caai⁴ *(translit.)*

A bare stick (swindler) meets a
bare firewood (swindler). (lit.)

A swindler takes in a swindler.

Diamond cut diamond.

A nip and tuck.

💡"光棍"為廣東人對騙子的叫法，但句
中的"光棍"本義是"光禿禿而沒皮的
木棍"而"冇皮柴"也是光禿禿而沒皮
的木棍，兩者既然同是一樣東西，廣
東人便以這"光棍"喻騙子的"光棍"，
全句意思是説"大家不相上下"而成為
騙中騙了，用於貶義方面。

0730　早知今日，何必當初？

zou² zi¹ gam¹ jat⁶, ho⁴ bit¹ dong¹ co¹
(translit.)

六
畫

Had this day been known earlier, why must it have been done? (lit.)

It is too late to ask oneself why one has gone astray when one knows the consequence to be so serious.

🈯指對過去的錯誤行為導致的後果，悔之已晚了。參閱 "早知今日，悔不當初" 條（0731）。

0731　早知今日，悔不當初

zou² zi¹ gam¹ jat⁶, fui³ bat¹ dong¹ co¹ *(translit.)*

Had one known the consequence of today, one would not have gone astray / done so. (lit.)

It is too late to repent for having gone astray / done so when one knows the consequence to be so serious.

🈯同 "早知今日，何必當初？"（0730）。

0732　早知燈係火，唔使黑摸摸

zou² zi¹ dang¹ hai⁶ fo², m⁴ sai² hak¹ mo² mo² *(translit.)*

If a lamp had been known to be fire, there would have been no need to feel about in the dark. (lit.)

It is too late to repent of one's previous ignorance.

It is too late to regret for having missed the opportunity to do something.

🈯指對過去無知或失去機會而不⋯⋯時，悔之已晚了。

0733　同一個鼻哥窿出氣

tung⁴ jat¹ go³ bei⁶ go¹ lung¹ ceot¹ hei³ *(translit.)*

Breathe from the same nose. (lit.)

Sing the same tune.

Echo somebody's nonsense.

🈯表示同某人有同一意見或跟人瞎說的意思。

0734　同人唔同命，同遮唔同柄

tung⁴ jan⁴ m⁴ tung⁴ meng⁶, tung⁴ ze¹ m⁴ tung⁴ beng³ *(translit.)*

Men are same but fate is different; umbrellas are same, but handles are different. (lit.)

Men were born with different fates.

No man has the same fortune.

🈯比喻人生際遇，各有不同。

0735　同⋯⋯有路

tung⁴ ... jau⁵ lou⁶ *(translit.)*

Have road with... (lit.)

Commit adultery with somebody.

Have illicit intercourse with somebody.

🈯即和某人通姦。

0736　同行如敵國

tung⁴ hong⁴ jyu⁴ dik⁶ gwok³ *(translit.)*

The same trade is like a hostile nation. (lit.)

Two of a trade never agree.

0737　同⋯⋯行埋咗

tung⁴ ... haang⁴ maai⁴ zo² *(translit.)*

Have walked closely with somebody. (lit.)

Have had a sexual intercourse with somebody.

Have made love with / to somebody.

🈯諱言和人發生了性關係的委婉語，但如果只說 "同⋯⋯行" 時，則表示和⋯⋯戀愛的意思而已。

Have somebody's steady date.
Fall in love with somebody.

0738　同……行得好埋

tung⁴ ... haang⁴ dak¹ hou² maai⁴ *(translit.)*

Walk very closely with somebody. *(lit.)*

Be on very familiar terms with somebody.

Get along very well with somebody.

🈯 和某人極為友好或和某人相處得很好。

0739　同枱食飯，各自修行

tung⁴ toi⁴ sik⁶ faan⁶, gok³ zi⁶ sau¹ hang⁴ *(translit.)*

Eating meal at the same table, everyone cultivates morality to become a Buddhist. *(lit.)*

Each does what he thinks is right.

Each cultivates his own virtue.

🈯 表示各人有自己的道德修養標準的意思。

0740　同撈同煲

tung⁴ lou¹ tung⁴ bou¹ *(translit.)*

Work and cook together. *(lit.)*

Share weal and woe with each other.

Live together through fair and foul.

🈯 相當於有福同享有禍同當。

0741　吊吊扐

diu⁶ diu¹ᐟ² fing³ *(translit.)*

Hang and let it sway. *(lit.)*

Swing this way and that way.
Not to reach a definite decision.
Be not assured.

🈯 本意是晃來晃去。後引伸表示事情未到決定階段或仍未獲得保證。

0742　吊砂煲

diu³ saa¹ bou¹ *(translit.)*

Hang up the earthen cooking pot. *(lit.)*

Be out of work.
Be too poor to have a meal.
Go hungry.

🈯 比喻失業，但亦喻斷炊或沒得吃。

0743　吊起嚟賣

diu³ hei² lai⁴ maai⁶ *(translit.)*

Hang up for sale. *(lit.)*

Hoard up for higher price.
Sell at a price.
Raise the market upon something.
Play the market.
Form an unduly high estimation of oneself.

🈯 表示奇貨可居或抬高身價的意思。

0744　吊靴鬼

diu³ hoe¹ gwai² *(translit.)*

The ghost that sticks to boots. *(lit.)*

A limpet.
The person who sticks somebody like a bur.

🈯 表示胡纏的意思，參閱"二仔底"（0091）條。

0745　吊癮

diu³ jan⁵ *(translit.)*

Hang up the addiction. *(lit.)*

Not to satisfy the craving for the time being.

🈯 相當於沒勁。

0746　因小失大

jan¹ siu² sat¹ daai⁶ *(translit.)*

六畫

Lose the big because of the small. *(lit.)*

Spoil a ship for a halfpenny worth of tar.

注 為了小緣故而貽誤大事。

0747　至多唔係……

zi³ do¹ m⁴ hai⁶... *(translit.)*

At most... (lit.)

If the worst comes to worst...

When things are at their worst...

注 表示"大不了"或"頂多是"。

0748　至到……

zi³ dou³... *(translit.)*

As to... (lit.)

As to...

注 表示到；及至；至於的意思，不過如果說"不至於"時，則意為"不會"，參閱該條（0286）。

0749　至無……

zi³ mou⁴... *(translit.)*

Even if... (lit.)

Even if...

Even so, ...

注 和"甚至無"同，參閱該條（1175）。

0750　至話

zi³ waa⁶ *(translit.)*

Just. (lit.)

Just now.

A moment ago.

Just.

Happen to.

As it happens.

注 和"正話"同，參閱該條（0495）。

0751　肉刺

juk⁶ cek³ *(translit.)*

The flesh itches. (lit.)

Make one's heart ache.

Be loath to part with.../leave...

Be reluctant to spend/have spent so much on something.

注 表示捨不得的意思。

0752　肉緊

juk⁶ gan² *(translit.)*

The flesh becomes tight. (lit.)

Be excited.

Feel anxious.

Be impatient.

注 表示緊張，着急或不耐煩。

0753　肉酸

juk⁶ syun¹ *(translit.)*

The flesh goes sour. (lit.)

Be ugly-looking.

Be creepy-crawly.

Make somebody's flesh creep.

Give somebody the creeps.

注 表示醜陋，難看，但亦表示令人身上發癢。

0754　肉隨砧板上

juk⁶ ceoi⁴ zam¹ baan² soeng⁶ *(translit.)*

The flesh is put on the chopping board. (lit.)

Be led by the nose.

Be bred at somebody's will.

Be laid by the heels.

注 比喻任人宰割或任人支配。

0755　年三十晚謝竈——好做唔做

nin⁴ saam¹ sap⁶ maan⁵ ze⁶ zou³ — hou² zou⁶ m⁴ zou⁶ *(translit.)*

Thank the god of kitchen at the lunar new year's eve — what should be done is undone. (lit.)

Do not do what one should do.

Did not do what one should have done.

注 前人多在年尾祭竈，以示謝意。在封建時代，有所謂官三民四蛋家五之説，意即階級分明，官方在農曆十二月廿三日，民間在十二月廿四日而蛋家則在十二月廿五日舉行，不容混亂，如果在除夕時舉行謝竈，則該做而不做了。

0756　年少老成

nin⁴ siu³ lou⁵ sing⁴ *(translit.)*

Young but mature. (lit.)

An old head on young shoulders.

0757　年晚煎堆——人有我有

nin⁴ maan⁵ zin¹ deoi¹ — jan⁴ jau⁵ ngo⁵ jau⁵ *(translit.)*

Deep oil fried pop-grain balls at the close of the year — others have and I have. (lit.)

Possess oneself of the same as others do.

注 廣東習俗無論貧富，在年晚時，例有煎堆（一種球形的油炸食物，中實以爆穀，外蓋芝麻），以取來年富有之意。

0758　朱義盛——不變色

zyu¹ ji⁶ sing² — baat¹ bin³ sik¹ *(translit.)*

Zyu Ji Sing — never change the colour. (lit.)

Be just as of old.

As before.

Be just the same.

Be the very person.

注 喻依然故我。在二三十年代，廣州市狀元坊有一朱義盛金飾店，專做鍍金首飾，以永不變色作號召，遂引致無人不知"不變色"，成為俚語。

0759　先入為主

sin¹ jap⁶ wai⁴ zyu² *(translit.)*

The first impression is the master. (lit.)

First impressions are unchangeable.

Have a prejudice against...

Preconceived ideas keep a strong hold.

0760　先下手為強

sin¹ haa⁶ sau² wai⁴ koeng⁴ *(translit.)*

It is stronger to attack first. (lit.)

Catch the ball before the bound.

It is more advantageous to shoot the first arrow.

Steal somebody's thunder.

Take the wind out of somebody's sails.

0761　先小人後君子

sin¹ siu² jan⁴ hau⁶ gwan¹ zi² *(translit.)*

Be a narrow-minded person first and then a gentleman. (lit.)

Make sure of every trifling matter before generosity.

Be narrow-minded before being generous.

注 指當雙方進行一項交易或合作時，應該先講好利益的分配，以免日後因財失義。至於彼此將來是否計較，此乃日後的事。

0762　先使未來錢

sin¹ sai² mei⁶ loi⁴ cin⁴ *(translit.)*

Spend the future money in advance. (lit.)

Anticipate one's wages / income.

Have one's corn in the blade.

注 參閱"寅食卯糧"條（1701）。

0763　先排

sin¹ paai² *(translit.)*

Previous days. (lit.)

Not long ago.

In the earlier days.

六畫

注 和"前喎排"意同，參閱該條（1278）。

0764　先斬後奏

sin¹ zaam² hau⁶ zau³ *(translit.)*

Behead a man first and then report to the emperor. (lit.)

Act before reporting.

Do something first and then tell somebody about it.

注 比喻先做完某事，造成既成事實，再向上級或有關方面報告。

0765　先敬羅衣後敬人

sin¹ ging³ lo⁴ ji¹ hau⁶ ging³ jan⁴ *(translit.)*

Respect silky clothes first and then the man. (lit.)

Fine clothes are in preference to man.

People usually open doors to fine clothes.

0766　先禮後兵

sin¹ lai⁵ hau⁶ bing¹ *(translit.)*

Politeness first and war later. (lit.)

A dog often barks before it bites.

Try peaceful means before force.

0767　丟生晒

diu¹ saang¹ saai³ *(translit.)*

Give all up. (lit.)

Be out of practice.

Show neglect of one's skill.

注 即荒疏。

0768　丟架

diu¹ gaa² *(translit.)*

Throw away the airs of greatness. (lit.)

Lose face.

Be disgraced.

Make an ass of oneself.

Make a sorry spectacle of oneself.

Commit a breach of etiquette.

注 本指"丟臉"或"出洋相"，參閱"出醜"（0618）條。這口語又作失禮的意思，參閱"抬棺材甩褲"（1009）條。

0769　丟疏咗

diu¹ so¹ zo² *(translit.)*

Without practice. (lit.)

Be out of practice.

Show neglect of one's skill.

注 同"丟生晒"（0767）

0770　竹紗

zuk¹ saa¹ *(translit.)*

Bamboo silk. (lit.)

Poplin.

注 即府綢（一種細，薄布）。

0771　竹織鴨——冇心肝

zuk¹ zik¹ aap³ — mou⁵ sam¹ gon¹ *(translit.)*

A duck knitted with bamboo tapes – without heart and liver (lit.)

An absent-minded person.

Be absent-minded.

注 參閱"心不在焉"條（0413）。

0772　自己工

zi⁶ gei² gung¹ *(translit.)*

Self work. (lit.)

Piece work.

Reckon by piece.

注 即計件工。

0773　自己身有屎

zi⁶ gei² san¹ jau⁵ si² *(translit.)*

One's own body is covered with manure. (lit.)

Be conscious of one's own fault / guilt.

Feel qualms about one's own action.

Feel compunction.

🈁 指作賊心虛，心中有鬼或問心有愧。
參閱 "心中有屎" 條（0414）。

0774 自打嘴巴

zi[6] daa[2] zeoi[2] baa[1] *(translit.)*

Smack on one's own mouth. (lit.)

Contradict oneself.

Be self-contradictory.

🈁 即自相矛盾。

0775 自投羅網

zi[6] tau[4] lo[4] mong[5] *(translit.)*

Fall into one's own trapping net on voluntary basis. (lit.)

Put one's own head in the noose.

0776 自梳

zi[6] so[1] *(translit.)*

Self comb. (lit.)

Make up one's mind to marry to no man.

Decide to be an old maid all one's life.

Remain a maid all one's life.

Live in maidenhood all one's life.

🈁 從前廣東順德、番禺、南海等縣的女子有終身不嫁的風氣，到了成年時，將辮子梳成髮髻，表示從此不嫁人，叫 "自梳" 或 "梳起"。並且集合志同道合者，組織所謂 "姑婆屋"，以備年老時互相照顧。

0777 自斟自酌

zi[6] zam[1] zi[6] zoek[3] *(translit.)*

Pour for oneself and drink all by oneself. (lit.)

Make an arbitrary decision and act peremptorily.

Be in the enjoyment of one's own life all by oneself.

🈁 指獨斷獨行或獨自享受個人生活。

0778 伊撈七

ji[1] lou[1] cat[1] *(translit.)*

Generally. (lit.)

Generally speaking...

🈁 這是插入式的口頭語，意為一般來說。

0779 行行出狀元

hong[4] hong[4] ceot[1] zong[6] jyun[4] *(translit.)*

Every trade has its own 'Zong Jyun'. (a title conferred on the scholar who came first in the Highest Imperial Examination) (lit.)

There is always an outstanding master in every trade.

Everyone can come to fame in his own trade.

0780 行行企企

hang[4] hang[4] kei[5] kei[5] *(translit.)*

Walk and stand. (lit.)

Lounge away.

Be of assistance to somebody.

🈁 指無所事事，但又相當於 "幫閒"。

0781 行得正，企得正

hang[4] dak[1] zeng[3] (zing[3]), kei[5] dak[1] zeng[3] (zing[3]) *(translit.)*

Both walk and stand in the right way. (lit.)

Be on one's best behaviours.

Play fair and square.

🈁 行為正直的意思。

0782 行船好過灣

haang[4] syun[4] hou[2] gwo[3] waan[1] *(translit.)*

Sailing is better than anchoring a boat. (lit.)

It is better to have a little to do than it is to do none.

🀄相當於 "不怕慢，只怕站"。

0783 行船爭解纜

haang⁴ syun⁴ zang¹ gaai² laam⁶ *(translit.)*

Fight to untie the cable (cast off) while beginning to set sail. (lit.)

Take the lead.

🀄指領先行動。

0784 行路打倒退

haang⁴ lou⁶ daa² dou³ tan³ *(translit.)*

Go backward while walking. (lit.)

Fall on evil days.

Misfortunes never come singly.

🀄全句本為 "衰起上嚟有頭有路，行路都會打倒退嘅"，意思是説 "當一個人倒霉時，甚至走路也會後退的"，但因為句子太長了，廣東人多只説 "行路打倒退"，簡單譯出來，便是 "倒霉" 或 "禍不單行"，參閱 "打倒退" 條（0460）。

0785 行運一條龍，失運一條蟲

haang⁴ wan⁶ jat¹ tiu⁴ lung⁴, sat¹ wan⁶ jat¹ tiu⁴ cung⁴ *(translit.)*

A person having good luck is a dragon but a man having ill luck is only but a worm. (lit.)

A man in luck walks heavy but a man out of luck cowers with humility.

🀄比喻走運的人，趾高氣揚，但倒霉的人則不敢見人。

0786 合晒心水

hap⁶ saai³ sam¹ seoi² *(translit.)*

Agree with the state of mind. (lit.)

After one's own heart.

To one's own liking.

🀄指合心意，參閱 "合晒合尺" 條（0787）。

0787 合晒合尺

hap⁶ saai³ ho⁴ ce¹ *(translit.)*

Correspond to 5 2 (the numbered musical notation). (lit.)

Be after one's own heart.

To one's own liking.

Fit in with...

Be fit like a glove.

Tight fit.

🀄表示合心意的意思，參閱 "合晒心水" 條（0786），但又表示完全符合的意思。"合" 讀作 "荷" 的低平聲，"尺" 則讀 "扯" 的高平聲。"合尺" 為粵樂的主音，相當於 5 2 音階，粵曲界無論唱者或玩樂器者，必先正線 "合尺" 音為較音標準，以免走音。普通話相應詞為 "合心意" 或 "對勁"。

0788 企喺城樓睇馬打

kei⁵ hai² sing⁴ / seng⁴ lau⁴ tai² maa⁵ daa² *(translit.)*

Stand on the gate tower to watch horses fighting. (lit.)

Make oneself stay out of the matter.

Keep oneself out of the affair.

🀄表示使自己置身度外。

0789 兇神惡煞

hung¹ san⁴ ok³ saat³ *(translit.)*

Brutal god and fierce devil. (lit.)

Be fiendish and devilish.

🀄形容人 "兇暴的" 的樣子。

0790 各自為政

gok³ zi⁶ wai⁴ zing³ *(translit.)*

Everyone governs in his own way.
(lit.)

Each one minds his own
business.

Each one cleaves his own
opinion.

🈯 指各自做自己的事或各持己見。

0791 各花落各眼

gok³ faa¹ lok⁶ gok³ ngaan⁵ *(translit.)*

Every flower falls to every man's
eyes. (lit.)

Beauty is but subjective.

Beauty exists in the eyes of the
beholder.

Different people make different
appraisals of beauty.

🈯 比喻每個人對美的不同看法。

0792 各適其適

gok³ sik¹ kei⁴ sik¹ *(translit.)*

Each enjoys what he enjoys. (lit.)

Each takes what he needs.

Each does what he thinks is
right.

Each takes what he likes to.

Each goes his own way.

🈯 指各取所需，各行其是或各取所愛。

0793 多個香爐多隻鬼

do¹ go³ hoeng¹ lou⁴ do¹ zek³ gwai²
(translit.)

One more censer, one more ghost.
(lit.)

The more the competitors, the
keener the competition.

The keener the competition is,
the narrower the margin of
profit will be.

🈯 比喻多一同業，多一競爭或多一同
業，利潤相應減少。

0794 交帶

gaau¹ daai³ *(translit.)*

Undertake for the job. (lit.)

Be responsible.

Bear responsibility for...

🈯 表示盡責或對⋯⋯負責的意思。

0795 充大頭鬼

cung¹ daai⁶ tau⁴ gwai² *(translit.)*

Pretend to be a big-headed ghost.
(lit.)

Put on the appearance of a man
of wealth.

Be shabby — genteel.

Live in genteel poverty.

🈯 指冒充闊氣或窮也要裝門面。

0796 羊毛出在羊身上

joeng⁴ mou⁴ ceot¹ zoi⁶ joeng⁴ san¹
soeng⁶ *(translit.)*

Wool comes from sheep's bodies.
(lit.)

Whatever is given is paid for.

All charges are shifted on to
consumers.

0797 羊牯

joeng⁴ gu² *(translit.)*

A ram. (lit.)

An outsider.

A layman.

An ignoramus.

A dupe.

A pigeon.

🈯 從前粵劇演員，稱觀眾為"羊牯"，
蓋譏為外行人，但後為騙子利用，作
為易受騙的笨人的代名詞。

0798 米已成炊

mai⁵ ji⁵ sing⁴ ceoi¹ *(translit.)*

The rice is well-cooked. (lit.)

The die is cast.

六
畫

注 指既成事實。

0799　江山易改，品性難移

gong¹ saan¹ ji⁶ goi², ban² sing³ naan⁴ ji⁴ *(translit.)*

It is easy to alter rivers and mountains but difficult to change a person's character. (lit.)

It is difficult to change one's skin.

The child is father to the man.

What is bred in the bone will come out in the flesh.

A leopard cannot change his spots.

0800　江西佬舞／打死馬騮——有家歸不得

gong¹ sai¹ lou² mou⁵／daa² sei² maa⁵ lau¹ — jau⁵ gaa¹ gwai¹ bat¹ dak¹ *(translit.)*

A native of Gong Sai makes his monkey dance／beats his monkey to death — having home but cannot go back. (lit.)

Be at the end of one's rope.

Be pushed to the wall.

Be beyond hope.

注 比喻陷入困境或進退兩難。從前廣州和佛山兩地，常有人在街頭耍猴子戲，藉以乞取生活費用，這些舞猴者，多為江西省人。假如他們賺錢的主角死了，他們便要淪落異鄉了。

0801　忙狼

mong⁴ long⁴ *(translit.)*

As busy as a wolf. (lit.)

Be in a hurry.

Make haste.

注 形容人匆匆忙忙的樣子。

0802　守得雲開見月明

sau² dak¹ wan⁴ hoi¹ gin³ jyut⁶ ming⁴ *(translit.)*

Await the clouds to open till the moon is seen. (lit.)

Wait till the clouds roll by.

0803　安分

on¹ fan⁶ *(translit.)*

Keep one's obligation. (lit.)

Know one's distance.

Dare not tempt one's fate.

Live to one's heart's content.

Rest content with one's present situation.

Not to go beyond one's bounds.

注 表示有自知之明不敢妄想或對目前境遇心滿意足的意思。

0804　安分守己

on¹ fan⁶ sau² gei² *(translit.)*

Keep one's obligation and good behaviours. (lit.)

Abide by laws and behave oneself well.

注 表示奉公守法，不作壞的勾當的意思。

0805　收山

sau¹ saan¹ *(translit.)*

Put away the mountain. (lit.)

Retire from one's work.

Retire from the world.

Live in retirement.

Wash one's hands of somebody.

注 表示退休，退隱，過退休生活或洗手不幹的意思。

0806　收手

sau¹ sau² *(translit.)*

Put away the hands. (lit.)

Stay one's hand.

Throw in one's hands.

注 表示住手不再幹或放棄的意思。

六畫

0807　收科

sau¹ fo¹ *(translit.)*

Bring to an end. (lit.)

End up./Put an end to...

Wind up.

Make something reach a satisfactory settlement.

Wash one's hand of...

Stay one's hand.

㊟本為粵劇 "煞科" （收場）的術語，但轉義為結束收手或使……圓滿解決。

0808　收檔

sau¹ dong³ *(translit.)*

Shut up the stall. (lit.)

Declare bankruptcy.

Close the stall/shop for the night.

Stop wagging the tongue.

Not to do it any more.

㊟本義為宣佈破產，關門休息。如果對人説時，則叫人不要再説或做下去。

0809　奸賴

gaan¹ laai³ *(translit.)*

Deny shamelessly. (lit.)

Disavow.

Refuse to confess.

㊟表示抵賴不認賬；耍賴皮。

0810　好人事

hou² jan⁴ si² *(translit.)*

Good man's kindness. (lit.)

Be affable.

Be kindhearted.

㊟意為心腸好，和藹。

0811　好人難做

hou² jan⁴ naan⁴ zou⁶ *(translit.)*

To be a good man is difficult. (lit.)

If you want to please everybody, you'll please nobody.

A sage is often regarded as a savage.

There are always those who are not satisfied with a good man.

㊟表示難以討好每一個人。

0812　好女兩頭瞞

hou² neoi² loeng⁵ tau⁴ mun⁴ *(translit.)*

A good daughter deceives both sides (families). (lit.)

Hide the truth of either of the two so as to please both.

Make the best of both worlds.

Sit on the hedge.

Cut both ways./Bear two faces in one head.

㊟指把兩方任何一方的真相隱瞞以取悦雙方，但引伸成為兩全其美，耍兩面派或兩邊倒。

0813　好天搵埋落雨米

hou² tin¹ wan² maai⁴ lok⁶ jyu⁵ mai⁵ *(translit.)*

While it is a fine day, look for rice for rainy days. (lit.)

Gather hay against a rainy day.

Make hay while the sun shines.

㊟表示未雨綢繆的意思。

0814　好水冇幾多朝

hou² seoi² mou⁵ gei² do¹ ziu¹ *(translit.)*

Good water won't come for many mornings. (lit.)

There is not much of such a good opportunity in one's life.

㊟比喻一生中好機會不多。

0815　好心地

hou² sam¹ dei² *(translit.)*

Good heart ground. (lit.)

六畫

Be kind-hearted.

注即心地善良。

0816　好心唔怕做

hou^2 sam^1 m^4 paa^3 zou^6 (translit.)

Be not afraid to be good-hearted.
(lit.)

Have one's heart in the right place.

Have a heart.

注鼓勵人行善。

0817　好心唔得好報

hou^2 sam^1 m^4 dak^1 hou^2 bou^3
(translit.)

Good heart is not well-repaid. (lit.)

Recompense good with evil.

Shoe the goose.

注同〝好心着雷劈〞。

0818　好心着雷劈〔殛〕

hou^2 sam^1 zoek^6 leoi^4 pek^3 (translit.)

Good heart meets with the strike of thunder. (lit.)

Bite the hand that feeds one.

Recompense good with evil.

注同〝好心唔得好報〞。

0819　好市

hou^2 si^5 (translit.)

Good market. (lit.)

Sell well.

Sell like hot cakes.

Command a ready sale.

注指暢銷或賣得快。

0820　好見飯

hou^2 gin^3 faan^6 (translit.)

See the cooked-rice well. (lit.)

The rice rises well when it is cooked.

注即〝出飯〞意指以同等份量的一種米

煮飯，比同等份量的另一種米出的飯多。

0821　好事不出門，壞事傳千里

hou^2 si^6 bat^1 ceot^1 mun^4, waai^6 si^6 cyun^4 cin^1 lei^5 (translit.)

Good things do not go out of the door, ill things spread a thousand li. (lit.)

Good news goes on clutchers but ill news flies apace.

注指壞事傳得極遠。

0822　好物沉歸底

hou^2 mat^6 cam^4 gwai^1 dai^2 (translit.)

Good things sink to the bottom. (lit.)

The best fish swim near the bottom.

注指好的東西在最後找到。

0823　好佬怕爛佬

hou^2 lou^2 paa^3 laan^6 lou^2 (translit.)

A good fellow fears a rascal. (lit.)

A pigeon makes no friends with a hawk.

A gentleman feels it beneath his dignity to argue with a rascal.

注表示好人或有教養的人不屑於和不講理的人或粗人爭吵或交往的意思。

0824　好食懶飛

hou^3 sik^6 laan^5 fei^1 (translit.)

Be fond of eating but lazy to fly. (lit.)

Eat one's head off.

注即好吃懶做。

0825　好眉好貌生沙蝨

hou^2 mei^4 hou^2 maau^6 saang^1 saa^1 sat^1 (translit.)

Good looking but having sand hoppers. (lit.)

A fair face hides a foul heart.

Be nice in appearance but defective in quality.

注 比喻人外表好但行為差劣或中看不中用。

0826　好馬不食回頭草

hou² maa⁵ bat¹ sik⁶ wui⁴ tau⁴ cou² *(translit.)*

A good horse never comes back to eat the grass. (lit.)

Once quit, never back.

A bird flying away from the cage will never come back to be fed.

注 比喻不再回頭受僱或一經放手，便再不回頭。

0827　好唱口

hou² coeng³ hau² *(translit.)*

A good singing mouth. (lit.)

Make irresponsible and sarcastic remarks.

Wag one's jaws.

注 本義好嗓子。但引伸作會説風涼話，但又表示口若懸河的意思。

0828　好啱偈

hou² ngaam¹ gai² *(translit.)*

Match well with. (lit.)

Be congenial to each other.

Get along well with each other.

注 表示彼此志趣相投或相處甚好的意思。

0829　好啱橋

hou² ngaam¹ kiu² *(translit.)*

Match well with. (lit.)

Be congenial to each other.

Get along well with each other.

注 意思和 "好啱偈" 相同，參閱（0828）條。

0830　好腳頭

hou² goek³ tau⁴ *(translit.)*

Good foot-head. (lit.)

Be born with good luck to the family.

Come with good luck to somebody.

注 指一出世或一到來便帶來幸運（指人或畜牲都可以）。

0831　好話唔好聽

hou² waa⁶ m⁴ hou² teng¹ *(translit.)*

Words are good but they are not good to listen to. (lit.)

Frankly speaking.

Be quite honest about it.

In a manner of speaking.

注 此為插入語，表示説實在的，老實説或不妨説的意思。

0832　好漢不吃眼前虧

hou² hon³ bat¹ hek³ ngaan⁵ cin⁴ kwai¹ *(translit.)*

A good fellow eats no loss immediately. (lit.)

It is better to show a clean pair of heels than it is to show a bare pair of hands.

It is better to avoid visible loss than it is to brave it out.

注 表示要避開眼前可見的損失。

0833　好聲好氣

hou² seng¹ hou² hei³ *(translit.)*

Good sound and good air. (lit.)

Speak in kindly manner.

注 形容心平氣和的説話態度。

0834　好戲在後頭

hou² hei³ zoi⁶ hau⁶ tau⁴ *(translit.)*

The good performance is at the later part of the entertainment. (lit.)

六畫

There will be something
interesting to see a little later.

注 暗喻還有事發生。

七 畫

0835 弄巧反拙

lung⁶ haau² faan² zyut³ *(translit.)*

*Try to make good of something but
end up with a blunder. (lit.)*

**Try to outsmart oneself but turn
out to be foolish.**

Ride one's horse to death.

注 本想用巧妙手段，結果反而做了蠢
事。

0836 弄假成真

lung⁶ gaa² sing⁴ zan¹ *(translit.)*

*Try to make believe but turn out to
be reality. (lit.)*

**What was make-believe has
become reality.**

注 本來是假做，結果變成了真的。

0837 吞口水養命

tan¹ hau² seoi² joeng⁵ meng⁶ *(translit.)*

*Swallow a mouth of water to live
on. (lit.)*

Hope to linger out longer.

**Linger on in a worsening
condition.**

注 表示苟延殘命（喘）的意思。

0838 吞吞吐吐

tan¹ tan¹ tou³ tou³ *(translit.)*

Swallowing and vomiting. (lit.)

Hum and haw.

Feel some hesitation in speaking.

Stick in one's throat.

注 參閱 "而依哦哦" 條（0708）。

0839 抌氣

dan³ hei³ *(translit.)*

Complain with angry breath. (lit.)

Nurse a grievance.

注 表示發洩怨氣，一肚子怨氣的意思。

0840 抌蝦籠

dan³ haa¹ lung² *(translit.)*

*Yank the bamboo cage for holding
shrimps. (lit.)*

Pick somebody's pocket.

注 比喻掏人的錢包。

0841 找晦氣

zaau² fui³ hei³ *(translit.)*

Look for gloomy air. (lit.)

**Go/Come to blame somebody to
vent one's spite.**

Seek a quarrel.

Denounce somebody for his...

注 表示譴責某人以洩憤，尋釁或痛斥某
人。

0842 批中

pai¹ zung³ *(translit.)*

Give a right criticism. (lit.)

As expected.

Anticipate the result.

注 在意料中或估計到的意思。

0843 扯皮條

ce² pei⁴ tiu⁴ᐟ² *(translit.)*

Drag leather straps. (lit.)

Procure for prostitutes.

注 指替娼妓介紹嫖客。

0844 扯風波

ce² fung¹ bo¹ *(translit.)*

Hoist a typhoon signal. (lit.)

Be heavy with child.

注 懷胎的詼諧説法。

0845　扯線

ce² sin²ᐟ³ *(translit.)*

Draw the line. (lit.)

Establish a relationship for both parties.

🈺給雙方拉關係。

0846　扯線公仔

ce² sin²ᐟ³ gung¹ zai² *(translit.)*

A wooden figure dragged by threads. (lit.)

A marionette.

A puppet.

A person who is led by the nose.

🈺即"牽線木偶"或"傀儡"，喻受人擺佈或支配的人。

0847　扯頭纜

ce² tau⁴ laam⁶ *(translit.)*

Draw the first cable. (lit.)

Take the lead.

🈺帶頭的意思，但有人説成"拉頭纜"的，參閱該條（1005）。

0848　扯貓尾

ce² maau¹ mei⁵ *(translit.)*

Pull a cat's tail. (lit.)

Collaborate with each other to hide the truth from somebody.

Each of the two acts in collaboration to pull the wool over the eyes of somebody.

🈺指兩人串通，互相呼應來瞞騙第三者，有時有人説成"拉或搤貓尾"，相當於"唱雙簧"。

0849　走馬看花

zau² maa⁵ hon³ faa¹ *(translit.)*

Ride a running horse to look at flowers. (lit.)

Take a scamper through something.

Gain a superficial understanding through cursory observation.

🈺指匆匆看過，未有深入了解。

0850　走唔過⋯⋯嘅手指罅

zau² m⁴ gwo³... ge³ sau² zi² laa³ *(translit.)*

Cannot run away from the gaps of somebody's fingers. (lit.)

See through somebody's tricks.

Twist somebody round one's finger.

🈺表示洞悉某人的陰謀或可以左右某人的意思。

0851　走眼

zau² ngaan⁵ *(translit.)*

The eyes run away. (lit.)

Slip from sight.

Be negligent in checking.

Misjudge somebody/something.

🈺表示看不到或判斷錯誤。參閱"有眼無珠"（0687），"睇差一皮"（1804）及"跌眼鏡"（1811）各條。

0852　走路

zau² lou² *(translit.)*

Run away. (lit.)

Desert.

Show a clean pair of heels.

Take to one's legs.

Make away/Make away with...

Run away.

🈺即逃跑，逃亡或挾帶⋯⋯而逃。參閱"趯更"條（2412）。

0853　走歸左

zau² gwai¹ zo² *(translit.)*

Run to the left. (lit.)

Go astray.

🈺比喻行差踏錯或誤入歧途。

七畫

0854　走雞

zau² gai¹ *(translit.)*

The hen runs away. (lit.)

Miss the opportunity.

Miss the bus.

Slip through one's fingers.

注 表示失去機會的意思。

0855　走寶

zau² bou² *(translit.)*

The treasure runs away. (lit.)

Slip through one's fingers.

Incur a heavy loss.

Miss a chance.

Lose one's maid's chastity.

注 比喻失之交臂或少女失貞。

0856　走趯

zau² dek³ *(translit.)*

Walk and run about. (lit.)

Run about.

Walk this way and that way.

Rush about on errands.

Be on the busy come-and-go.

Do legwork.

Play a role of bit.

Be a legman / a utility man.

注 表示四處走動，但引伸表示替人活
動，奔波，做人跑腿或跑龍套的意思。

0857　扰心扰肺

jiu¹ sam¹ jiu¹ fai³ *(translit.)*

*Pierce both the heart and the
lungs. (lit.)*

Break somebody's heart.

Go to somebody's heart.

注 令人很傷心的意思。

0858　折墮

zit³ do⁶ *(translit.)*

Break off and fall. (lit.)

**Be reduced to poverty by God's
denouncement.**

Obtain one's deserts.

注 表示因受天譴而墮落或得到應有的報
應。

0859　扮傻

baan⁶ so⁴ *(translit.)*

Pretend to be mad. (lit.)

Play the fool.

Feign ignorance.

Pretend to be ignorant of...

注 即"裝瘋賣傻"，"裝蒜"或對……
詐作不知。

0860　扮嘢

baan⁶ je⁵ *(translit.)*

In disguise. (lit.)

Strike an attitude.

Make believe.

注 表示裝腔作勢的意思。

0861　扮豬食老虎

baan⁶ zyu¹ sik⁶ lou⁵ fu² *(translit.)*

Feign to be a pig to eat a tiger. (lit.)

Play the fool.

Feign oneself to be foolish.

A wise man often acts the fool.

Feign ignorance.

注 意即裝笨相。

0862　扮蟹

baan⁶ haai⁵ *(translit.)*

Tie a crab. (lit.)

Tie somebody up.

**Bind somebody's hands behind
him.**

Be tied up./Be bound up.

Be trussed up.

注 表示把某人綁住，被人綁住或拘押的
意思。

0863　扻／砍頭埋牆

ham^2 tau$^{2/4}$ maai^4 coeng^4 *(translit.)*

Knock the head against the wall. (lit.)

Show repentance for having been foolish／ignorant.

🈲表示曾因無知做錯事而事後悔恨的意思。

0864　扻心口

dam^2 sam^1 hau^2 *(translit.)*

Knock the mouth of heart. (lit.)

Fleece somebody of his money.

Extort money from somebody.

Be repentant of something wrong.

Be heart-broken.

Nurse a grief.

🈲即敲詐，又喻作悔恨或傷心。

0865　均真

gwan^1 zan^1 *(translit.)*

Equalize. (lit.)

Be fair-minded.

Be impartial to...

See fair.

🈲表示公平或公正的意思。

0866　扭六壬

nau^2 luk^6 jam^4 *(translit.)*

Wring out six points (the ninth of the ten heavenly stems). (lit.)

Rack one's brains.

Resort to manoeuvres.

🈲表示絞盡腦汁或玩弄花招的意思。

0867　扭計

nau^2 gai^2 *(translit.)*

Wring out a plan. (lit.)

Naughty;mischievous.

Employ all kinds of base devices.

Resort to manoevres.

Scheme against each other.

🈲相當於淘氣；頑皮或出鬼點子難人；搞鬼；跟人勾心鬥角。

0868　扭屎窟花

nau^2 si^2 fat^1 faa^1 *(translit.)*

Twist hips in the shape of a flower. (lit.)

Try some tricks.

🈲即"耍花招"。

0869　扭紋柴

nau^2 man^4 caai^4 *(translit.)*

Cross-grained firewood. (lit.)

A regular mischief.

A little mischief.

🈲比喻小孩子脾氣蠻橫或淘氣。

0870　扭擰

nau^2 ning^6 *(translit.)*

Twist around. (lit.)

Strike attitudes.

Put on poses.

🈲表示扭扭捏捏（即羞澀不大方的姿態）的意思。

0871　把火

baa^2 fo^2 *(translit.)*

A column of fire. (lit.)

Be filled with rage.

Be hot with rage／anger.

🈲意和"一把火"同，參閱該條（0023）。

0872　把屁

baa^2 pei^3 *(translit.)*

Useless fart. (lit.)

Be of no use.

Be useless.

What is the use of...?

What is the use to do something?

七畫

注 參閱 "把鬼"（0873）條。此外作反問語時，表示有甚麼用處的意思。相當於 "頂個屁用"。

0873　把鬼

baa² gwai² (translit.)

Muddle the ghost. (lit.)

Be of no use.

Be useless.

It wastes one's energy / time to...

注 表示毫無用處的意思外，還含有白費氣力或時間的意思。

0874　把幾火

baa² gei² fo² (translit.)

More than a column of fire. (lit.)

Flare out.

Be hot with rage.

Burn with anger.

Be filled with rage.

注 大致上意和 "一把火"（0023）及 "把火"（0871）同，但意思和語氣較強。

0875　枬失

ngat¹ sat¹ (translit.)

Too miserly. (lit.)

Square accounts to the smallest details.

Haggle over every penny.

注 指斥斤計較。

0876　杉木靈牌 —— 唔做得主

caam³ muk⁶ leng⁴ / ling⁴ paai⁴ — m⁴ zou⁶ dak¹ zyu² (translit.)

An ancestral tablet made of pine — it cannot be used as a real ancestral tablet. (lit.)

Be not in a position to decide / to make a decision.

注 廣東習俗在長輩死後，必為他設置用栗木做的神主牌作供奉之用，（相傳原出於春秋時介之推在被晉文公焚山求

他出仕時，抱栗木而死，文公為着紀念他，砍那棵栗木作木屐穿着，後人遂用栗木做神主牌。）但在未 "上高" 前，用杉木作為臨時靈牌，故有杉木靈牌唔做得主（神主牌）這一句話。相當於 "丫鬟帶鑰匙 —— 當家不作主"。

0877　求人不如求己

kau⁴ jan⁴ bat¹ jyu⁴ kau⁴ gei² (translit.)

Begging others is not like begging oneself. (lit.)

Turn one's own hand to do one's own business.

God help those who help themselves.

注 即 "天助自助者"。

0878　求先

kau⁴ sin¹ (translit.)

Just now. (lit.)

A moment ago.

Just now.

注 表示片刻之前或剛才的意思，和 "頭先" 同義，參閱該條（2260）。"頭先" 和 "求先" 之分，是由於鄉音問題而已。

0879　求求其其

kau⁴ kau⁴ kei⁴ kei⁴ (translit.)

Casual. (lit.)

Slap together.

Huddle up.

In a slapdash manner.

Casually.

At random.

Anything / Anybody will do.

注 表示隨便或馬馬虎虎的意思。在選擇方面而言，參閱 "是是但但"（1204）條。

0880　車天車地

ce¹ tin¹ ce¹ dei⁶ (translit.)

Turn both the sky and earth. *(lit.)*

Have an idle talk with somebody.

Make an extravagant remark.

Make an extravagant boast of oneself.

🈺 指和人瞎扯，吹牛或過分吹噓自己。

0881 豆腐刀——兩便面

dau⁶ fu⁶ dou¹ — loeng⁵ bin⁶ min² *(translit.)*

A knife used to cut beancurd — both sides are cutting blades. (lit.)

Sit on both sides of the hedge.

Cut both ways.

🈺 即"耍兩面派"；"銅板切豆腐——兩面光"。

0882 奀嫋鬼命

ngan¹ liu¹ gwai² meng⁶ *(translit.)*

As thin and brittle as ghost's life. (lit.)

Be in delicate health.

🈺 形容人十分瘦弱的樣子。

0883 夾手夾腳

gap³ sau² gap³ goek³ *(translit.)*

Link hands and feet together. (lit.)

Co-operate closely with each other.

🈺 緊密合作的意思。

0884 夾份

gaap³ / gap³ fan² *(translit.)*

Crowd shares together. (lit.)

Club together.

Club shares.

Pool shares.

🈺 表示湊份子，湊錢，合夥；分攤的意思。參閱"田雞東"（0519）。

0885 夾計

gaap³ / gap³ gai² *(translit.)*

Put the plots together. (lit.)

Lay our / your / their heads together.

Gang up with somebody.

Plot together.

Collude with somebody.

🈺 即和某人聯合起來，串謀或串通。

0886 步步為營

bou⁶ bou⁶ wai⁴ jing⁴ *(translit.)*

Take care pace by pace. (lit.)

Pick one's steps.

Do something by inches.

Be on the alert against...

🈺 表示小心翼翼提高警覺的意思。

0887 見人講人話，見鬼講鬼話

gin³ jan⁴ gong² jan⁴ waa², gin³ gwai² gong² gwai² waa² *(translit.)*

Seeing a man, speak man's language; seeing a ghost, speak ghost words. (lit.)

Speak to a saint like a saint, to a devil like a devil.

Scratch somebody where he feels an itch.

🈺 即説投人所好的話的意思。

0888 見山就拜

gin³ saan¹ zau⁶ baai³ *(translit.)*

Worship the grave as soon as one sees it. (lit.)

Wrongly make sure of somebody / something without getting to the bottom.

Take A for B without making sure.

🈺 比喻不問究竟，一眼望去便誤認甲為乙。

0889 見地不平擔鉀鑹

gin³ dei⁶ bat¹ ping⁴ daam¹ bong¹

七畫

caan[2] *(translit.)*

Take a hoe and shovel when seeing the uneven ground. (lit.)

Cry out against injustice.

Ready to take up the cudgels for somebody / something.

Stand up for the weak sister.

注即抱打不平。

0890　見步行步

gin[3] bou[6] haang[4] bou[6] *(translit.)*

See a step, walk with a step. (lit.)

Pick one's steps.

Meet the situation step by step.

注相當於"走一步，見一步"。

0891　見屎窟郁唔見米白

gin[3] si[2] fat[1] juk[1] m[4] gin[3] mai[5] baak[6] *(translit.)*

See the hips moving but not see the rice turn white. (lit.)

Pretened to be hard at work without getting anything done.

注貌似積極幹，毫無實效。

0892　見高就拜，見低就踩

gin[3] gou[1] zau[6] baai[3], gin[3] dai[1] zau[6] caai[2] (jaai[2]) *(translit.)*

Worship the high one and tread the low one. (lit.)

Be snobbish.

Look down on somebody below one but fawn upon somebody far superior to one.

注表示諂上欺下的意思。

0893　見過鬼就怕黑

gin[3] gwo[3] gwai[2] zau[6] paa[3] hak[1] *(translit.)*

After seeing a ghost, one becomes afraid of darkness. (lit.)

A burnt child dreads the fire.

Once bitten, twice shy.

注相當於"一朝被蛇咬，三年怕草繩"。

0894　足水

zuk[1] seoi[2] *(translit.)*

Enough water. (lit.)

Be contented with one's luck.

Be pleased with oneself.

注表示心滿意足或自鳴得意。

0895　吟詩都吟唔甩

jam[4] si[1] dou[1] jam[4] m[4] lat[1] *(translit.)*

Cannot get rid of it in spite of chanting. (lit.)

There is no way to evade... (doing something).

Fail to shirk.

注同"秀才遇老虎 —— 吟詩都吟唔甩"（0905）。

0896　別致

bit[6] zi[3] *(translit.)*

Special and fine. (lit.)

Be new and unusual.

注即新奇而不尋常。

0897　吹鬚轆眼

ceoi[1] sou[1] luk[1] ngaan[5] *(translit.)*

Blow the beard and roll the pupils of eyes. (lit.)

Fall into a rage.

Tear one's hair.

注相當於"吹鬍子，瞪眼"。

0898　吼

hau[1] *(translit.)*

Have a look at. (lit.)

Watch.

Take notice of...

Buy / Patronize

Hope for... / Woo...

Pursue

Take a fancy to...

🈷廣東人用"吼"作動詞用。意為看守、注意，光顧或買及向……（異性）追求等。

0899　吼斗

hau¹ dau² *(translit.)*

Would like to have. (lit.)

Hope for...

Woo...

Take a fancy to...

Can do with...

🈷表示希望得到或想要。

0900　告枕頭狀

gou³ zam² tau⁴ zong² *(translit.)*

Bring in a pillow indictment. (lit.)

Lay a complaint against somebody in the presence of one's husband.

0901　我都冇你咁好氣

ngo⁵ dou¹ mou⁵ nei⁵ gam³ hou² hei³ *(translit.)*

I have no such good air as yours. (lit.)

I am now at my ease.

I am carefree now.

I won't have to strive for...

I'll close my eyes to...

I'll snap my fingers at...

I'll talk no more.

I am not going to talk to you any more.

🈷表示自己生活優遊或已達要求目的，不必再和人競爭的意思。此外又有不屑一顧或不願再談下去的意義。

0902　利口便辭

lei⁶ hau² bin⁶ ci⁴ *(translit.)*

Be eloquent. (lit.)

Have a ready or silver tongue.

🈷表示口才敏捷的意思。

0903　利口唔利腹

lei⁶ hau² m⁴ lei⁶ fuk¹ *(translit.)*

Benefit the mouth but not the belly. (lit.)

Good for mouth but bad for health.

🈷表示好吃的東西會損害健康的意思。

0904　秀才手巾 —— 包書"輸"

sau³ coi⁴ sau² gan¹ — baau¹ syu¹ *(translit.)*

A scholar's handkerchief — wrap books with (surely to lose) (lit.)

Stand to lose.

🈷相當於"孔子搬家 —— 淨書（輸）"。（按："書"和"輸"同音）

0905　秀才遇老虎 —— 吟詩都吟唔甩

sau³ coi⁴ jyu⁶ lou⁵ fu² — jam⁴ si¹ dou¹ jam⁴ m⁴ lat¹ *(translit.)*

A scholar meets a tiger — he cannot get rid of it even though he chants. (lit.)

Fail to shirk.

There is no way to evade... (doing something)

🈷比喻勢難逃避。

0906　秀才遇着兵 —— 有理講不清

sau³ coi⁴ jyu⁶ zoek⁶ bing¹ — jau⁵ lei⁵ gong² bat¹ cing¹ *(translit.)*

A scholar meets a soldier — having reason but unable to be understood. (lit.)

Be unable to persuade somebody with reason.

Fail to reason with somebody for / against...

七畫

注 表示不可理喻的意思。

0907　私己

si¹ gei² *(translit.)*

Personal effects. (lit.)

Private savings.

Personal effects.

注 即私房錢或私有財產（尤指家中婦女
所積蓄的財物）。

0908　兵來將擋，水來土掩

bing¹ loi⁴ zoeng³ dong², ceoi² loi⁴
tou² jim² *(translit.)*

*Soldiers coming will be turned
away by a general; water coming
will be covered with soil. (lit.)*

A Roland for an Oliver.

Pay tit for tat.

注 表示針鋒相對的意思；參閱 "你做初
一，我做十五"（0929）條。

0909　佔上風

zim³ soeng⁶ fung¹ *(translit.)*

Usurp the top wind. (lit.)

**Take the wind out of somebody's
sails.**

Have the advantage of somebody.

注 表示佔得別人的好處或比別人有利的
意思。

0910　佔便宜

zim³ pin⁴ ji⁴ *(translit.)*

Usurp small gains. (lit.)

**Gain extra advantage by unfair
means.**

Profit at other's expense.

0911　作死

zok³ sei² *(translit.)*

Want to die. (lit.)

Take the road to ruin oneself.

注 表示自尋死路的意思。

0912　作狀

zok³ zong⁶ *(translit.)*

Attitudinize. (lit.)

Strike a pose.

Put on an act.

Act in affected manners.

注 即裝腔作勢或裝模作樣。參閱 "扮嘢"
條（0860）。

0913　作怪

zok³ gwaai³ *(translit.)*

Do something queer. (lit.)

Make trouble.

Do mischief.

注 即搞鬼。

0914　作威作福

zok³ wai¹ zok³ fuk¹ *(translit.)*

Show power and blessing. (lit.)

Come the bully over somebody.

Play the bully.

Throw one's weight about.

注 表示妄自尊大，濫用權勢，盛氣凌人
的意思。

0915　作賊心虛

zok³ caak⁶ sam¹ heoi¹ *(translit.)*

*Be timid at heart for being a thief.
(lit.)*

Have a guilty conscience.

A bully fears to face the law.

注 參閱 "心中有屎"（0414）及 "自己
身有屎" 條（0773）。

0916　作嘔

zok³ au² *(translit.)*

Feel like vomiting. (lit.)

**Be filled with nausea at the sight
of...**

Make one feel sick.

注 表示要嘔吐，令人噁心的意思。

七
畫

0917 作賤自己

zok³ zin⁶ zi⁶ gei² *(translit.)*

Make onself cheap. (lit.)

Run oneself down.

Spoil oneself.

0918 低庄／莊

dai¹ zong¹ *(translit.)*

The amount of bank is low. (lit.)

Be regardless of one's own social status.

Put oneself to a step lower.

Be mean about money matters.

注 表示不理個人社會地位，降低自己或吝嗇的意思。

0919 低低地躓鋪

dai¹ dai¹ dei² gwaan³ pou¹ *(translit.)*

Stumble lowly for once. (lit.)

Put one's pride in one's pocket and yield oneself.

Say uncle to somebody.

Say 'sorry' to somebody.

Admit being defeated.

注 表示承認失敗，向人道歉或認輸。

0920 低頭切肉，把眼看人

dai¹ tau⁴ cit³ juk⁶, baa² ngaan⁵ hon³ jan⁴ *(translit.)*

Bow the head down to cut meat and judge the customer. (lit.)

Choose a pigeon to cheat.

Pluck a pigeon.

注 比喻先看對方是否可欺，再作決定。所謂＂知己知彼＂，亦即此意。

0921 低聲下氣

dai¹ sing¹ (seng¹) haa⁶ hei³ *(translit.)*

Lower one's voice and compress one's air. (lit.)

Put one's pride in one's pocket.

Bear and forbear.

Be meek and submissive.

注 一忍再忍或逆來順受的意思。

0922 你有半斤，我有八兩

nei⁵ jau⁵ bun³ gan¹, ngo⁵ jau⁵ baat³ loeng² *(translit.)*

You have half a catty, I have eight taels. (lit.)

Six of one and half a dozen of the other.

Be much of a muchness.

注 參閱＂半斤八兩＂（0584），＂石地堂，鐵掃把＂（0513），＂你有張良計，我有過牆梯＂（0924）及＂你有乾坤，我有日月＂（0923）各條。

0923 你有乾坤，我有日月

nei⁵ jau⁵ kin⁴ kwan¹, ngo⁵ jau⁵ jat⁶ jyut⁶ *(translit.)*

You have 'Kin Kwan'; I have the sun and the moon. (lit.)

'Kin' — the first of the eight diagrams, standing for 'heaven'.

'Kwan' — the seventh of the eight diagrams, standing for 'earth'.

When Greek meets Greek, there is the tug of war.

Neck and neck.

Be well-matched.

Be on a par with...

注 參閱＂半斤八兩＂，（0584）＂石地堂，鐵掃把＂（0513）；＂你有張良計，我有過牆梯＂（0924）各條。

0924 你有張良計，我有過牆梯

nei⁵ jau⁵ zoeng¹ loeng⁴ gai³, ngo⁵ jau⁵ gwo³ coeng⁴ tai¹ *(translit.)*

You have Zoeng Loeng's devise and I have a ladder long enough for me to climb over the wall. (lit.)

Be evenly matched.

七畫

Be six of one and half a dozen of the other.

注 相當於你有關門計，我有跳牆法。參閱 "半斤八兩"（0584）；"石地堂，鐵掃把"（0513）；"你有乾坤，我有日月"（0923）各條。

0925　你／佢有寶呀？

nei⁵／keoi⁵ jau⁵ bou² aa⁶
(translit.)

Do you／Does he...have treasured objects? (lit.)

What is unusual about you／him...?

Who cherishes you／him...?

Who cares about you／him...?

注 這是對人表示輕蔑的用語，意為你／他有甚麼了不起，或誰稀罕你／他。

0926　你走你嘅陽關路，我過我嘅獨木橋

nei⁵ zau² nei⁵ ge³ joeng⁴ gwaan¹ lou⁶, ngo⁵ gwo³ ngo⁵ ge³ duk⁶ muk⁶ kiu⁴ *(translit.)*

You walk your road to Joeng Gwaan and I walk over my single-plank bridge. (lit.)

Each has his role to play.

Each goes his own way.

Each follows his bent.

注 表示各行其是，各走各的路，互不侵犯的意思。

0927　你／佢真開胃

nei⁵／keoi⁵ zan¹ hoi¹ wai⁶ *(translit.)*

You really have／He really has a good appetite. (lit.)

You are／He is too avaricious／greedy.

注 即你／他真貪得無厭或貪婪。

0928　你唔嫌我籮疏，我唔嫌你米碎

nei⁵ m⁴ jim⁴ ngo⁵ lo¹ so¹, ngo⁵ m⁴ jim⁴ nei⁵ mai⁵ seoi³ *(translit.)*

You do not cold-shoulder my dispersive bamboo basket and neither do I detest your smashed rice. (lit.)

Neither of the two detests the weak points of either side.

Be two of a kind.

注 比喻彼此互不嫌棄或臭味相投。

0929　你做初一，我做十五

nei⁵ zou⁶ co¹ jat¹, ngo⁵ zou⁶ sap⁶ ng⁵
(translit.)

You do the first day of the month; I do the fifteenth. (lit.)

Tit for tat.

Eye for eye.

注 表示以牙還牙或針鋒相對的意思。

0930　你敬我一尺，我敬你一丈

nei⁵ ging³ ngo⁵ jat¹ cek³, ngo⁵ ging³ nei⁵ jat¹ zoeng⁶ *(translit.)*

You offer me one foot, I'll offer you ten feet in return. (lit.)

I'll give you an ell for an inch.

I'll show greater respect for you if you do a little to me.

注 比喻互相尊重。

0931　你／佢想點就點

nei⁵／keoi⁵ soeng² dim² zau⁶ dim²
(translit.)

Mark as you like／he likes to mark. (lit.)

Do／Does what you want／he wants to.

You／He can do what you／he can at random.

Do／Does as you like／he likes to.

Do / Does as you see / he sees fit.

Do / Does as your / his convenience.

📝 大意和 "隨便你 / 佢" 條同，參閱該
條（2297）或 "隨得……"（2298）。

0932　你嗰槓嘢我都有得出賣

nei⁵ go²′³ lung⁵ je⁵ ngo⁵ dou¹ jau⁵
dak¹ ceot¹ maai⁶ *(translit.)*

I have the same thing as that in
your trunk for sale. (lit.)

That is a game two people can
play.

📝 即你這套詭計，大家都會。

0933　身在福中不知福

san¹ zoi⁶ fuk¹ zung¹ bat¹ zi¹ fuk¹
(translit.)

The one that lives in weal does not
know the weal. (lit.)

Disregard the happy life one
enjoys.

Not to appreciate the enjoyment
of a happy life one is in.

0934　身當命抵

san¹ dong¹ meng⁶ dai² *(translit.)*

The body undertakes and the life
deserves. (lit.)

Have only onself to blame.

Lay the blame on oneself.

📝 即自承其咎。

0935　佛口蛇心

fat⁶ hau² se⁴ sam¹ *(translit.)*

Buddha's mouth but snake's
heart. (lit.)

Be kind-mouthed but vicious-
hearted.

Be hypocritical and malignant.

📝 表示口慈心毒或口蜜腹劍。

0936　佛都有火

fat⁶ dou¹ jau⁵ fo² *(translit.)*

Even Buddha could have fire (get
angry). (lit.)

It would try the patience of a
saint.

It would provoke God to anger.

📝 表示難以容忍的意思。

0937　坐一望二

zo⁶ jat¹ mong⁶ ji⁶ *(translit.)*

Sit one and hope for two. (lit.)

Hope for another after gaining
one.

📝 形容貪心不足。

0938　坐定粒六

zo⁶ ding⁶ lap¹ luk⁶ *(translit.)*

Fix al the dice to six. (lit.)

Feel sure of oneself.

Consider oneself to be a sure fire
winner.

Have full confidence.

📝 比喻很有把握，十拿九穩；穩拿。

0939　坐食山崩

zo⁶ sik⁶ saan¹ bang¹ *(translit.)*

Sitting and eating will cause a
mountain collapse. (lit.)

Sit idle without work and the
whole fortune will be at last
used up.

📝 即 "坐吃山空"。

0940　坐穩釣魚船

co⁵ wan² diu³ jyu⁴ syun⁴ *(translit.)*

Sit firmly in a fishing boat. (lit.)

Be on firm ground.

Success is within one's grasp.

📝 表示成功在握的意思。

0941　谷住度氣

guk¹ zyu⁶ dou⁶ hei³ *(translit.)*

Hold one's temper. (lit.)

七
畫

Eat the leek.

ⓘ 表示被迫忍受。

0942　谷起泡腮 / 顋

guk¹ hei² paau¹ (pau¹) soi¹ *(translit.)*

Puff out the cheeks. (lit.)

Be displeased.

Be out of sorts.

ⓘ 表示不滿的意思。

0943　含血噴人

ham⁴ hyut³ pan³ jan⁴ *(translit.)*

Hold in a mouthful of blood and spurt it at somebody. (lit.)

Smite with the tongue.

Make malicious remark upon somebody.

Make slanderous accusations.

ⓘ 指對人作出誹謗或指控。

0944　含冤莫白

ham⁴ jyun¹ mok⁶ baak⁶ *(translit.)*

Hold a wrong and can't be righted. (lit.)

Suffer an unrighted wrong.

ⓘ 指被人冤枉。

0945　肚皮打鼓

tou⁵ pei⁴ daa² gu² *(translit.)*

The skin of the abdomen is like a drum being beaten. (lit.)

Be as hungry as a hunter.

ⓘ 表示腹如雷鳴的意思。

0946　肚裏蟲

tou⁵ leoi⁵ cung⁴ *(translit.)*

The worm in the belly. (lit.)

A mind reader.

ⓘ 即明白別人心意的人。

0947　冷手執個熱煎堆

laang⁵ sau² zap¹ go³ jit⁶ zin¹ deoi¹ *(translit.)*

Pick up a hot deep-fried popgrain ball with a cold hand. (lit.)

Gain an unexpected advantage.

Gain pennies from heaven.

ⓘ 比喻得到意外的便宜。

0948　沐恩弟子 —— 周身債

muk⁶ jan¹ dai⁶ zi² – zau¹ san¹ zaai³ *(translit.)*

A disciple steeped in gods' bounties — his whole body is covered with debts. (lit.)

Be over head and ears in debt.

Run into debt.

ⓘ 有的人迷信且信奉多神，每遇逆境，輒向諸神許以三牲酬謝為條件，祈求所願，倘所願果真實現時，則稱為沐恩弟子，必要履行諾言。但求神時不只祈求一神，因而弄到滿身都是諾言債。廣東人便以此喻 "債台高築" 的意思。

0949　沙沙滾

saa⁴ saa⁴ gwan² *(translit.)*

Make hiss. (lit.)

Play the field.

ⓘ 表示不踏實，粗心大意或東搞西搞，不專一的意思。

0950　沙哩弄銃

saa⁴ᐟ⁶ li¹ lung³ᐟ⁶ cung³ *(translit.)*

Act in improper way. (lit.)

Act rashly.

Take thoughtless action.

ⓘ 表示魯莽輕率，莽撞的意思。

0951　沙 / 砂煲刁眼角

saa¹ bou¹ diu¹ ngaan⁵ gok³ *(translit.)*

Earthen rice-cookers take sidelong glances at each other. (lit.)

Go hungry.

Suffer from hunger.

七畫

注 比喻斷炊，無米下鍋。參閱"吊砂煲"
（0742）條。

0952 沙／砂煲兄弟

saa¹ bou¹ hing¹ dai⁶ *(translit.)*

Brothers cook with the same earthen rice-cooker. (lit.)

Friends under stress of weather.

Friends in the same boat.

注 指結幫拜把的兄弟，又比喻患難與共
的朋友。

0953 沙塵

saa¹ can⁴ *(translit.)*

Sandy dust. (lit.)

With colours flying and band playing.

Make a boast of oneself.

Take pride in oneself.

注 形容人輕浮、驕傲，目中無人，又有
好出風頭，愛誇誇其談，炫耀自己的
意思。參閱"白霍"（0561）條。

0954 沙灣燈籠——何府"苦"

saa¹ waan¹ dang¹ lung⁴ — ho⁴ fu² *(translit.)*

Sa Wan lanterns — Ho's houses (why so). (lit.)

What needs?

Why so?

For what reason?

Why bother?

Is it worth the trouble?

注 沙灣為在廣州附近，離市橋不遠的一
個鄉村，村中人絕大多數人為姓何
的，且多望族。富有者常在門外懸
掛大燈籠一對，上書"何府"二字，
"府"和"苦"同音，因此諧音作"為
了甚麼"或"為甚麼要這樣"的意思。

0955 快刀斬亂麻

faai³ dou¹ zaam² lyun⁶ maa⁴ *(translit.)*

Quick knife cuts off tangled hemp. (lit.)

Cut the Gordian knot.

Take quick action.

Give a quick hand at something.

Cut the Gordian knot.

注 表示乾脆利落，速戰速決的意思。

0956 初哥

co¹ go¹ *(translit.)*

Be initiative. (lit.)

A beginner.

A new hand.

For the first time.

注 指第一次做某種事的人；生手。

0957 初歸心抱（新婦），落地孩兒

co¹ gwai¹ sam¹ pou⁵ (san¹ fu⁵), lok⁶ dei⁶ haai⁴ ji⁴ *(translit.)*

The newly-married daughter-in-law and the newly born baby. (lit.)

It is too late to teach an old dog new tricks.

Bend a tree while it is young.

Babyhood is the time when a baby is bred.

注 暗喻小孩或新人應要及早教導。（按
"心抱"實為"新婦"的音誤。）

0958 忍唔住

jan² m⁴ zyu⁶ *(translit.)*

Stand it no more. (lit.)

Be out of patience with...

Swallow a camel.

A worm will turn.

注 參閱"忍無可忍"條（0959）。

0959 忍無可忍

jan² mou⁴ ho² jan² *(translit.)*

Can't stand it any more. (lit.)

七
畫

Be out of patience with...
Swallow a camel.
A worn will turn.

🈲表示難於容忍的意思。

八 畫

0960　奉旨"子"成婚

fung⁶ zi² sing⁴ fan¹ *(translit.)*

Be forced to get married under an imperial decree 'by a child'. (lit.)

Take a shotgun marriage.

🈲取"旨"和"子"的諧音來嘲人因有孕而不得不結婚。

0961　青頭仔

ceng¹ tau⁴ zai² *(translit.)*

A green-headed boy. (lit.)

A young man without sexual experience.

🈲指未有性經驗的青少年。

0962　青磚沙梨

ceng¹ zyun¹ saa¹ lei²/⁴ *(translit.)*

A russet pear made out of black brick. (lit.)

Not only a penny-pincher but also money snatcher.

🈲比喻視財如命而且在別人身上打算盤的人。

0963　長痛不如短痛

coeng⁴ tung³ bat¹ jyu⁴ dyun² tung³ *(translit.)*

Prefer to have a short ache than a long ache. (lit.)

Better a finger off than aye waging.

🈲表示寧願承受短期痛苦,不願承受長

期更大的痛苦。

0964　長腳蜢

coeng⁴ goek³ maang² *(translit.)*

Long-legged grasshoppers. (lit.)

A person with long legs.
Be long-legged.
Be much of a walker.

🈲比喻長腿的人,走得快或善於走路的人。

0965　拋生藕

paau¹ saang¹ ngau⁵ *(translit.)*

Throw a raw lotus-root. (lit.)

Bewitch a man by means of coquetry.
Coquette with a man.

🈲指女人以甜言蜜語向男人賣弄風情。

0966　拋浪頭

paau¹ long⁶ tau⁴ *(translit.)*

Toss the head of wave. (lit.)

Come the bully over somebody.

🈲表示虛張聲勢來嚇人的意思。

0967　拋頭露面

paau¹ tau⁴ lou⁶ min⁶ *(translit.)*

Toss the head and show the face. (lit.)

(of a woman in feudal society) show one's face in public.
Show oneself to make a living.

🈲原指婦女出現在大庭廣眾中(封建道德認為是丟臉的事)。現一般指公開露面。

0968　花天酒地

faa¹ tin¹ zau² dei⁶ *(translit.)*

Flowery sky and wine earth. (lit.)

Indulge oneself in dissipation.
Lead a life of debauchery.

🈲形容荒淫腐化的生活。

0969 花心

faa¹ sam¹ *(translit.)*

Flowery heart. (lit.)

Be insatiable in love.

Not to give one's mind to one's lover.

Play the field.

㊟形容人愛情不專一。

0970 花心蘿蔔

faa¹ sam¹ lo⁴ baak⁶ *(translit.)*

Flowery-hearted radish. (lit.)

The person who is not constant in love.

The person who is not singleminded on his lover.

㊟比喻"愛情不專一的男人"。

0971 花弗 (扶)

faa¹ fit¹ *(translit.)*

Be flowery. (lit.)

Be flashy without substance.

Be gaudy like a peacock.

㊟表示愛打扮或趕時髦的意思。相當於 "花俏"。

0972 花多眼亂

faa¹ do¹ ngaan⁵ lyun⁶ *(translit.)*

Too many flowers make eyes become perturbed. (lit.)

There are too many to choose.

Cannot see the wood for the trees.

㊟表示多得無從選擇的意思。

0973 花言巧語

faa¹ jin⁴ haau² jyu⁵ *(translit.)*

Flowery words and clever speech. (lit.)

Fine words.

Have a sweet tongue.

Be clever at blandishment.

㊟形容虛假而動聽的言語。

0974 花花公子

faa¹ faa¹ gung¹ zi² *(translit.)*

A play-boy. (lit.)

A dandy.

A coxcomb.

A fop.

㊟形容只會吃喝玩樂的男子。

0975 花花綠綠

faa¹ faa¹ luk⁶ luk⁶ *(translit.)*

Flowery and green. (lit.)

Be full of colours.

Be brightly coloured.

Money note.

Money paper.

㊟除表示色彩繽紛的意思外;還喻紙幣。

0976 花門

faa¹ mun² *(translit.)*

Slide out of the door. (lit.)

Slip away.

Sneak out of one's job at the last moment.

㊟粵劇演員稱同伴不告而別或在臨上演前一走了之為"花門",後被引用於口頭俚語來表示上述同樣意義。

0977 花紅

faa¹ hung⁴ *(translit.)*

Flowery red. (lit.)

Bonus.

Dividend.

㊟即紅利或獎金。

0978 花靚仔

faa¹ leng¹ zai² *(translit.)*

Flowery handsome kid. (lit.)

A youngster.

A young boy as green as grass.

A play-boy.

八畫

A youngster of rascality.

🈂指沒經驗的青少年，但貶義則喻不三不四的人。

0979　抽水

cau¹ seoi² *(translit.)*

Draw water. (lit.)

Take a cut off the winnings in gambling.

🈂指在賭博時，抽贏家的一部分錢。

0980　抽佣

cau¹ jung² *(translit.)*

Draw commission. (lit.)

Draw a commission on the sale.

🈂即抽取佣金的簡稱。

0981　抽後腳

cau¹ hau⁶ goek³ *(translit.)*

Draw a hind leg. (lit.)

Pull somebody's leg.

Capitalize upon somebody's vulnerable statement.

🈂指把人説過的話重複來嘲弄他。相當於"抓辮子"。

0982　抽秤 / 揕

cau¹ cing³ *(translit.)*

Pick and weigh. (lit.)

Find fault with somebody.

Pick holes in...

Do nit-picking.

🈂表示挑剔或找錯的意思。相當於"找碴兒"。

0983　抽絲剝繭

cau¹ si¹ mok¹ gaan² *(translit.)*

Draw silk and strip cocoons. (lit.)

Trace a fox to its den.

Analyse a cace to find out the truth.

🈂表示逐步追查真相或找出原因的意思。

0984　拐帶

gwaai² daai³ *(translit.)*

A man who kidnaps children. (lit.)

Kidnap.

🈂即誘拐小孩。

0985　拃亂戈柄

zaa⁶ lyun⁶ gwo¹ beng³ *(translit.)*

Disturb the dagger-axes and their handles. (lit.)

Make an interruption.

Put sand in the wheels.

Cause a hindrance.

🈂表示打斷別人的話或妨礙別人。

0986　拖泥帶水

to¹ nai⁴ daai³ seoi² *(translit.)*

Drag through mud and water. (lit.)

Be sloppy in one's work.

🈂表示做事拖拉，不利落。

0987　拍心口

paak³ sam¹ hau² *(translit.)*

Slap the mouth of heart (chest). (lit.)

Readily promise to undertake responsibility.

Be ready to do one's best to help somebody.

🈂表示拍胸膛一口承擔的意思。

0988　拍成佢

paak³ seng⁴ keoi⁵ *(translit.)*

Cause it to succeed. (lit.)

Make two sides agree to a deal.

Go between with the hope of making a match.

🈂指促使雙方成功。

0989　拍烏蠅

paak³ wu¹ jing¹ *(translit.)*

Slap flies. (lit.)

Have a dull market.

Have a slack business.

注 暗喻生意清淡。

0990　拍硬檔

paak³ ngaang⁶ dong³ *(translit.)*

Slap the stall hard. (lit.)

Set one's shoulder to the wheel.

Help each other to work on.

Come to one's assistance.

Assist somebody with something.

Pool together our efforts.

注 表示緊密地合作，互相配合的意思。

0991　拍膊頭

paak³ bok³ tau⁴ *(translit.)*

Tap somebody's shoulder. (lit.)

Hope for somebody to set his shoulder to the wheel.

Cry on somebody's shoulder.

Intend to have great facilities for friend's sake.

注 指希望別人給自己方便或企求別人的同情。

0992　拍薑咁拍

paak³ goeng¹ gam³ paak³ *(translit.)*

Slap somebody like flattening a piece of ginger with a kitchen chapper. (lit.)

Give somebody a hard smack.

Knock the tar out of somebody.

注 指把人痛打一頓。

0993　拍檔

paak³ dong³ *(translit.)*

Slap the stall. (lit.)

A partner.

A companion who works together with somebody.

注 即夥伴。

0994　拆穿西洋鏡

caak³ cyun¹ sai¹ joeng⁴ geng³ *(translit.)*

Unmask a weatern mirror. (lit.)

Become aware of the camouflage.

Expose the fraud.

Give the lie to something.

注 表示洞悉欺騙或揭露某事的虛偽。相當"撕開畫皮"。

0995　抵死

dai² sei² *(translit.)*

Deserve the death. (lit.)

It serves somebody right.

Deserve the punishment/death.

Carry a sting. (of speech or article)

注 相當於該死，活該的意思。有時又表示別人的説話或文章有刺的意思。

0996　抵到爛

dai² dou³ laan⁶ *(translit.)*

Very cheap indeed. (lit.)

Get the best value for one's money.

注 表示價錢很便宜的意思。

0997　抵得諗

dai² dak¹ nam² *(translit.)*

Can bear hardship. (lit.)

Can bear the burden of work and complaint.

注 表示能任勞任怨的意思。

0998　抵賴

dai² laai⁶ *(translit.)*

Have another to blame. (lit.)

Shift the blame on to other

shoulders.

Lay the blame on the wrong shoulders.

Disavow.

Make a denial of something.

注 表示推卸責任，或不承認的意思。

0999　拘執

keoi¹ zap¹ *(translit.)*

Be particular with. (lit.)

Bother oneself about small matters.

Be punctilious.

Stand on ceremony.

注 指計較小節或拘禮。

1000　拉人裙冚自己腳

laai¹ jan⁴ kwan⁴ kam² zi⁶ gei² goek³ *(translit.)*

Drag another person's skirt to cover one's own legs. (lit.)

Dress oneself in borrowed plumes.

注 表示靠別人的聲望來抬高自己的意思。

1001　拉牛上樹

laai¹ ngau⁴ soeng⁵ syu⁶ *(translit.)*

Pull a bull up a tree. (lit.)

Have difficulty in teaching somebody.

注 比喻某人不易教導。

1002　拉埋天窗

laai¹ maai⁴ tin¹ coeng¹ *(translit.)*

Pull close the skylight. (lit.)

Establish a family.

Get married.

注 指男女結合，成婚。

1003　拉埋……落水

laai¹ maai⁴ ... lok⁶ seoi² *(translit.)*

Drag ... into the water. (lit.)

Lay part of the blame upon somebody (for something).

Include one/somebody in the subject of conversation.

Drag somebody in...

Involve one/somebody in the trouble.

Make somebody join in...

注 即拉人下水，表示把部分責任歸咎某人，把某人包括在話題內或把某人拉進（行動／事情）內的意思。

1004　拉柴

laai¹ caai⁴ *(translit.)*

Drag firewood. (lit.)

Meet one's fate.

Die a death.

注 指死亡。參閱"瓜直"（0567），"瓜柴"（0568）及"瓜老襯"（0566）。

1005　拉頭纜

laai¹ tau⁴ laam⁶ *(translit.)*

Pull the first cable. (lit.)

Take the lead.

注 意和"扯頭纜"同，參閱該條（0847）。

1006　幸災樂禍

hang⁶ zoi¹ lok⁶ wo⁶ *(translit.)*

Lucky to see other's calamity and happy over other's misfortune. (lit.)

Gloat upon other's misfortune.

Take pleasure in other's calamity.

注 見人有難而高興。

1007　招搖過市

ziu¹ jiu⁴ gwo³ si⁵ *(translit.)*

Faunting through the streets. (lit.)

Be fond of showing oneself in the streets.

八畫

Be fond of limelight.

注 表示喜歡在公眾場合炫耀或出風頭的
意思。

1008　招搖撞騙

ziu¹ jiu⁴ zong⁶ pin³ *(translit.)*

Act ostentatiously and swindle.
(lit.)

Put on a good bluff.

注 即假借名義行騙。

1009　抬棺材甩褲 —— 失禮死人

toi⁴ gun¹ coi⁴ lat¹ fu³ — sat¹ lai⁵ sei²
jan⁴ *(translit.)*

One's trousers come down while
one is carrying a coffin — be
discourteous to the dead man.
(lit.)

Cut a sorry figure.

Commit a breach of etiquette.

注 不像樣子，不成體統；失禮。

1010　亞斗官

aa³ dau² gun¹ *(translit.)*

Master Aa Dau. (lit.)

A person / fop who spends money
like water.

注 比喻揮金如土的人或紈袴子弟。原句
本為 "大良亞斗官"（大良為順德縣
一村）。

1011　亞昆洗鑊 —— 內外都咁乾
淨

aa³ kwan¹ sai² wok⁶ — noi⁶ ngoi⁶
dou¹ gam³ gon¹ zeng⁶ *(translit.)*

Aa Kwan washes a frying
pan — both inside and outside
are so clean. (lit.)

Be out of pocket.

Be broke to the world.

Turn one's pockets inside out.

Lose all one's money in
gambling.

注 比喻一貧如洗或賭錢輸光。

1012　亞茂整餅 —— 冇個樣整個
樣

aa³ mau² zing² beng² — mou⁵ go²
joeng⁶ zing² go² joeng⁶ *(translit.)*

Aa Mau makes cakes — making
new shapes out of none. (lit.)

Affect / Try to be different from
others.

Display originality.

Blaze a new path.

Have a unique style.

Be in a class by oneself.

Strike an attitude.

注 比喻與眾不同，獨出心裁，別具一格，
別開生面，甚至裝腔作勢等。

1013　亞保亞勝

aa³ bou² aa³ sing³ *(translit.)*

Aa Bou and Aa Sing. (lit.)

Every Tom, Dick and Harry.

注 泛指任何一個人，即 "張三李四" 的
意思。

1014　亞崩叫狗 —— 越叫越走

aa³ bang¹ giu³ gau² — jyut⁶ giu³ jyut⁶
zau² *(translit.)*

A man with hare-lip calls a
dog — the more he calls, the
farther it runs. (lit.)

Kick over the traces.

Run away without obedience.

Be unable to restrain somebody.

注 比喻不服從或無法約束。

1015　亞崩劏羊 —— 咩（哶）都
冇得咩（哶）

aa³ bang¹ tong¹ joeng⁴ — nge¹
(me¹) dou¹ mou⁵ dak¹ nge¹ (me¹).
(translit.)

八
畫

A man with hare-lip slaughters a goat — it bleats no more. (lit.)

Have lost one's tongue.

Hold one's tongue.

Not a sound is uttered.

Be forced to keep silence.

🈯比喻啞口無言或被迫禁止發言。

1016　亞崩養狗 ── 轉性

aa³ bang¹ joeng⁵ gau² — zyun³ sing³ *(translit.)*

A man with hare-lip rears a dog, — it changes its nature. (lit.)

Have a change of nature.

Change skin.

🈯比喻人的性格改變。

1017　亞超着褲 ── 焗住

aa³ ciu¹ zoek³ fu³ — guk⁶ zyu⁶ *(translit.)*

Aa Ciu wears trousers — being oppressed. (lit.)

Be forced to do something.

Be driven by stress of...

Need must when the devil drives.

🈯比喻被迫。

1018　亞單睇榜 ── 一眼睇晒

aa³ daan¹ tai² bong² — jat¹ ngaan⁵ tai² saai³ *(translit.)*

A single-eyed man reads a list of successful candidates — one eye sees all. (lit.)

See with half an eye.

See at a glance.

Be clear at a glance.

That's the all and the one one can see.

🈯比喻一目了然或全部見到。

1019　亞駝〈馱〉行路 ── 春春 "中中" 地

aa³ to² haang⁴ lou⁶ — zung¹ zung¹ dei² *(translit.)*

A hump-back walks, — bending down (strike the happy medium). (lit.)

Strike the happy medium.

Be in moderation.

Be medium.

Take a mean course.

Be fair to middling.

🈯比喻採取中庸之道處理或形容人或物過得去（還算好的意思）。

1020　亞駝〈馱〉賣蝦米 ── 大家都唔掂

aa³ to² maai⁶ haa¹ mai⁵ — daai⁶ gaa¹ dou¹ m⁴ dim⁶ *(translit.)*

A hump-back sells dried shrimps — both are not stright (alright). (lit.)

All play in hard luck.

All (will) have a lot of trouble.

🈯比喻彼此都倒霉或大家都會有麻煩。至於 "現在倒霉" 抑或 "將有麻煩" 則以説話的情況或上文下理而定。（按："掂" 本意為 "直"，但轉義為 "沒有麻煩"，"唔掂" 即 "不是沒有麻煩" ── 負負得正）。

1021　亞蘭嫁亞瑞 ── 大家累鬥累

aa³ laan⁴ gaa³ aa³ seoi⁶ — daai⁶ gaa¹ leoi⁶ dau³ leoi⁶ *(translit.)*

Aa Laan marries to Aa Seoi — one implicates another. (lit.)

Be implicative of each other.

Drag in one another.

🈯比喻互相牽累。

1022　亞蘭賣豬 ── 一千唔賣，賣八百

aa³ laan²′⁴ maai⁶ zyu¹ — jat¹ cin¹ m⁴

maai⁶, maai⁶ baat³ baak³ *(translit.)*

Aa Laan sells pigs — she doesn't sell them for one thousand dollars but for only eight hundred. (lit.)

Be forced to devalue something/oneself after having missed an opportunity.

Bargain away something.

Sell something at sale price.

注 指錯過機會後，被迫把自己降低身價或把物件賤價出售，但亦可簡單意為賤價把物件出賣。

1023 亞聾送殯 — 唔聽枝死人笛

aa³ lung⁴ sung³ ban³ — m⁴ teng¹ zi¹ sei² jan⁴ dek⁶ *(translit.)*

A deaf man attends the funeral procession, — not to listen to the pipe blown for the dead man. (lit.)

Turn a deaf ear to somebody.

注 比喻充耳不聞或不願聽。參閱 "借咗聾陳隻耳" 條（1446）。

1024 亞聾燒炮 —— 散晒

aa³ lung⁴ siu¹ paau³ — saan² saai³ *(translit.)*

A deaf man fires a firecracker — all scatter about. (lit.)

Be disbanded./Be dissolved.

Break off the friendly relation with somebody.

Fizzle out.

Meet with a failure.

注 比喻散夥，解散，關係終止，事情告吹或甚至遭到失敗。

1025 拗手瓜

ngaau² sau² gwaa¹ *(translit.)*

Join arms in collusion. (lit.)

Measure one's strength or power with somebody.

Show power against another.

注 比喻和人較量實力。

1026 拗頸

aau³ geng² *(translit.)*

Twist the neck. (lit.)

Argue against somebody.

Have a debate with somebody.

注 表示爭執或抬槓的意思。

1027 抆頭

fing⁶ tau²ᐟ⁴ *(translit.)*

Shake the head. (lit.)

Shake one's head over something.

Say no.

Shake one's head to show disgust/to express sorry feeling.

注 即搖頭，表示不答應，否認，厭惡或難過的意思（有時說成抆頭抆髻）。

1028 直程

zik⁶ cing⁴ *(translit.)*

Straight way. (lit.)

Keep straight on.

Directly.

Straightway.

Sure enough.

To be sure.

注 表示直接，逕直或當然，肯定的意思。

1029 直腸直肚

zik⁶ coeng⁴ zik⁶ tou⁵ *(translit.)*

Have straight intestines and tripe. (lit.)

Speak straightforward.

Be outspoken in the expression of one's opinions.

注 比喻坦率陳詞。

1030 直頭

zik⁶ tau⁴ *(translit.)*

八畫

Straight ahead. (lit.)

Straightway.

注 表示一直，直接的意思。

1031　枉作小人

wong² zok³ siu² jan⁴ *(translit.)*

It is a vain attempt to be a mean person. (lit.)

Play the villain, but fail to gain any profit.

注 枉費心機。

1032　林沈

lam³ᐟ⁶ sam² *(translit.)*

Odds and ends. (lit.)

Something nondescript.

Odds and ends.

Something like skin disease.

注 即不三不四的東西，零零碎碎的東西或皮膚病之類。

1033　枕住

zam² zyu⁶ *(translit.)*

Rest on. (lit.)

注 同 "枕長" （1034）。

1034　枕長

zam² coeng⁴ *(translit.)*

Rest for long. (lit.)

Often.

Throughout.

All along.

Year in and year out.

注 經常地，長期，一貫地或長年累月地的意思。

1035　東家唔打打西家

dung¹ gaa¹ m⁴ daa² daa² sai¹ gaa¹ *(translit.)*

Be dismissed by the eastern shop but employed by the western one. (lit.)

Lose at sunrise and gain at sunset.

Make up on the roundabouts what one loses on the swings.

Lose employment in one but get a job in the other.

注 表示在職業方面失之東隅收之桑榆的意思。

1036　東莞佬賣蓆——你生定死㗎？

dung¹ gun² lou² maai⁶ zek⁶ — nei⁵ saang¹ ding⁶ sei² gaa³ *(translit.)*

Natives of Dongguan sell mats — you are live or dead? (lit.)

Stretch one's legs according to one's own blanket.

注 傳言東莞人短小精幹所製臘腸，亦短而粗大，同時所織草蓆亦較他地出產品較短，苟有人問他們為甚麼這樣短的，他們便反問説 "你生定死㗎！" 彼等意思是 "死人則直臥，便不夠長，活人則可屈膝而臥，即便夠長的。" 後來被人轉義為 "人是能屈能伸的" 更而喻 "人是要隨機應變的"。參閱 "大丈夫能屈能伸" 條（0187）。

1037　事不關己，己不勞心

si⁶ bat¹ gwaan¹ gei², gei² bat¹ lou⁴ sam¹ *(translit.)*

The matter that does not concern one is not worried about. (lit.)

Mind one's own business.

Never trouble trouble till trouble troubles you.

Saw wood.

注 比喻不管別人的事。

1038　事在人為

si⁶ zoi⁶ jan⁴ wai⁴ *(translit.)*

Things are done by men. (lit.)

Where there is a will, there is a way.

All depends on human effort.

🈯 事情的成功與否決定於人的努力。

1039 事後孔明

si⁶ hau⁶ hung² ming⁴ *(translit.)*

After the event, everyone can be the man named Hung Ming. (lit.)

Hung Ming was Military Councillor of Suk⁶ Hon³ in the period of Three Kingdoms — B. C.221 — 253.He was said to be able to forsee everything.

Be wise after the event.

The wit after the event is the wit of everybody.

🈯 同"馬後炮"。

1040 事頭

si⁶ tau² *(translit.)*

The head of matters. (lit.)

The boss.

A proprietor.

🈯 對東家或老闆的稱呼。

1041 事頭婆

si⁶ tau⁴ po⁴ *(translit.)*

The woman of the head of matters. (lit.)

A proprietress.

🈯 對老闆娘的稱呼。

1042 兩公婆扒艇 —— 你有你事

loeng⁵ gung¹ po²ᐟ⁴ paa⁴ teng⁵ — nei⁵ jau⁵ nei⁵ si⁶ *(translit.)*

A husband and a wife row a sampan — you have your own affairs.

Mind your own business.

🈯 相當於"敲鑼賣糖" —— 各幹一行。

1043 兩公婆見鬼 —— 唔係你就係我

loeng⁵ gung¹ po⁴ gin³ gwai² — m⁴ hai⁶ nei⁵ zau⁶ hai⁶ ngo⁵ *(translit.)*

The husband and the wife saw a ghost — either you or I. (lit.)

Either of the two.

1044 兩個和尚擔水食，三個和尚冇水食

loeng⁵ go³ wo⁴ soeng² daam¹ seoi² sik⁶, saam¹ go³ wo⁴ soeng² mou⁵ seoi² sik⁶ *(translit.)*

Two monks carry water to cook with, three monks have no water to cook with. (lit.)

Too many cooks make no broth.

Everybody's business is nobody's business.

🈯 比喻眾人的事沒有人理。

1045 兩睇

loeng⁵ tai² *(translit.)*

See either this side or that one. (lit.)

Be either definite or indefinite.

Not make up one's mind yet.

Betwixt and between.

🈯 表示兩可之間或尚未決定的意思。（有人說"兩開"，意思相同。）

1046 兩頭唔到岸

loeng⁵ tau⁴ m⁴ dou³ ngon⁶ *(translit.)*

Fail to reach ashore at both sides. (lit.)

Neither sink nor swim in the middle of the sea.

Be on the horns of a dilemma.

Be in a dilemma.

🈯 表示進退兩難的意思。

八畫

1047　兩頭唔受中間受

loeng⁵ tau⁴ m⁴ sau⁶ zung¹ gaan¹ sau⁶ *(translit.)*

Both sides do not accept it but the middle does. (lit.)

Line one's pocket.

Feather one's nest.

Neither of both parties but the third one takes...

注 指中飽私囊，但亦指雙方不要，由第三者接受。

1048　兩頭蛇

loeng⁵ tau⁴ se⁴ *(translit.)*

A two-headed snake. (lit.)

A tale teller.

A discord sower.

A fence sitter / rider.

A Jack on both sides.

注 比喻挑撥是非的人或騎牆派。

1049　兩騎牛

loeng⁵ ke⁴ ngau²ᐟ⁴ *(translit.)*

Ride on two bulls. (lit.)

Take an equivocal attitude.

Sit on the fence.

Be a double-dealer.

注 指態度模棱兩可或騎牆派。

1050　來者不善，善者不來

loi⁴ ze² bat¹ sin⁶, sin⁶ ze² bat¹ loi⁴ *(translit.)*

The person who comes is not kind; the person who is kind does not come. (lit.)

No coward dares to come.

He who comes harbours ulterior motives.

He who comes harbours malicious intentions.

注 表示膽小的就不來或既來就是不懷好

意的意思。

1051　來說是非者，便是是非人

loi⁴ syut³ si⁶ fei¹ ze², bin⁶ si⁶ si⁶ fei¹ jan⁴ *(translit.)*

The person coming to tell tales is a gossip monger. (lit.)

The person who speaks ill of others will speak ill of you.

注 愛搬弄是非的人，本身就是製造是非的人。

1052　到埠

dou³ bou⁶ *(translit.)*

Reach the wharf. (lit.)

Arrive (at / in...).

注 即到達。

1053　到家

dou³ gaa¹ *(translit.)*

Reach home. (lit.)

Reach a very high level.

Be excellent in...

注 表示達到很高水平或在⋯⋯方面極為傑出的意思。

1054　到處楊梅一樣花

dou³ cyu³ joeng⁴ mui⁴ jat¹ joeng⁶ faa¹ *(translit.)*

Red bayberries in every place bring forth the same flowers. (lit.)

Same trees at all places bear same fruits.

All tarred with the same brush.

注 表示任何地方情況也是一樣的意思，但亦引伸喻一路貨色。

1055　到喉唔到肺

dou³ hau⁴ m⁴ dou³ fai³ *(translit.)*

Reach to the throat not to the lungs. (lit.)

Not enough to satisfy one's appetite.

八畫

Not enough to one's heart's content.

注本指不滿足食慾，但引伸喻意猶未足。

1056 叔姪縮窒

suk¹ zat⁶ suk¹ zat⁶ *(translit.)*
Both uncle and nephew; shrink and stop. (lit.)

Be happy over having retreated from having to open one's purse.

注廣東諺語難懂，不僅外省人，甚至廣東人也有同感。以這句而言，的確使人瞠目不知所云，"縮窒"為"叔姪"的諧音，意為本來非破財不可，但由於各嗇而縮手，結果正因縮手，不費分文，事後深自欣慰。

1057 虎父無犬子

fu² fu⁶ mou⁴ hyun² zi² *(translit.)*
A tiger father has not a dog son. (lit.)

Like father, like son.
Like begets like.

1058 虎落平陽被犬欺

fu² lok⁶ ping⁴ joeng⁴ bei⁶ hyun² hei¹ *(translit.)*
A tiger coming down to the plain is bullied by dogs. (lit.)

Out of one's sphere of influence, out of one's power.

注比喻一個人不在自己的勢力範圍內便沒有勢力。參閱"龍游淺水遭蝦戲"（2286）。

1059 虎頭蛇尾

fu² tau⁴ se⁴ mei⁵ *(translit.)*
Tiger's head with snake's tail. (lit.)

Do something by halves.
Leave one's work half-done.
A brave beginning but a weak ending.

In like a lion, but out like a lamb.

注參閱"有頭威，冇尾陣"（0698）。喻做事有始無終。

1060 明人不做暗事

ming⁴ jan⁴ bat¹ zou⁶ am³ si⁶ *(translit.)*
A bright person never does invisible things. (lit.)

Make no secret of everything.
An open-hearted person often acts in open manner.

注指心地光明的人不在暗地裏做見不得人的事。

1061 明刀明槍

ming⁴ dou¹ ming⁴ coeng¹ *(translit.)*
Visible knife and visible spear. (lit.)

Before somebody's very eyes.
Conduct an evil activity in the open.
Do something openly.

注指公開地行事。參閱"擺明車馬"條（2357）。

1062 明火打劫

ming⁴ fo² daa² gip³ *(translit.)*
Rob in the bright fire. (lit.)

Rob in the light of day.

注表示明目張膽地做壞事。

1063 明槍易擋，暗箭難防

ming⁴ coeng¹ ji⁶ dong², am³ zin³ naan⁴ fong⁴ *(translit.)*
It is easy to stop a visible spear but hard to guard against an invisible arrow. (lit.)

Better to suffer an attack by overt than by covert.

注比喻公開的攻擊易對付，暗中的攻擊難提防。

1064　易過借火

ji⁶ gwo³ je³ fo² *(translit.)*

It is easier than borrowing fire. (lit.)

Be as easy as pie.

Be as easy as my eye.

🈯表示易如反掌的意思。

1065　忠忠直直，終須乞食

zung¹ zung¹ zik⁶ zik⁶, zung¹ seoi¹ hat¹ sik⁶ *(translit.)*

The person who is honest and straight may beg for food in the end. (lit.)

The properer one's behaviours are, the less luckier one will be.

🈯指為人太忠直會一貧如洗。

1066　呷醋

haap³ cou³ *(translit.)*

Sip vinegare. (lit.)

Be jealous of one's own rival in love.

Get angry out of envy.

🈯即吃醋（指男女關係上的妒忌）。

1067　制唔過

zai³ m⁴ gwo³ *(translit.)*

Not worth doing. (lit.)

It doesn't pay...

It is not to one's profit.

🈯和“唔制得過”意同，參閱該條（1384）。

1068　制得過

zai³ dak¹ gwo³ *(translit.)*

It is worth doing. (lit.)

It will pay to do something.

It is worth while doing something.

🈯相當於“划得來”或“值得做”。（廣東話“制”意為“做”。）

1069　知人口面不知心

zi¹ jan⁴ hau² min⁶ bat¹ zi¹ sam¹ *(translit.)*

Know a man's mouth and face but know not his heart. (lit.)

Be familiar with somebody but ignorant of his true nature.

🈯指只看人的外表不能了解他的為人。

1070　知己知彼

zi¹ gei² zi¹ bei² *(translit.)*

Know oneself and know others. (lit.)

Besides knowing itself, an old fox has to know a fox-hunter.

It needs to understand both oneself and others.

🈯表示正確的了解自己。

1071　知子莫若父

zi¹ zi² mok⁶ joek⁶ fu⁶ *(translit.)*

A father knows his son better. (lit.)

No one knows a boy better than his father.

🈯指父親最了解自己的兒子。

1072　知其一不知其二

zi¹ kei⁴ jat¹ bat¹ zi¹ kei⁴ ji⁶ *(translit.)*

Know only one aspect of something not two. (lit.)

Have only one-sided view.

Have a smattering of…

Be aware of one aspect but ignorant of the other.

🈯指僅知事物的一部分，而不知其他的部分。

1073　知情識趣

zi¹ cing⁴ sik¹ ceoi³ *(translit.)*

Know what somebody is feeling and interested in. (lit.)

Know how to behave oneself to

cope with somebody's feeling and interest.

🈁 表示善於體會別人的意圖。

1074　知無不言，言無不盡

zi[1] mou[4] bat[1] jin[4], jin[4] mou[4] bat[1] zeon[6] *(translit.)*

Say what is known and say all. (lit.)

Say all what one knows.

Say all one knows without reserve.

🈁 將所知的全盤説出。

1075　物以罕為貴

mat[6] ji[5] hon[2] wai[4] gwai[3] *(translit.)*

Rare things are more expensive. (lit.)

Precious things are never found in heaps.

The rarer it is, the more it is worth.

🈁 表示事物越罕有越貴重。

1076　物以類聚

mat[6] ji[5] leoi[6] zeoi[6] *(translit.)*

Things of the same kind gather together. (lit.)

Birds of a feather flock together.

🈁 表示性質相近的東西常聚集在一起。

1077　物輕情義重

mat[6] hing[1] cing[4] ji[6] zung[6] *(translit.)*

The thing is light but the friendship is weighty. (lit.)

A gift of trifling value conveys affection.

🈁 表示禮物價值雖不高，但代表深厚情意。

1078　物離鄉貴，人離鄉賤

mat[6] lei[4] hoeng[1] gwai[3], jan[4] lei[4] hoeng[1] zin[6] *(translit.)*

Things leaving home are expensive; men leaving their native land become cheap. (lit.)

Articles leaving home become precious, but men, demeaned.

🈁 表示離開產地越遠，產品就越珍貴。

1079　刮龍

gwaat[3] lung[2] *(translit.)*

Scrape a dragon. (lit.)

Coin money by unfair means.

Coin one's brains by illegal means.

Reap huge profit.

🈁 指利用不法手段去賺錢或動腦筋謀取暴利的行為，如貪污。

1080　和尚食狗肉——一件穢，兩件又穢

wo[4] soeng[2] sik[6] gau[2] juk[6] — jat[1] gin[6] wai[3], loeng[5] gin[6] jau[6] wai[3] *(translit.)*

A monk eats dog's flesh — it is sinful to eat one piece or two pieces. (lit.)

It is equally disgraceful to do such an ill deed for once or even once more again.

🈁 比喻做一次壞事和再做多一次是一樣不光彩的。

1081　和味

wo[4] mei[6] *(translit.)*

Good taste. (lit.)

Be delicious.

Taste wonderful.

Have a wide margin of profits.

A good sum of money.

🈁 表示味美；利潤多及大筆款項的意思。

1082　和過

wo[4] gwo[2] *(translit.)*

A draw. (lit.)

A dead heat.

A drawn game.

八畫

Neither win nor lose.

注 無勝無負的平局，和局。

1083 使銅銀夾大聲

sai² tung⁴ ngan⁴ gaap³ daai⁶ seng¹ *(translit.)*

Use false silver coins with a loud voice. (lit.)

Thunder threats at somebody.
Seize the catch before the hound.
Take the wind out of somebody's sails.

注 喻理虧在先，還要兇。銅銀為偽做硬幣。在當時政府尚未接納蘇聯經濟專家"李茲羅斯"建議將白銀收歸國有前，國人仍使用純銀硬幣。狡黠者以銅鍍上銀色亂真。因往時民風敦厚，如使銅銀者大聲夾惡，每易得逞。

1084 使頸

sai² geng² *(translit.)*

Use the neck. (lit.)

Harden the neck for one's will.
Fly into a temper.
Feel wronged and act rashly.
Take huff for dissatisfaction.

注 相當於"使性子"，耍脾氣；賭氣。

1085 依挹 / 依依挹挹

ji¹ jap¹ / ji¹ ji¹ jap¹ jap¹ *(translit.)*

Get in carnal touch. (lit.)

Have illicit intercourse.
Carry on a clandestine love affair.

注 喻男女間的私通或偷情。

1086 依時依候

ji¹ si⁴ ji¹ hau⁶ *(translit.)*

According to time. (lit.)

On time.
In time.
Be punctual.

According to schedule.

注 表示按時，準時或按照預定時間。

1087 的起心肝

dik¹ hei² sam¹ gon¹ *(translit.)*

Take up the heart and liver. (lit.)

Pull up one's socks.
Brace oneself up.
Bestir oneself.
Make up one's mind.

注 表示鼓起勇氣，下定決心及振作精神的意思。

1088 近山不可燒枉柴，近河不可洗枉水

gan⁶ saan¹ bat¹ ho² siu¹ wong² caai⁴, gan⁶ ho⁴ bat¹ ho² sai² wong² seoi² *(translit.)*

Those living near a mountain do not waste firewood, and those living near a river do not waste water. (lit.)

Waste not, want not.

注 比喻不浪費便不會缺乏。

1089 近水樓台先得月

gan⁶ seoi² lau⁴ toi⁴ sin¹ dak¹ jyut⁶ *(translit.)*

The avilion near the water gets the moonlight first. (lit.)

Be in a favourable situation.

注 比喻得地利，參閱"近住城隍廟求炷好香"（1090）；"近官得力"（1091）及"近廚得食"（1092）各條。

1090 近住城隍廟求炷好香

gan⁶ zyu⁶ sing⁴ wong⁴ miu² kau⁴ zyu³ hou² hoeng¹ *(translit.)*

Living near the temple of the City-god, one can ask for a good set of incense-sticks. (lit.)

Hope to curry favour with

somebody.

Intend to be favoured with what one asks for.

注 參閱 "近水樓台先得月"（1089）、
"近官得力"（1091）及 "近廚得食"
（1092）各條。

1091 近官得力

gan[6] gun[1] dak[1] lik[6] *(translit.)*

Near officials, one can obtain power. (lit.)

It is much more convenient to have a friend in court.

注 參閱 "近水樓台先得月"（1089）、"近
住城隍廟求炷好香"（1090）及 "近廚
得食"（1092）各條。

1092 近廚得食

gan[6] ceoi[4] dak[1] sik[6] *(translit.)*

Near the kitchen, one can get a lot to eat. (lit.)

Be in a favourable position to gain advantage.

注 參閱 "近水樓台先得月"（1089）、"近
住城隍廟求炷好香"（1090）及 "近官
得力"（1091）各條。

1093 返去舊時嗰度

faan[1] heoi[3] gau[6] si[4] go[2] dou[6] *(translit.)*

Go back to the old place. (lit.)

Be gathered to one's fathers.
Go west.

注 暗喻死亡。

1094 金盆洗手

gam[1] pun[4] sai[2] sau[2] *(translit.)*

Wash hands in a gold basin. (lit.)

Wash one's hands of...
Hang up one's axe.

注 指洗手不幹。

1095 金睛火眼

gam[1] zing[1] fo[2] ngaan[5] *(translit.)*

Gold pupils and firy eyes. (lit.)

Keep one's eyes polished.

Be lynx-eyed.

Be up to one's eyes in work.

注 本義表示提高警覺或留心着的意思，
但引伸喻工作忙得不可開交。

1096 命根

meng[6] gan[1] *(translit.)*

The root of life. (lit.)

One's life blood.
One's beloved.
One's favourite.

注 指特別寵愛的人或物。相當於 "命根
子"。

1097 受人二分四

sau[6] jan[4] ji[6] fan[1] sei[3] *(translit.)*

Accept one-third of ten cents. (lit.)

Be in the employ of a boss.

注 從前使用硬幣時代廣東的稱為小洋，
每個銀圓（值一圓）純銀重量為七錢
二分，二角的為一錢四分四厘，一角
的為七分二厘。在當時一間大商號的
在事或稱司理（即今日的經理職位）
月薪亦不過十圓多些，普通職員不會
多過十圓。因此受人二分四（即一角
的三分一）是指 "受僱於人" 的意思。

1098 受人錢財，替人消災

sau[6] jan[4] cin[4] coi[4], tai[3] jan[4] siu[1] zoi[1] *(translit.)*

The payee should endure the calamity on place of the payer. (lit.)

Accept suffering as payment for a debt.

After being paid, one must take one's life in one's hand to do something for somebody.

注 收了別人錢，給人做事。

八畫

1099　受唔住

sau⁶ m⁴ zyu⁶ *(translit.)*

Cannot accept it. (lit.)

Can't stand it.

Can't bear for somebody to do something.

注 表示忍不住或不能容忍某人做（某事）。

1100　受氣

sau⁶ hei³ *(translit.)*

Accept the air. (lit.)

Suffer wrong.

Take the rap.

注 表示受虐待，受不公正待遇或捱罵。

1101　受軟唔受硬

sau⁶ jyun⁵ m⁴ sau⁶ ngaang⁶ *(translit.)*

Bear softness but refuse hardness. (lit.)

Submit to gentle manners but refuse to submit bully ones.

Prefer to be coaxed rather than threatened.

注 相當於“吃軟不吃硬”。

1102　受硬唔受軟

sau⁶ ngaang⁶ m⁴ sau⁶ jyun⁵ *(translit.)*

Bear hardness but not accept softness. (lit.)

Submit to somebody's pressure after first turning down his gentle manners.

Browbeat the weak but fear the strong.

注 表示欺軟怕硬的意思。

1103　受落

sau⁶ lok⁶ *(translit.)*

Accept. (lit.)

Accept something.

Feel greatly flattered by somebody's praise.

注 表示接受或被人稱讚後感到榮幸的意思。

1104　爭

zaang¹ *(translit.)*

Contend for. (lit.)

Strive for...

Scramble for...

Differ from...

Fall short of...

Be out of balance.

Owe somebody something.

注 表示爭取某人／物或差，欠，缺，短的意思。

1105　爭交

zaang¹ gaau¹ *(translit.)*

Strive for negotiation. (lit.)

Stop people from fighting with each other.

Dissude people from fighting each other.

注 表示勸架或勸阻打架的意思。

1106　爭住……

zaang¹ zyu⁶... *(translit.)*

Strive for... (lit.)

Show partiality to somebody.

Be behind with something.

Owe somebody something.

Be in arrears with one's payment.

Vie with each other in doing something.

注 表示偏袒某人，拖欠或爭先做……的意思。

1107　爭住先

zaang¹ zyu⁶ sin¹ *(translit.)*

Strive first. (lit.)

Be behind with something
temporarily.

Owe somebody something
temporarily.

Be in arrears with one's payment
temporarily.

🈯 暫時拖欠的意思。

1108 肥肥白白

fei⁴ fei⁴ baak⁶ baak⁶ *(translit.)*

Fat and white. (lit.)

Fair and plump.

🈯 即又白又胖；皮膚白嫩，豐滿。

1109 肥缺

fei⁴ kyut³ *(translit.)*

A fat job. (lit.)

A gravy train.

An armchair job.

1110 周身刀——有張利

zau¹ san¹ dou¹ — mou⁵ zoeng¹ lei⁶
(translit.)

*There are knives on the whole
body — no one is sharp. (lit.)*

**Jack of all trades and master of
none.**

Jack-of-all-trades.

🈯 比喻博而不專的人。

1111 周身唔聚財

zau¹ san¹ m⁴ zeoi⁶ coi⁴ *(translit.)*

*The whole body cannot gather
wealth. (lit.)*

**Be uncomfortable / uneasy all
over.**

Be in a terrible fidget.

Fidget with one's tie.

🈯 表示坐立不安的意思。

1112 狗上瓦桁——有條路

gau² soeng⁵ ngaa⁵ haang¹ — jau⁵ tiu⁴
lou⁶ *(translit.)*

*A dog goes up to the roof — there
is a road. (lit.)*

With ulterior motives.

Have an aim.

🈯 表示"別有用心"的意思。相當於耗
子鑽水溝——各有各的路。

1113 狗咬呂洞賓——不識好人心

gau² ngaau⁵ leoi⁵ dung⁶ ban¹ — bat¹
sik¹ hou² jan⁴ sam¹ *(translit.)*

*A dog bites Leoi Dung Ban (one of
the eight immortals of Taoism)
— not know the good man's
heart. (lit.)*

Not know chalk from cheese.

**Not know the good from the
bad.**

🈯 比喻不分好歹的意思。

1114 狗咬狗骨

gau² ngaau⁵ gau² gwat¹ *(translit.)*

Dogs eat dogs' bones. (lit.)

Put up an internecine fight.

There is no love between them.

🈯 比喻狗咬狗；互相勾心鬥角。

1115 狗眼看人低

gau² ngaan⁵ hon³ jan⁴ dai¹ *(translit.)*

*A dog's eyes look down on people.
(lit.)*

Hold somebody in contempt.

Put on airs with despise.

**Look down on somebody like a
snob.**

🈯 比喻為人勢利，看不起別人。

1116 夜長夢多

je⁶ coeng⁴ mung⁶ do¹ *(translit.)*

*A long night brings many dreams.
(lit.)*

Too long a delay causes hitches.

🈯 指事情拖得太長便會引起障礙。

八
畫

1117　夜遊神

je⁶ jau⁴ san⁴ (translit.)

A night-strolling god. (lit.)

A night owl.

注 比喻深宵不睡的人或過慣夜生活的
人。"夜貓子"。

1118　放下心頭大石

fong³ haa⁶ sam¹ tau⁴ daai⁶ sek⁶
(translit.)

*Lay down the stone of the heart.
(lit.)*

Be free from anxiety.

注 表示消除憂慮的意思。

1119　放水

fong³ seoi² (translit.)

Let out the water. (lit.)

**Make an exception to favour
somebody.**

**Accommodate somebody with
good intention.**

**Convenience somebody for
private reason.**

注 表示作出例外以利某人，故意通融或
私下給人方便的意思。

1120　放白鴿

fong³ baak⁶ gap³ (translit.)

Set a pigeon free. (lit.)

Play a confidence game / trick.

注 二人串通行騙，尤指騙子夫婦串通，
女的改嫁給別人後，把錢財席捲而逃
的一種騙局。

1121　放屁

fong³ pei³ (translit.)

Break wind. (lit.)

Talk rot.

Stuff and nonsense.

注 相當於"胡説八道"。

1122　放虎歸山

fong³ fu² gwai¹ saan¹ (translit.)

*Let the tiger go back to the
mountain. (lit.)*

Lay trouble for the future.

注 比喻引來後患。

1123　放路溪錢──引死人

fong³ lou⁶ kai¹ cin⁴ ─ jan⁵ sei² jan⁴
(translit.)

*The paper-money (used in idolatry)
scattered along roads ─ leading
a dead man. (lit.)*

Tease cocks.

Be very attractive.

Be very charming.

注 在出殯行列前，例有人沿途散放紙
錢（溪錢），取意是賄賂途中遊魂野
鬼，讓其引導死者到他的安息地。
"引死人"的"引"是"帶引"的意
思，但相關語則作"吸引"的"引"，
因此便借這相關語來喻女子的美色
吸引異性。

1124　放聲氣

fong³ seng¹ hei³ (translit.)

Send out the sound and air. (lit.)

Leak out some information.

Give a hint.

Spread information.

注 表示放風聲，露口風的意思。

1125　盲公布袋──自開自解

maang⁴ gung¹ bou³ doi⁶ ─ zi⁶ hoi¹ zi⁶
gaai² (translit.)

*A blind man's cloth-bag ─ self
opening and self tying. (lit.)*

Give comfort to oneself.

Console oneself.

Seek consolation for oneself.

注 表示自我安慰的意思。因廣東人把
"開解"兩字作"安慰"解。

八畫

1126　盲佬貼符——倒貼

maang⁴ lou² tip³ fu⁴ — dou³ tip³ *(translit.)*

A blind man sticks a Taoist magic incantation — sticking it upside down. (lit.)

A female goes to the expense of a man.

🈯女人給男人錢用，或養着男人。（注：借"貼"字雙關而成為"津貼"的"貼"字。）

1127　盲拳打死老師傅

maang⁴ kyun⁴ daa² sei² lou⁵ si¹ fu² *(translit.)*

Blind fists hit the old master to death. (lit.)

A poor hand may put the old master to death.

🈯表示新手有時也會比老手強。

1128　盲眼

maang⁴ ngaan⁵ *(translit.)*

Blind eye. (lit.)

Blind.

🈯即瞎眼，失明。

1129　盲婆餵奶——亂塞

maang⁴ po⁴ wai³ naai⁵ — lyun⁶ sak¹ *(translit.)*

A blind woman gives her baby the breast — stuff at random. (lit.)

Force somebody to accept what is given out.

Stuff a box / bag...with something.

🈯表示強人接受物件或把物件胡亂地向盛器裏塞進去的意思。

1130　盲摸摸

maang⁴ mo² mo² *(translit.)*

Feel the way in the dark. (lit.)

Do something without a plan.

Go about one's job in a haphazard way.

Do one's job without experience.

🈯意指瞎幹或做事無經驗。

1131　盲頭烏蠅

maang⁴ tau⁴ wu¹ jing¹ *(translit.)*

A blind-headed fly. (lit.)

A bull in a china shop.

A blind flying person.

An absent-minded professor.

🈯比喻魯莽的人，漫無目的或無知的人。

1132　炒冷飯

caau² laang⁵ faan⁶ *(translit.)*

Fry cooked-rice which was left over night. (lit.)

Lift the conception out of other's writing.

Act as a plagiarist.

Serve a standing dish.

🈯比喻重複別人説過的話或做過的事，沒新內容。

1133　炕沙

hong³ saa¹ *(translit.)*

Be stranded on the sand. (lit.)

Go aground.

Come to a deadlock.

Be in low water.

Be immovable.

🈯本義為船隻擱淺，比喻作陷入僵局，拮据或動彈不得（指物）。

1134　沬水舂牆

mei⁶ seoi² zung¹ coeng⁴ *(translit.)*

Dive and come into the wall. (lit.)

Go through fire and water.

🈯即赴湯蹈火。（"沬水"即"潛水"，

八畫

"舂牆"即"撞牆"。）

1135　河水不犯井水

ho⁴ seoi² bat¹ faan⁶ zeng² seoi²
(translit.)

River-water does not offend well-water. (lit.)

Have no conflict with each other.

Each follows his bent.

Live and let live.

🈯 指互不侵犯。參閱"你走你嘅陽關路，我過我嘅獨木橋"條（0926）。

1136　油瓶

jau⁴ peng² *(translit.)*

An oil jar. (lit.)

Stepchild on mother's side.

🈯 指隨母改嫁的孩子，含貶意。

1137　泥水佬開門口 —— 過得自己過得人

nai⁴ seoi² lou² hoi¹ mun⁴ hau² — gwo³ dak¹ zi⁶ gei² gwo³ dak¹ jan⁴
(translit.)

A brick-layer cuts a door in the wall — let oneself pass through and let others pass through. (lit.)

Live and let live.

The hand that gives gathers.

🈯 意思是説為自己設想，也要為人設想或自己方便時也要給人方便。

1138　泥菩薩過江 —— 自身難保

nai⁴ pou⁴ saat³ gwo³ gong¹ — zi⁶ san¹ naan⁴ bou² *(translit.)*

A clay stature of god crosses the river — it fails to protect itself. (lit.)

Cannot protect oneself.

Be unable even to fend for oneself.

Be too busy with one's own work to help anybody.

🈯 指自己無法保全自己避過災禍。

1139　波羅雞 —— 靠黐

bo¹ lo⁴ gai¹ — kaau³ ci¹ *(translit.)*

Paper-pasted hens made in Bo Lo — depending on stickiness. (lit.)

The person who always profits himself at other people's expense.

A grabber of petty advantages.

🈯 比喻專揩油的人。波羅為廣州八景之一（波羅浴日）。該地有一波羅廟，每逢神誕，不少善男信女在拜神祈福後，購買"紙雞"返家，以取吉利。該種"紙雞"栩栩如生，但因紙製，必用漿糊黐黏，但廣東人把"黐"又作"沾"（揩油的意思）解，一義之轉便諧格了。

1140　定晒形

ding⁶ saai³ jing⁴ *(translit.)*

Fix the figure. (lit.)

Be stupefied.

Trance oneself.

🈯 表示發楞或發呆的意思。

1141　定過抬油

ding⁶ gwo³ toi⁴ jau⁴ *(translit.)*

Be calmer than carrying two pots of oil on the shoulder. (lit.)

Compose oneself.

Keep one's head.

Be unperturbed.

Be bound to succeed.

Have the game in one's hands.

Have the ball at one's feet.

🈯 除表示鎮定外還有勝券在握的意思。

1142　官仔骨骨

gun¹ zai² gwat¹ gwat¹ *(translit.)*

八畫

Be like the son of high official. *(lit.)*

Be well-groomed and dressed in fine clothes.

注指打扮得俊俏的男子。

1143　官字兩個口

gun[1] zi[6] loeng[5] go[3] hau[2] *(translit.)*

The Chinese character '官' (official) has two mouths. (lit.)

Official jargon may mean this or that.

Speak in bureaucratese.

注借中國字的"官"字字形，喻從政者或當官的人打官腔。

1144　官官相衞

gun[1] gun[1] soeng[1] wai[6] *(translit.)*

Officials protect officials. (lit.)

Devils help devils.

Officials scratch the back of one another.

Bureaucrats shield one another.

注指做官的人互相遮掩過失。

1145　空口講白話

hung[1] hau[2] gong[2] baak[6] waa[6] *(translit.)*

Empty mouth says vain words. (lit.)

Words pay no debts.

Fine words butter no parsnips.

注表示空言無用或口惠而實不至的意思。參閱"口爽荷包立"條（0251）。

1146　空心老倌

hung[1] sam[1] lou[5] gun[1] *(translit.)*

An actor with a hollow heart. (lit.)

A person without real ability and learning.

A phony rich man.

A person who lives in genteel poverty.

注"老倌"為廣東人對粵劇演員的稱呼。"空心老倌"本指"徒有虛名的演員"，但後來引伸比喻沒有真才實學的人，空頭富翁或家境貧窮卻虛擺場面的人。

1147　門當戶對

mun[4] dong[1] wu[6] deoi[3] *(translit.)*

Doors should match with doors of the same rank. (lit.)

Let beggars match with beggars.

注結婚的雙方家庭經濟和社會地位相等。

1148　牀下底破柴——撞大板

cong[4] haa[6] dai[2] po[3] caai[4] — zong[6] daai[6] baan[2] *(translit.)*

Split firewood under the bed — knock against the big board. (lit.)

Meet with a rebuff.

Be rebuked.

Run into snags.

Make a mistake.

Do wrong.

注除相當於"半夜叫城門——碰釘子"外，還表示做錯的意思。

1149　屈尾十

wat[1] mei[5] sap[6] *(translit.)*

Bend the tail to ten. (lit.)

Turn around and come back.

注表示掉頭回來的意思。

1150　屈質

wat[1] zat[1] *(translit.)*

Be confined. (lit.)

Be cramped.

Be confined and limited.

注指地方侷促或狹窄。

1151　妹仔大過主人婆

mui[1] zai[2] daai[6] gwo[3] zyu[2] jan[4] po[4] *(translit.)*

A waiting maid is bigger than a

八畫

hostest. (lit.)

Put the trivial above the important.

Spend much more on the trivial than on the important.

The tail wags the dog.

Put the cart before the horse.

🈲比喻做事沒分寸，或輕重倒置。

1152　姑勿論……

gu[1] mat[6] leon[6]... *(translit.)*

Temporarily speak nothing. (lit.)

Not to speak of...

🈲暫且不說……的意思。

1153　姐

ze[1/2] *(translit.)*

Elder sister. (lit.)

Sister.

A general term for addressing a woman of one's own age.

A term for maidservant.

🈲對平輩婦女的稱呼，一般跟在名字後邊，或對女傭人的稱呼（ze[1]）。

1154　姐手姐腳

ze[2] sau[2] ze[2] goek[3] *(translit.)*

Maid's hands and feet. (lit.)

Be as weak as a cat.

Be feeble like a lady.

Work with a light hand.

🈲形容人手足無力或做事太斯文。

1155　阿箇

o[1] go[6] *(translit.)*

Overdo. (lit.)

Be extremely unnatural and affected.

Overdo in affected manners.

Be inflexible.

Be restrained.

Be overscrulous.

🈲表示過分矯揉造作，拘束，或過分拘泥細節的意思。

1156　陀衰家

to[4] seoi[1] gaa[1] *(translit.)*

The calamity involves the family in trouble. (lit.)

A person of rough luck implicates others.

A person who brings his bad luck to somebody.

🈲指牽連別人的人。

九　畫

1157　契家佬

kai[3] gaa[1] lou[2] *(translit.)*

A kept lover. (lit.)

An adulterer.

A male cohabitant.

🈲即情夫，姘頭。

1158　契家婆

kai[3] gaa[1] po[2/4/6] *(translit.)*

A kept mistress. (lit.)

An adulteress.

A female cohabitant.

🈲即情婦，姘頭。

1159　毒鬥毒

duk[6] dau[3] duk[6] *(translit.)*

Poison for poison. (lit.)

Pay tit for tat.

Like for like.

Like cures like.

Use poison as an antidote to poison.

🈲除表示行為上的針鋒相對外，還含有醫學上的 "以毒攻毒" 的意思。

1160　苦口婆心

fu² hau² po⁴ sam¹ *(translit.)*

Bitter mouth with old woman's heart. (lit.)

Bitter pills may have wholesome effects.

Words importunate but heart compassionate.

注 表示以真誠的態度竭力勸告他人。

1161　苦瓜乾嗷嘅面口

fu² gwaa¹ gon¹ gam² ge³ min⁶ hau² *(translit.)*

The face as well as the mouth looks like a dried bitter gourd. (lit.)

Pull a long face.

注 即"哭喪着臉"，"耷拉着臉"的樣子。

1162　苦過弟弟

fu² gwo³ di⁴ di² *(translit.)*

Bitter than a duckling. (lit.)

Go through all kinds of hardships.

Sink into the abyss of misery.

Find oneself in a tight corner.

注 指嘗盡苦楚，陷入苦海或身處困境的意思。

1163　若要人不知，除非己莫為

joek⁶ jiu³ jan⁴ bat¹ zi¹, ceoi⁴ fei¹ gei² mok⁶ wai⁴ *(translit.)*

If one does not want people to know, one must not do it. (lit.)

There are eyes even in the dark.

One cannot conceal what one has done.

What is done by night will appear by day.

注 指隱藏的事必敗露。

1164　英雄重英雄

jing¹ hung⁴ zung⁶ jing¹ hung⁴ *(translit.)*

A hero respects a hero. (lit.)

Like knows like.

注 有能力的人彼此尊重。

1165　英雄莫問出處

jing¹ hung⁴ mok⁶ man⁶ ceot¹ cyu³ *(translit.)*

Not to ask the source of a hero. (lit.)

Not every great man was born with a silver spoon in his mouth.

注 不必講究出身背景。

1166　挑蟲入屎窟

tiu¹ cung⁴ jap⁶ si² fat¹ *(translit.)*

Pick a worm and lead it into the rectum. (lit.)

Prepare a rod for one's own back.

Fry in one's own grease.

Invite trouble for oneself.

注 比喻自作自受或自找麻煩。

1167　指天篤地

zi² tin¹ duk¹ dei⁶ *(translit.)*

Point at the sky and pierce the earth. (lit.)

Talk nonsense.

Sheer rubbish.

Drivel.

注 相當於"胡說八道"。

1168　指手劃腳

zi² sau² waak⁶ goek³ *(translit.)*

Point with fingers and draw with feet. (lit.)

Order somebody about.

Lord it over somebody.

Be a backseat driver.

Give dictates to somebody.

九畫

注 形容人那副作威作福發施號令的神態。

1169　指冬瓜話葫蘆

zi² dung¹ gwaa¹ waa⁶ wu⁴ lou⁴ *(translit.)*

Point at a hard-skinned cucumber and say it is a cucurbit. (lit.)

Talk nonsense.

Call black white.

Confound right with wrong.

Distort the facts.

注 意即胡説八道，顛倒黑白（或是非）或歪曲事實。

1170　指住禿奴罵和尚

zi² zyu⁶ tuk¹ nou⁴ maa⁶ wo⁴ soeng² *(translit.)*

Point at a bald head to heap abuse on a Buddism monk. (lit.)

Talk at somebody.

Make an oblique accusation / Make oblique accusations.

注 即指桑罵槐。

1171　指擬

zi² ji⁵ *(translit.)*

Depend on. (lit.)

Count on somebody.

Rely on somebody / something.

Look to somebody for something.

注 指望或依賴他人。

1172　拼死無大害

pun² sei² mou⁴ daai⁶ hoi⁶ *(translit.)*

There is no harm is spite of death. (lit.)

Do something at the risk of...

Risk everything on a single throw.

Run one's head against a wall.

注 表示不惜冒險去做的意思。

1173　拼啤

pun² pe² *(translit.)*

Consider nothing. (lit.)

Act shamelessly.

Act for better or worse.

Disregard one's dignity.

Be perverse.

Leave oneself to sink or swim.

注 相當於耍無賴或耍賴，撒野。

1174　拼爛

pun² laan² *(translit.)*

Disregard everything. (lit.)

注 同 “拼啤” （1173）。

1175　甚至無……

sam⁶ zi³ mou⁴... *(translit.)*

Even if... (lit.)

Even though...

Even if...

Even so,

注 即使，甚至或就算是……的意思。

1176　捋吓鼓邊

lat³ haa⁵ gu² bin¹ *(translit.)*

Beat the rim of a drum. (lit.)

Have a small talk with somebody to sound out his reaction / the actual situation.

Sound somebody out on a question.

注 表示用説話試探某人的反應或事情的真相或試探某人對一個問題的意見。參閱 “敲鼓邊” 條（2106）。

1177　捋埋

lat³ maai⁴ *(translit.)*

Hide somewhere. (lit.)

Hide oneself.

九畫

Hide out. / Cover up one's tracks.

Be on the dodge.

🈩 和"匿埋"同義（1541），不過"捌埋"較為粗鄙。

1178　胡胡混混

wu⁴ wu⁴ wan⁶ wan⁶ *(translit.)*

Muddle away the life. (lit.)

Live a mediocre life.

Lead an aimless life.

🈩 庸庸碌碌或無目的的生活的意思。

1179　胡帝胡天 / 胡天胡帝

wu⁴ dai³ wu⁴ tin¹ / wu⁴ tin¹ wu⁴ dai³ *(translit.)*

Mess up both the sky and the emperor. (lit.)

Behave foolishly.

Be mischievous.

Run wild.

🈩 表示胡鬧，亂搞亂鬧。

1180　南嘸佬遇鬼迷

naam⁴ mo⁴ lou² jyu⁶ gwai² mai⁴ *(translit.)*

A Taoist priest is enchanted by ghost. (lit.)

An expert marksman misses the target.

An old horse loses its way.

🈩 和"張天師遇鬼迷"同義，意為專家也會失手。參閱"老貓燒鬚"條（0648）。

1181　柑咁大個鼻

gam¹ gam³ daai⁶ go³ bei⁶ *(translit.)*

The nose is as large as a loose-skinned orange. (lit.)

Turn up one's nose at...

Look down one's nose at somebody.

🈩 形容驕傲的樣子。

1182　相見好，同住難

soeng¹ gin³ hou², tung⁴ zyu⁶ naan⁴ *(translit.)*

It is good to see each other sometimes but difficult to live together constantly. (lit.)

Familiarity breeds contempt.

🈩 見面相安無事，同住卻很困難。

1183　相睇

soeng¹ tai² *(translit.)*

See one another. (lit.)

Make a blind date.

🈩 以前民風保守，婚嫁多由媒人安排男女雙方在一個地方相會，這便是"相睇"。二三十年代，廣州西關的"陶陶居"茶樓二樓，幾乎成為此類"相睇"的固定地點。

1184　查家宅

caa⁴ gaa¹ zaak⁶ *(translit.)*

Inspect somebody's family and house. (lit.)

Get to the bottom of somebody / something.

See the root stock.

🈩 比喻向人查根問底。

1185　要風得風，要雨得雨

jiu³ fung¹ dak¹ fung¹, jiu³ jyu⁵ dak¹ jyu⁵ *(translit.)*

Have wind when wind is needed; have rain when rain is needed. (lit.)

Be able to gain what is wanted.

Do as one list.

🈩 隨心所欲。

1186　面左左

min⁶ zo² zo² *(translit.)*

Turn the face to the left. (lit.)

Turn one's back upon somebody.

九畫

There is no love lost between
them.
Be at odds with one another.
Be at loggerhead with one
another.

注比喻彼此不和。

1187　面皮厚

min⁶ pei⁴ hau⁵ *(translit.)*

Thick-skinned face. (lit.)

Have a thick skin.
Be shameless.
Be thick-skinned.

注比喻沒有羞恥心。

1188　面紅

min⁶ hung⁴ *(translit.)*

The face becomes red. (lit.)

Blush for shyness / shame.
Blush with anger.

注指因害羞或忿怒而面紅。

1189　面紅面綠

min⁶ hung⁴ min⁶ luk⁶ *(translit.)*

*The face becomes red and green.
(lit.)*

Be red with anger.
Blush for excitement.

注表示非常憤怒。

1190　面懵心精

min⁶ mung² sam¹ zeng¹ *(translit.)*

*Stupid on the face but clever in
the heart. (lit.)*

Play the fool.
Feign oneself to be foolish.

注參閱"扮豬食老虎"（0861）條。

1191　耐不耐

noi⁶ bat¹ noi² *(translit.)*

Sometimes. (lit.)

Once in a [long] while.

Occasionally.

注表示偶爾，有時或不經常的意思。

1192　耐中

noi⁶ zung¹ *(translit.)*

Sometimes. (lit.)

Once in a [long] while.
Occasionally.

注同"耐不耐"（1191）及"耐唔中"
（1193）。

1193　耐唔中

noi⁶ m⁴ zung¹ *(translit.)*

Sometimes. (lit.)

Once in a [long] while.
Occasionally.

注同"耐不耐"條（1191）。

1194　耍太極

saa² taai³ gik⁶ *(translit.)*

Play 'Taichi'. (lit.)

Decline tactfully with all sorts of
lame excuse.
Give the runaround.
Give an equivocal replay.
Shirk one's duty with tactful
tactics.

注比喻藉詞推搪的手段或模棱兩可的態
度或方法。不過亦喻婉詞推卸責任。

1195　耍花槍

saa² faa¹ coeng¹ *(translit.)*

*Braudish spears in a showy way.
(lit.)*

Have a quarrel for fun.
Make a joke on each other of the
couple.

注夫婦間的調情。

1196　耷尾

dap¹ mei⁵ *(translit.)*

Hang down the tail. (lit.)

九
畫

With the tail between the legs.
Be crestfallen.
Lose courage.
Lose one's spirits.
Show a complete lack of reserve
strength.
Have no staying power.

注 利用打敗的狗那副神態來喻人灰溜溜
地，垂頭喪氣或缺乏後勁。

1197　耷頭佬
dap¹ tau⁴ lou² *(translit.)*
*A man with his head hanging
down. (lit.)*
A man full of schemes and tricks.
An artful villian.

注 比喻詭計多端的人。（古老傳説，"男
怕望地，女怕望天"，意謂這兩種人
心術不正。）

1198　耷頭耷腦
dap¹ tau⁴ dap¹ nou⁵ *(translit.)*
*Hang down the head and brains.
(lit.)*
Be crestfallen.
Lose one's spirits.
Be listless.

注 垂頭喪氣，精神不振作或沒精打采的
意思。

1199　省鏡
saang² geng³ *(translit.)*
Save a mirror. (lit.)
Be very beautiful.
Have a good-looking face.

注 形容女性美麗。

1200　是必要……
si⁶ bit¹ jiu³... *(translit.)*
Must... (lit.)
Must...
Ought to...

Have to...
Be bound to...

注 表示一定要，應該要或必須的意思。

1201　是非只為多開口
si⁶ fei¹ zi² wai⁶ do¹ hoi¹ hau²
　　(translit.)
Too much talk leads to error. (lit.)
Loquacity leads to troubles.

注 意即言多語失。

1202　是非皆因強出頭
si⁶ fei¹ gaai¹ jan¹ koeng⁵ ceot¹ tau⁴
　　(translit.)
*Trouble comes merely because of
taking the lead. (lit.)*
**A busybody often invites
troubles.**

注 好出頭露面，易招惹是非。

1203　是非鬼 / 啄
si⁶ fei¹ gwai² / doeng¹ *(translit.)*
The ghost who carries tales. (lit.)
A scandalmonger.

注 相當於"是非簍子"。

1204　是是但但
si⁶ si⁶ daan⁶ daan⁶ *(translit.)*
At convenience. (lit.)
Slap together.
Huddle a job through.
Anything / Anybody will do.

注 參閱"求求其其"（0879）條。

1205　眈天望地
daam¹ tin¹ mong⁶ dei⁶ *(translit.)*
*Look up at the sky and down at
the ground. (lit.)*
Glance this way and that way.
Pay no attention to...
Be inattentive.

注 東張西望或毫不留心的意思。

九
畫

1206 咧啡

le5 fe5 *(translit.)*

Be untidy. (lit.)

Be in one's shirt sleeve.

Be dressed in casual wear.

Be sloppy-dressed.

Sloppy Joe.

Slap dash.

Do a sloppy job.

注 形容人衣冠不整，不修邊幅或工作馬虎，吊兒郎當。

1207 思思縮縮

si1 si1 suk1 suk1 *(translit.)*

Cower and cower. (lit.)

Have not an easy manner.

Do not carry oneself with ease and confidence.

Walk gingerly.

Cower with cold.

Be indecisive/hesitant.

注 拘束；躡手躡腳；冷得打哆嗦或舉棋不定的意思。

1208 喺契爺咁喺

ngai1 kai3 je4 gam3 ngai1 *(translit.)*

Beg like begging an adoptive father. (lit.)

Keep on begging a favour of somebody in real earnest.

注 表示不斷向人懇求的意思。

1209 喺喺西西

ngai1 ngai1 sai1 sai1 *(translit.)*

Beg and beg again. (lit.)

Keep on pleading with somebody.

Beg a favour of somebody.

注 表示懇求的意思。

1210 咬耳仔

ngaau5 ji5 zai2 *(translit.)*

Bite ears. (lit.)

Have a word in one's ear.

Whisper to somebody.

注 即附耳而語。

1211 咬實牙齦

ngaau5 sat6 ngaa4 gan1 *(translit.)*

Bite the gums firemly. (lit.)

Have patience with...

Endure hardship.

Swallow the leek.

注 指極度忍耐或忍受痛苦或屈辱等。

1212 咪拘

mai5 keoi1 *(translit.)*

Not to be bigoted. (lit.)

Don't trouble me, please.

No. Thank you. I won't take/accept it.

注 用於推卻時的口語。

1213 缸瓦船打老虎——盡地呢一煲（鋪）

gong1 ngaa5 syun4 daa2 lou5 fu2 — zeon6 dei2 nei1 jat1 bou1 (pou1) *(translit.)*

The man in the boat loaded with earthenwares beats a tiger – finishing with the last pot (game). (lit.)

Shoot one's last bolt.

Bet one's bottom dollar.

Put all one's eggs in one basket.

注 表示孤注一擲的意思。

1214 拜神唔見雞

baai3 san4 m4 gin3 gai1 *(translit.)*

Lose a hen (as a sacrifice) while worshiping an idol. (lit.)

Bustle in and out with a murmur.

Complain with a murmur.

Go on uttering.

㊟ 形容人口中唸唸有詞忙來忙去的樣子。

1215　看牛不及打馬草

hon[1] ngau[4] bat[1] gap[6] daa[2] maa[5] cou[2] *(translit.)*

Watching cows cannot be compared with gathering hay for horses. (lit.)

It wastes time for a busy man to have a chat with an idler.

㊟ 看牛是悠閒的工作，但打馬草是急不容緩的任務，所以這俚語便喻一個趕急的人和從容的人閒談是會浪費時間或甚至誤事的。

1216　看風駛悝

hon[3] fung[1] sai[2] lei[5] *(translit.)*

See the wind to set sails. (lit.)

Trim the sails.

Run before the wind.

Take advantage of...

㊟ 即見風使舵，把握時機。

1217　香爐墩

hoeng[1] lou[4] dan[2] *(translit.)*

The mound of an incense burner (an earthen pot for holding incense sticks). (lit.)

One's sole inheritor / heir.

One's sole son to carry on ancestral traditions.

㊟ 即唯一的繼承的兒子或接續香煙的獨子。

1218　重係……

zung[6] hai[6]... *(translit.)*

Be still... (lit.)

All the same.

Nevertheless.

Had better...

㊟ 仍是，仍然或還是的意思。但如果説"重係（接動詞）好"時，則表示還是……的好或最好莫如……的意思。

1219　俗骨

zuk[6] gwat[1] *(translit.)*

Vulgar bones. (lit.)

Be vulgar.

Be in bad taste.

㊟ 即俗氣。

1220　係噉意

hai[6] gam[2] ji[2] *(translit.)*

With such an idea. (lit.)

Do it is as a token.

It is but a symbol.

Be symbolized.

㊟ 表示稍表心意而已或象徵性的意思。

1221　係威係勢

hai[6] wai[1] hai[6] sai[3] *(translit.)*

With awe-inspiring and power. (lit.)

Make a false show of being in sad earnest.

Have a good backing.

㊟ 指像煞有介事或大有來頭的樣子。

1222　信邪

seon[3] ce[2] *(translit.)*

Believe in evil spirits. (lit.)

Have belief in meeting with misfortune.

㊟ 表示相信會遭遇不幸。

1223　皇天不負有 / 苦心人

wong[4] tin[1] bat[1] fu[6] jau[5] / fu[2] sam[1] jan[4] *(translit.)*

Heaven will not forget those who have minds. (those whose hearts are bitter). (lit.)

God tempers the wind to the shorn lamb.

九畫

God helps those who help themselves.

ⓘ 即天助自助者。

1224　皇帝女——唔憂嫁

wong⁴ dai³ neoi² — m⁴ jau¹ gaa³ *(translit.)*

An emperor's daughter — she doesn't worry about her marriage. (lit.)

A hoard / A person / A commodity / An object / Something everybody strives for / makes every endeavour to obtain.

ⓘ 比喻為人極力爭取的珍品／人／商品／對象或東西，亦即所謂奇貨可居。

1225　皇帝唔急太監急

wong⁴ dai³ m⁴ gap¹ taai³ gaam³ gap¹ *(translit.)*

The emperor does not feel worried but the eunuch does. (lit.)

Key oneself up over other's business.

Feel both anxious and nervous at other's business.

ⓘ 即為別人着急。參閱〝水上扒龍船，岸上夾死仔〞條（0357）。

1226　食七咁食

sik⁶ cat¹ gam³ sik⁶ *(translit.)*

Be like eating in a mourning feast taken place on every other seventh day after the death of a man. (lit.)

Gorge oneself.

Have a good stomach.

ⓘ 比喻狼吞虎嚥的吃或大吃大喝。家有喪事時，例於死者死後的每個第七天設置飲食，招待前來拜祭的親朋，但有些根本和死者家人毫無關係的貪食者亦來大吃一頓。主人家明知此事，毫不禁止或驅逐，任由他們吃個痛快。

1227　食人唔𦟌骨

sik⁶ jan⁴ m⁴ loe¹ gwat¹ *(translit.)*

Eat men without vomiting bones. (lit.)

Be insatiable of profits.

Be covetous of everything.

Be greedy for gain.

ⓘ 貪得無厭的意思。

1228　食少啖多覺瞓

sik⁶ siu² daam⁶ do¹ gaau³ fan³ *(translit.)*

Eat less, sleep more. (lit.)

Play for safety.

Earn no danger money.

ⓘ 表示為安全計，不做危險的事或賺不義之財。

1229　食生菜咁食

sik⁶ saang¹ coi³ gam³ sik⁶ *(translit.)*

Eat like eating lettuce. (lit.)

It is as easy as rolling a log.

It is as easy as pie.

ⓘ 比喻極其容易。參閱〝易過借火〞條（1064）。

1230　食西北風

sik⁶ sai¹ bak¹ fung¹ *(translit.)*

Eat the northwest wind. (lit.)

Live in poverty.

Suffer from hunger.

Have nothing to eat.

ⓘ 生活貧困，缺乏糧食或捱餓。

1231　食死貓

sik⁶ sei² maau¹ *(translit.)*

Eat a dead cat. (lit.)

Be unjustly blamed.

Endure the calamity for others.

Be made a scapegoat.

注 替人受過的意思。相當於"背黑鍋"。

1232　食夾棍

sik[6] gaap[3] gwan[3] *(translit.)*

Eat torture instruments. (lit.)

Jump a claim.

Make a grab at what somebody should gain.

Take the wind out of somebody's sails.

注 指攫取或利用手段去奪他人所應得的利益。"食夾棍"本為賭場術語,意指如莊閒兩家也有同一手牌贏錢時,則莊家有優先贏錢的權利。

1233　食君之祿,擔君之憂

sik[6] gwan[1] zi[1] luk[6], daam[1] gwan[1] zi[1] jau[1] *(translit.)*

Eat emperor's emolument, undertake emperor's worriments. (lit.)

Do one's duty / Take somebody's duty since one is paid.

注 指既受人用,應盡己責。

1234　食拖鞋飯

sik[6] to[1] haai[2] faan[6] *(translit.)*

Eat cooked-rice of slippers. (lit.)

Sponge upon one's wife / girlfriend.

注 指靠自己的妻子或女友賣色相過活的人。參閱"食軟飯"(1241)條。

1235　食枉米

sik[6] wong[2] mai[5] *(translit.)*

Eat rice without purpose. (lit.)

A person of no use.

An idler / an idle bread eater.

注 指白吃飯的人,參閱"食塞米"條(1250)。

1236　食咗人隻車

sik[6] zo[2] jan[4] zek[3] geoi[1] *(translit.)*

Eat another's chariot. (lit.)

Take the wind out of somebody's sails.

Be overcovetous of everything.

Intend to drive somebody to his death.

注 本為中國象棋的術語,但引伸比喻先發制人而佔盡上風,妄圖佔有一切或要人老命。

1237　食咗人隻豬

sik[6] zo[2] jan[4] zek[3] zyu[1] *(translit.)*

Have eaten somebody's pig. (lit.)

Have raped / seduced a maid / virgin.

注 喻姦污了一個處女的委婉語。

1238　食咗火藥

sik[6] zo[2] fo[2] joek[6] *(translit.)*

Have eaten gun-powder. (lit.)

Be hot with rage.

Be beside oneself with rage.

注 比喻怒不可遏。

1239　食砒霜杜狗

sik[6] pei[1] (fei[1]) soeng[1] dou[6] gau[2] *(translit.)*

Eat arsenic to put an end to a dog. (lit.)

Be at disadvantage before gaining an advantage.

注 暗喻自己先受其害。

1240　食屎食着豆

sik[6] si[2] sik[6] zoek[6] dau[2] *(translit.)*

One happens to find out beans to eat while eating ordure. (lit.)

Have a fault on the right side.

Get a piece of good luck out of misfortune.

注 表示因禍得福的意思,參閱"錯有錯着"條(2276)。

九畫

1241　食軟飯

sik⁶ jyun⁵ faan⁶ *(translit.)*

Eat soft cooked-rice. (lit.)

**Sponge upon one's
wife / girlfriend.**

🔸同"食拖鞋飯"（1234）條。

1242　食得禾米多

sik⁶ dak¹ wo⁴ mai⁵ do¹ *(translit.)*

*Have eaten plenty of unhulled rice.
(lit.)*

**Have made lots of people fall
into one's dupery.**

🔸表示騙得人多的意思。

1243　食得鹹，就要抵得渴

sik⁶ dak¹ haam⁴, zau⁶ jiu³ dai² dak¹
hot³ *(translit.)*

*Since one can eat very salty food,
one must be able to stand thirst.
(lit.)*

**Since one has the courage of
one's convictions, one must
be prepared to accept the
consequences.**

🔸即"敢做敢當"的意思。喻一個人既
然敢做出自己認為正確的事，便要準
備承擔後果。

1244　食葱送飯

sik⁶ cung¹ sung³ faan⁶ *(translit.)*

*Eat cooked-rice with green onion.
(lit.)*

Stand to sense.

🔸即通情達理。

1245　食碗面，反碗底

sik⁶ wun² min², faan² wun² dai²
(translit.)

*Eat with the top of the bowl but
turn over the bottom of it. (lit.)*

Go back upon somebody.

Play somebody false.

Betray a friend.

🔸比喻忘恩負義或背叛朋友。

1246　食過夜粥

sik⁶ gwo³ je⁶ zuk¹ *(translit.)*

Have eaten night-congee. (lit.)

**Know Chinese martial arts (kung
fu).**

**Serve one's apprenticeship with a
master.**

🔸比喻懂得武術（功夫），但亦引伸為
經過學徒階段。

1247　食過翻尋味

sik⁶ gwo³ faan¹ cam⁴ mei⁶ *(translit.)*

*Look for the taste again after
having eaten. (lit.)*

Would like to try once again.

**Go for more after being satisfied
with the initial gain.**

1248　食飽無憂米

sik⁶ baau² mou⁴ jau¹ mai⁵ *(translit.)*

Eat worriless rice to the full. (lit.)

Have nothing to worry about.

Lead a happy life.

Lead an idle life.

🔸指生活無憂無慮或毫無牽掛。

1249　食飽飯等屎屙

sik⁶ baau² faan⁶ dang² si² o¹ *(translit.)*

*Wait to ease manure after eating
to the full. (lit.)*

Have nothing to do.

Live like an idle wheel.

🔸表示無所事事。

1250　食塞米

sik⁶ sak¹ (sat¹) mai⁵ *(translit.)*

*A person who eats and waste rice.
(lit.)*

A person of no use.

An idler.

注比喻白吃飯而沒用的人，有人説成
"食枉米"（sik⁶ wong² mai⁵）。

1251 食豬血屙黑屎——立刻見功

sik⁶ zyu¹ hyut³ o¹ hak¹ si² — lap⁶ hak¹ gin³ gung¹ *(translit.)*

Ease black manure as soon as one eats pig-blood — see the effect instantly. (lit.)

Get the instant results.

The effect comes out at once.

注表示立竿見影。

1252 食穀種

sik⁶ guk¹ zung² *(translit.)*

Eat seed-corns. (lit.)

Live on one's fat.

注即吃老本。

1253 食貓麵

sik⁶ maau¹ min⁶ *(translit.)*

Eat noodles with cat's flesh. (lit.)

Incur blame for something.

Get it in the neck.

Have a stomach full of somebody's abuse.

注捱罵，受申斥。

1254 食齋不如講正話

sik⁶ zaai¹ bat¹ jyu⁴ gong² zing³ waa⁶ *(translit.)*

It is better to speak correct words than it is to go vegetarian. (lit.)

It is better to be truthful.

It is better to speak the truth.

1255 食鹽多過食飯，行橋多過行路

sik⁶ jim⁴ do¹ gwo³ sik⁶ faan⁶, haang⁴ kiu⁴ do¹ gwo³ haang⁴ lou⁶ *(translit.)*

Having eaten more salt than cooked-rice and walked over more bridges than on roads. (lit.)

Have seen more elephants.

Have been weather-beaten a lot more.

Experience does it.

1256 風水佬呃你十年八年，唔呃得一世

fung¹ seoi² lou² ak¹ nei⁵ sap⁶ nin⁴ baat³ nin⁴, m⁴ ak¹ dak¹ jat¹ sai³ *(translit.)*

A master of geomancy can fool you for eight or ten years, but he cannot fool you a whole life. (lit.)

Time can witness to a fact.

注暗喻"時間會證明一切"或"事實會證明"。

1257 風水輪流轉

fung¹ seoi² leon⁴ lau⁴ zyun² *(translit.)*

The wind and water (geomancy) goes around like a wheel. (lit.)

Every dog has his day.

Every cloud has a silver lining.

注比喻每人都有得志日，大致上和"世界輪流轉"（0502）所表示的意思相同，但"風水輪流轉"則着重所見到的結果，而"世界輪流轉"則較着眼於人生命運的因果循環。

1258 風生水起

fung¹ saang¹ seoi² hei² *(translit.)*

The wind blows and the water rises. (lit.)

Be prosperous.

Be getting on in life.

Have a rise in the world.

九畫

Be prospering with each passing day.

Have one's day.

📑 表示正在發跡，飛黃騰達或正在得意之時。

1259　風吹荒蓤——衰"垂"到貼地

fung¹ ceoi¹ jyun⁴ sai¹ — seoi¹ (seoi⁴) dou³ tip³ dei² *(translit.)*

The wind blows the coriander — it becomes on the wane (droops) to the ground. (lit.)

Fall upon very unlucky days.

Meet with very bad luck.

Be the end of one's rope.

Come to a sticky end.

📑 借 "垂" 字諧音作 "衰"，意為倒霉透了。

1260　風吹雞蛋殼——財散人安樂

fung¹ ceoi¹ gai¹ daan⁶ hok³ — coi⁴ saan³ jan¹ on¹ lok⁶ *(translit.)*

The wind blows the shells of eggs — the money is given out for ease of mind. (lit.)

Pay a price for one's safety / security.

Pay a sum of money for being well / the recovery of health / the ease of mind.

📑 表示付出代價才獲得安全 / 復原（疾病）或安心的意思。

1261　風流

fung¹ lau⁴ *(translit.)*

Dissolute; loose. (lit.)

Seek or be in the limelight.

Leisurely and carefree mood.

📑 即出風頭或閒情逸致。

1262　風頭火勢

fung¹ tau⁴ fo² sai³ *(translit.)*

Be in the head of wind and the power of fire. (lit.)

Be in the state of full blast.

Be at the trend of an event.

Be at the tendency of a movement.

📑 比喻正在緊張或全盛的時期。

1263　風頭薑

fung¹ tau⁴ dan² *(translit.)*

The bulk of wind head. (lit.)

The person who is fond of limelight.

📑 指好引人注目的人，愛出風頭的人。

1264　風擺柳

fung¹ baai² lau⁵ *(translit.)*

The willow waved by the wind. (lit.)

A person who takes no firm resolution.

Be changeful in ideas.

Be undecided.

📑 比喻猶豫不定或隨形勢而改變主意的人。

1265　怨命

jyun³ meng⁶ *(translit.)*

Repine the lot of life. (lit.)

Murmur against one's own lot.

Submit to one's own destiny.

Admit to having been determined by fate.

Acknowledge oneself predestined.

📑 自怨命運不濟或認命的意思。

1266　急時抱佛腳

gap¹ si⁴ pou⁵ fat⁶ goek³ *(translit.)*

While urgency comes, hold Buddha's feet. (lit.)

Seek help at the last moment.

Ask God for mercy when danger comes.

1267 急驚風遇着慢郎中

gap[1] ging[1] fung[1] jyu[6] zoek[6] maan[6] long[4] zung[1] *(translit.)*

The child who is attacked by acute infantile convulsions meet with a slow-moving physician. (lit.)

Be too impatient to wait.

Be very impatient of somebody's phlegmatic temperament.

🈯 表示對別人慢條斯理的個性極不耐煩的意思。

1268 計正

gai[3] zeng[3] / zing[3] *(translit.)*

Count right. (lit.)

In the course of nature.

In the ordinary course of things.

Under normal conditions.

Accurately speaking.

🈯 即按理説；本來；在正常情形下或準確地説。

1269 度水

dok[6] seoi[2] *(translit.)*

Measure water. (lit.)

Ask for money.

🈯 即要錢（詼諧的説法）。

1270 度住屎窟裁褲

dok[6] zyu[6] si[2] fat[1] coi[4] fu[3] *(translit.)*

Measure one's hips to cut trousers. (lit.)

Cut one's coat according to one's cloth.

Pinch pennies.

Make both ends meet.

🈯 比喻量入為出，參閲 "睇餸食飯，睇燭喃嘸〈謨〉"（1807）。

1271 施恩莫望報

si[1] jan[1] mok[6] mong[6] bou[3] *(translit.)*

Showing favour is not the purpose of being repaid. (lit.)

Throw one's bread upon the waters.

🈯 表示付出不要計較有沒有收穫。

1272 姜太公封神 —— 漏咗自己

Goeng[1] taai[3] gung[1] fung[1] san[4] — lau[6] / laai[6] zo[2] zi[6] gei[2] *(translit.)*

Grand Duke Goeng offered gods high posts — omitting himself. (lit.)

Leave out / Omit oneself.

🈯 歇後語便是注腳。凡分配，點名等等忘了自己那一份，廣東人便説 "姜太公封神"，源自《封神榜》中的一段故事。

1273 姜太公釣魚 —— 願者上釣

Goeng[1] taai[3] gung[1] diu[3] jyu[2] — jyun[6] ze[2] soeng[5] diu[3] *(translit.)*

Grand Duke Goeng fished — those who were willing jumped at the bait. (lit.)

Swallow the bait of one's own accord.

Put one's own head in the noose.

Take a voluntary action.

Do something on a voluntary basis.

🈯 自願做某事。

1274 前人種果後人收

cin[4] jan[4] zung[3] gwo[2] hau[6] jan[4] sau[1] *(translit.)*

Ancestors planted the fruit, descendants reap it. (lit.)

Descendants reap what their ancestors sowed.

The good deeds the forerunners

did will go down to their posterity.

🈲表示前人處事的後果會由後人承受。

1275　前世唔修

cin⁴ sai³ m⁴ sau¹ *(translit.)*

Did not cultivate moral characters in the previous life. (lit.)

Suffer retribution for all ill deeds done in the previous existence.

🈲意思是説由於前生不修身，所以今生受到應得的報應。

1276　前世撈亂骨頭

cin⁴ sai³ lou¹ lyun⁶ gwat¹ tau⁴ *(translit.)*

The bones of the dead in the previous life were turned upside down. (lit.)

Be hostile to each other.

Feel hostility towards each other.

🈲比喻彼此仇視。

1277　前言不對後語

cin⁴ jin⁴ bat¹ deoi³ hau⁶ jyu⁵ *(translit.)*

Previous words do not accord with the later ones. (lit.)

One's words do not hang together.

One's remarks are incoherent.

One's accounts are self-contradictory.

🈲指所説的話，前後不符或自相矛盾。

1278　前嗰排

cin⁴ go² paai²ᐟ⁴ *(translit.)*

The other days. (lit.)

Not long ago.

In the earlier days.

🈲前些日子的意思。

1279　炮仗頸

paau³ zoeng² geng² *(translit.)*

A neck like firecrackers. (lit.)

Be short-tempered.

Be apt to fly into rage and calm down soon.

🈲比喻脾氣暴躁，但不久平靜無事。

1280　剃眼眉

tai³ ngaan⁵ mei⁴ *(translit.)*

Shave eyebrows. (lit.)

Not to spare somebody's sensibilities.

Not to save somebody's face.

Criticize somebody to his face.

Bring humiliation upon somebody.

🈲指令人丟臉，當面批評人或使人當場出醜的行為。

1281　為口奔馳

wai⁶ hau² ban¹ ci⁴ *(translit.)*

Run about for the mouth. (lit.)

Labour for food in the field.

Be on the run to make a living.

🈲指為生活而奔波。

1282　為食鬼

wai⁶ sik⁶ gwai² *(translit.)*

A gluttonous ghost. (lit.)

A glutton.

🈲即饞嘴者。

1283　為食貓

wai⁶ sik⁶ maau¹ *(translit.)*

A gluttonous cat. (lit.)

A glutton.

🈲比喻饞嘴的人，參閱"為食鬼"條（1282）。

1284　為意

wai⁴ ji³ *(translit.)*

Pay attention to. (lit.)

Be aware of

🈲同"在意"。（0656）

九畫

1285　洒手擰頭

saa² sau² ning⁶ tau² *(translit.)*

Wave the hand and shake the head. (lit.)

Shake one's head (over something).

Say no.

Give a flat refusal.

ℹ️ 大致上和 "抌頭" （1027）同義，但此語還含有 "斷然拒絕" 的意思。

1286　洗碗有相砍

sai² wun² jau⁵ soeng¹ ham² *(translit.)*

Bowls would run up against each other when they are being washed. (lit.)

Familiarity would sometimes have a brush.

Familiarity breeds contempt.

ℹ️ 比喻大家相處日久，難免有矛盾或衝突。

1287　洗腳唔抹腳

sai² goek³ m⁴ mut³ (maat³) goek³ *(translit.)*

Wash feet without wiping them. (lit.)

Money burns a hole in one's pocket.

Splash one's money about.

Play ducks and drakes with one's money.

ℹ️ 比喻揮霍。

1288　洗濕個頭

sai² sap¹ go³ tau⁴ *(translit.)*

Wet the head. (lit.)

Hold a wolf by the ears.

Needs must when the devil drives.

Have no way to back down.

ℹ️ 比喻勢成騎虎，勢在必行或騎虎難下。

1289　派 / 派頭

paai¹ / paai¹ tau⁴ *(translit.)*

Fashionable / fashionable style. (lit.)

Stylish / Be well-dressed.

Put on quite a show. / Live in grand style.

Extravagant and ostention display.

1290　派行水 / 派片

paai³ hang⁴ seoi² / paai³ pin² *(translit.)*

Give out walking water. / Send away slices. (lit.)

Grease the palm of somebody.

Offer somebody levies of money.

ℹ️ "派行水" 為二三十年代向盜賊給予保護費的一種行為，亦即所謂 "買通" 或 "行賄" 的意思。至於 "派片" 為近代廉政公署未成立前，向部分治安人員或黑社會分子交出所謂保護費的行為，名稱雖異，作用實同。

1291　恃老賣老

ci⁵ lou⁵ maai⁶ lou⁵ *(translit.)*

Rely upon old age and sell seniority. (lit.)

Act like a Dutch uncle.

ℹ️ 指因年長或經驗豐富而自覺有能力。

1292　恃熟賣熟

ci⁵ suk⁶ maai⁶ suk⁶ *(translit.)*

Rely on familiarity and sell familiarity. (lit.)

Be too familiar with each other to stand on ceremony.

ℹ️ 由於彼此很熟而不拘禮節的意思。

1293　恨死隔籬

han⁶ sei² gaak³ lei⁴ *(translit.)*

Make neighbours envy to death.
(*lit.*)

Become the envy of others.

注 表示成為他人羨慕的目標。

1294　穿煲／穿崩

cyun¹ bou¹ / cyun¹ bang¹ (*translit.*)

Punch a hole in an earthen pot./Punch and break apart. (*lit.*)

Let the cat out of the bag./Spill one's guts.

Spill the beans./Split on an accomplice.

Expose the flaw/fault/sham.

注 不慎泄露了秘密，説漏了嘴，告發同犯，露出破綻的意思。（嚴格説來，"穿煲"和"穿崩"是有些分別的。前者多指事情或秘密方面，而後者較着重指表演技藝方面。）

1295　穿櫃桶底

cyun¹ gwai⁶ tung² dai² (*translit.*)

Puncture the bottom of the drawer. (*lit.*)

Embezzle／Misappropriate the funds of the shop／store／company...

注 表示挪用或侵吞公司／店舖款項的意思。（"穿櫃桶底"和"櫃桶底穿"兩者的分別是前者為主動，後者為被動。）

1296　客氣

haak³ hei³ (*translit.*)

A guest's politeness. (*lit.*)

Stand on ceremony.

Be too polite.

Be too modest.

注 太客氣的意思。

1297　客家佔地主

haak³ gaa¹ zim³ dei⁶ zyu² (*translit.*)

A guest occupies the position of a host. (*lit.*)

Reverse the positions of the host and the guest.

It is presumptuous of somebody to usurp on the owner's right.

Be like the camel which kicked its master out of the tent.

注 喧賓奪主的意思。

1298　扁鼻佬戴眼鏡 —— 冇得頂

bin² bei⁶ lou² daai³ ngaan⁵ geng² — mou⁵ dak¹ ding² (*translit.*)

A flat-nosed man wears spectacles — nowhere to support. (*lit.*)

Be more than a match for somebody／something.

Without equal.

注 "頂"的意思，在廣東人意為"支撐"，但廣東人又把"頂"轉義為"競爭"或"比較"，這句俚語的歇後，便取這個意思了。因此便表示無可競爭或好極了，無可比擬的意思。

1299　神不知鬼不覺

san⁴ bat¹ zi¹ gwai² bat¹ gok³ (*translit.*)

Neither gods nor ghosts know it. (*lit.*)

In top secret.

Without anybody knowing it.

Nobody knows it.

注 表示秘密進行。

1300　神主牌都會郁

san⁴ zyu² paai² dou¹ wui⁵ juk¹ (*translit.*)

Ancestral tablets can also move. (*lit.*)

Play big luck.

Meet with one's fortune.

注 比喻人走了大運。

九畫

1301 神主牌都會擰轉面

san⁴ zyu² paai¹ dou¹ wui⁵ ning⁶ zyun³
min⁶ *(translit.)*

*Ancestral tablets also turn round
their faces. (lit.)*

**Once one becomes a leper,
one brings disgace on one's
forefathers.**

🈲麻瘋病患者，為人避之唯恐不及，甚
至連祖宗也蒙羞，這句話便是含有這
個意思。

1302 神台貓屎——神憎鬼厭

san⁴ toi⁴ maau¹ si² — san⁴ zang¹
gwai² jim³ *(translit.)*

*The cat's manure on the
altar — gods hate and ghosts
abominate. (lit.)*

An accused target.

**The person at whom everybody
shake his finger.**

Be abominated by everybody.

Be accusable.

Be accursed.

🈲喻惹人憎惡或討人厭的人。

1303 神前桔——陰乾

san⁴ cin⁴ gat¹ — jam¹ gon¹ *(translit.)*

*The tangerines placed at the
presence of gods, — they are
dried in the shade. (lit.)*

**The longer the sum of money is
saved, the smaller and smaller
it becomes.**

**The longer something is kept, the
smaller and smaller/the less
and less it becomes.**

**The older one grows, the thinner
and thinner one gets.**

🈲比喻越放越少（金錢或物）或越長越
瘦（人）。

1304 神神化化

san⁴ san⁴ faa³ faa³ *(translit.)*

Divinitified. (lit.)

Be silly and curious.

Be elusive.

Be not quite right in the mind.

🈲表示神經不正常或行為使人捉摸不
定。

1305 神神地

san⁴ san⁴ dei² *(translit.)*

Deificationally. (lit.)

Be not right in the mind.

Be abnormal in the mind.

Not to work properly.

🈲形容人神經不正常或機械運行不正
常。

1306 神推鬼擁

san⁴ teoi¹ gwai² ung² *(translit.)*

Both god and ghost push. (lit.)

One can't help oneself.

In spite of oneself.

🈲表示不由自主或身不由己的意思。

1307 神魂顛倒

san⁴ wan⁴ din¹ dou² *(translit.)*

*Spirit and soul get upside down.
(lit.)*

Be out of one's head.

Be infatuated with...

🈲表示精神恍惚。

1308 神憎鬼厭

san⁴ zang¹ gwai² jim³ *(translit.)*

*Gods hate and ghosts abominate.
(lit.)*

Be abominated by everybody.

Be accusable.

Be accursed.

An accused target.

九
畫

The person at whom everybody shakes his finger.

注 表示令人討厭的意思，參閱 "神台貓屎" 條〔1302〕。

1309　閂後門

saan¹ hau⁶ mun² (*translit.*)

Bolt the back door. (*lit.*)

Express one's own poor situation beforehand in order to stop somebody from asking for a loan.

Feign oneself to live in poverty before somebody begins to borrow money.

注 指預先哭窮，以免對方開口借錢。

1310　屋漏更兼逢夜雨

uk¹ lau⁶ gang³ gim¹ fung⁴ je⁶ jyu⁵ (*translit.*)

Not only does the roof of the house leak but also the night rain pours. (*lit.*)

Misfortunes never come singly.

It never rains but pours.

注 比喻禍不單行。參閱 "越窮越見鬼，肚餓打瀉米" 條〔1748〕。

1311　屎忽關刀 —— 聞「文」唔得，舞「武」唔得

si² tam⁵ gwaan¹ dou¹ — man⁴ m⁴ dak¹, mou⁵ m⁴ dak¹ (*translit.*)

General Gwaan's knife in the manure pool — be neither smelled nor played with (be good at neither polite letters nor martial arts). (*lit.*)

Be capable of neither mental nor manual labour.

注 這俚語是利用歇後語的 "聞" 和 "舞" 兩字來諧音 "文" 和 "武"，比喻一個人既不能文也不能武。

1312　屎急開坑

si² gap¹ hoi¹ haang¹ (*translit.*)

Not dig a pit until one has to go to stool. (*lit.*)

Make no timely preparations.

Make a frantic last-minute effort.

Have a cloak made when it begins to rain.

注 表示臨渴掘井的意思。

1313　屎窟生瘡 —— 冇眼睇

si² fat¹ saang¹ cong¹ — mou⁵ ngaan⁵ tai² (*translit.*)

Have a boil on one of the hips — have no eyes to see it. (*lit.*)

Close one's eyes to...

Bear no sight of...

注 表示不忍目睹或不願看一眼的意思。

1314　屎橋

si² kiu² (*translit.*)

Useless plot. (*lit.*)

A useless plan.

An impractical device.

注 比喻不實用的計策或方法。

1315　眉精眼企

mei⁴ zing¹ ngaan⁵ kei⁵ (*translit.*)

Eyebrows are clever and eyes are upright. (*lit.*)

Know a trick or two.

Be as smart as a steel trap.

注 形容人長得機靈，精明能幹。

1316　眉頭一皺，計上心頭

mei⁴ tau⁴ jat¹ zau³, gai³ soeng⁵ sam¹ tau⁴ (*translit.*)

As soon as eyebrows frown, an idea comes into the heart. (*lit.*)

Hit upon an idea.

Have a sudden inspiration.

（注）表示心生一計的意思。

1317　姣屍扽篤

haau⁴ si¹ dan³ duk¹ *(translit.)*

Be coquettish. (lit.)

Coquette in a lustful manner.

（注）形容女人故作嬌媚姿態。

1318　姣婆遇着脂粉客

haau⁴ po⁴ jyu⁶ zoek⁶ zi¹ fan² haak³
(translit.)

A dissolute woman meets a luster.
(lit.)

Be two of a kind.

People of a kind come together.

**Two of promiscuous sexes love
each other at first sight.**

（注）廣義是表示臭味相投的意思，狹義是
亂交的男女一見鍾情。

1319　架步

gaa³ bou⁶ *(translit.)*

The step of a shelf. (lit.)

Den.

Vice spots.

Unlicensed brothel.

Unlicensed gambling den.

（注）這“架步”和那“駕步”（見該條
2233）音同義異，這“架步”意為進
行非法活動的地方或巢穴，或非法妓
寨及賭館之類。

1320　架勢

gaa³ sai³ *(translit.)*

Posture of superiority. (lit.)

Magnificent.

Gorgeous.

Luxurious.

Swell with pride.

Terrific.

（注）南北皆有“架勢”這口語。但兩者意
義不同。廣東人的所謂“架勢”意為

堂皇、威風、豪華、華麗或了不起的
意思。

1321　架樑

gaa³ loeng² *(translit.)*

Erect a beam. (lit.)

Pour oil on the flames.

**Try to help one of the fighting
sides.**

（注）表示推波助瀾或幫助打架的一方的意
思。

1322　飛

fei¹ *(translit.)*

Flying. (lit.)

**Be sharp / formidable. (of
person with meaning of
condemnation)**

**Be smart / clever. (of person with
meaning of praise)**

（注）在貶義方面意為厲害的或難以駕御
的，在褒義方面，意為精明能幹的或
聰明的，試觀下列兩例：（1）“你
而家飛咯”，意為“你現在不受駕御
了”。這是貶義，但（2）“你嗰個
女好飛嘅”意為“你的女兒很精明能
幹的”這是褒義。褒貶之分，視乎語
氣而定。

1323　飛擒大咬

fei¹ kam⁴ daai⁶ ngaau⁵ *(translit.)*

Fly to catch and have a big bite.
(lit.)

Show one's horn.

**Extort money from somebody to
excess.**

Show one's lustful manner.

（注）表示露出兇相，過分敲詐或露出色相
等意思。

1324　紅光滿面

hung⁴ gwong¹ mun⁵ min⁶ *(translit.)*

The face is full of red light. (lit.)

One's face glows with health.

1325 紅鬚軍師

hung^4 sou^1 gwan^1 si^1 *(translit.)*

Red-breaded military counsellor. (lit.)

A thoughtless adviser.

A misadviser.

注指給人錯誤指導的人。

十畫

1326 班馬

baan^1 maa^5 *(translit.)*

Collect horses. (lit.)

Call for more persons...

Gang up with more persons...

注表示糾集多些人參加行動的意思。

1327 揼坭

dau^6 nai^4 *(translit.)*

Earth-like. (lit.)

Look shabby.

Be shabby in dress.

Be inferior.

Be of poor quality.

注形容人衣着襤褸或物品質量低劣。

1328 馬仔

maa^5 zai^2 *(translit.)*

Baby horse. (lit.)

Hatchet man.

Bodyguard.

Page.

Retinue.

Attendant.

注凡"打手"，"保鏢"或"侍從"之類，廣東人皆通稱之為"馬仔"。

1329 馬死落地行

maa^5 sei^2 lok^6 dei^6 haang^4 *(translit.)*

Begin to walk after the death of a horse. (lit.)

One should help oneself when there is no help for one.

Stand on one's legs if dependence vanishes into the void.

注比喻無所依賴時，便要自力更生。

1330 馬屎憑官勢

maa^5 si^2 pang^4 gun^1 sai^3 *(translit.)*

The manure of a horse depends upon officials' power. (lit.)

Throw one's weight about.

Pull one's rank on...

注比喻仗勢欺人或利用職權。

1331 起快（起筷）

hei^2 faai^2 *(translit.)*

Raise fast. (Raise chopsticks) (lit.)

Help yourself to the food.

Cut and come again.

注"起快"亦即"起筷"。"起筷"其實是"起箸"，廣東省多水上人（艇戶），"箸"和"住"同音，"住"有停滯的意思，彼等迷信如"停滯不前"，則屬不吉，何況"箸"又稱"筷箸"，因此索性改稱為"起快"取順風順水，進行快速之意。"快"和"筷"同音，而"筷"為正字，逐漸成為"起筷"，意為不要客氣隨便夾菜或較粗俗的說隨便盡量吃罷。

1332 起尾注

hei^2 mei^5 zyu^3 *(translit.)*

Grab the end bet. (lit.)

Usurp somebody's gains.

注比喻吞沒別人的利潤。

1333 起飛腳

hei^2 fei^1 goek^3 *(translit.)*

Raise a flying leg. (lit.)

Intend to fly high over somebody.
Rise in rebellion / revolt against
somebody.
Try to flaunt one's superiority
and outshine somebody.

注 指懷有雄心，企圖超越某人。

1334　起眼

hei² ngaan⁵ *(translit.)*
Raise eyes. (lit.)
Be worthy of notice.
Draw attention.

注 引人注意。

1335　起痰

hei² taam⁴ *(translit.)*
Cause phlegm. (lit.)
Lick one's chop.
Show greed for...
Have a strong desire for...
Cast greedy eyes on...

注 表示起了不良的慾念，或對……饞涎
欲滴的意思。

1336　茶瓜送飯 —— 好人有限

caa⁴ gwaa¹ sung³ faan³ — hou² jan⁴
jau⁵ haan⁶ *(translit.)*
*Have cooked-rice with cucumber
stips in sugar-salted — Good
men are limited. (lit.)*
Not to behave oneself as well as
one is expected.
Be not such a good person as
expected.

注 即斷非好人。病人（不是健康的好人）
在禁口時，只好用茶瓜（一種糖水浸
漬的瓜）送飯。反過來說，用茶瓜送
飯的人決非好（健康好的）人。此"好
人"和行為良好的"好人"語帶雙關。

1337　埋牙

maai⁴ ngaa⁴ *(translit.)*

Near to teeth. (lit.)
Start fighting.
Come to blows.
Begin to exchange blows.
Be spoiling for a fight.

注 表示動手打架的意思。

1338　埋堆

maai⁴ deoi¹ *(translit.)*
Put piles up. (lit.)
Form a small coterie / clique.

注 搞小集團或拉幫結派。

1339　埋櫃

maai⁴ gwai² *(translit.)*
Close the counter. (lit.)
Close the turnover of day.
Phunder a shop of its turnover of
the day

注 表示結算當天的營業額，也被引伸作
搶劫商店的意思。

1340　捉用神

zuk³ jung⁶ san⁴ *(translit.)*
Catch the spirit. (lit.)
Guess at what somebody
means / thinks / likes.
Make a guess at something.

注 表示猜測別人的用意或所好。

1341　捉字虱 / 蝨

zuk³ zi⁶ sat¹ *(translit.)*
Catch fleas in a word. (lit.)
Find fault with the meaning of a
Chinese character or a word.
Pick hole in the meaning of a
sentence or a word.

注 相當於"摳字眼"或"挑字眼"。

1342　捉到鹿都唔會脫角

zuk³ dou² luk⁶ᐟ³ dou¹ m⁴ wui⁵ tyut³
gok³ *(translit.)*

十
畫

Not to know how to take off its horns after catching a deer. (lit.)

Let the opportunity slip.

Miss the bus.

🈯 比喻有機會都不會利用。

1343　捉黃腳雞

zuk³ wong⁴ goek³ gai¹ *(translit.)*

Catch a yellow-legged cock. (lit.)

Extort money from a man by setting a sex-trap.

🈯 男子冒稱一女子的丈夫，進房捉拿並指控被此女子勾引的男子與其妻幽會或勾引其妻，如此那冒牌丈夫便乘機敲詐一筆金錢。

1344　捉豬問地腳

zuk³ zyu¹ man⁶ dei⁶ goek³ *(translit.)*

Catch a pig to ask for the foundation. (lit.)

Seek out the negotiator / the agent handling the job.

🈯 表示經手是問的意思。

1345　捉錯用神

zuk³ co³ jung⁶ san⁴ *(translit.)*

Wrongly catch the idea. (lit.)

Misunderstand somebody's intention.

🈯 表示誤解別人用意，或 "表錯情"。

1346　捉蟲入屎窟

zuk³ cung⁴ jap⁶ si² fat¹ *(translit.)*

Catch a worm and put it into anus. (lit.)

Invite or ask for trouble.

Bring vexation on oneself.

🈯 表示自尋煩惱，自討苦吃或自找麻煩的意思。但亦可說成 "挑蟲入屎窟"。參閱該條（1166）。

1347　劀

cok³ *(translit.)*

Jerk. (lit.)

Jerk.

Tease somebody to tell the truth / to say that...

Coax somebody into telling the truth / saying that...

🈯 表示用力一拉（本意）或逗引人說出真相或講出……

1348　劀住度氣

cok³ zyu⁶ dou⁶ hei³ *(translit.)*

Jerk the breath. (lit.)

Be forced to swallow the leek.

Be compelled to hold back one's rage.

Be forced to submit to humiliation.

🈯 被迫忍氣吞聲。

1349　真金不怕洪爐火，石獅不怕雨滂沱

zan¹ gam¹ bat¹ paa³ hung⁴ lou⁴ fo², sek⁶ si¹ bat¹ paa³ jyu⁵ pong⁴ to⁴ *(translit.)*

Genuine gold fears no fire and stone lions fear no heavy rain. (lit.)

A person of integrity can stand severe tests.

A person of ability can withstand all trials and tribulations.

🈯 比喻正直或有才幹的人是經得起考驗的。

1350　桃榔樹——一條心

fong² long⁴ syu⁶ — jat¹ tiu⁴ sam¹ *(translit.)*

A coir-palm tree — only one heart. (lit.)

Love somebody heart and soul.

Apply one's mind to the person one loves.

Be single-minded in love.

Be constant in love.

🈁表示愛情專一。

1351　桐油埕

tung⁴ jau⁴ cing⁴ *(translit.)*

The large jar for wood oil. (lit.)

A man sticking to his old job like a bur.

A man doing the same job without any change.

🈁比喻改變不了自己職業的人，相當於
"桐油罐子無二用"。

1352　核突

wat⁶ dat⁶ *(translit.)*

Creeply and disgusting. (lit.)

Give somebody the creeps.

Make somebody's flesh creep.

Creepy-crawly.

Be nauseating.

🈁令人肉麻的，令人作嘔（討厭）的，
參閱"肉酸"條（0753）。

1353　索油

sok³ jau⁴ *(translit.)*

Soak up oil. (lit.)

Intend to make a pass at a lady.

Tease a lady to amuse oneself.

🈁抱着不良動機有意接近女人，企圖佔
便宜或調戲婦女。

1354　原封不動

jyun⁴ fung¹ bat¹ dung⁶ *(translit.)*

The original seal is kept unmoved. (lit.)

Be kept in its integrity.

Be kept intact.

🈁比喻保持原狀。

1355　鬥

dau³ *(translit.)*

Fight. (lit.)

Touch.

Vie with somebody / Compete against somebody for... / in doing something.

Enter into rivalry with somebody for...

Resort to manoeuvres with somebody.

Have a battle of wits with somebody.

Be at odds with somebody.

🈁表示觸摸，和人競爭……/ 做……，
和人角逐……，和人耍花招，和人鬥
智，或和人鬧彆扭等意思。

1356　鬥氣

dau³ hei³ *(translit.)*

Fight for airs. (lit.)

Be at odds with somebody.

Have the sulks.

Do something in a fit of pique.

Take a pique against somebody.

🈁賭氣，慪氣，鬧彆扭或和人有爭執的
意思。

1357　鬥嘥

dau³ saai¹ *(translit.)*

Have a battle if waste. (lit.)

Slander / Defame / Calumniate each other.

Vie with somebody in squandering something.

🈁表示互相詆譭，互相誹謗或和人爭相
浪費……的意思。

1358　鬥踩

dau³ caai² / jaai² *(translit.)*

Vie to tread on each other. (lit.)

Slander / Defame / Calumniate each other.

十

畫

註意和"鬥嘥"同，參閱該條（1328），但和競相浪費絕無關係。

1359　戙起牀板

dung⁶ hei² cong⁴ baan² *(translit.)*

Stand the bed-plates. (lit.)

Burn the midnight oil.

註表示工作至深夜的意思，參閱"開夜車"條（1897）。

1360　戙起幡竿有鬼到

dung⁶ hei² faan¹ gon¹ jau⁵ gwai² dou³ *(translit.)*

Set up the banner calling the soul home and ghosts will come. (lit.)

People will come as soon as they know the location.

註表示有人知所在地，自會前來的意思。

1361　柴台

caai⁴ toi⁴ *(translit.)*

Hooting. (lit.)

Give a Bronx cheer.

Give somebody the bird.

Make cat calls.

註喝倒彩。

1362　柴哇哇

caai⁴ waa¹ waa¹ *(translit.)*

Mess up. (lit.)

Run wild.

Make a mess like sheep without a shepherd.

Play a joke.

Bustle with joy and excitement.

註表示隨隨便便，馬馬虎虎，鬧着玩或喧鬧一番的意思。

1363　財不可露眼

coi⁴ bat¹ ho² lou⁶ ngaan⁵ *(translit.)*

Money should not be exposed to eyes. (lit.)

Opportunity makes the thief.

註表示漫藏誨盜。

1364　財可通神

coi⁴ ho² tung¹ san⁴ *(translit.)*

Money can tempt gods. (lit.)

Money makes the mare go.

Money talks.

註參閱"有錢使得鬼推磨"條（0700）。

1365　財到光棍手─有去冇回頭

coi⁴ dou³ gwong¹ gwan³ sau² ─ jau⁵ heoi³ mou⁵ wui⁴ tau⁴ *(translit.)*

The money reaches a swindler's hand ─ once go never come back. (lit.)

Give a bone to a dog.

No one can get it back when the bone is given to a dog.

註表示被騙的錢沒法收回，相當於"肉包子打狗──一去不回頭"。

1366　唔一定

m⁴ jat¹ ding⁶ *(translit.)*

Cannot fix yet. (lit.)

Be not sure.

It is indefinite.

Can give no affirmative answer.

No definite answer can be given.

註表示不肯定的意思。

1367　唔三唔四

m⁴ saam¹ m⁴ sei³ *(translit.)*

Not three not four. (lit.)

Neither fish, flesh nor fowl.

Neither one thing nor the other.

Be nondescript.

註不倫不類的；形容不出的。

1368　唔止……重兼……

m⁴ zi²... zung⁶ gim¹... *(translit.)*

Not only...but also... (lit.)

十畫

Not only... but also...

注 此為連接詞，有人說成"不特……重
兼 / 而且……"。

1369 唔中用

m[4] zung[1] jung[6] *(translit.)*

Be not useful. (lit.)

Be good for nothing.

Be ne'eve-do-well.

Won't do.

注 表示不管用，無能，不成器或不行的
意思。

1370 唔化

m[4] faa[3] *(translit.)*

Not sublimate. (lit.)

Be too stubborn.

Be not enlightened / openminded.

Be not liberal in one's views.

Not realize the ways of the world.

注 固執，不開通或不覺醒的意思。

1371 唔打唔相識

m[4] daa[2] m[4] soeng[1] sik[1] *(translit.)*

No blows, no friendship grows. (lit.)

No discord, no concord.

注 又作"不打不相識"。

1372 唔在行

m[4] zoi[6] hong[4] *(translit.)*

Not in the trade. (lit.)

Be out of one's beat.

Be out of one's line.

注 指自己不熟悉的事或並非自己本行業
的範圍。

1373 唔同牀唔知被爛

m[4] tung[4] cong[4] m[4] zi[1] pei[5] laan[6]
(translit.)

*One that does not sleep in the
same bed does not know that
the quilt is worn out. (lit.)*

**No one knows what the other
side of the world looks like.**

注 比喻局外人難知局中事，參閱"一家
唔知一家事"條（0050）。

1374 唔自在

m[4] zi[6] zoi[6] *(translit.)*

Be uneasy. (lit.)

Be unwell.

Feel awkward and ill at ease.

注 表示不舒服或局促不安。

1375 唔自量

m[4] zi[6] loeng[6] *(translit.)*

Not to measure oneself. (lit.)

Not to understand oneself.

**Be ignorant of one's own
ability / situation.**

注 表示不自量力。

1376 唔似樣

m[4] ci[5] joeng[2] *(translit.)*

Not alike. (lit.)

It is most imporper.

**It is unreasonable for somebody
to...**

It is outrageous that...

**Bear no resemblance to
somebody / something.**

注 指在禮貌上要別人做……不成體統或
太不像話，或指在別人的行為或態度
上，有令人難以容忍的含義。此外又
表示在外表方面和……不類似的意
思。

1377 唔好手腳

m[4] hou[2] sau[2] goek[3] *(translit.)*

Hands and feet are not good. (lit.)

Have a tendency of theft.

Get used to stealing.

注 即"手腳不乾淨"，有偷竊傾向或慣
於偷竊。

十
畫

1378　唔志在

m⁴ zi³ zoi⁶ *(translit.)*

Not mind about. (lit.)

Not to care a fig.

Not to mind.

㊟即不在乎的意思。

1379　唔見得光

m⁴ gin³ dak¹ gwong¹ *(translit.)*

Cannot see the light. (lit.)

Cannot be exposed to the light of day.

㊟即不能公開的意思。

1380　唔見棺材唔流眼淚

m⁴ gin³ gun¹ coi⁴ m⁴ lau⁴ ngaan⁵ leoi⁶ *(translit.)*

Not to shed a tear until seeing the coffin. (lit.)

Refuse to be convinced until facing the grim reality.

㊟不見到最後結果不死心或事到臨頭才知危害。

1381　唔見過鬼都唔怕黑

m⁴ gin³ gwo³ gwai² dou¹ m⁴ paa³ hak¹ *(translit.)*

One that hasn't seen a ghost does not fear darkness. (lit.)

Any child that hasn't been burned dreads no fire.

A burned child dreads the fire.

㊟參閱 "見過鬼就怕黑" 條（0893）。

1382　唔抵得瘀

m⁴ dai² dak¹ jyu² *(translit.)*

Cannot stand the extravasated blood. (lit.)

Cannot bear the sight of...

Frown upon...

Cannot bear the waste.

㊟表示看不下去或捨不得浪費。

1383　唔抵得頸

m⁴ dai² dak¹ geng² *(translit.)*

Cannot stand the neck. (lit.)

Cannot control one's temper.

Be unable to contain oneself for it.

㊟氣不過，忍不住性子或憋不住的意思。

1384　唔制得過

m⁴ zai³ dak¹ gwo³ *(translit.)*

Not worth doing. (lit.)

It doesn't pay...

It is not to one's profit.

㊟即不划算或划不來的意思，參閱 "制唔過" 條（1067）。

1385　唔知個 "醜" 字點寫

m⁴ zi¹ go³ cau² zi⁶ dim² se² *(translit.)*

Do not know how to write the Chinese character "醜". (lit.)

Be dead to shame.

Be thick-skinned.

㊟形容人厚顏無恥。

1386　唔使指擬

m⁴ sai² zi² ji⁵ *(translit.)*

Not to depend upon. (lit.)

Hold no hope of it.

Have no fond dream about it.

㊟別指望或別夢想。

1387　唔使恨

m⁴ sai² han⁶ *(translit.)*

Have no wish for. (lit.)

Cherish no hope for somebody / something.

Pin none of one's hope on somebody / something.

㊟表示不用指望，對某人 / 物不抱有希望的意思。

1388 唔使問亞貴

m⁴ sai² man⁶ aa³ gwai³ *(translit.)*

There is no need to ask Aa Gwai. (lit.)

Be as sure as eggs is eggs.

There is no need to ask if a duck will swim.

注 比喻不言而喻或事情便是這樣，用不着問。

1389 唔使畫公仔畫出腸

m⁴ sai² waak⁶ gung¹ zai² waak⁶ ceot¹ ceong² *(translit.)*

It is not necessary to draw intestines while drawing a figure. (lit.)

It goes without saying in details.

It is not necessary to ask if a duck will swim.

注 表示不言而喻的意思，參閱 "唔使問亞貴" 條（1388）。

1390 唔使慌

m⁴ sai² fong¹ *(translit.)*

Don't be scared. (lit.)

Don't be afraid.

Don't worry about...

Take it easy.

Pin none of one's hope.

Pin no hope on the fact that...

注 表示不必害怕（本義），不用擔心或不必發愁的意思。當説此語而帶勉強的語氣時，則是表示別指望了的幽默反義語。

1391 唔使擒擒青

m⁴ sai² kam⁴ kam² ceng¹ *(translit.)*

There is no need to be in such a hurry. (lit.)

First catch your hare, then cook him.

Easy does it.

There is no hurry about it.

注 即不必着急。

1392 唔爭在⋯⋯

m⁴ zaang¹ zoi⁶ *(translit.)*

Not to fight for it. (lit.)

Can do without.

Can dispense with...

注 不差，不計較或沒有也行的意思。

1393 唔爭氣

m⁴ zaang¹ hei³ *(translit.)*

Not to fight for air. (lit.)

Fail to live up to one's expectation.

Disappoint somebody.

Let one down.

注 表示不符期望，令人失望或辜負期望的意思。

1394 唔忿氣

m⁴ fan⁶ hei³ *(translit.)*

Not to give the air up. (lit.)

Be unreconciled to...

Be reluctant to give in/up.

Be unwilling to confess the defeat.

注 不服氣，不甘心於⋯⋯或不願放棄/讓步/承認失敗的意思。

1395 唔怕官至怕管

m⁴ paa³ gun¹ zi³ paa³ gun² *(translit.)*

Not to be afraid of the senior officials but afraid of the junior clerk who governs. (lit.)

Had better obey the person in direct charge.

A mouse fears nobody but the cat that would catch it.

注 相當於 "不怕官就怕管"。

1396 唔怪之得／唔怪得之

m⁴ gwaai³ zi¹ dak¹／m⁴ gwaai³ dak¹

十畫

zi¹ *(translit.)*

There is no wonder. (lit.)

Little wonder that...

...so that is why...

注 難怪，引語，用於表示忽然明白原因時引出下句。

1397　唔要斧頭唔得柄甩

m⁴ jiu³ fu² tau² m⁴ dak¹ beng³ lat¹ *(translit.)*

Through the axe is not wanted any more, it is difficult to get its helve off. (lit.)

Hold a wolf by the ears.

Up a gum tree.

Cannot help carrying on.

注 比喻欲罷不能。

1398　唔咬弦

m⁴ ngaau⁵ jin⁴ *(translit.)*

Do not bite the string of the musical instrument. (lit.)

Be out of tune with somebody.

Not to speak the same language.

Not to get along so well with somebody.

注 比喻和某人談不來或合不來。

1399　唔係是必要……

m⁴ hai⁶ si⁶ bit¹ jiu³... *(translit.)*

Need not... (lit.)

Do not need to...

There is no need for somebody to...

It is not necessary for somebody to...

注 即不必要。

1400　唔係猛龍唔過江，唔係毒蛇唔打霧

m⁴ hai⁶ maang⁵ lung⁴ m⁴ gwo³ gong¹, m⁴ hai⁶ duk⁶ se⁴ m⁴ daa²

mou⁶ *(translit.)*

If it were not a fierce dragon, it would not cross the river; if it were not a deadly snake, it would not breathe mist. (lit.)

He who dares to come is surely not a coward.

If one were not so despotic, one would not come.

Only the man of power dares to come.

注 參閱 "來者不善，善者不來"（1050）。

1401　唔係路

m⁴ hai⁶ lou⁶ *(translit.)*

Not the way. (lit.)

Be not on the right track.

It doesn't seem to be normal / right.

It doesn't seem to be encouraging.

It is far from good.

注 即不對勁，不對頭或事情不妙的意思。

1402　唔係講玩

m⁴ hai⁶ gong² waan² *(translit.)*

Not speaking to play. (lit.)

It is no joke.

注 不是玩兒的或這不是開玩笑的事的意思。

1403　唔信命都信吓塊鏡

m⁴ seon³ meng⁶ dou¹ seon³ haa⁵ faai³ geng³ *(translit.)*

If one does not believe in one's own fate, one should believe in the mirror. (lit.)

It is wise to know oneself.

It is wise to have self-knowledge.

注 表示要有自知之明的意思。

1404　唔食羊肉一身臊

m⁴ sik⁶ joeng⁴ juk⁶ jat¹ san¹ sou¹ *(translit.)*

The whole body gets full of lamb odour without eating mutton. (lit.)

Invite unexpected trouble.

Be involved in an unexpected troublesome case.

🈲 相當於〝不吃羊肉空惹一身膻〞。

1405　唔食得豬

m⁴ sik⁶ dak¹ zyu¹ *(translit.)*

Eat no pigs. (lit.)

Be non-virginal.

A maid without moral integrity of virginity.

🈲 南番順各地，向重女性貞操，故迎娶時，慣例必有燒豬回門，以示新娘仍屬處女，若回門時，不備燒豬，藉作暗示新娘已非原璧。因此這俚語便用以婉說一個女子並非處女，倘女子被人說〝你唔食得豬〞時，便認為莫大的侮辱。

1406　唔計帶

m⁴ gai³ daai³ *(translit.)*

Neither count nor bring. (lit.)

Do not mind.

Do not care about...

Do not haggle about.

🈲 表示不介意或不計較的意思。

1407　唔恨

m⁴ han⁶ *(translit.)*

Without wish. (lit.)

Not to care about.

Do not mind.

🈲 表示不稀罕，不想或不在乎的意思。

1408　唔埋得個鼻

m⁴ maai⁴ dak¹ go³ bei⁶ *(translit.)*

Cannot get near the nose. (lit.)

Make a long nose.

Turn up one's nose at...

Look down one's nose at...

🈲 原意為〝臭不堪聞〞，引伸為對人表示鄙視，瞧不起。大致相當於〝一錢不值〞，〝沒甚麼了不起〞。

1409　唔理三七二十一

m⁴ lei⁵ saam¹ cat¹ ji⁶ sap⁶ jat¹ *(translit.)*

Not to care if three times seven equal to twenty-one. (lit.)

Chance the duck.

Cast all caution to the wind.

Pay no regard to the consequences.

🈲 表示不顧一切的意思。參閱〝唔理得咁多〞條（1410）。

1410　唔理得咁多

m⁴ lei⁵ dak¹ gam³ do¹ *(translit.)*

Not to care for such a good many. (lit.)

Cast all caution to the wind.

Pay no regard to the consequences.

Rain or shine.

For better or worse.

🈲 相當於〝唔理三七二十一〞。

1411　唔啱蕎

m⁴ ngaam¹ kiu² *(translit.)*

With wrong ideas. (lit.)

Do not get along well with each other.

Do not sing the same tune.

Be at odds with each other.

🈲 即合不來或意見不合的意思。

1412　唔做中唔做保，唔做媒人三代好

m⁴ zou⁶ zung¹ m⁴ zou⁶ bou², m⁴ zou⁶

mui⁴ jan⁴ saam¹ doi⁶ hou² *(translit.)*

Neither being a middleman or a guarantor nor being a match-marker will make three later generations better. (lit.)

He that does no business of a middleman and the like will have worthy descendence.

🈺 這是勸人不要多管別人的事或做中間人的口頭語。

1413　唔淨只……
m⁴ zing⁶ zi²... *(translit.)*
Not only... (lit.)
Not only...
🈺 相當於 "不單只"。

1414　唔通……
m⁴ tung¹... *(translit.)*
Could...? (lit.)
Isn't it that...?
Could...possibly...?
🈺 即難道。多用於疑問句中以加強語氣。

1415　唔通氣
m⁴ tung¹ hei³ *(translit.)*
Not to let air out. (lit.)
Be not sensible.
Not to know to behave in a delicate situation.
🈺 表示不知趣（妨礙別人）的意思。參閱 "電燈膽"（1972）條。

1416　唔敢當
m⁴ gam² dong¹ *(translit.)*
Not so bold to deserve it. (a polite and humble expression spoken by the first person) (lit.)
Thank you, but I feel ashamed to obtain my desert.
🈺 不敢當。

1417　唔睇白鴿，都睇吓堆屎
m⁴ tai² baak⁶ gap³, dou¹ tai² haa⁵ deoi¹ si² *(translit.)*
Not to look at the pigeon itself, but have to look at its manure. (lit.)
A straw shows which way the wind blows.
From his ostentation or extravagance, one can find a clue to how wealthy somebody is.
🈺 比喻見微知著。（指從某人的排場便知某人的家世的意思。）

1418　唔睇僧面，都睇吓佛面
m⁴ tai² zang¹ min⁶, dou¹ tai² haa⁵ fat⁶ min⁶ *(translit.)*
Not to look at the face of a monk, look at the face of Buddha. (lit.)
Not for everybody's sake but for somebody's sake.
🈺 這是用於懇求別人幫忙時的插語，意思即是説 "如你不賞臉給我，也請你賞臉給某人"。相當於 "不看僧面看佛面"。

1419　唔嗱耕
m⁴ naa¹ gaang¹ *(translit.)*
Have no relation. (lit.)
Have nothing to do with...
Bear no relation to...
Be not concerned in...
Be as different as chalk from cheese.
Beside the point.
Be wide of mark.
🈺 表示毫不相干，和某人毫無關係，"不着邊際或不切題" 的意思。

1420　唔湯唔水
m⁴ tong¹ m⁴ seoi² *(translit.)*
Neither soap nor water. (lit.)

十畫

Neither fish nor fowl.

Be done by halves.

Hang in half-way.

🈷 表示不倫不類或工作做得一半而未徹
底完成的意思。

1421　唔嗅米氣

m⁴ cau³ mai⁵ hei³ *(translit.)*

Haven't yet smelt the odour of rice. (lit.)

One's mouth is full of pap.

Be too childish.

🈷 比喻無知或幼稚。

1422　唔嗲唔吊

m⁴ de² m⁴ diu³ *(translit.)*

Neither care nor pay attention to... (lit.)

Be casual.

🈷 相當於 "大大咧咧的"，意指不緊不
慢，愛理不理或對甚麼都無所謂的態
度。

1423　唔話得

m⁴ waa⁶ dak¹ *(translit.)*

Have nothing to say. (lit.)

Have nothing to complain of...

Be really good.

🈷 表示沒有甚麼可説的，沒有可埋怨的
話或確實是好人的意思。（對人或事
表示滿意，提不出甚麼意見。）

1424　唔該借一借

m⁴ goi¹ ze³ jat¹ ze³ *(translit.)*

Please lend me a loan. (lit.)

Excuse me.

Give way to me, please.

Make room for me, please.

🈷 參閱 "唔該借歪啲" 條（1425）。

1425　唔該借歪啲

m⁴ goi¹ ze³ me² di¹ *(translit.)*

Please, lend a little. (lit.)

Excuse me.

Give way to me, please.

Make room for me, please.

🈷 意為借光，請讓開一些！用於請對方
"讓路" 或 "讓坐"。

1426　唔經大腦

m⁴ ging¹ daai⁶ nou⁵ *(translit.)*

Not to pass through the cerebrums. (lit.)

Not to rack one's brains.

Leap without thinking.

🈷 表示未經考慮便説出或做出某事的意
思。

1427　唔算數

m⁴ syun³ sou³ *(translit.)*

Not to count the sum. (lit.)

Go back on one's words.

Play fast and loose.

🈷 表示食言或反覆無常，參閱 "唔認
賬 / 數" 條（1428）。

1428　唔認賬 / 數

m⁴ jing⁶ zoeng³ / sou³ *(translit.)*

Deny the account (sum). (lit.)

Go back on one's words.

Play fast and loose.

🈷 參閱 "唔算數" 條（1427）。

1429　唔⋯⋯罷就

m⁴ ... baa⁶ zau⁶ *(translit.)*

Drop the matter if not... (lit.)

Forget it / Drop it / Let it pass if / since somebody does / will not...

🈷 即不⋯⋯便算了。

1430　唔覺眼

m⁴ gok³ ngaan⁵ *(translit.)*

Have no feeling in the eyes. (lit.)

十
畫

Pay no attention to...

Not to keep one's eyes open.

📝沒注意。

1431　唔覺意

m⁴ gok³ ji³ (translit.)

Have no feeling in the mind. (lit.)

Take no care.

One's mind is absent.

Have no intention of...

Not to mean to...

📝不留神，不小心。

1432　唔黐家

m⁴ ci¹ gaa¹ (translit.)

Not to stick home. (lit.)

Not to be a home-bird.

Not to stick indoors.

📝表示不喜歡或不經常留在家中的意思。

1433　蚊都瞓

man¹ dou¹ fan³ (translit.)

Mosquitoes also sleep. (lit.)

It will be too late to...

📝表示某人行動慢吞吞的，等到他做……時，為時已晚的意思。

1434　蚊髀同牛髀

man¹ bei² tung⁴ ngau⁴ bei² (translit.)

The leg of a mosquito and the leg of an ox. (lit.)

By long chalks.

Cannot measure with each other.

There is no comparison between the two.

Not to be compared with each other.

📝比喻無法作互相比較或有天淵之別。

1435　骨子

gwat¹ zi² (translit.)

Smallboned. (lit.)

Be delicate and exquisite.

📝形容嬌小玲瓏的意思。

1436　骨痹

gwat¹ bei³ (translit.)

The bones become numbled. (lit.)

Be filled with nausea.

Cause somebody to be disgusting.

📝即令人肉麻的意思。

1437　恩將仇報

jan¹ zoeng¹ cau⁴ bou³ (translit.)

Revenge for kindness. (lit.)

Bite the hand that feeds.

Quit love for hate.

📝同"以怨報德"。

1438　趷路

gat⁶ lou⁶ (translit.)

Walk in the road with a limp! (lit.)

Scram!

Get out!

Beat it!

Get out of my sight!

📝參閱"躝屍"條（2467）及"躝屍趷路"條（2468）。

1439　氣羅氣喘

hei³ lo⁴ hei³ cyun² (translit.)

The air grasps. (lit.)

Be out of breath.

Grasp for air.

Be panting.

📝即氣喘。

1440　特登

dak⁶ dang¹ (translit.)

On purpose. (lit.)

Intentionally.

Deliberately.

On purpose.

十畫

For a special purpose.

🈂故意地或有目的地的意思。

1441　笑到肚刺

siu³ dou³ tou⁵ cek³ *(translit.)*

One's belly aches with laughter. (lit.)

Split one's sides with laughter.

Laugh one's head off.

🈂同"笑到肚都攣埋"。

1442　倀／撐雞

caang⁴ gai¹ *(translit.)*

Be like a fighting cock. (lit.)

Be passionate and violent.

Be shrewish.

🈂潑婦似的。

1443　倀／撐雞妹

caang⁴ gai¹ mui¹ *(translit.)*

A girl like a fighting cock. (lit.)

A girl of passionate disposition and violent temper.

🈂指性兇惡而又易怒的少女。

1444　借刀殺人

ze³ dou¹ saat³ jan⁴ *(translit.)*

Borrow a knife to kill people. (lit.)

Murder with a borrowed knife.

Make use of somebody/something to get rid of one's adversary.

🈂比喻假他人之手去害人。

1445　借花敬佛

ze³ faa¹ ging³ fat⁶ *(translit.)*

Borrow flowers to offer to Buddha. (lit.)

Make use of the gift from another to show respect to somebody.

🈂即借花獻佛。

1446　借咗聾陳隻耳

ze³ zo² lung⁴ can² zek³ ji⁵ *(translit.)*

Borrow an ear from the deaf Mr. Chan. (lit.)

Turn a deaf ear to somebody.

🈂比喻充耳不聞，參閱"亞聾送殯"條（1023）。

1447　借艇割禾

ze³ teng⁵ got³ wo⁴ *(translit.)*

Borrow a boat to cut paddies. (lit.)

Make use of somebody to profit oneself.

Enlist somebody's help to fulfill one's own purpose.

🈂指利用別人來謀取利益或借助別人的幫忙來實踐自己的企圖的一種手段。

1448　借題發揮

ze³ tai⁴ faat³ fai¹ *(translit.)*

Take advantage of the subject to call into play. (lit.)

Make use of the subject under discussion to put over one's own ideas.

Seize on an incident/a subject to talk at/make an assault on somebody.

1449　倒吊冇滴墨水

dou³ diu³ mou⁵ dik⁶ mak⁶ seoi² *(translit.)*

Have not a drop of ink even being hung upside down. (lit.)

Be uncivilized.

Haven't been educated.

Be uneducated.

🈂形容人沒文化，沒受過教育。

1450　倒吊荷包

dou³ diu³ ho⁴ baau¹ *(translit.)*

Hang the purse upside down. (lit.)

Invite losses for oneself.

Stand in one's own light.

注 比喻自招損失或甘願蝕本。參閱 "倒米" 條（1451）。

1451　倒米

dou² mai⁵ *(translit.)*

Dump rice. (lit.)

**Cause oneself or one's own side
to suffer a loss.**

Stand in one's own light.

注 表示使自己或自己一方蒙受損失或損害自己利益的意思。參閱 "倒吊荷包" 條（1450）。

1452　倒米壽星

dou² mai⁵ sau⁶ sing¹ *(translit.)*

*The god of longevity dumps rice.
(lit.)*

**The person who causes himself
or his own side to suffer
a loss.**

**A person who stands in his own
light.**

注 比喻自招損失或損害自己一方利益的人。

1453　倒掛臘鴨——滿口／嘴油

dou³ gwaa³ laap⁶ aap²ᐟ³ — mun⁵
hau² / zeoi² jau⁴ *(translit.)*

*A cured duck hung upside
down — its bill is full of oil. (lit.)*

Have a glib tongue.

Oil one's tongue.

注 形容人油腔滑調。

1454　倒瀉籮蟹

dou² se² lo⁴ haai⁵ *(translit.)*

*Upset a bamboo-basket of crabs.
(lit.)*

Be all in a muddle.

**Be very busy with either this or
that.**

注 形容手忙腳亂的樣子。

1455　倒瓤冬瓜

dou² nong⁴ dung¹ gwaa¹ *(translit.)*

*A big hard-skinned wax gourd with
rotten pulp. (lit.)*

**A person who is strong in
appearance but poor in health.**

**A person who is outwardly
wealthy but inwardly poor.**

注 比喻外表壯碩但實際不健康的人或外表富有但實際貧窮的人。

1456　修遊

sau¹ jau⁴ *(translit.)*

Unhurried. (lit.)

Be calm and unhurried.

Lead an easy life.

注 形容從容不迫或過着悠閒的生活。

1457　修遊淡定

sau¹ jau⁴ daam⁶ ding⁶ *(translit.)*

Keep cool and calm. (lit.)

Be calm and composed.

**Keep one's head and make no
hast.**

注 這句話只表示從容不迫的態度。

1458　個蜆個肉

go³ hin² go³ juk⁶ *(translit.)*

*A small clam has only one lump of
flesh. (lit.)*

Just one for just one.

注 相當於 "一個蘿蔔一個坑"。

1459　俾人揸住痛腳

bei² jan⁴ zaa¹ zyu⁶ tung³ goek³
(translit.)

*Let somebody hold one's aching
leg. (lit.)*

Give somebody a handle.

Become fair game.

注 即給人抓住把柄或成為人有隙可擊的對象。

十畫

1460　俾心機

bei² sam¹ gei¹ *(translit.)*

Give heart to... (lit.)

Pay attention to...

Concentrate on...

Devote one's time and effort to...

🈯 表示留心或下功夫的意思。

1461　俾個心你食都當狗肺

bei² go³ sam¹ nei⁵ sik⁶ dou¹ dong³ gau² fai³ *(translit.)*

The heart given you to eat is regarded as dog's lungs. (lit.)

Not to know chalk from cheese.

Not to know what is good for one.

Be ignorant of good from bad.

🈯 指對方不知好歹。

1462　俾個頭你

bei² go³ tau⁴ nei⁵ *(translit.)*

Give you the head. (lit.)

No, I won't give you.

I'll give you nothing.

🈯 表面肯定實際是否定的賭氣語。真意是拒絕給對方東西。

1463　俾蕉皮／西瓜皮人踩

bei² ziu¹ pei⁴ / sai¹ gwaa¹ pei⁴ jan⁴ caai² *(translit.)*

Give somebody banana skin / the skin of water-melon to tread on. (lit.)

Make somebody meet with failure / loss...

Make somebody stand on slippery ground.

Make somebody slip up.

🈯 指使人遭受失敗，損失或站在不可靠的地步或令人犯錯誤。

1464　隻眼開，隻眼閉

zek³ ngaan⁵ hoi¹, zek³ ngaan⁵ bai³ *(translit.)*

One eye opens and one eye shuts. (lit.)

Wink at...

Close one's eyes to...

Turn one's blind eye to...

🈯 相當於"睜一隻眼，閉一隻眼"；假裝沒看見。

1465　臭檔

cau³ dong³ *(translit.)*

Stinking stall. (lit.)

Be notorious.

A notorious scoundrel.

A stinkard.

🈯 形容人臭名昭著，卑鄙，或聲名狼藉。

1466　烏〔黑〕狗得食，白狗當災

wu¹〔hak¹〕gau² dak¹ sik⁶, baak⁶ gau² dong¹ zoi¹ *(translit.)*

A black dog gains the food to eat but a white dog suffers from the disaster. (lit.)

Be a whipping boy.

Carry the can.

Be a scapegoat.

🈯 比喻代人受過，做代罪羔羊。

1467　烏卒卒

wu¹ zeot¹ zeot¹ *(translit.)*

All is black. (lit.)

Be at a complete loss.

Be entirely ignorant.

Be as black as one's hat.

Be as black as night.

🈯 即無知，參閱"烏啄啄"（1468）及"烏蛇蛇"（1469）各條，但又表示漆黑的意思。

十畫

1468　烏啄啄

wu¹ doeng¹ doeng¹ *(translit.)*

In the dark. (lit.)

Be at a complete loss.

Be entirely ignorant.

注 懵然不知，參閱 "烏卒卒" （1467）
及 "烏蛇蛇" （1469）條。

1469　烏蛇蛇 （借音字）

wu¹ soe²ᐟ⁴ soe⁴ *(translit.)*

In the dark. (lit.)

Be at a complete loss.

Be entirely ignorant.

注 參閱 "烏卒卒"（1467）及 "烏啄啄"
（1468）條。

1470　烏喱馬扠

wu¹ lei¹ maa⁵ caa⁵ *(translit.)*

Black out all and write at random.
(lit.)

Be illegible and sloppy.

注 形容字跡潦草。

1471　烏喱單刀

wu¹ lei¹ daan¹ dou¹ *(translit.)*

Black out the single knife. (lit.)

Be all in a muddle.

Be in an awful state.

注 一塌糊塗的意思。

1472　烏煙瘴氣

wu¹ jin¹ zoeng³ hei³ *(translit.)*

Black smoke and malaria. (lit.)

Be all in a muddle.

Be in an awful state.

注 形容人事或環境黑暗混亂。

1473　烏龍

wu¹ lung² *(translit.)*

A black dragon. (lit.)

Make a muddle of...

Muddle something together.

A muddy thinker.

注 指做事糊塗，錯誤百出。

1474　烏蠅摟馬尾──一拍兩散

wu¹ jing¹ lau¹ maa⁵ mei⁵ — jat¹ paak³
loeng⁵ saan³ *(translit.)*

Flies gather to hold on the tail of a
horse — one slap disperses two.
(lit.)

Rather make a mess of
something then let either side
monopolize it.

Smash up a monopoly.

注 寧可把事情搞糟兩方面都得不到好處
或不讓人獨佔。

1475　鬼五馬六

gwai² ng⁵ maa⁵ luk⁶ *(translit.)*

Ghost five and horse six. (lit.)

Act in a grotesque way.

Grotesque.

Shady-looking.

Be not serious.

注 形容人或物樣子怪誕的或不正經的。

1476　鬼打你

gwai² daa² nei⁵ *(translit.)*

The ghost beats you. (lit.)

You are possessed / obsessed.

注 罵人話，即 "活見鬼"，"鬼迷心竅"。

1477　鬼打鬼

gwai² daa² gwai² *(translit.)*

Ghosts fight ghosts. (lit.)

Put up an internecine fight.

Be at odds with each other.

Have an internal dissension.

注 內閧。參閱 "狗咬狗骨" 條（1114）。

1478　鬼打都冇咁醒

gwai² daa² dou¹ mou⁵ gam³ sing²
(translit.)

A ghost's strike is not so alarming.
(lit.)

Be on the alert.

🈲 表示非常警覺。

1479 鬼拍後尾枕 —— 不打自招

gwai[2] paak[3] hau[6] mei[5] zam[2] — bat[1]
daa[2] zi[6] ziu[1] *(translit.)*

A ghost taps one's
occiput — confess oneself
without being beaten. (lit.)

Confess without pressure.

Make a confession without
duresse.

Unintentionally reveal one's own
secret to somebody.

🈲 比喻自己承認罪狀或過失或不自覺地
泄露自己的秘密，參閱 "不打自招"
（0285）條。

1480 鬼食泥噉聲

gwai[2] sik[6] nai[4] gam[2] seng[1] *(translit.)*

Make the sound like a ghost eating
mud. (lit.)

Give utterance to one's
complaint/rage.

Murmur against...

🈲 形容人口中唸唸有詞，發出怨言或絮
絮不休的自言自語的神態。

1481 鬼馬

gwai[2] maa[5] *(translit.)*

Ghostly horse. (lit.)

Have a whole bag of tricks.

Be as crafty as a fox.

Be comical.

🈲 形容人狡猾或滑稽。

1482 鬼鬼鼠鼠〈祟祟〉

gwai[2] gwai[2] syu[2] syu[2] *(translit.)*

Devilish and mischievous. (lit.)

Sneak around.

Be furtive in one's movement.

🈲 鬼鬼祟祟或偷偷摸摸的意思。

1483 鬼揞/掩眼

gwai[2] am[2] ngaan[5] *(translit.)*

A ghost covers one's eyes with
hands. (lit.)

Be muddled to make a mistake.

A mistake slips in.

🈲 比喻糊裏糊塗地出錯。

1484 鬼畫符

gwai[2] waak[6] fu[4] *(translit.)*

The incantations that ghosts draw.
(lit.)

Be like an illegible scrawl.

🈲 諷刺筆跡潦草。

1485 鬼猾

gwai[2] wat[6]/waat[6]/waak[6] *(translit.)*

Ghostly cunning. (lit.)

Crafty.

Be as crafty as a fox.

Cunning.

🈲 狡猾或詭計多端的意思。

1486 鬼聲鬼氣

gwai[2] seng[1] gwai[2] hei[3] *(translit.)*

Ghost's voice and breath. (lit.)

Speak in strange voice.

🈲 即怪聲怪氣。

1487 倔情

gwat[6] cing[4] *(translit.)*

Blunt feeling. (lit.)

Be unamiable.

Be unamenable to reason.

🈲 指對人冷淡的；不易親近的或不近人
情的。

1488 師姑

si[1] gu[1] *(translit.)*

Master's aunt. (lit.)

A Buddhist nun.

注 即尼姑。

1489　針冇兩頭利

zam[1] mou[5] loeng[5] tau[4] lei[6] *(translit.)*

Not a needle is sharp at both ends. (lit.)

There is no rose without a thorn.

Nothing is good for both respects.

Nothing can satisfy rival claims.

注 比喻沒有十全十美的事，相當於 "甘蔗沒有兩頭甜"。

1490　針唔拮到肉唔知痛

zam[1] m[4] gat[1] dou[3] juk[6] m[4] zi[1] tung[3] *(translit.)*

One does not feel the ache until a needle stings one. (lit.)

No one but the wearer knows better where the shoe pinches.

Do not stand in the shoe that pinches.

注 比喻不置身於痛苦的地位不知痛苦。

1491　針鼻削鐵

zam[1] bei[6] soek[3] tit[3] *(translit.)*

Scrape iron off the nose of a needle. (lit.)

Gain the narrowest margin of profit.

注 利潤極少。

1492　拿手好戲

naa[4] sau[2] hou[2] hei[3] *(translit.)*

One's dexterous performance. (lit.)

One's strong suit.

Be expert in...

注 指最擅長的本領。

1493　拿拿聲

naa[4] naa[2/4] seng[1] *(translit.)*

Make a sound of 'Naa Naa'. (lit.)

Make haste to do something.

In haste.

Quicken one's steps to do something.

注 形容趕快或加快步伐。

1494　胭脂馬 —— 難騎

jin[1] zi[1] maa[5] — naan[4] ke[4] *(translit.)*

A rouged horse — It is hard to be ridden. (lit.)

An uncontrollable person.

注 比喻不受控制或難以駕馭的人。

1495　狼

long[4] *(translit.)*

Wolf-natured. (lit.)

Be ferocious.

注 形容人兇狠，兇猛。

1496　狼忙

long[4] mong[4] *(translit.)*

As busy as a wolf. (lit.)

Be in a hurry.

Be in a hurry-skurry.

注 表示急忙，匆忙或慌張，手忙腳亂。

1497　狼胎

long[4] toi[1] *(translit.)*

Wolf-foetused. (lit.)

Be both fierce and malicious.

Be both ferocious and relentless.

Be too covetous.

注 形容兇狠或過分貪婪。

1498　狼過華秀隻狗

long[4] gwo[3] waa[4] sau[3] zek[3] gau[2] *(translit.)*

More fierce than Waa Sau dog. (lit.)

Be more rapacious than a hawk.

Stick out for something by hook or crook.

十畫

Be very ferocious.
Bare one's fangs.

📝 表示貪得無厭，不擇手段要……或露出兇相的意思。

1499　留得青山在，哪怕有柴燒

lau⁴ dak¹ cing¹ saan¹ zo⁶, naa⁵ paa³ mou⁵ caai⁴ siu¹ *(translit.)*

As long as the green mountain exists, one need not worry about having no firewood to burn. (lit.)

Life is safe and gains will surely be safe.

1500　留番啖氣暖吓肚

lau⁴ faan¹ daam⁶ hei³ nyun⁵ haa⁵ tou⁵ *(translit.)*

Reserve a puff of breath to warm the belly. (lit.)

Maintain a strict silence on...
Button up one's mouth.
Bite the tongue.

📝 表示保持緘默的意思。

1501　留番嚟攝灶罅

lau⁴ faan¹ lai⁴ sip³ zou³ laa³ *(translit.)*

Put by a daughter to fill in the gap of the furnace. (lit.)

Let one's own daughter stay unmarried.

📝 比喻任由自己女兒作老處女，終身不嫁。

1502　高不成，低不就

gou¹ bat¹ sing⁴, dai¹ bat¹ zau⁶ *(translit.)*

Neither achieve the height nor accomplish the low. (lit.)

Be neither willing to stoop to conquer nor able to match with...
Be neither unfit for a higher

position nor willing to take a lower one.

📝 參閱"半天吊"〔0583〕條。

1503　高竇

gou¹ dau³ *(translit.)*

A high nest. (lit.)

Be as proud as a peacock.
Have not a word to throw at a dog.

📝 傲慢。

1504　差一皮

caa¹ jat¹ pei⁴ *(translit.)*

Fall short of a skin-depth. (lit.)

Be inferior (to...)
Be lower-graded (than...)
Be on a lower level.

📝 即差一等或低一級。

1505　差唔多

caa¹ m⁴ do¹ *(translit.)*

Almost. (lit.)

Much of a muchness.
Be not very different from...
Be about the same.
Almost.
Nearly.

📝 表示很相像或相差不大，但亦表示幾乎的意思。

1506　差遲

caa¹ ci⁴ *(translit.)*

Error. (lit.)

Fault.
Mistake.
Slip.

📝 過失，差錯，失誤，漏洞或意外事故的意思。

1507　送羊入虎口

sung³ joeng⁴ jap⁶ fu² hau² *(translit.)*

十畫

Send a goat into the mouth of a tiger. (lit.)

Put oneself / somebody to death.

Put one's chick under the care of a wolf.

注 即等於把……送死。

1508　送佛送到西

sung³ fat⁶ sung³ dou³ sai¹ *(translit.)*

See Buddha off, go with him to the west. (lit.)

Help somebody, help him from end to end.

Help a lame dog, help it over the stile.

Carry something through to the end.

Be thorough in one's work.

注 比喻幫人幫到底或做事要徹底。

1509　粉板 / 牌字 —— 唔啱就抹咗佢

fan² baan² / paai² zi⁶ — m⁴ ngaam¹ zau⁶ mut³ / maat³ zo² keoi⁵ *(translit.)*

Words / Characters on the blackboard — wipe them away if they are incorrect. (lit.)

Forget it if what is said is incorrect / disapproved.

注 當你表達意見，不知對方是否同意或所説的是否正確，因此借黑板（廣東人叫做粉板或粉牌）上的字來表示所説的可以隨時不算或作廢。

1510　迷頭迷腦

mai⁴ tau⁴ mai⁴ nou⁵ *(translit.)*

Bury one's head and brains. (lit.)

Indulge oneself in...

Concentrate one's attention on...

注 表示沉迷於某事或全神貫注的意思，也有人説成 "埋頭埋腦"。

1511　逆次次

ngaak⁶ ci³ ci³ *(translit.)*

Go against. (lit.)

Feel embarrassed not to comply with somebody's request.

Be not amenable to reason.

Rebel against somebody's will.

注 表示由於不順應他人意思而感為難或逆人意向的意思。

1512　酒後吐真言

zau² hau⁶ tou³ zan¹ jin⁴ *(translit.)*

Tell the truth after having wine. (lit.)

Truth is exposed in wine.

注 酒後將平時不敢講或不該講的話都説出來。

1513　酒醉三分醒

zau² zeoi³ saam¹ fan¹ seng² *(translit.)*

Be drunk but still a little clear-minded. (lit.)

Be in wine but still a little conscious.

Be in muddle but still know what to do.

注 與 "爛醉如泥" 相反。

1514　消 / 宵夜

siu¹ je² *(translit.)*

While away the night. (lit.)

Have a midnight snack.

Midnight supper.

Refreshments taken late at night.

注 晚飯後的一餐。

1515　海上無魚蝦自大

hoi² soeng⁶ mou⁴ jyu⁴ haa¹ zi⁶ daai⁶ *(translit.)*

Were there no fish in the sea, a shrimp would become the biggest. (lit.)

A dwarf in Liliput would be

thought as a superbeing.

1516　海水沖倒龍王廟 —— 自己人不識自己人

hoi² seoi² cung¹ dou² lung⁴ wong⁴ miu² — zi⁶ gei² jan⁴ bat¹ sik¹ zi⁶ gei² jan⁴ *(translit.)*

Seawater washes down the Temple of the Dragon King of the sea (Chinese Neptune) — One's own man does not know one's own man. (lit.)

Not to recognize another member / other members on one's own side.

Not to know the person(s) belonging to the same group.

1517　流口水

lau⁴/⁶ hau² seoi² *(translit.)*

Dribble mouth water. (lit.)

Lick one's chops.

Show greed for...

Be inferior.

Be of poor quality.

Be low-graded.

注 表示饞涎欲滴。如形容物件為劣質時，"流"字作lau⁶音。

1518　流馬尿

lau⁴/⁶ maa⁵ niu⁶ *(translit.)*

Flow horse's urine. (lit.)

Shed tears.

Cry out tears.

注 譏諷人流淚。

1519　流嘢

lau⁴ je⁵ *(translit.)*

Poor thing. (lit.)

An article of poor quality.

Be low-graded.

Be low-levelled.

注 形容成績或質量低劣，差。

1520　家有一老，如有一寶

gaa¹ jau⁵ jat¹ lou⁵, jyu⁴ jau⁵ jat¹ bou² *(translit.)*

Having an old person at home is like having a gem. (lit.)

An old-timer in the family is an adviser of rich experience.

注 指家中的老人是一個經驗豐富的顧問。

1521　家和萬事興

gaa¹ wo⁴ maan⁶ si⁶ hing¹ *(translit.)*

A family of peace can establish ten thousand things. (lit.)

Harmony makes a family prosperous.

注 和睦共處則家庭興旺。

1522　家家有本難唸的經

gaa¹ gaa¹ jau⁵ bun² naan⁴ nim⁶ dik¹ ging¹ *(translit.)*

Every family has a Buddhist Scripture that one finds it difficult to chant. (lit.)

Each and every family has its own problems.

注 指每個家庭有自己的問題。

1523　家醜不可外傳

gaa¹ cau² bat¹ ho² ngoi⁶ cyun⁴ *(translit.)*

The shameful business of a family cannot be exposed outside. (lit.)

It is an ill bird that fouls its own nest.

Not to wash dirty linen in public.

注 家裏的醜事不可給外人知道。

1524　害人終害己

hoi⁶ jan⁴ zung¹ hoi⁶ gei² *(translit.)*

Hurting others will hurt oneself

十畫

instead in the end. (lit.)

Harm watch, harm catch.

Harm set, harm get.

🈺 又作害人害己。

1525　害死亞堅

hoi⁶ sei² aa³ gin¹ *(translit.)*

Harm Aa Gin to death. (lit.)

Be encumbered by somebody.

Be encumbered with something.

Make somebody come to an end.

🈺 比喻為……所累或累死某人。

1526　冤有頭，債有主

jyun¹ jau⁵ tau⁴, zaai³ jau⁵ zyu² *(translit.)*

Enmity has cause and debt has its debtor. (lit.)

There must be an agent for what is done.

🈺 比喻凡事都有原因或主使者。

1527　冤枉嚟瘟疫去

jyun¹ wong² lai⁴ wan¹ jik⁶ heoi³ *(translit.)*

Come from a wrong, go for plague. (lit.)

Ill gotten, ill spent.

🈺 表示悖入悖出的意思。

1528　冤屈

jyun¹ wat¹ *(translit.)*

A wrong. (lit.)

Grievance.

False charge.

🈺 "冤枉"的同義詞。

1529　冤家

jyun¹ gaa¹ *(translit.)*

An enemy. (lit.)

An opponent.

One's destined lover.

🈺 指對立的人，有時又指自己命中注定的愛人或妻子。

1530　冤家宜解不宜結

jyun¹ gaa¹ ji⁴ gaai² bat¹ ji⁴ git³ *(translit.)*

Enmity should be untied and should not be tied. (lit.)

It is better for enemies to have their hatred slaked than it is to contract enmity.

It is better to bury the hatchet.

1531　冤家路窄

jyun¹ gaa¹ lou⁶ zaak³ *(translit.)*

Opponents in the narrow road. (lit.)

Enemies are bound to meet.

1532　冤豬頭都有盟鼻菩薩

jyun¹ zyu¹ tau⁴ dou¹ jau⁵ mang⁴ bei⁶ pou⁴ saat³ *(translit.)*

A foul pig's head would be appreciated by the god with bad nose. (lit.)

A lover has no judge of beauty.

Love is blind.

Beauty exists in a lover's eyes.

Beauty exists in a beholder.

🈺 相當於"臭豬頭有爛鼻子來聞"，意為美麗是沒有準則的，參閱"情人眼裏出西施"條（1699）。

1533　冤孽

jyun¹ jip⁶ *(translit.)*

The curses for evil deeds. (lit.)

The retribution for ancestors' evil deeds.

Predestinated connection.

Evil connection.

🈺 指上一代敗德所留下的報應或命中注定的關係。

1534　剝光豬

mok¹ gwong¹ zyu¹ *(translit.)*

Make a pig bare. *(lit.)*

Strip oneself / somebody to the skin.

Gamble away.

Be robbed of all one's money.

Take somebody to the cleaners.

🈳 比喻脱光衣服，輸光或被人搶光。

1535　剝花生

mok[1] faa[1] sang[1] *(translit.)*

Strip off the husks of peanuts. (lit.)

Become a peanut when going with somebody to have a heavy date.

🈳 比喻陪人去談情説愛，自己處於無聊的地位。

1536　除笨有精

ceoi[4] ban[6] jau[5] zeng[1] *(translit.)*

Besides foolishness, there is cleverness. (lit.)

Bait a hook with a small fish to catch a bigger one.

Make the best of a bad bargain.

🈳 形容笨人偶爾也有聰明之處，或除了吃虧也會佔便宜。

1537　除褲屙屁 —— 多此一舉

ceoi[4] fu[3] o[1] pei[3] — do[1] ci[2] jat[1] geoi[2] *(translit.)*

Take off trousers to break wind — take an unnecessary action. (lit.)

Carry coals to Newcastle.

🈳 表示做不必要的、多餘的事。

1538　紗紙

saa[1] zi[2] *(translit.)*

Gauze paper. (lit.)

A certificate.

A diploma.

🈳 沙紙（sand paper）和紗紙（gauze paper）音同異義，前者為用以打磨木器的一種用品，而後者為中國特產，因其像紗布，故名 "紗紙"，這種紙富有韌性，不易折斷，而且歷久不霉，古時書寫契約或字據之類文件，必用這種紙張，後人遂引伸喻作文憑或證書。

1539　紙紮下扒

zi[2] zaat[3] haa[6] paa[4] *(translit.)*

The paper chin. (lit.)

Talk at random.

Talk through one's neck.

Only cackle without laying an egg.

🈳 比喻大放厥詞，亂説一通或講空話。

十一　畫

1540　春瘟雞

zung[1] wan[1] gai[1] *(translit.)*

A plagued hen. (lit.)

A person who walks in a drunken manner.

A person who knocks round this way and that way.

🈳 比喻行路像喝醉酒的人或亂碰亂撞的人。

1541　匿埋

lei[1] maai[4] *(translit.)*

Hide somewhere. (lit.)

Hide oneself.

Hide out. / Cover up one's tracks.

Be on the dodge.

🈳 即藏起來或無固定住處以逃避拘捕。參閲 "捐埋" 條（1177）。

1542　現眼報

jin[6] ngaan[5] bou[3] *(translit.)*

The visible recompense. (lit.)

十一畫

Deserve an immediate
retribution.

注 指做了壞事，馬上得到報應。相當於
"現世現報"。

1543　掛羊頭賣狗肉

gwaa³ joeng⁴ tau⁴ maai⁶ gau² juk⁶
(translit.)

*Hang a goat's head but sell dog's
flesh. (lit.)*

Foist something on somebody.
Label vinegar as vintage.
Cry up wine and sell vinegar.

注 表示名不符實。

1544　掛臘鴨

gwaa³ laap⁶ aap³ *(translit.)*
Hang a cured duck. (lit.)

Hang oneself.

注 謔喻上吊自殺。（掛臘鴨時，是用繩
子繫着鴨頸的。）

1545　揢拃

ngaa⁶ zaa⁶ *(translit.)*
Infringe space. (lit.)

Occupy too much space.
Be overbearing.
Occupy space with a high hand.

注 形容東西佔地方，形容人霸道，以高
壓手段霸佔地方。

1546　捱世界

ngaai⁴ sai³ gaai³ *(translit.)*
Endure the world. (lit.)

Live from hand to mouth.
Keep the wolf from the door.

注 熬苦日子。

1547　捱更抵夜

ngaai⁴ gaang¹ dai² je⁶ *(translit.)*
*Endure the beating of watch-man's
drum and bear the night. (lit.)*

Sit up all night.
Sit up late.
Turn night into day.

注 即"熬夜"。

1548　捱夜

ngaai⁴ je² *(translit.)*
Endure the night. (lit.)

Sit up late.

注 同"捱更抵夜"（1547）。

1549　捱騾仔

ngaai⁴ leoi⁴ zai² *(translit.)*
Endure like an ass. (lit.)

Labour up to live on.
Work like a horse.
Be beaten like a mule.

注 辛辛苦苦過日子。

1550　掉忌

zaau⁶ gei⁶ *(translit.)*
It is too bad. (lit.)

It is too bad.
It is under taboo.

注 即不妙了的意思。

1551　荳丁

dau⁶ ding¹ *(translit.)*
Small like a bean. (lit.)

Tiny.
Bean-like.
A little chap.

注 表示小得可憐或小傢伙意思，含有輕
蔑的意思。

1552　推三推四

teoi¹ saam¹ teoi¹ sei³ *(translit.)*
Push three and push four. (lit.)

Cook up a lame excuse.
Shift on to somebody else.
Decline with all sorts of excuses.

注 藉詞推卻的意思。

1553　推心置腹

teoi¹ sam¹ zi³ fuk¹ *(translit.)*

Push the heart and place it into another's belly. (lit.)

Place confidence in somebody.

Take somebody into one's confidence.

注 表示絕對信任某人或把某人當作知心人。

1554　推波助瀾

teoi¹ bo¹ zo⁶ laan⁴ *(translit.)*

Push small waves and help big waves. (lit.)

Pour oil on the flames.

Make waves.

1555　推莊

teoi¹ zong¹ *(translit.)*

Push the bank away. (lit.)

Decline.

Shirk one's duty towards...

Beat a retreat.

注 表示拒絕負上責任，逃避對⋯⋯的責任或放棄的意思，參閱"打退堂鼓"條（0469）。

1556　頂包

ding² baau¹ *(translit.)*

Support the package. (lit.)

Take somebody's place by assuming his name.

Pass somebody / something off as...

注 冒名頂替或以假充真。

1557　頂尖

ding² zim¹ *(translit.)*

At the tip-top. (lit.)

To the queen's taste.

Choose the best.

Aim at perfection.

注 表示務求盡善盡美的意思。

1558　頂肚

ding² tou⁵ *(translit.)*

Fill up the abdomen. (lit.)

Have something to appease one's hunger.

Allay one's hunger with something.

注 即充飢，解餓。

1559　頂唔住

ding² m⁴ zyu⁶ *(translit.)*

Cannot support. (lit.)

Cannot stand it.

Fail to put up with...

Be unable to...any more.

注 表示受不了，吃不消或再不能⋯⋯了的意思，參閱"頂唔順"條（1560）。

1560　頂唔順

ding² m⁴ seon⁶ *(translit.)*

Cannot support any more. (lit.)

Cannot stand it.

Fail to put up with...

Be unable to...any more.

注 同"頂唔住"，參閱該條（1559）。

1561　頂硬上

ding² ngaang⁶ soeng⁵ *(translit.)*

Tolerate the torment. (lit.)

Compel oneself to do something against one's own will.

Brace oneself up and bear with it.

注 表示硬着頭皮頂着或忍耐着，忍受着的意思。

1562　頂撞

ding² zong⁶ *(translit.)*

Support and knock against. (lit.)

Offend somebody.

十一畫

Offer an affront to somebody.

🈁指冒犯或當眾侮辱。

1563 頂頭上司

ding² tau⁴ soeng⁶ si¹ *(translit.)*

The boss direct on one's head. (lit.)

One's direct superior.

🈁即直接主管。

1564 頂頭陣

ding² tau⁴ zan⁶ *(translit.)*

Support the heading formation. (lit.)

Set out in anticipation to make arrangements.

Act as a pioneer.

Take the lead.

Be in the van of movement/fight.

🈁指打前站或打頭陣，參閱前篇"打頭陣"條（0481）。

1565 頂頸

ding² geng² *(translit.)*

Support the neck. (lit.)

Squabble with somebody.

Quarrel with somebody.

Refute.

Talk back.

Retort sarcasm for sarcasm.

🈁表示雙方的拌嘴、抬槓或單方的反唇相譏的意思，參閱（2066）"駁嘴"條。

1566 頂檔

ding² dong³ *(translit.)*

Support the stall. (lit.)

Serve as a stopgap.

🈁臨時代替，頂替。

1567 頂籠

ding² lung² *(translit.)*

Support the cage. (lit.)

Fulfil the quota.

Full-loaded.

Full up.

Full house.

Reach the limit.

🈁表示滿額，滿員，滿座，全滿，引伸作齊全。

1568 執二攤

zap¹ ji⁶ taan¹ *(translit.)*

Pick at a second-hand stall. (lit.)

Have/Buy something second hand.

Marry a widow/a non-virgin/a loose woman.

🈁指購買二手貨；娶寡婦或非處女等為妻。

1569 執人口水溦

zap¹ jan⁴ hau² seoi² mei¹/⁵ *(translit.)*

Pick up somebody's mouth water. (lit.)

Take a leaf out of somebody's book.

Say after somebody.

Follow the words of somebody.

Echo somebody.

Echo somebody's nonsense.

🈁人云亦云，拾人牙慧。

1570 執手尾

zap¹ sau² mei⁵ *(translit.)*

Pick up the hand and tail. (lit.)

Deal with the work left over.

Deal with the aftermath of...

🈁指收拾丟下未完的工作或清理善後。相當於"擇魚頭"。

1571 執死雞

zap¹ sei² gai¹ *(translit.)*

Pick up a dead hen. (lit.)

Take what others give up.

Obtain a real bagain.

📕 比喻人棄我取或購得非常便宜的東西，買退票。

1572　執到襪帶累身家

zap[1] dou[2] mat[6] daai[3] leoi[6] san[1] gaa[1] *(translit.)*

The garters picked up implicate the whole wealth. (lit.)

Lose a pound for gaining a penny.

Penny wise and pound foolish.

📕 比喻因小失大。

1573　執笠

zap[1] lap[1] *(translit.)*

Pick a bamboo basket. (lit.)

Shut up the shop.

Go bankrupt.

Close down.

📕 即倒閉的意思。

1574　執番條命

zap[1] faan[1] tiu[4] meng[6] *(translit.)*

Pick back the life. (lit.)

Escape with bare life.

📕 即死裏逃生。

1575　執輸

zap[1] syu[1] *(translit.)*

Pick up a loss. (lit.)

Take no wind out of somebody's sails.

Miss the bus.

Lose an opportunity.

Not to take an immediate action in time.

📕 表示佔下風，吃虧，失去機會或未採取立即行動的意思。

1576　執輸行頭，慘過敗家

zap[1] syu[1] hang[4] tau[4], caam[2] gwo[3]

baai[6] gaa[1] *(translit.)*

It is more distressful not to pack up the baggage in time than it is to ruin a family. (lit.)

It would be disadvantageous not to take an immediate action in time.

📕 譏諷那些行動遲緩而讓人佔了上風的人。

1577　執頭執尾

zap[1] tau[4] zap[1] mei[5] *(translit.)*

Pick odds and ends. (lit.)

Do odd jobs.

📕 指無指定的工作做，做零碎工作。

1578　掟煲

deng[3] bou[1] *(translit.)*

Throw down an earthen pot. (lit.)

Break up.

Break off.

📕 男女因感情破裂而分手的意思，相當於"吹了"。

1579　捩咁嚟

lai[2] gam[3] he[3] *(translit.)*

Busy about. (lit.)

Be all in a muddle.

Make a muddle of something.

Be all in a fluster.

📕 形容狼狽或手足無措的神態。

1580　捩橫折曲

lai[2] waang[4] zit[3] kuk[1] *(translit.)*

Turn round and bend. (lit.)

Swear black is white.

Confound right with wrong.

📕 表示指鹿為馬的意思。

1581　掘尾龍——攪風攪雨

gwat[6] mei[5] lung[2] — gaau[2] fung[1] gaau[2] jyu[5] *(translit.)*

A blunt-tailed dragon — stirring wind and rain. *(lit.)*

The person who stirs up strife.

The person who plays some ones off against one another.

注 指煽風點火的人。

1582 勒時間

laak⁶ si⁴ gaan¹ *(translit.)*

Immediately. (lit.)

All at once.

All of a sudden.

Out of the blue.

注 即忽然間，突然間。

1583 勒實褲頭帶

laak⁶ sat⁶ fu³ tau⁴ daai³ *(translit.)*

Tighten the belt of trousers. (lit.)

Tighten one's belt.

注 暗喻忍受飢餓。

1584 帶花

daai³ faa¹ *(translit.)*

Put on a flower. (lit.)

Stop a bullet.

注 比喻受槍傷或受傷。（多為黑社會人語。）

1585 帶挈

daai³ hit³ *(translit.)*

Look after. (lit.)

Keep an eye on somebody.

Help somebody on.

Guide and support somebody.

注 即關照或提攜。

1586 乾手淨腳

gon¹ sau² zeng⁶ goek³ *(translit.)*

Dry hands and clean feet. (lit.)

Save trouble.

Make a snappy.

In a straightforward way.

With nothing to worry about in the days to come.

注 表示省卻麻煩，直截了當的意思。

1587 乾時緊月

gon¹ si⁴ gan² jyut⁶ *(translit.)*

Dry time and tight months. (lit.)

Be hard up for money.

注 指手頭拮据。

1588 乾塘

gon¹ tong⁴ *(translit.)*

The pool becomes dry. (lit.)

Be in low water.

Fall short of money.

Be penniless.

注 水塘乾涸則無水，以水喻錢，因此 "乾塘" 意即 "不名一文"。

1589 梗板

gang² baan² *(translit.)*

Rigid plank. (lit.)

Be inflexible.

Be as stiff as a poker.

注 表示呆板，死板，或固定不變的意思。

1590 梳起

so¹ hei² *(translit.)*

Comb up. (lit.)

Make up one's mind to marry to no man.

Decide to be an old maid all one's life.

Remain a maid all one's life.

Live in maidenhood all one's life.

注 同 "自梳"，參閱該條（0776）。

1591 斬腳趾避沙蟲

zaam² goek³ zi² bei⁶ saa¹ cung² *(translit.)*

Cut off the toes to avoid siphonworm. (lit.)

十一畫

Trim the toes to fit the shoes.

Abandon the greatest to save the smallest.

Make a sacrifice in order to avoid trouble.

🈁比喻為了避免小麻煩，不惜作較大犧牲。

1592　斬纜

zaam² laam⁶ *(translit.)*

Cut the rope. (lit.)

Break off with somebody.

Make a cle an break with somebody.

Break off relations with somebody / between A and B.

🈁比喻和人一刀兩斷，分手或絕交，參閱 "掟煲" 條（1578）。

1593　軟皮蛇

jyun⁵ pei⁴ se⁴ *(translit.)*

A soft-skinned snake. (lit.)

A person who neither cuts up stiff nor reacts to blames.

A person who acts in a slick way.

🈁比喻對譴責無反應及不易發怒的人或疲疲沓沓，對甚麼都無所謂的人。

1594　專登

zyun¹ dang¹ *(translit.)*

In purpose. (lit.)

Intentionally.

Deliberately.

On purpose.

For a special purpose.

🈁參閱 "特登" 條（1440）。

1595　曹操都有知心友，關公亦有對頭人

Cou⁴ Cou¹ dou¹ jau⁵ zi¹ sam¹ jau⁵, Gwaan¹ Gung¹ jik⁶ jau⁵ deoi³ tau⁴ jan⁴ *(translit.)*

Cou Cou had his bosom friends and Gwaan Gung had his enemies. (lit.)

Cou Cou — the person standing for craftiness.

Gwaan Gung — the person standing for uprightness.

A devil has friends to sup with and a saint has foes worthy of his steel.

🈁比喻壞人有其支持者，而好人也有其反對者。

1596　豉油撈飯 —— 整色水

si⁶ jau⁴ lou¹ faan⁶ — zing² sik¹ seoi² *(translit.)*

Mix cooked-rice with soy sause — making colours. (lit.)

Stand upon one's dignity by intention.

Put on airs.

🈁比喻故作尊嚴或擺架子。

1597　爽手

song² sau² *(translit.)*

Brisk hands. (lit.)

Be generous in giving money / consent / help...to others.

Be as nimble as a squirrel.

Be quick.

Quicken one's hands / steps.

🈁本義為用手觸摸東西時，有軟滑舒服的感覺。但此語為轉義詞形容人慷慨或爽快。這一語有人說成 "手爽"。此外又形容人利索，敏捷。

1598　眼大睇過籠 / 界

ngaan⁵ daai⁶ tai² gwo³ lung⁴ / gaai³ *(translit.)*

The eyes are so big that they see beyond the line. (lit.)

Be too careless to see anything.

注 心粗看不細。

1599 眼中釘

ngaan⁵ zung¹ deng¹ *(translit.)*

The nail in the eye. (lit.)

A thorn in one's flesh.

A pain in the neck.

注 比喻極憎惡而急於除去的事物。

1600 眼火爆

ngaan⁵ fo² baau³ *(translit.)*

The fire of eyes bursts. (lit.)

See red.

Fly into a rage.

注 指看到令人氣憤的事而憤怒。

1601 眼甘甘

ngaan⁵ gam¹ gam¹ *(translit.)*

Look fixedly. (lit.)

Fix one's eyes upon...

Not to take one's eyes off...

注 形容貪婪地，目不轉睛地盯着看的樣子。

1602 眼坦坦

ngaan⁵ taan² taan² *(translit.)*

Show the whites of eyes. (lit.)

In a desperate state.

To an unbearable degree.

To the state of fatigue.

In a situation of complete defeat.

注 照字面看，似和普通話的“翻白眼”意同。但廣東話的含義應為在絕望中，到了難以忍受的地步或處於完全失敗的境地。部分意義和“攤攤腰”相同，參閱該條（2432）。

1603 眼眉毛長過辮

ngaan⁵ mei⁴ mou⁴ coeng⁴ gwo³ bin¹ *(translit.)*

The eyebrows are longer than a pigtail. (lit.)

Be very lazy.

Not to stir a finger.

注 諷刺人懶得動也不動。

1604 眼眉毛雕通瓏

ngaan⁵ mei⁴ mou⁴ diu¹ / tiu¹ tung¹ lung² *(translit.)*

The eyebrows are carved to be tubular. (lit.)

Be up to snuff.

There are no flies on one.

Be sharp-witted.

Have a keen insight into matters.

注 比喻精明，不易受騙或明察秋毫。

1605 眼紅

ngaan⁵ hung⁴ *(translit.)*

Eyes become red. (lit.)

Be jealous of...

Feel envy at...

注 表示妒忌的意思。

1606 眼唔見為伶俐

ngaan⁵ m⁴ gin³ wai⁴ ling⁴ lei⁶ *(translit.)*

Anything that is not seen by eyes is clear / clean. (lit.)

Out of sight, out of mind.

注 相當於“眼不見，心不煩”。

1607 眼冤

ngaan⁵ jyun¹ *(translit.)*

The grievance of eyes. (lit.)

Be disgusted at...

Take an aversion to...

Feel a repugnance to...

注 指看見不好的事物或情景就討厭，反感。

1608 眼掘掘

ngaan⁵ gwat⁶ gwat⁶ *(translit.)*

Keep the eyes fixed. *(lit.)*

Glare hate at somebody.

Stare at somebody with hostility.

🈟 表示以仇恨的眼光或敵意盯着人的意思。

1609 眼斬斬

ngaan⁵ zaam² zaam² *(translit.)*

The eyes wink. (lit.)

Be expressionless.

A dull look passes over one's face.

🈟 指無表情或臉上顯出無可奈何的神色。

1610 眼淺

ngaan⁵ cin² *(translit.)*

The eyes are shallow. (lit.)

Be narrow-minded.

Be intolerant of...

Be jealous of...

Be apt to be moved to tears.

🈟 指人小氣，心胸狹窄，妒忌或易受感動而流淚。

1611 眼睩睩

ngaan⁵ luk¹ luk¹ *(translit.)*

The eyes roll. (lit.)

Look at somebody with angry eyes.

Glower at somebody.

🈟 即怒目而視。

1612 眼噬噬

ngaan⁵ sai⁶ sai⁶ *(translit.)*

The eyes seem to swallow up. (lit.)

Look sideways at somebody in order to prevent him from doing something.

🈟 同"眼矖矖"條（1615）。

1613 眼濕濕

ngaan⁵ sap¹ sap¹ *(translit.)*

The eyes are getting wet. (lit.)

One's eyes are filled with tears.

🈟 眼睛帶着淚花的樣子。

1614 眼闊肚窄

ngaan⁵ fut³ tou⁵ zaak³ *(translit.)*

Eyes are broad but the belly is narrow. (lit.)

Bite off more than one can chew.

🈟 表示貪心不足或心有餘而力不足的意思。

1615 眼矖矖

ngaan⁵ lai⁶ lai⁶ *(translit.)*

Give a signal with eyes. (lit.)

Look sideways at somebody in order to stop him from doing something.

🈟 即斜視着某人意圖制止他做某事。

1616 啞仔食黃連 —— 有苦自己知 / 有口難言

aa² zai² sik⁶ wong⁴ lin⁴ — jau⁵ fu² zi⁶ gei² zi¹ / jau⁵ hau² naan⁴ jin⁴ *(translit.)*

A dumb eats coptis roots — knowing the bitterness by himself.

— having mouth but finding it hard to speak. (lit.)

Swallow the leek.

Have lost one's tongue.

Take the bitter without a word.

🈟 表示難以啟齒。

1617 啞仔食雲吞 —— 心中有數

aa² zai² sik⁶ wan⁴ tan¹ — sam¹ zung¹ jau⁵ sou³ *(translit.)*

A dumb eats stuffed dumplings — his mind knows the number. (lit.)

十一畫

Know what to do.

Know a thing or two.

Know what is what.

注 對事情清楚把握。

1618　晦氣

fui³ hei³ (translit.)

Gloomy air. (lit.)

Show somebody a querulous and
discontent attitude.

Be too querulous and
discontented to be friendly.

注 表示對人不滿及滿腹牢騷的態度。
（廣東人説的"晦氣"和普通話説的
"晦氣"意義不同。）

1619　異相

ji⁶ soeng³ (translit.)

Odd-looking. (lit.)

Unsightly.

Odd-looking.

注 形容人或物難看或樣子古怪。

1620　蛇有蛇路，鼠有鼠路

se⁴ jau⁵ se⁴ lou⁶, syu² jau⁵ syu² lou⁶
(translit.)

Snakes have their won way and
mice also have their way. (lit.)

Gang one's own gait.

Play a lone hand.

Each follows his own bent.

注 表示各有各的打算或各行各是的意
思。

1621　蛇見硫磺

se⁴ gin³ lau⁴ wong⁴ (translit.)

Snakes see sulphur. (lit.)

Everybody has his vanquisher.

Diamond cut diamond.

注 表示各有相克的意思，參閱"一物治
一物，糯米治木蝨"條（0031）。

1622　蛇無頭不行

se⁴ mou⁴ tau⁴ bat¹ hang⁴ (translit.)

A snake cannot crawl without a
head. (lit.)

Without a man in the lead, all
the others move no farther.

注 表示沒有人帶頭，事情難成。

1623　蛇鼠一窩

se⁴ syu² jat¹ wo¹ (translit.)

Snakes and mice live together in
the same den. (lit.)

Gang up with each other.

Be in collusion with each other.

Play booty.

注 朋比為奸的意思。

1624　蛇頭鼠眼

se⁴ tau⁴ syu² ngaan⁵ (translit.)

Snake's head and rat's eyes. (lit.)

Be as crafty as a fox.

Be wily.

注 相當於"鬼頭蛤蟆眼"。

1625　唱衰人

coeng³ seoi¹ jan⁴ (translit.)

Sing somebody to be on the wane.
(lit.)

Paint somebody in dark colour.

Put false colours upon
somebody.

注 公開把人説得一錢不值。

1626　喎咗

wo⁵ zo² (translit.)

All failed. (lit.)

Fell flat.

Fell down.

Fizzled out.

注 表示完全失敗的意思。相當於"告吹
了"。

十一畫

1627　患得患失

waan⁶ dak¹ waan⁶ sat¹ *(translit.)*

Worry about personal gains and losses. (lit.)

Be swayed by considerations of success and failure.

注 沒有得到以前怕得不到，得到後又怕失去。

1628　患難見真情

waan⁶ naan⁶ gin³ zan¹ cing⁴ *(translit.)*

Calamity exposes the true affection. (lit.)

A friend in need is a friend indeed.

Calamity is the true touchstone.

注 苦難最能考驗友情。

1629　啱心水

ngaam¹ sam¹ seoi² *(translit.)*

Suit one's heart. (lit.)

After one's own heart.

After one's fancy.

注 表示合意的意思。參閱"合晒心水"條(0786)及"合晒合尺"條(0787)。

1630　啱啱

ngaam¹ ngaam¹ *(translit.)*

Just. (lit.)

Just as...

Just now.

Only...

注 即剛剛的意思。

1631　啱啱好

ngaam¹ ngaam¹ hou² *(translit.)*

Just right. (lit.)

To the turn of a hair.

Be as right as nails.

注 表示剛好，絲毫不差或十分正確的意思。

1632　啲咁多

di¹ gam³ do¹ *(translit.)*

A little. (lit.)

A little bit.

A wee bit.

注 表示極少，一點點兒，一丁點兒。

1633　啋

coi¹ *(translit.)*

Go with you! (lit.)

Bah!

注 婦女多用以表示嫌棄或斥責的感歎詞，相當於"去你的"。

1634　眾事莫理，眾定莫企

zung³ si⁶ mok⁶ lei⁵ , zung³ deng⁶ mok⁶ kei⁵ *(translit.)*

Neither handle public affairs nor stand at the public place. (lit.)

Put neither your hand between the bark and the tree nor yourself in a bustling place.

Neither poke your nose into everybody's business nor go with the crowd.

注 這是老一輩的"獨善其身"的做人道理，表示不要理人家的事或大眾的事，也不要流連在熱鬧的地方。

1635　崩口人忌崩口碗

bang¹ hau² jan⁴ gei⁶ bang¹ hau² wun² *(translit.)*

A man with hare-lip shuns the bowl with broken brim. (lit.)

Not to stroke somebody's hair the wrong way.

Avoid touching somebody on the raw.

Not to sting somebody to the quick.

注 表示避諱或別觸及人的痛處，相當於

"別當着矮人説短話"。

1636　移礀就船

ji⁴ ham³ zau⁶ syun⁴ *(translit.)*

Move the bund to the ship. (lit.)

If the mountain will not come to Mohammed, Mohammed must go to the mountain.

注 比喻女求男去男子的家中幽會或降貴屈尊去遷就某人。

1637　笨手笨腳

ban⁶ sau² ban⁶ goek³ *(translit.)*

Foolish hands and legs. (lit.)

One's fingers are all thumbs.
A stumblebum.

注 即行動遲鈍。

1638　笨頭笨腦

ban⁶ tau⁴ ban⁶ nou⁵ *(translit.)*

Foolish head and brains. (lit.)

Be block-headed.

注 即頭腦愚笨。

1639　做日和尚唸日經

zou⁶ jat⁶ wo⁴ soeng² nim⁶ jat⁶ ging¹ *(translit.)*

Be a day's monk, chant a day's Buddhist Sutra. (lit.)

Wear through the day.
Be a happy-go-lucky person.
Take a passive attitude towards one's work.

注 相當於"做一天和尚撞一天鐘"。

1640　做世界

zou⁶ sai³ gaai³ *(translit.)*

Do the world. (lit.)

Do an evil deed.
Rob or steal.

注 指為非作歹，幹行兇，偷盜，搶劫等勾當。

1641　做好做醜

zou⁶ hou² zou⁶ cau² *(translit.)*

Be both good and bad. (lit.)

Both coax and coerce.
With an iron hand in a velvet glove.

注 軟硬兼施或又唱紅臉又唱白臉。

1642　做咗人豬仔 / 俾人賣豬仔

zou⁶ zo² jan⁴ zyu¹ zai² / bei² jan⁴ maai⁶ zyu¹ zai² *(translit.)*

Become somebody's piglet / Be sold as a piglet. (lit.)

Be sold / betrayed by somebody.
Be shanghaied into going to... (somewhere).

注 指被人出賣或背叛或被人誘拐去……（地方）。

1643　做咗鬼會迷人

zou⁶ zo² gwai² wui⁵ mai⁴ jan⁴ *(translit.)*

Enchant people after becoming a ghost. (lit.)

Once a beggar is set on horse back, he will work for devils.

注 比喻小人得志便會害人。

1644　做鬼都唔靈

zou⁶ gwai² dou¹ m⁴ leng⁴ *(translit.)*

Even though one becomes a ghost, one does not turn out to be marvellous. (lit.)

Be good-for-naught.

注 形容人毫無長處。

1645　做慣乞兒懶做官

zou⁶ gwaan³ hat¹ ji⁴ laan⁵ zou⁶ gun¹ *(translit.)*

Be too lazy to be an official because of being accustomed to being a beggar. (lit.)

Get used to living in idleness.

注 表示安於目前悠閒自在或懶惰的生活。

1646 做磨心

zou⁶ mo⁶ sam¹ *(translit.)*

Be an axis of a grinder. (lit.)

Be in a dilemma.

Have difficulty in taking the sides with both parties.

Find it difficult to be partial to either side.

Be an arbitrator.

注 處於為難境地，各方的關係不好處理，或作調停人的意思。

1647 做薑唔辣，做醋唔酸

zou⁶ goeng¹ m⁴ laat⁶, zou⁶ cou³ m⁴ syun¹ *(translit.)*

It is not hot if it is used as ginger; it is not sour if it is used as vinegar. (lit.)

It is far from sufficient for something/the purpose.

注 距離所需要的數目太遠（尤指金錢方面）。

1648 做醜人

zou⁶ cau² jan² *(translit.)*

Be a bad person. (lit.)

Be scapegoat.

Carry the can.

Speak for somebody.

注 當捱罵的人或替人説話或辯護。

1649 偷偷摸摸

tau¹ tau¹ mo² mo² *(translit.)*

Act stealthly. (lit.)

On the sly.

Do something under the rose.

Act surreptitiously.

注 即行動鬼祟。

1650 偷龍轉鳳

tau¹ lung⁴ zyun² fung⁶ *(translit.)*

Steal a dragon and change it for a phoenix. (lit.)

Make a secret substitution.

Substitute A for B.

注 比喻以甲換乙。

1651 偷雞

tau¹ gai¹ *(translit.)*

Steal hens. (lit.)

Loaf on the job.

Be idle.

Avail oneself of a leisure moment.

Jery-build.

Scamp the work and stint materials.

注 沒正當理由缺席，開小差，曠課，逃學或偷工減料。

1652 偷雞唔到蝕揸米

tau¹ gai¹ m⁴ dou² sit⁶ zaa¹ mai⁵ *(translit.)*

Try to steal a hen but end up with a loss of a handful of rice. (lit.)

Go for wool and come home shorn.

注 比喻得不到益處，反受損失。

1653 偏心

pin¹ sam¹ *(translit.)*

Slenting-hearted. (lit.)

Be biassed (towards...)

Show partiality to somebody.

注 即對某人偏袒。

1654 兜住

dau¹ zyu⁶ *(translit.)*

Wrap up. (lit.)

Save somebody from embarrassment.

Help somebody out of an

十一畫

awkward position.

Bring about a change of somebody's wrong remarks in order to save his face.

注 表示幫助別人從尷尬局面中解脫或扭轉別人的誤説而挽回他的面子。

1655　兜踎

dau¹ mau¹ *(translit.)*

Be in humble circumstances. (lit.)

Be poverty-striken.

Be shabby in dress.

注 比喻貧困或衣衫襤褸。

1656　兜篤將軍

dau¹ duk¹ zoeng¹ gwan¹ *(translit.)*

Turn around to discover check. (lit.)

Shoot a Parthian arrow.

Rip up the back of somebody.

注 比喻向人背後放暗箭或背後中傷或攻擊。

1657　得寸進尺

dak¹ cyun³ zeon³ cek³ *(translit.)*

Gain an inch and then go for a foot. (lit.)

Gain an inch and then take an ell.

Be greedy for gains.

注 指得一想二。

1658　得上牀掀被冚

dak¹ soeng⁵ cong⁴ hin¹ pei⁵ kam² *(translit.)*

After being permitted to get into bed, one tries to pull a coverlet to cover oneself. (lit.)

Gain an inch and then take an ell.

Be greedy for gains.

注 比喻得寸進尺，貪得無厭。

1659　得米

dak¹ mai⁵ *(translit.)*

Have got the rice. (lit.)

Meet with success.

Achieve one's goal.

注 比喻得手或達到目的。

1660　得把聲

dak¹ baa² seng¹ *(translit.)*

Have only the sound. (lit.)

Go on cackling without laying an egg.

In word but not in deed.

注 諷刺人只會説而不見諸行動。

1661　得些好意須回手

dak¹ se¹ hou² ji³ seoi¹ wui⁴ sau² *(translit.)*

Pull in one's hand after gaining a little profit. (lit.)

One should leave some leeway after having got some advantage.

Stop before going too far.

Not to overdo it.

注 指得到好處便應留有餘地或勸人切勿過分。

1662　得咗

dak¹ zo² *(translit.)*

Have got it. (lit.)

Come off with flying colours.

Meet with success.

注 參閱"得米"（1659）條。

1663　得個吉

dak¹ go³ gat¹ *(translit.)*

Gain an emptiness. (lit.)

Come to nothing.

End up with nothing.

Draw water with a sieve.

注 表示落空或毫無收穫，參閱"筲箕打

十一畫

水"條（2010）。

比喻悔之已晚。

1664 得戚

dak¹ cik¹ *(translit.)*

Get an imperial order. (lit.)

Have one's head swelled by being favoured.

Hold one's head high.

Crow over oneself.

注 洋洋自得，得意忘形的意思。

1665 得啖笑

dak¹ daam⁶ siu³ *(translit.)*

Have a puff of laughter. (lit.)

Laugh out of court.

Carry off with a laugh.

注 即樂一樂。

1666 得棚牙

dak¹ paang⁴ ngaa⁴ *(translit.)*

Have only the haw of teeth. (lit.)

Have a loose tongue.

Wag one's tongue.

注 諷刺人絮絮叨叨地説話，但亦可和 "得把聲"同義，參閱該條（1660）。

1667 得過且過

dak¹ gwo³ ce² gwo³ *(translit.)*

Pass and let oneself pass. (lit.)

Muddle along.

Fair to muddling.

Not to put undue stree on...

注 即草率。

1668 船到江心補漏遲

syun⁴ dou³ gong¹ sam¹ bou² lau⁶ ci⁴ *(translit.)*

It is too late to plug a leak when the boat reaches the midstream. (lit.)

It is too late to mend.

It is too late to repent.

1669 船到橋頭自然直

syun⁴ dou³ kiu⁴ tau⁴ zi⁶ jin⁴ zik⁶ *(translit.)*

When the ship reaches the head of the bridge, it will be naturally straight. (lit.)

Let things slide.

Be submissive to God's will.

Leave it chance.

Don't cross the bridge until you come to it.

注 比喻事到臨頭自然會有辦法，多用於 安慰對方。相當"車到山前必有路"。

1670 船頭慌鬼，船尾慌賊

syun⁴ tau⁴ fong¹ gwai², syun⁴ mei⁵ fong¹ caak⁶ *(translit.)*

Fear to see a ghost at the prow and a thief at the stern. (lit.)

One's heart misgives one about this and that.

Be between the devil and the deep sea.

Get into a hobble.

Be in a cleft stick.

注 表示擔心這樣，又擔心那樣或進退兩 難的意思。

1671 "貪"字變個"貧"

taam¹ zi⁶ bin³ go³ pan⁴ *(translit.)*

The Chinese character "貪" (read 'taam', means 'greed') changes to the character "貧" (read 'pan', means 'poverty'). (lit.)

Grasp all, lose all.

注 借兩個形狀近似的漢字來比喻貪心反 而損失。

1672 貪得無厭

taam¹ dak¹ mou⁴ jim³ *(translit.)*

十一畫

Be too greedy to be insatiable. (lit.)

Be too greedy for gains.

Be as greedy as a hawk.

🈯非常貪心。

1673　貧不與富敵，富不與官爭

pan[4] bat[1] jyu[5] fu[3] dik[6], fu[3] bat[1] jyu[5] gun[1] zaang[1] *(translit.)*

The poor cannot match against the rich;the rich cannot fight against the authorities. (lit.)

Money speaks louder and kings have long arms.

🈯指有錢人和官員往往可以為所欲為。

1674　逢場作興

fung[4] coeng[4] zok[3] hing[3] *(translit.)*

Enjoy oneself for once. (lit.)

Join in the enjoyment on occasion.

🈯碰到一定的場合，湊湊熱鬧，樂呵樂呵。

1675　夠皮

gau[3] pei[2] *(translit.)*

Have enough skin. (lit.)

Just sufficient to cover the cost.

Just sufficient to pay one's expenses.

Have had enough.

It is too much for one.

More than one can...

🈯賺夠消費之用，夠本或多得吃不消了的意思。

1676　麻雀雖小，五臟俱全

maa[4] zoek[3] seoi[1] siu[2], ng[5] zong[6] keoi[1] cyun[4] *(translit.)*

A sparrow is small, but it has all five visera. (lit.)

There is a life in a mussel though it is small.

🈯比喻事物雖小，卻齊全。

1677　麻麻地

maa[4] maa[2] dei[2] *(translit.)*

Rather. (lit.)

Be neither good nor bad.

Exceptionally do one / somebody a favour to...

Make a virtue of necessity.

Be constrained to...

🈯表示尚好，例外地幫一幫忙或裝出非做不可的勉強。

1678　瓷器棺材 ── 不漏汁

ci[4] hei[3] gun[1] coi[4] ─ bat[1] lau[6] zap[1] *(translit.)*

A porcelain coffin — it does not leak juice. (lit.)

A person who haggles over every penny.

A person who profits nobody.

A person who preoccupies his own losses.

🈯比喻精打細算的人，斤斤計較的人或不會給人利益的人。

1679　望天打卦

mong[6] tin[1] daa[2] gwaa[3] *(translit.)*

Wish heaven to cast lots. (lit.)

Be left to the mercy of God.

Wish to be the mercy of God.

By the finger of God.

🈯靠天吃飯，希望上蒼垂憐的意思，參閱 "摩囉差拜神" 條（2221）。

1680　望長條頸

mong[6] coeng[4] tiu[4] geng[2] *(translit.)*

Hope makes a neck longer. (lit.)

Pin one's hopes on...

Hanker after...

Be looking forward to...

🈯表示渴望的意思。

1681　牽腸掛肚

hin¹ coeng⁴ gwaa³ tou⁵ *(translit.)*

Drag intestines and hang abdomen. (lit.)

Feel deep anxiety about somebody.

注 即掛念〔某人〕。

1682　羞家

sau¹ gaa¹ *(translit.)*

Shame the family. (lit.)

For shame!

Shame on you/him...!

Make somebody die of shame.

注 羞，羞人，丟臉的意思。

1683　粗人

cou¹ jan⁴ *(translit.)*

Rough person. (lit.)

A vulgarian.

注 指沒有教養的人。

1684　粗口爛舌

cou¹ hau² laan⁶ sit⁶ *(translit.)*

Rough mouth and rotten tongue. (lit.)

Speak contemptible words.

Speak coarse language.

注 即説下流粗鄙的話。

1685　粗手粗腳

cou¹ sau² cou¹ goek³ *(translit.)*

Thick hands and thick feet. (lit.)

A clumsy person.

Have clumsy fingers.

注 即笨手笨腳。

1686　粗心大意

cou¹ sam¹ daai⁶ ji³ *(translit.)*

Careless mind and big idea. (lit.)

Be inadvertent.

注 不細心，馬馬虎虎。

1687　粗枝大葉

cou¹ zi¹ daai⁶ jip⁶ *(translit.)*

Thick branches and big leaves. (lit.)

Be crude and careless.

Be slapdash.

A sloppy job.

注 做事不認真，不細緻。

1688　粗重工夫

cou¹ cung⁵ gung¹ fu¹ *(translit.)*

Heavy work. (lit.)

Heavy work.

注 即體力勞動較多的工作。

1689　粗茶淡飯

cou¹ caa⁴ daam⁶ faan⁶ *(translit.)*

Bad tea and tasteless cooked rice. (lit.)

Simple fare.

A homely meal.

Fare plainly.

注 即家常便飯。

1690　粗製濫造

cou¹ zai³ laam⁶ zou⁶ *(translit.)*

Rough manufactured and indiscriminately done. (lit.)

Be slipshod in one's work.

Make something in a slipshod way.

注 表示不夠細緻。

1691　粗魯

cou¹ lou⁵ *(translit.)*

Rough. (lit.)

Be rough and rude.

注 指不斯文，動作大。

1692　清官難審家庭事

cing¹ gun¹ naan⁴ sam² gaa¹ ting⁴ si⁶ *(translit.)*

It is hard for an upright official to

十一畫

bring family affairs to trial. (lit.)

Outsiders find it hard to understand the cause of a family quarrel.

注 指外人無法明白別人的家庭糾紛。

1693　添食

tim¹ sik⁶ *(translit.)*

Add more to eat. (lit.)

Ask for one / some more.

Do once more again.

Get an encore.

Give anencore.

注 要多一些，再來一次或重演 / 奏的意思。

1694　混水摸魚

wan⁶ seoi² mo² jyu⁴ *(translit.)*

Grope for fish in turbid waters. (lit.)

Fish in trouble waters.

1695　混吉

wan⁶ gat¹ *(translit.)*

Give trouble. (lit.)

Do something in a haphazard way.

Ask [a shop-assistant] for this and that without making a purchase.

注 表示瞎抓，瞎擺弄或看這樣看那樣而不購買的意思。

1696　混混 / 渾渾噩噩

wan⁶ wan⁶ ngok⁶ ngok⁶ *(translit.)*

Be unintelligent. (lit.)

Be as innocent as a baby.

Be chaotic-headed.

注 表示頭腦渾沌無知的意思。

1697　淨係

zing⁶ hai⁶ *(translit.)*

Only. (lit.)

Alone.

Only.

Merely.

Simply.

注 意和 "單係" 同，參閱該條（1816）。

1698　淘古井

tou⁴ gu² zeng² *(translit.)*

Clean out an ancient well. (lit.)

Marry with a widow lady of great wealth.

注 比喻娶富有的寡婦。

1699　情人眼裏出西施

cing⁴ jan⁴ ngaan⁵ leoi⁵ ceot¹ sai¹ si¹ *(translit.)*

Sai Si comes out of a lover's eyes. (lit.)

Sai Si — one of the four beauties in ancient China.

Love is blind.

Beauty exists in a lover's eyes.

注 表示美麗是沒有標準的，參閱 "冤豬頭都有盟鼻菩薩" 條（1532）。

1700　掂過碌蔗

dim⁶ gwo³ luk¹ ze³ *(translit.)*

Straighter than a sugar-cane. (lit.)

Come off well.

Have something in the bag.

Have not any trouble with...

Take a path strewn with roses.

注 表示一切順利或生活安樂的意思。

1701　寅食卯糧

jan⁴ sik⁶ maau⁵ loeng⁴ *(translit.)*

At the third of the Twelve Earthly Branches (the period of the day from 3 a.m. to 5 a.m.), eat the cereals which are to be earned at the fourth of the twelve Earthly Branches (the period of the day from 5 a.m. to 7 a.m.). *(lit.)*

Anticipate one's wages / income.

Have one's corn in the blade.

😊 即提前使用工資的意思，參閱"先使未來錢"條（0762）。

1702 密底算盤

mat⁶ dai² syun³ pun⁴ *(translit.)*

An abacus with sealed bottom. (lit.)

Penny pincher.

A person who takes much count of every dollar.

😊 比喻精打細算的人。

1703 密斟

mat⁶ zam¹ *(translit.)*

A secret talk. (lit.)

A private conversation.

Talk in secret.

😊 密談。

1704 密實姑娘假正經

mat⁶ sat⁶ gu¹ noeng⁴ gaa² zing³ ging¹ *(translit.)*

A girl of silent disposition has false seriousness. (lit.)

A girl of few words may not be so serious as she should be.

😊 "密實"即沉默寡言的意思。

1705 密鑼緊鼓

mat⁶ lo⁴ gan² gu² *(translit.)*

Beat the gong and drum very fast. (lit.)

The noose is hanging.

Be intense in preparation for an undertaking.

😊 即籌備得如火如荼。

1706 問師姑攞梳 —— 實冇

man⁶ si¹ gu¹ lo² so¹ — sat⁶ mou⁵ *(translit.)*

Ask a nun for a comb — sure to have none. (lit.)

Ask the wrong person for something.

Come to the wrong shop.

😊 相當於"和尚廟裏借梳子 —— 走錯門了"。

1707 屙尿遞草紙

o¹ niu⁶ dai⁶ cou² zi² *(translit.)*

Offer toilet tissue to the one who is discharging one's urine. (lit.)

Offer an unnecessary help.

😊 比喻給予不必要的幫忙。

1708 屙屎唔出賴地硬，屙尿唔出賴風猛

o¹ si² m⁴ ceot¹ laai⁶ dei⁶ ngaang⁶, o¹ niu⁶ m⁴ ceot¹ laai⁶ fung¹ maang⁵ *(translit.)*

Put the blame on the hard ground for failure to defecate and on the strong wind for being unable to discharge one's urine. (lit.)

Bad workmen often blame their tools.

Lay the blame upon somebody / something.

😊 比喻歸咎某人 / 物或怪這怪那。相當於"拉不出屎賴茅房"。

1709 強中自有強中手

koeng⁴ zung¹ zi⁶ jau⁵ koeng⁴ zung¹ sau² *(translit.)*

There is a stronger man among the strong. (lit.)

Catch a tartar.

😊 表示遇到勁敵的意思。

1710 將……一軍

zoeng¹...jat¹ gwan¹ *(translit.)*

Challenge somebody. (lit.)

十一畫

Embarrass somebody.

Lay a complaint against somebody with...

注 表示使某人窘迫或向……告某人一狀的意思。

1711　將心比己

zoeng¹ sam¹ bei² gei² *(translit.)*

Compare oneself with other's heart. (lit.)

Measure another's foot by one's own last.

Measure other's corn by one's own bushel.

注 以己度人的意思。

1712　將佢拳頭扰佢嘴

zoeng¹ keoi⁵ kyun⁴ tau⁴ dam² keoi⁵ zeoi² *(translit.)*

Knock somebody's mouth with his own fist. (lit.)

Pay somebody back in his own coin.

Return like for like.

Turn somebody's battery against himself.

Give somebody a gift of the same value as that he has given out.

注 比喻"以其人之道還治其人之身"，"以子之矛攻子之盾"或用同等價值的禮物回敬。

1713　將計就計

zoeng¹ gai³ zau⁶ gai³ *(translit.)*

Let the plot be the plot. (lit.)

Turn somebody's tricks against him.

1714　將就

zoeng¹ zau⁶ *(translit.)*

Compromise. (lit.)

Make do with...

Put up with...

Accommodate oneself to...

注 勉強適應不滿意的事物或環境。

1715　將錯就錯

zoeng¹ co³ zau⁶ co³ *(translit.)*

Let the mistake be the mistake. (lit.)

Make the best of a bad job.

Make the best of a mistake.

Over shoes over boots.

注 既然錯了，索性利用錯誤去補償的意思。

1716　將 / 攞……嚟教飛

zoeng¹ / lo²...lai⁴ gaau³ fei¹ *(translit.)*

Look for somebody / something to be taught to fly. (lit.)

Put somebody / something to trial.

注 指把某人 / 某物作試驗品。

1717　蛋家婆打仔——唔慌你走得上坦

daan⁶ gaa¹ po² daa² zai² — m⁴ fong¹ nei⁵ zau² dak¹ soeng⁵ taan² *(translit.)*

A Tanka (the boat people of Canton) woman beats her son — not fearing you can run to the sand. (lit.)

Put somebody at the dead end.

Drive somebody to bay.

注 相當於"大缸擲骰子——沒跑兒"，意謂"無路可走"。

1718　蛋家婆打醮——冇壇「彈」

daan⁶ gaa¹ po² daa² ziu³ — mou⁵ taan⁴ *(translit.)*

Tanka women celebrate the feast of 'All Souls' — No altar (no criticism). (lit.)

Be above criticism.

Be beyond reproach.

十一畫

注 蛋家以艇為家，打醮酬神時，限於地方，不能擺設祭壇，"壇"和"彈"同音，借這諧音喻無可批評或指責。

1719　蛋家婆摸蜆——第二篩「世」

daan⁶ gaa¹ po² mo² hin² — dai⁶ ji⁶ sai¹ᐟ³ *(translit.)*

Tanka women grope for clams — until next sieve (generation). (lit.)

Have hope in nine cases out of ten.

Have difficulties in realizing one's aspiration as long as one lives.

注 比喻今生已成絕望，唯有希望來世（第二世）。"世"是"篩"的諧音。

1720　蛋家雞——見水唔得飲

daan⁶ gaa¹ gai¹ — gin³ seoi² m⁴ dak¹ jam² *(translit.)*

The chickens of Tanka — they are unable to drink the water in sight. (lit.)

The person who fails to obtain an advantage in spite of being in a favourable position.

Always have opportunities to near somebody one loves on the sly but never have an opportunity to win her/him.

注 蛋家在艇上養雞，但雞並不因身處近水的地方而能喝到見到的水，因此這俚語在廣義上喻並不因自己身處有利的地位而得到好處，在狹義上則喻雖常有機會接近自己暗中熱戀的人，但從沒有機會得到她（他）。

1721　通天

tung¹ tin¹ *(translit.)*

Open the sky. (lit.)

Expose something without any reserve.

Make no secret of something.

The secret has been let out.

注 表示毫無保留地把事件暴露出來，對事情毫不掩飾或秘密已經泄露了的意思。

1722　通水

tung¹ seoi² *(translit.)*

Let out the water. (lit.)

Give information to somebody.

Disclose secret information.

注 通風報信的意思。

1723　通氣

tung¹ hei³ *(translit.)*

Ventilate. (lit.)

Have more sense than to hinder somebody.

Show somebody every consideration.

注 形容人通情達理得不致於妨礙別人或體貼人。

1724　陸雲庭睇相——冇衰攞嚟衰／冇衰整成衰

luk⁶ wan⁴ ting⁴ tai² soeng³ — mou⁵ seoi¹ lo² lai⁴ seoi¹ / mou⁵ seoi¹ zing² seng⁴ seoi¹ *(translit.)*

A man named Luk Wan Ting had his phylognomy read, — not so poor but pretended to reduce to poverty.

— not in distress but invited the distress himself. (lit.)

Feign oneself to be poor.

Bring disgrace to oneself.

Offer an insult to oneself.

Pocket an insult.

注 軍閥陸雲庭化裝成貧民去找一位享譽甚高的相士看相，目的想考驗那相士的相術，及知自己的前途，詎料該相士一看便看出他不是普通人，於是把他譏諷一番。"冇衰整成衰"意謂扮窮，"冇衰攞嚟衰"意謂被人譏諷或自取其辱。

1725　陳皮

can[4] pei[4] *(translit.)*

Old skin. (lit.)

Dried orange peel.

Old-fashioned.

Be stale.

🈺 "陳皮"本為廣東三寶（陳皮，老薑及禾稈草）之一，是由柑皮曬乾而成，用作藥材。貯藏年份越久價值越高，正由此因，遂轉喻陳舊的或舊式樣。

1726　陳村種

can[4] cyun[1] zung[2] *(translit.)*

The clan of Csan Cyun. (lit.)

A fop with money to burn a hole in his pocket.

🈺 比喻有錢便要花光的人。（陳村為順德縣屬的一小村落）。

1727　陰濕

jam[1] sap[1] *(translit.)*

Both gloomy and wet. (lit.)

Be vicious.

Be insidious.

🈺 形容人狡猾，陰險。

1728　陪太子讀書

pui[4] taai[3] zi[2] duk[6] syu[1] *(translit.)*

Accompany the Crown Prince to study. (lit.)

Bear somebody company.

Do something with somebody for company.

🈺 比喻陪人做某事。

1729　細水長流

sai[3] seoi[2] coeng[4] lau[4] *(translit.)*

A small stream flows long. (lit.)

Waste not, want not.

A bit at a time causes no letup.

🈺 比喻節約，有計劃的用錢可保持不缺。有時也用來比喻經常不間斷地做某事。

1730　細心

sai[3] sam[1] *(translit.)*

Small-hearted. (lit.)

Be tender to attend upon somebody.

Be attentive to somebody / something.

Attend upon somebody with meticulous care.

🈺 表示當心照料或體貼入微的意思。

1731　細佬哥剃頭

sai[3] lou[2] go[1] tai[3] tau[4] *(translit.)*

A small child has his head shaved. (lit.)

Will be ready / finished in no time.

Will soon complete / finish...

🈺 比喻事物很快便準備好 / 完成或很快便完成……（工作）。

1732　細時偷雞，大時偷牛

sai[3] si[4] tau[1] gai[1], daai[6] si[4] tau[1] ngau[4] *(translit.)*

Stealing hens in young days will lead to steal cows in the days of adulthood. (lit.)

Young pilferer, old robber.

A child who maltreats animals in his childhood will become a killer in his young days.

🈺 比喻兒時犯錯，長大成人犯罪。

1733　終須有日龍穿鳳

zung[1] seoi[1] jau[5] jat[6] lung[4] cyun[1] fung[6] *(translit.)*

A dragon will one day marry a
phoenix. *(lit.)*

Every cloud has a silver lining.

Every dog has his day.

Everyone would have a chance to
stand head and shoulder above
others.

Will free oneself from misery one
day.

🈟指人人皆有出頭日。

十二 畫

1734 替死鬼

tai³ sei² gwai² *(translit.)*

*The ghost takes somebody's place
to die. (lit.)*

A whipping boy.

The person who carries the can.

A scapegoat.

🈟比喻代人受過的人，參閱"烏〔黑〕
狗得食，白狗當災"（1466）或"做
醜人"（1648）條。

1735 揸大葵扇

zaa¹ daai⁶ kwai⁴ sin³ *(translit.)*

*Hold a big fan made out of mallow
leaves. (lit.)*

Be a match-maker.

Act as a go-between.

🈟即作媒。在一般人心目中，至少在戲
劇角色的造型上，大凡媒婆都手拿葵
扇，象徵把男女雙方"撥成"（撮
合）。

1736 揸住雞毛當令箭

zaa¹ zyu⁶ gai¹ mou⁴ dong³ ling⁶ zin³
(translit.)

Hold a fowl's feather as an arrow-

token of authority. *(lit.)*

Steal the show of an authoritative
person.

Put on airs.

Bully somebody on other's
power.

🈟即"狐假虎威"，借別人的權勢唬人。

1737 揸頸就命

zaa¹ geng² zau⁶ meng⁶ *(translit.)*

*Grasp the neck to procrastinate
the life. (lit.)*

Bear and forbear to save life.

Suffer from the patience of Job.

Submit to humiliation to cope
with the situation.

🈟忍辱偷生或為應付目前環境而忍氣吞
聲的意思。

1738 揸鐵筆

zaa¹ tit³ bat¹ *(translit.)*

Hold an iron pen. (lit.)

Carry off somebody's lover.

Cut the ground from under
somebody's feet.

Snatch the business from one's
competitor.

🈟比喻奪人的愛人或生意。相當於"挖
牆腳"，參閱"撬牆腳"條（2153）。

1739 揸鑊鏟

zaa¹ wok⁶ caan² *(translit.)*

Hold a frying-spade. (lit.)

Be a cook.

Wake up a heavy sleeper.

🈟指任廚子職位的自嘲説法，但又比喻
喚醒不易起牀的懶人的諧趣語。

1740 捹手唔成勢

laa² sau² m⁴ sing⁴ sai³ *(translit.)*

*Set a hand to something but fail to
make a formation. (lit.)*

十二畫

Be tied up in knots due to lack of preview.

Find it difficult to work in a hopeless mess.

注 棘手，難辦，或在一團糟的情形下，做起來樣樣事都棘手。

1741 揦西

laa² sai¹ *(translit.)*

Rough out something. (lit.)

Scamp one's work.

注 工作馬虎或隨便。

1742 揦屎上身

laa² si² soeng⁵ san¹ *(translit.)*

Grasp manure and bring it on to the body. (lit.)

Invite trouble.

Wake a sleeping dog.

Make a rod for one's own back.

注 比喻自找麻煩或自作自受，參閱"木匠擔枷"條（0277）。

1743 揦起塊面

laa² hei² faai³ min⁶ *(translit.)*

Stretch the face tight. (lit.)

Pull a long face.

注 相當於耷拉着臉。

1744 揦高肚皮

laa² gou¹ tou⁵ pei⁴ *(translit.)*

Lift up the skin of belly. (lit.)

Give the show away.

Expose one's own weak sides.

注 暴露自己弱點的意思。

1745 揦脷

laa² lei⁶ *(translit.)*

Sting the tongue. (lit.)

Haggle over every penny.

Be high-priced.

Open one's mouth wide.

注 比喻因要價過高或成本太高，受不了的意思。

1746 揼堆

dam³ deoi¹ *(translit.)*

Lack of pace. (lit.)

Be both doddery and obtuse.

Be penniless and frustrated.

注 形容老態龍鍾，參閱"論盡"（2210）條，但又表示貧困潦倒的意思。

1747 越搇越出屎

jyut⁶ gam⁶ jyut⁶ teot¹ si² *(translit.)*

The more pressure, the more manure. (lit.)

The more one speaks, the more secret one lets out.

The harder somebody is pressed to say, the more secret he reveals.

注 這俚語可用於主動或被動兩方面，主動意為越講越泄漏多些內幕，被動則意為被迫越越甚，所泄漏的秘密也越多。

1748 越窮越見鬼，肚餓打瀉米

jyut⁶ kung⁴ jyut⁶ gin³ gwai², tou⁵ ngo⁶ daa² se² mai⁵ *(translit.)*

The poorer one is, the more ghosts one sees; one upsets all the rice when one feels hungry. (lit.)

Misfortunes never come singly.

Go from bad to worse.

So much the worse.

注 表示更加糟糕或禍不單行的意思，參閱"屋漏更兼逢夜雨"條（1310）。

1749 趁手

can³ sau² *(translit.)*

Take advantage of the hand. (lit.)

In passing.

At one's convenience.

When it is convenient.
Take the opportunity.

🈲順手或乘機的意思。

1750　提心吊膽

tai⁴ sam¹ diu³ daam² *(translit.)*

Lift up the heart and hang the gall. *(lit.)*

Have one's heart in one's mouth.
Be in a blue funk.
Be on tenterhooks.

🈲形容非常擔心，害怕，慌恐不安。

1751　揭盅

kit³ zung¹ *(translit.)*

Lift up the cover of a teacup. *(lit.)*

Make known.
Bring to light.

🈲即揭鍋或披露。

1752　搵丁

wan² ding¹ *(translit.)*

Look for the foolish ones. *(lit.)*

🈲同"搵老襯"（1754）。

1753　搵……（人）過橋

wan²...gwo³ kiu² *(translit.)*

Look for somebody to walk across the bridge. *(lit.)*

Make use of somebody as a cat's paw.
Play upon somebody.

🈲用不正當手段利用別人達到自己目的。

1754　搵老襯

wan² lou⁵ can³ *(translit.)*

Look for a dupe. *(lit.)*

Attract somebody to rise to a bait.
Fool somebody into doing something.

Fool money out of somebody.
Make somebody fall into dupery.

🈲騙人；使人上當受騙；使人吃虧。

1755　搵笨

wan² ban⁶ *(translit.)*

Look for the foolish ones. *(lit.)*

🈲騙人；騙；討便宜。同"搵丁"（1752）。

1756　搵得嚟，使得去

wan² dak¹ lai⁴, sai² dak¹ heoi³ *(translit.)*

Find it and spend it. *(lit.)*

Easy come, easy go.
Light come, light go.

🈲比喻金錢"來的容易去的快"。

1757　煮到嚟就食

zyu² dou³ lai⁴ zau⁶ sik⁶ *(translit.)*

Eat what is cooked for. *(lit.)*

Submit oneself to the circumstances.
Adapt oneself to what happens to one.
Submit oneself to one's own fate.

🈲使自己適應環境，對所發生的事處之泰然或順應天命的意思。

1758　煮重米

zyu² cung⁶ mai⁵ *(translit.)*

Cook much more rice. *(lit.)*

Paint somebody in the darkest colour.
Lodge an exaggerated complaint against somebody.

🈲參閱"煮鬼"條（1759）。

1759　煮鬼

zyu² gwai² *(translit.)*

Boil a ghost. *(lit.)*

Rip up the back of somebody.
Lay complaints against somebody.

十二畫

Paint somebody in dark colour behind his back.

注 表示在人背後指控的意思，參閱 "煮重米"（1758）及 "督背脊"（1974）條。

1760　揞／撳住良心

am³ zyu⁶ loeng⁴ sam¹ *(translit.)*

Cover the good heart with a hand. (lit.)

Be conscience-smitten.

Have the conscience to do something.

注 表示自受良心責備或竟敢不顧良心而厚着臉皮去做……。

1761　揞／撳住嘴嚓笑

am³ zyu⁶ zeoi² lai⁴ siu³ *(translit.)*

Cover the mouth with a hand and laugh. (lit.)

Laugh at somebody in one's sleeve.

注 暗暗譏笑某人的意思。

1762　報效

bou³ haau⁶ *(translit.)*

Offer service. (lit.)

Be free of charge.

注 即免費。

1763　惡人先告狀

ok³ jan⁴ sin¹ gou³ zong²ᐟ⁶ *(translit.)*

An evil man brings in an indictment first. (lit.)

Take a preemptive step.

注 即先發制人，參閱 "使銅銀夾大聲" 條（1083）。

1764　惡人自有惡人磨

ok³ jan⁴ zi⁶ jau⁵ ok³ jan⁴ mo⁴ *(translit.)*

An ill person will be ill-treated by other evil persons. (lit.)

Diamond cut diamond.

Devils devil devils.

1765　惡有惡報

ok³ jau⁵ ok³ bou³ *(translit.)*

Evil doings recompense evil returns. (lit.)

Sow the wind and reap the whirl-wind.

Curses come home to roost.

Recompense somebody for his misdeeds.

1766　惡死能登

ok³ si²／sei² nang⁴ dang¹ *(translit.)*

Give a fierce look. (lit.)

Be ferocious／vicious.

注 即惡狠狠的。

1767　惡到凸堆

ok³ dou³ dat⁶ deoi¹ *(translit.)*

Be ferocious to the top degree. (lit.)

Play the bully.

注 形容恃強凌弱的姿態。

1768　惡恐人知便是大惡

ok³ hung² jan⁴ zi¹ bin⁶ si⁶ daai⁶ ok³ *(translit.)*

The ferociousness that is hidden is a great piece of ferociousness. (lit.)

The sins dissembled are deadly sins indeed.

1769　惡揢揢

ok³ tan⁴ tan⁴ *(translit.)*

Fierce. (lit.)

Look ferocious (usually of women).

注 （樣子）很兇的（常指女人）。

1770　黃皮樹鷯哥——唔熟唔食

wong⁴ pei⁴ syu⁶ liu⁴ go¹ — m⁴ suk⁶ m⁴ sik⁶ *(translit.)*

The mynah on a whampee tree — It does not eat the unripe fruit. (lit.)

The person who swindles money out of his familiar friends.

The person who sells a pup to his close friends.

🈯 歇後語中的 "熟" 字和 "食" 字，都是語帶雙關的。意為專欺騙熟人或向熟人推銷次品。

1771　黃泡髧熟

wong⁴ paau¹ dam³ suk⁶ *(translit.)*

Yellow and swollen. (lit.)

A swollen face with yellow complexion.

🈯 形容人面目浮腫或臉色萎黃。

1772　黃面婆

wong⁴ min⁶ po²ᐟ⁴ *(translit.)*

A yellow-faced woman. (lit.)

One's old woman.

One's wife.

🈯 指男人自稱自己妻子的謔稱。

1773　黃馬褂

wong⁴ maa⁵ gwaa³ *(translit.)*

A yellow riding jacket. (Yellow riding jackets were given to royalties by the emperors of the T'sing Dynasty as a mark of honour.) (lit.)

The clerk related to the boss.

🈯 比喻和老闆有親屬關係的職員。由於 "黃馬褂" 為清代的一種官服，巡行扈從大臣，如御前大臣、內大臣、內廷王大臣、侍衛什長皆例准穿黃馬褂，有功大臣也特賜穿着，表彰他的功勳，因而得這口頭語。

1774　黃腫腳 —— 不消蹄「提」

wong⁴ zung² goek³ — bat¹ siu¹ tai⁴ *(translit.)*

Dropsy leg — the swelling of the trotter is not dispersed. (lit.)

Make no mention of it.

(The character ' 蹄 ' which means 'trotter' is the homonym to the character ' 提 ' which means 'mention'.)

🈯 借 "蹄" 字諧音作 "提" 用，意為不必提了。

1775　黃綠醫生

wong⁴ luk⁶ ji¹ sang¹ *(translit.)*

Yellow and green doctor. (lit.)

A charlatan.

🈯 指庸醫，不學無術的大夫，醫術不高明，靠行醫騙錢。

1776　散水

saan³ seoi² *(translit.)*

Disprese the water. (lit.)

Escape in every direction.

Everybody takes his way.

🈯 表示各自逃走的意思，參閱 "田雞過河" 條（0520）。

1777　散更鑼

saan³ gaang¹ lo⁴ *(translit.)*

The last alarm of a watchman's gong. (lit.)

A flourish of trumpets.

A horn-blower.

The person who bandies something about.

(The last alarm of watchman's gong is beaten at dawn, indicating that it is going to be daybreak)

🈯 比喻到處散播謠言或其他消息的人（尤指婦女）。往時廣東省各地有更夫報時，夜裏每隔一段時間便敲小鼓及小鑼，到黎明時，密敲小鑼，意味天明，這便是 "散更鑼"。

1778　散檔

saan³ dong³ *(translit.)*

Disassemble the stall. (lit.)

Disband.

Break off the partnership with somebody.

Make trouble.

Undermine somebody.

注 表示散夥或結束，但亦表示搗亂或拆台的意思。

1779　揸金龜

dap³ gam¹ gwai¹ *(translit.)*

Knock a gold tortoise. (lit.)

Put the arm on one's wife.

Ask one's wife for money.

注 指向妻子要錢花。

1780　揩

saang² *(translit.)*

Brush. (lit.)

Brush up something with sand / sand-paper / cleanser...

Rebuke somebody.

Dress down somebody.

注 表示用沙之類刷洗（本義），但引伸表示訓斥某人的意思。

1781　揩牛黃

saang² ngau⁴ wong⁴ *(translit.)*

Seize cow bezoa. (lit.)

Bully somebody and snatch something from him.

注 強取或強佔他人的東西；勒索。

1782　揩到（人）鑞鑞睖

saang² dou³ ... laap³ laap³ ling³ *(translit.)*

Brush...to shine brightly. (lit.)

Scathingly denounce somebody.

Sharply dress somebody down.

注 痛斥某人一頓或狠狠地揍某人一頓的意思。

1783　朝上有人好做官

ciu⁴ soeng⁶ jau⁵ jan⁴ hou² zou⁶ gun¹ *(translit.)*

It is easy to be an official if one has a friend at court.(lit.)

Make convenience of a friend at court.

注 自己的朋友有了地位或權力自己總得個方便或辦事容易。

1784　朝種樹，晚剝板

ziu¹ zung³ syu⁶, maan⁵ gaai³ baan² *(translit.)*

Plant trees in the morning and cut them into planks in the evening. (lit.)

Live from hand to mouth.

Live beyond one's means.

注 比喻不足溫飽或朝食晚糧。

1785　喪家狗

song³ gaa¹ gau² *(translit.)*

Homeless dog. (lit.)

Be in a state of anxiety.

Be seized with fear.

注 比喻失魂落魄或惶惶不可終日的人。（"喪"字廣東人多誤讀為song¹音。）

1786　棋高一着

kei⁴ gou¹ jat¹ zoek⁶ *(translit.)*

One move ahead. (lit.)

Be a stroke above somebody.

注 表示比對手高明。

1787　棋差一着

kei⁴ caa¹ jat¹ zoek⁶ *(translit.)*

Make a careless move. (lit.)

Lose a move to somebody.

注 表示不小心走錯一步。

1788 棋逢敵手

kei⁴ fung⁴ dik⁶ sau² *(translit.)*

Meet a rival in the chess tournament. (lit.)

Be well-matched.

Nip and tuck.

🈯 旗鼓相當或技藝不相上下的意思。

1789 棚尾拉箱

paang⁴ mei⁵ laai¹ soeng¹ *(translit.)*

Drag trunks at the end of a shed. (lit.)

Come to a disgraceful end.

Meet with an ignominious fate.

🈯 指遭遇並不光榮的下場。粵劇演員叫演出的地方為"戲棚"。如在演出時，開面，做手或唱工偶有出錯，便被對粵劇有認識的觀眾大喝倒彩，而這個演員就要下台，靜悄悄地由後台（棚尾）拉箱（搬走衣箱的意思）而去了。

1790 硬晒軚

ngaang²ᐟ⁶ saai³ taai⁵ *(translit.)*

The steer becomes stiff. (lit.)

Bring to a deadlock.

Be immovable.

🈯 指事情鬧僵了，完全沒希望了。但又形容動彈不得。

1791 虛浮

heoi¹ fau⁴ *(translit.)*

Be both void and floating. (lit.)

Be impractical.

Be superficial.

🈯 表示膚淺或不實際的意思。

1792 量地官

loeng⁴ dei⁶ gun¹ *(translit.)*

An official of measuring land. (lit.)

Be out of job.

A job hunter.

Be unemployed.

A person looking for an employment.

A person without a job.

🈯 失業者的幽默解嘲語。

1793 貼錯門神

tip³ co³ mun⁴ san⁴ *(translit.)*

Stick the paper portrait of door gods in the wrong ways. (lit.)

There is no love between them.

Be at odds with each other.

Turn one's back upon somebody.

Be at loggerheads with each other.

🈯 比喻彼此不和，互相仇視或互相敵對，相當於"反貼門神"。（按："門神"的正確貼法為面對面左右分貼的。）

1794 貼錢買難受

tip³ cin⁴ maai⁵ naan⁶ sau⁶ *(translit.)*

Pay out money to buy calamity to suffer. (lit.)

Pay for troubles.

🈯 比喻付出代價，反惹麻煩。

1795 睇人口面

tai² jan⁴ hau² min⁶ *(translit.)*

Look at somebody's mouth and face. (lit.)

Consult somebody's wishes / pleasure.

Be dependent on other's pleasure.

Be slavishly dependent.

🈯 看人臉色行事或仰仗他人。

1796 睇小

tai² siu² *(translit.)*

Look small. (lit.)

Look down on somebody.

Despise somebody / something.

Belittle somebody / something.

十二畫

注 即小看或輕視。

1797　睇水

tai² seoi² *(translit.)*

Watch water. (lit.)

Keep watch.

Take a sharp lookout.

注 把風，放風。

1798　睇化

tai² faa³ *(translit.)*

See the solution of life. (lit.)

Understand one's life thoroughly.

Awaken to life.

Realize why life should be so.

注 表示看透了世事的意思。相當於〝看透了〞。

1799　睇白／睇死

tai² baak⁶／tai² sei² *(translit.)*

See the white. / See the death. (lit.)

Can anticipate that...

It is to be expected that...

According to expectation,

Assert that...

Stand to one's assertion that...

注 斷定，意料到……或正如所料的意思。（〝睇白〞多用於事後表示自己在事情發生前早就料到。〝睇死〞則帶有輕視態度於事前所作的斷定。）

1800　睇穿

tai² cyun¹ *(translit.)*

See through. (lit.)

Gain an insight [into...]

注 表示對於……看得一清二楚的意思。

1801　睇起

tai² hei² *(translit.)*

See up. (lit.)

Regard somebody with special favour.

Take a bright view of somebody.

注 表示對某人瞧得起。

1802　睇唔過眼

tai² m⁴ gwo³ ngaan⁵ *(translit.)*

Not agree to the eyes. (lit.)

Cannot bear the sight of...

Frown upon...

注 表示看不過去；有看見不公平的事氣不過的意思。

1803　睇衰

tai² seoi¹ *(translit.)*

Look at the wane. (lit.)

Look down on somebody.

Despise somebody.

Belittle somebody.

注 蔑視，看不起，小看。大意和〝睇小〞相同。但分別處為〝睇小〞可用於人或物，而〝睇衰〞則只限用於人。

1804　睇差一皮

tai² caa¹ jat¹ pei⁴ *(translit.)*

Give a wrong look. (lit.)

Commit an error in judgement.

Form a wrong estimation of somebody／something.

注 表示判斷錯誤的意思，參閱〝有眼無珠〞條（0687），〝走眼〞條（0851）及〝跌眼鏡〞（1811）各條，語出自〝番攤〞（賭博的一種）。

1805　睇開啲嘞！

tai² hoi¹ di¹ laa¹ *(translit.)*

See it open! (lit.)

Don't mind it!

Turn a blind eye to it!

注 這是叫人〝不要計較〞或〝裝看不見好了〞的一句口頭語。

1806　睇嚟湊

tai² lai⁴ cau³ *(translit.)*

See the condition. *(lit.)*

It depends on the situation.

注 看着辦，根據情況而定。

1807 睇餸食飯，睇燭喃嘸〈謨〉

tai² sung³ sik⁶ faan⁶, tai² zuk¹ naam⁴ mo⁴ *(translit.)*

Watch the dainties to eat cooked-rice and watch the candle-sticks to say 'Namah' (Sanskrit, meaning 'to trust in Buddha). (lit.)

Cut one's coat according to one's cloth.

Make both ends meet.

Live with one's means.

注 表示量入為出的意思，參閱"度住屎窟裁褲"（1270）條。

1808 喱啦

li¹ / lei¹ laa¹ *(translit.)*

Shoot off the mouth. (lit.)

Run off at the mouth.

Have a loose tongue.

Be fond of gossip.

Be nosy.

注 多嘴，順口開河，愛講閒話或多管閒事的意思。

1809 跌咗個橙，執番個桔

dit³ zo² go³ caang², zap¹ faan¹ go³ gat¹ *(translit.)*

Drop an orange but pick up a tangerine in return. (lit.)

Make up on the roundabouts what one loses on the swings.

Lose at sunrise and gain at sunset.

注 比喻"失之東隅，收諸桑榆"。

1810 跌倒搲番揸沙

dit³ dou² laa² faan¹ zaa⁶ saa¹ *(translit.)*

Stumbled but pretended to pick up

a handful of sand. *(lit.)*

Invent a lame excuse to save face in spite of failure / making mistakes.

Put one's fault in the right side.

注 比喻失敗或做錯也不承認，措詞來挽回面子或"文過飾非"。

1811 跌眼鏡

dit³ ngaan⁵ geng²/³ *(translit.)*

Drop the spectacles. (lit.)

Have an error in judgement.

注 相當於"走了眼"，參閱"走眼"（0851），"有眼無珠"（0687）及"睇差一皮"（1804）各條。

1812 跛腳鷯哥自有飛來蜢

bai¹ goek³ liu¹ go¹ zi⁶ jau⁵ fei¹ loi⁴ maang² *(translit.)*

A lame mynah naturally has grasshoppers flying to it. (lit.)

God tempers the wind to the shorn lamb.

注 指呆人有呆福。

1813 單刀直入

daan¹ dou¹ zik⁶ jap⁶ *(translit.)*

Enter straight with a single knife. (lit.)

Come straight to the point.

Speak out without beating about the bush.

注 直截了當地說出目的，參閱"開門見山"（1898）條。

1814 單手獨拳

daan¹ sau² duk⁶ kyun⁴ *(translit.)*

Single hand and lone fist. (lit.)

Pull a lone oar.

注 表示無人協助，單獨去做的意思。

1815 單身寡仔

daan¹ san¹ gwaa² zai² *(translit.)*

Single body and widower boy. (lit.)

Be a single man / a bachelor.

Remain unmarried.

A celibate.

注 即單身漢。

1816　單係

daan¹ hai⁶ *(translit.)*

Only. (lit.)

Alone.

Only.

Merely.

Simply.

注 表示光是，只是等意思，參閱 "淨係" 條（1697）。

1817　單料銅煲

daan¹ liu² tung⁴ bou¹ *(translit.)*

The water-boiler made of the thinnest plate copper. (lit.)

The person who instantly makes friends with a stranger.

The person who takes a stranger for an old friend at the first meeting.

注 指跟陌生人一見如故的人，尤指女性。

1818　單眼仔睇榜——一目了然

daan¹ ngaan⁵ zai² tai² bong² — jat¹ muk⁶ liu⁵ jin⁴ *(translit.)*

A single-eyed guy looks at the list of successful candidates — one eye makes clear. (lit.)

See with half an eye.

See at a glance.

Be clear at a glance.

注 "亞單睇榜" 的另一說法，參閱（1018）該條。

1819　單單打打

daan¹ daan¹ daa² daa² *(translit.)*

Dash and dash and beat and beat. (lit.)

Satirize and make a mock of somebody.

Pour ridicule on somebody. / Talk at somebody.

Make oblique accusations at somebody.

注 指不明言地諷刺或嘲笑，指雞罵狗或指桑罵槐，參閱 "指住禿奴罵和尚" 條（1170）及 "靠諦" 條（2199）。

1820　單筷子批（即攪拌）豆腐——攪喎晒

daan¹ faai³ zi² fak³ dau⁶ fu⁶ — gaau² wo⁵ saai³ *(translit.)*

Stir bean curd with a single chopstick — it becomes muddy. (lit.)

Make a mess of things.

Muddle things up.

注 比喻把事情弄糟。

1821　喺口唇邊

hai² hau² seon⁴ bin¹ *(translit.)*

At the edge of lips. (lit.)

Have something at the tip of one's tongue.

注 指一時想不起。

1822　喺乞兒兜揦飯食

hai² hat¹ ji¹ dau¹ laa² faan⁶ sik⁶ *(translit.)*

Snatch cooked-rice to eat out of a begging bowl. (lit.)

Rob the poor.

Juice the hay.

Squeeze wool for water.

注 指打窮人的主意或壓榨窮人。

1823　喺孔夫子面前賣文章

hai² hung² fu¹ zi² min⁶ cin⁴ maai⁶

man⁴ zoeng¹ *(translit.)*

Sell literary works before the face of Confucius. (lit.)

Teach one's grandmother how to suck eggs.

Display one's slight skill in the presence of an expert.

🈟即"班門弄斧"。

1824　喺門角落頭燒炮仗

hai² mun⁴ gok³ lok¹ tau² siu¹ paau³ zoeng² *(translit.)*

Let off fireworks at the corner of the door. (lit.)

All dressed and nowhere to go.

🈟比喻炫耀自己的光彩不得其法。

1825　喺沉

ngam⁴ cam⁴ *(translit.)*

Be wordy. (lit.)

Be long-winded.

Keep on murmuring.

🈟形容人絮叨或多怨言。

1826　買水嗽嘅頭

maai⁵ seoi² gam² ge³ tau² *(translit.)*

Be like the head of a mourning son who is buying water for his dead father. (lit.)

Be crestfallen.

Be dejected.

Sing the blues.

🈟指垂頭喪氣的神態。（舊時俗例父母死後，長子必到附近河邊，投入銅錢，取些河水為屍體抹臉，這便是"買水"，在去"買水"途中，身穿孝服，垂頭流涕，痛失至親，自不待言了。）

1827　買生不如買熟

maai⁵ saang¹ bat¹ jyu⁴ maai⁵ suk⁶ *(translit.)*

Buying from a stranger is not like

buying from a familiar. (lit.)

Feel secure to make a purchase in a familiar shop.

🈟指在熟識的店買東西較可靠。

1828　黑口黑面

hak¹ hau² hak¹ min⁶ *(translit.)*

Black-mouthed and black-faced. (lit.)

Look displeased.

Nurse a grievance.

🈟形容人滿臉不高興的樣子或心懷不滿的神色。

1829　無孔不入

mou⁴ hung² bat¹ jap⁶ *(translit.)*

Not to enter where there is no hole. (lit.)

Seize every opportunity.

🈟表示把握每一個機會的意思，含貶義。

1830　無功不受祿

mou⁴ gung¹ bat¹ sau⁶ luk⁶ *(translit.)*

Not to get a reward for not having merit. (lit.)

Refuse to be paid for doing nothing.

🈟表示沒有功勞不接受賞賜。

1831　無名小卒

mou⁴ ming⁴ siu² zeot¹ *(translit.)*

A nameless soldier. (lit.)

A mere nobody.

🈟指不見經傳的小人物。

1832　無私顯見私

mou⁴ si¹ hin² gin³ si¹ *(translit.)*

In spite of being not selfish, the selfish motives are clearly seen. (lit.)

Reveal oneself's own guilty

十二畫

conscience in spite of being irrelative with the trouble.

🈯 表示事件雖和自己無關，但亦不經心地流露出自己的心虛的意思。

1833　無事不登三寶殿

mou⁴ si⁶ bat¹ dang¹ saam¹ bou² din⁶ *(translit.)*

If one had nothing, one would not go up to the temple-hall of Buddhist Trinity. (lit.)

Have an axe to grind.

🈯 比喻沒有事不上門。

1834　無事生非

mou⁴ si⁶ saang¹ fei¹ *(translit.)*

Cause trouble out of nothing. (lit.)

Make trouble out of nothing.

🈯 無緣無故挑起事端，製造麻煩。參閱"無風三尺浪"（1838）條。

1835　無事忙

mou⁴ si⁶ mong⁴ *(translit.)*

Busy for nothing. (lit.)

Make much ado about nothing.
Be busy with nothing.

🈯 表示忙於正務以外的事。

1836　無事獻殷勤，非奸即盜

mou⁴ si⁶ hin³ jan¹ kan⁴, fei¹ gaan¹ zik¹ dou⁶ *(translit.)*

When somebody pays attentions to you without any cause, he is either an artful villain or a thief. (lit.)

Too much solicitous hospitality without any cause would be considered as an ill deed.

🈯 指有人無緣無故對你好，即懷有不軌企圖。

1837　無官一身輕

mou⁴ gun¹ jat¹ san¹ hing¹ / heng¹

(translit.)

It makes the body lighter to have no office. (lit.)

Without burdens, without worries.
Free from office, free from care.

🈯 比喻一旦卸下責任，輕鬆得多。

1838　無風三尺浪

mou⁴ fung¹ saam¹ cek³ long⁶ *(translit.)*

Three-foot-high waves rise without wind. (lit.)

Invent a baseless slander.
Make trouble out of nothing.

🈯 參閱"無事生非"（1834）條。

1839　無風不起浪

mou⁴ fung¹ bat¹ hei² long⁶ *(translit.)*

There are no waves without wind. (lit.)

There is no smoke without fire.
Nothing is stolen without hands.
Every why has its wherefore.

🈯 比喻事出有因，參閱"冇檳榔唔嚼得出汁"（0339）條。

1840　無聊賴

mou⁴ liu⁴ laai⁶ *(translit.)*

Have not any resources. (lit.)

Feel bored.
Be dispirited.
Idle away one's time / days.

🈯 無聊或無事可幹而虛度時光。

1841　無情白事

mou⁴ cing⁴ baak⁶ si⁶ *(translit.)*

Have not anything. (lit.)

Without reason or cause.
All of a sudden.

🈯 表示無緣無故或忽然間的意思，參

閱 "無端端"（1845）, "無端白事"
（1844）及 "無嘮嘮"（1842）各條。

1842　無嘮嘮

mou⁴ naa¹ naa¹ *(translit.)*

Have not any hints. (lit.)

Without reason or cause.

All of a sudden.

🈯 參閱 "無端端"（1845）, "無端白事"
（1844）及 "無情白事"（1841）各條。

1843　無債一身輕

mou⁴ zaai³ jat¹ san¹ hing¹ / heng¹
(translit.)

*It makes the body lighter to have
no debts. (lit.)*

Out of debt, out of burden.

🈯 比喻一旦沒有債務，輕鬆得多。

1844　無端白事

mou⁴ dyun¹ baak⁶ si⁶ *(translit.)*

Have not any hints. (lit.)

Without reason or cause.

All of a sudden.

🈯 參閱 "無端端"（1845）, "無情白事"
（1841）及 "無嘮嘮"（1842）各條。

1845　無端端

mou⁴ dyun¹ dyun¹ *(translit.)*

Have not any clues. (lit.)

Without reason or cause.

All of a sudden.

🈯 參閱 "無端白事"（1844）, "無情
白事"（1841）及 "無嘮嘮"（1842）
各條。

1846　無端端發達

mou⁴ dyun¹ dyun¹ faat³ daat⁶ *(translit.)*

Suddenly become rich. (lit.)

Strike oil.

Shake the pagoda tree.

🈯 忽然發了大財的意思。

1847　無聲狗，咬死人

mou⁴ sing¹ / seng¹ gau² , ngaau⁵ sei²
jan⁴ *(translit.)*

*Noiseless dog bites a man to
death. (lit.)*

**A dumb's bite is worse than a
barking dog's.**

**A man of no words gives it
somebody hot.**

🈯 比喻不聲不響使用陰謀的人最可怕。

1848　無氈無扇，神仙難變

mou⁴ zin¹ mou⁴ sin³, san⁴ sin¹ naan⁴
bin³ *(translit.)*

*Even a benignant spirit cannot
change without a blanket and a
fan. (lit.)*

**No one can make bricks without
straw.**

**No one can make a silk purse out
of a sow's ear.**

🈯 比喻巧婦難為無米之炊。

1849　筍嘢

seon² je⁵ *(translit.)*

A very cheap thing. (lit.)

A real bargain.

**A job with wide margin of
profits.**

🈯 比喻好東西，真便宜的東西或利潤大
的工作。

1850　順口

seon⁶ hau² *(translit.)*

Smoothen the mouth. (lit.)

Read smoothly.

🈯 表示（字句或文章等）啷啷上口而易
讀的意思。

1851　順水人情

seon⁶ seoi² jan⁴ cing⁴ *(translit.)*

The human nature with the

downstream. (lit.)

The favour done at one's
convenience.

🈯即順便的幫忙。

1852　順水推舟

seon⁶ seoi² teoi¹ zau¹ *(translit.)*

Push a boat with the downstream.
(lit.)

Make use of an opportunity to
win one's end.

Take advantage of the tide to...

Take advantage of the tide to
refuse somebody's request.

🈯指趁着機會做……參閱＂順風駛悝＂
條（1855），但亦表示乘機推卻他人
的請求的意思。

1853　順手

seon⁶ sau² *(translit.)*

At hand. (lit.)

Be handy.

With ease.

Without extra trouble.

Carry on with doing something.

Right after doing something.

🈯表示順便，方便，跟着做……或接着
做……的意思。

1854　順手牽羊

seon⁶ sau² hin¹ joeng⁴ *(translit.)*

Lead away the goat at hand. (lit.)

Go on the scamp.

Make away with something.

Make free with something.

Take something off on the sly.

🈯即乘人不備，順手拿走東西的行為。

1855　順風駛悝

seon⁶ fung¹ sai² lei⁵ *(translit.)*

Make sails in the favourable wind.
(lit.)

Trim the sails.

Take advantage of the
opportunity to do something.

Grasp at an opportunity.

🈯順着趨勢行事。參閱＂順水推舟＂條
（1852）。

1856　順眼

seon⁶ ngaan⁵ *(translit.)*

Agree to the eyes. (lit.)

Be pleasing to the eyes.

Be pleasant to look at...

🈯表示看起來悦目的意思。

1857　順得「德」人

seon⁶ dak¹ jan² *(translit.)*

Yes man. (lit.)

A person who always says yes to
everyone.

A person who never refuses.

A person who always complies
with what he is asked to do.

🈯龍山和龍江本為順德縣屬下的鄉鎮，
但龍江鄉人和龍山鄉人從不承認他們
的鄉鎮是隸屬於順德縣。所以有＂兩
龍不認順＂的一句話。但順德鄉人則
常以＂順德人＂為自豪。＂德＂和＂得＂
為一音之轉，意義便成＂能夠順人意
的人＂的意思了。

1858　順得哥情失嫂意

seon⁶ dak¹ go¹ cing⁴ sat¹ sou² ji³
(translit.)

Obey elder brother's will but lose
the idea of sister-in-law. (lit.)

Find it hard to be partial to
either side of the two.

🈯左右為難。

1859　順喉

seon⁶ hau⁴ *(translit.)*

Smoothen the throat. (lit.)

十二畫

Be mild to the throat.

注 形容味醇的（指煙酒等）。

1860　順攤

seon⁶ taan¹ *(translit.)*

Be easy. (lit.)

Be smooth.

Can be dealt with without a hitch.

Be running smoothly / without a hitch.

注 表示容易應付的（人）或順當（事）的意思。

1861　傍友

bong⁶ jau² *(translit.)*

A dependant. (lit.)

A hanger-on.

A person sponging upon his friend / boss.

注 指食客或依賴朋友或上司生活的人。

1862　飲咗門官茶

jam² zo² mun⁴ gun¹ caa⁴ *(translit.)*

Have drunk the tea offered to the god of door. (lit.)

Split one's sides with laughter.

Always wear a smiling face.

注 即笑口常開。

1863　飲頭啖湯

jam² tau⁴ daam⁶ tong¹ *(translit.)*

Drink the first sip of soup. (lit.)

Gain the initial advantage.

Take a first sip of somebody's soup.

注 比喻獲得他人尚未得到的好處，相當於“試頭水”。

1864　腌尖

jim¹ zim¹ *(translit.)*

Find faults. (lit.)

Strain at a gnat.

Split hairs over something.

Pick and choose.

Pick hole in something.

注 愛挑剔的或好吹毛求疵的。

1865　腌尖腥悶

jim¹ zim¹ seng¹ mun⁶ *(translit.)*

Be hard to please. (lit.)

Be hard to please.

Be choosey.

Pick and choose.

注 指難以取悅的或因愛挑剔，太講究而令人討厭的。

1866　腌悶

jim¹ mun⁶ *(translit.)*

Be vexed. (lit.)

Vex oneself.

Be upset.

注 表示獨自煩惱或心煩的意思。如說對方為“腌悶”時，則為“腌尖腥悶”的簡略語，見 1865 條。

1867　猴急

hau⁴ gap¹ *(translit.)*

The monkey hurries. (lit.)

Be of a hasty disposition.

Be impetuous.

注 指心急或性急，相當於“急性子”。

1868　猴擒

hau⁴ kam⁴ *(translit.)*

The monkey snatches. (lit.)

注 同“猴急”（1867）。

1869　詐型

zaa³ jing⁴ *(translit.)*

Feign. (lit.)

Put on an act.

Play the fool.

注 即裝模作樣。

十二畫

1870　詐假意

zaa³ gaa¹ ji¹ *(translit.)*

Pretend to be true. (lit.)

Make believe.

Feign oneself to be / to do something.

Make a joke.

Be but a joke.

注 假裝或鬧着玩的意思。

1871　詐嬌

zaa³ giu¹*(translit.)*

Pretend to be pampered. (lit.)

Pretend to get angry at displeasure.

Look somewhat displeased.

Behave like a spoiled child.

注 即"撒嬌"。

1872　詐諦

zaa³ dai³ *(translit.)*

Pretend to know nothing. (lit.)

Feign oneself to be ignorant of something.

Make a pretence of ignorance.

注 假裝，裝作，相當於"裝蒜"。

1873　就嚟

zau⁶ lai⁴ *(translit.)*

Come soon. (lit.)

Coming.

Just a second.

注 答覆對方的催促時説的口頭語，表示快要來了。

1874　就嚟⋯⋯

zau⁶ lai⁴... *(translit.)*

Will... soon. (lit.)

Will / Shall ... quite / very soon.

注 當後面接上動詞時，意為快要⋯⋯了，例如"佢就嚟搬屋咯"（他快要搬家了）或"就嚟落雨喇"（天快要

十二畫

1875　着起龍袍唔似太子

zoek³ hei² lung⁴ pou⁴ m⁴ ci⁵ taai³ zi²
(translit.)

Not to look like the Crown Prince in spite of putting on an emperor's robe. (lit.)

A beggar in a dress-suit still looks like a beggar.

注 比喻一個無才無貌或才貌不出眾的人，無論怎樣打扮或處於任何地位，也仍是庸才，難登大雅。

1876　着緊

zoek⁶ gan² *(translit.)*

Care for. (lit.)

Pay too much attention to...

Give one's mind to...

Care for...

Be worried about...

注 表示對人特別關心或焦慮的意思。

1877　着數

zoek⁶ sou³ *(translit.)*

Profit oneself from something. (lit.)

Gain extra advantage.

Take the lead in doing something.

Be favoured.

Be in a favourable situation.

Be reasonable in price.

Get one's money's worthwhile.

注 表示獲得額外利益，在行動上佔優勢，處於有利地位或合算的意思。

1878　善財難捨，冤枉甘心

sin⁶ coi⁴ naan⁴ se², jyun¹ wong² gam¹ sam¹ *(translit.)*

It is difficult to give money for philanthropy, but pleased to spend it in a wrong way. (lit.)

Be reluctant to give money to some good purposes, but ready to play ducks and drakes with it.

注 比喻寧揮霍也不願花錢花得有意義。

1879　善靜

sin[6] zing[6] *(translit.)*

Good and silent. (lit.)

Be kind and silent.

注 善良且沉靜的意思。

1880　惗善

nam[4] sin[6] *(translit.)*

Soft and kind. (lit.)

Be good and kind.

Be of an even temper.

注 表示善良或性情平和。

1881　勞氣

lou[4] hei[3] *(translit.)*

Labour the breath. (lit.)

Fly into a temper.

Show temper.

注 即勞神，動氣的意思。

1882　勞嘈

lou[4] cou[4] *(translit.)*

Be angry and noisy. (lit.)

Make noisy clamour.

Get busy about...

Be eager about...

注 大吵大鬧，生氣或急於⋯⋯的意思。

1883　湊啱

cau[3] ngaam[1] *(translit.)*

By any chance. (lit.)

Happen to de something.

In the nick of time.

As luck would have it.

注 剛好，湊巧或恰巧的意思，有時廣東人把“湊蹺”和“湊啱”互相換用。

1884　渣嘢

zaa[2] je[5] *(translit.)*

Poor thing. (lit.)

An article of poor quality.

Be low-graded.

Be low-levelled.

注 參閱“流嘢”條（1519）及“二打六”條（0088）。

1885　滋油

zi[1] jau[4] *(translit.)*

Slow at movement. (lit.)

Act or speak leisurely and unhurriedly.

注 指談吐及行動慢條斯理的。不慌不忙，悠然自得。

1886　滋油淡定

zi[1] jau[4] daam[6] ding[6] *(translit.)*

Slow and calm at movements. (lit.)

A slow coach.

Of phlegmatic temperament.

注 指從容不迫的態度，亦即“慢條斯理”的意思。

1887　滋陰／滋微

zi[1] jam[1]／zi[1] mei[1] *(translit.)*

Nourish the negative element in the body./Nourish the slightest. (lit.)

Pinch pennies.

Haggle over every penny.

注 表示精打細算或斤斤計較的意思。

1888　補鑊唔見枳

bou[2] wok[6] m[4] gin[3] zat[1] *(translit.)*

While mending a frying-pan, one loses a cotton-cork. (lit.)

Find oneself in a fix.

Be in a tight corner.

Be all in a fluster.

注 比喻狼狽或手足無措。鑊即炒菜鍋。

十二畫

從前用以炒菜的鍋為生鐵製的。佛山
為產地，用破了可以修補。廣州佛山
兩地，常有鑄鑊的退休工人轉業上
街替人補鑊，其法是把鐵沙燒熔後，
先用布紮成的布塞（枳）放在要補的
地方下面，再把鐵漿倒在上面，再用
另一布塞（枳）把鐵漿壓平，俟其冷
卻，便告修好。如果在這工序上失去
布枳，情形怎樣，可以想見了。

1889　開刀

hoi¹ dou¹ *(translit.)*

Open knife. (lit.)

Perform an operation on a patient.

Fleece somebody of his money.

Cut down.

Reduce.

Fire somebody. (of workers or staff)

Dismiss somebody. (-do-)

🈺 表示在病人身上動手術（本義），向
人敲竹槓，勒索金錢，或裁減或開除
的意思。

1890　開大價

hoi¹ daai⁶ gaa³ *(translit.)*

Open a big price. (lit.)

Open one's mouth wide.

1891　開口及着脷

hoi¹ hau² gap⁶ zoek⁶ lei⁶ *(translit.)*

Bite the tongue as soon as the mouth is opened. (lit.)

Cause offence to somebody as soon as one begins to speak.

Talk at somebody as soon as one starts talking.

🈺 指一開口便觸怒或諷刺某人。

1892　開口埋口都話……

hoi¹ hau² maai⁴ hau² dou¹ waa⁶...
(translit.)

Whenever opening and shutting the mouth, say that... (lit.)

Whenever one speaks, one says that...

Always sing the same old tune that...

🈺 老是説……的意思。

1893　開天索價，落地還錢

hoi¹ tin¹ saak³ gaa³, lok⁶ dei⁶ waan⁴ cin⁴ *(translit.)*

One opens the sky to ask for a price and another comes down to the ground to cut the charge. (lit.)

Drive a hard bargain over something.

🈺 指賣方要價很高，而買方則給予低價
的一種討價還價行為。相當於“瞞天
要價，就地還錢”。

1894　開心見誠

hoi¹ sam¹ gin³ sing⁴ *(translit.)*

Open the heart to show sincerity. (lit.)

Show one's card on the table.

Be open-hearted.

Wear one's heart upon one's sleeve.

🈺 表示開誠相見或毫不隱瞞的意思，參
閱“開明車馬”條（1896）及“擺到
明”條（2356）。

1895　開古

hoi¹ gu² *(translit.)*

Reveal the story. (lit.)

Make known.

Reveal the answer to the riddle.

Let the cat out of the bag.

🈺 表示揭曉，揭謎底或揭露秘密。參閱
“揭盅”條（1751）。

1896 開明車馬

hoi[1] ming[4] geoi[1] maa[5] *(translit.)*

Apparently move the chariot and horse. (lit.)

Be open-hearted.

Wear one's heart upon one's sleeve.

Lay one's card on the table.

注 説明意圖。參閱 " 開心見誠 " 條（1894）及 " 擺到明 " 條（2356）。

1897 開夜車

hoi[1] je[6] ce[1] *(translit.)*

Drive a night train. (lit.)

Work late into the night.

Burn midnight oil.

注 參閱 " 佷起牀板 " 條（1359）。

1898 開門見山

hoi[1] mun[4] gin[3] saan[1] *(translit.)*

Opening the door, one sees the mountain. (lit.)

Come straight to the point.

Not to mince one's words.

Not to put too fine a point on it.

Put it bluntly.

注 參閱 " 單刀直入 " 條（1813）。

1899 開荒牛

hoi[1] fong[1] ngau[4] *(translit.)*

A bull opening up wasteland. (lit.)

A person who does pioneering work.

注 比喻開基創業的先驅者。

1900 開埋井俾人食水

hoi[1] maai[4] zeng[2] bei[2] jan[4] sik[6] seoi[2] *(translit.)*

Excavate a well for somebody to drink water. (lit.)

Do pioneering work with great labour but let somebody sit with folded arms and enjoy the results.

注 比喻努力創業，但任人坐享其成。

1901 開啱……嗰樋

hoi[1] ngaam[1]...go[2/3] lung[5] *(translit.)*

Open the very trunk of somebody. (lit.)

Hit somebody's fancy.

Be after somebody's fancy.

To somebody's liking.

Hit one's very ability.

注 正合某人心意或正是某人的所長的意思。

1902 開通

hoi[1] tung[1] *(translit.)*

Be opened and ventilated. (lit.)

Be liberal.

Be enlightened.

注 即開明或不守舊。

1903 開齋

hoi[1] zaai[1] *(translit.)*

Break fast. (lit.)

Conclude an initial transaction of the day.

Get an initial winning after losing a lot.

注 表示達成一天的第一宗交易或輸了不少錢後才第一次贏錢的意思，參閱 " 發市 " 條（1909）。

1904 開籠雀

hoi[1] lung[4] zoek[3/2] *(translit.)*

The bird in the opened cage. (lit.)

Talk away.

Wag one's tongue.

注 一開口便滔滔不絕。

1905 閒閒地

haan[4] haan[4] dei[2] *(translit.)*

十二畫

Easily. (lit.)

Easily.

Casually.

Without any difficulties.

Without making an effort.

It is a cinch that...

🈲表示輕而易舉地，隨隨便便地或沒問題地的意思。

1906　韌皮

ngan⁶ pei⁴ *(translit.)*

Tough-skinned. (lit.)

Naughty.

Mischievous.

Disobedient.

🈲皮，頑皮或調皮。參閱＂跳皮（調皮）＂條（1990）但又含有不服從的意義。

1907　發木獨

faat³ muk⁶ duk⁶ *(translit.)*

Be inflexible. (lit.)

Be in a trance.

Look like an idiot.

🈲發愕或發呆的意思，參閱＂發吽哣＂條（1911）。

1908　發毛

faat³ mou¹ *(translit.)*

Grow hair. (lit.)

Go mouldy.

🈲即發霉。

1909　發市

faat³ si⁵ *(translit.)*

Expand the market. (lit.)

Conclude an initial transaction of the day.

Get an initial winning after losing a lot.

🈲即＂開市＂或＂開齋＂，參閱該條（1903）。

1910　發矛

faat³ maau⁴ *(translit.)*

Raise a spear with anger. (lit.)

Fly into a rage.

Go off the hooks with anger.

🈲指人因過於衝動而不顧一切，紅了眼。參閱＂發啷厲＂條（1913）。

1911　發吽哣

faat³ ngau⁶ dau⁶ *(translit.)*

With a silly look (lit.)

Be in a trance.

Look like an idiot.

🈲發愕，發呆。參閱＂發木獨＂條（1907）。

1912　發吟發話

faat³ ngam⁴ faat³ waa²ᐟ⁶ *(translit.)*

Issue words. (lit.)

Talk rubbish.

Talk nonsense.

🈲即説廢話或胡説八道。參閱＂發噏風＂條（1916）。

1913　發啷厲

faat³ long¹ lai² *(translit.)*

Raise an anger. (lit.)

Suddenly fly into a rage.

Go off the hooks with anger.

Suddenly fly into temper with anger.

🈲突然發脾氣，大發雷霆。

1914　發盟憎

faat³ mang² zang² *(translit.)*

Be displeased with oneself. (lit.)

Quarrel with one's own shadow.

🈲指莫明其妙地自己生自己的氣。

1915　發夢冇咁早

faat³ mung⁶ mou⁵ gam³ zou² *(translit.)*

It is too early to be in a dream. (lit.)

It is not the time for somebody to
talk nonsense / to rave.
Not to have a fond dream in the
day time.

🈁 即別説夢話。

1916　發噏風

faat³ ngap¹ fung¹ *(translit.)*
Issue the wind. (lit.)
Talk nonsense.
Throw the bull.
Talk through one's hat.

🈁 胡説八道，胡言亂語。

1917　發窮惡

faat³ kung⁴ ok³ *(translit.)*
Raise an anger of poverty. (lit.)
Be angered by poverty.

🈁 因窮而心境不好，發脾氣來發泄。

1918　發錢寒

faat³ cin² hon⁴ *(translit.)*
Shiver with the cold of money. (lit.)
Be infatuated with money.

🈁 財迷心竅，想錢想瘋了。

1919　發爛渣

faat³ laan⁶ zaa² *(translit.)*
Make dregs become ferment. (lit.)
Disregard one's dignity.
Be reckonless of consequences.

🈁 這是比較新一點的口頭語，意謂不顧
尊嚴或不顧後果。

1920　幾大就幾大

gei² daai² zau⁶ gei² daai² *(translit.)*
*How big is how big. / Not to care
how big it is. (lit.)*
For good or for evil.
In for a penny, in for a pound.
Rain or shine.

🈁 無論如何或不顧一切。

1921　幾乎

gei¹ fu⁴ *(translit.)*
Almost. (lit.)
Almost.
Nearly.
By a hair's breadth.

1922　幾係㗎

gei² hai⁶ gaa³ *(translit.)*
Considerably. (lit.)
It is a little too much to bear.
It is too much to cope with.
It is hard to bear.
It is quite an ordeal.

🈁 表示"有些那個"，"夠甚麼的"，"夠
受的"或"夠勁兒"的意思。用於表
達已經達到相當程度，但甚麼程度又
不明言，例如説"呢間酒家收費都幾
係㗎"（夠高了），又或"今日行咗好
遠路，幾係㗎"（夠受了）等等。

1923　幾係幾係，五郎救弟

gei² hai⁶ gei² hai⁶, ng⁵ long⁴ gau³ dai⁶
(translit.)
*It was hard to bear when Brother
V saved his younger brother. (lit.)*
**It is considerably / fairly cold
today.**

🈁 這句口語真是令人難解的，原來意為
"今天多麼冷啊"。"五郎"為坊間小
説"楊門女將"或劇目"楊家將"中
的"楊五郎"，故事家喻戶曉，至於為
甚麼竟轉義成為"今天很冷"則無從
考證了。

1924　幾難至得……

gei² naan⁴ zi³ dak¹... *(translit.)*
*Have difficulties before gaining...
(lit.)*

🈁 和"幾難先至……"同義，參閲該條
（1925）。

十二畫

1925　幾難先至……

gei² naan⁴ sin¹ zi³... *(translit.)*

Have difficulties before... (lit.)

Have a hard time before...

Meet with great difficulty before...

注 即好容易才……。

十三　畫

1926　搭沉船

daap³ cam⁴ syun⁴ *(translit.)*

Make the ship sink. (lit.)

One's bad luck implicates others.

The person whose bad luck causes others to suffer a loss.

注 比喻招致別人損失的不祥的人，參閱"陀衰家"條（1156）。

1927　搭單

daap³ daan¹ *(translit.)*

Join hands. (lit.)

Take advantage of somebody's convenience to ask him to do something.

Join as a partner.

Join in a bet.

注 乘着別人之便請他也做……，搭夥或參加賭注的意思。

1928　搭錯賊船

daap³ co³ caak⁶ syun⁴ *(translit.)*

Wrongly take a pirate ship. (lit.)

Be misled to suffer a loss.

Tread in somebody's wrong steps.

注 因被誤導而招致損失或"跟錯風"的意思。

1929　搭錯線

daap³ co³ sin³ *(translit.)*

Get in touch with the wrong line. (lit.)

Dial the wrong number.

Misunderstand what somebody means and give an irrelevant answer.

注 本指撥錯電話號碼，但引伸比喻誤會別人意思而答非所問。

1930　搏一搏

bok³ jat¹ bok³ *(translit.)*

Gamble for once. (lit.)

Take a risk.

Risk the jump.

注 表示冒一冒險的意思。

1931　搏命

bok³ meng⁶ *(translit.)*

Fight for life. (lit.)

Make every effort.

For dear life.

注 即拚命。

1932　搏唔過

bok³ m⁴ gwo³ *(translit.)*

Not worth to bet. (lit.)

It is not worth while running such a risk.

注 表示不值得冒險的意思。

1933　搏亂

bok³ lyun⁶ *(translit.)*

Make use of the confusion. (lit.)

Fish in trouble water.

Take advantage of the confused situation.

注 即混水摸魚，參閱該條（1694）。

1934　搏懵

bok³ mung² *(translit.)*

Try to gain a muddle of something. (lit.)

Hope for an advantage by
making use of somebody's
negligence.

注 即利用別人不留神，不警惕而得到好
處。相當於"鑽空子"。

1935 萬事起頭難

maan⁶ si⁶ hei² tau⁴ naan⁴ *(translit.)*

*It is difficult to begin the head of
ten thousand things. (lit.)*

**It is difficult to begin a new
business.**

1936 萬事俱備，只欠東風

maan⁶ si⁶ keoi¹ bei⁶, zi² him³ dung¹
fung¹ *(translit.)*

*Ten thousand things are all ready
to wait for the eastern wind.
(lit.)*

Ready to the last gaiter button.
**All is ready except what is
crucial.**

注 表示一切均已做好準備，只差最後一
個重要條件。

1937 萬無一失

maan⁶ mou⁴ jat¹ sat¹ *(translit.)*

*There is not a miss in ten thousand
times. (lit.)*

There is no risk to worry about.
Be as sure as a surefooted horse.

注 絕對不會出差錯。

1938 萬變不離宗

maan⁶ bin³ bat¹ lei⁴ zung¹ *(translit.)*

*Ten thousand changes cannot get
rid of the origin. (lit.)*

**Myriads of changes base
themselves on the origin.**

注 無論形式怎樣千變萬化，但最基本的
東西沒有變或無論事情怎樣變化其宗
旨（目的）不變。

1939 落力

lok⁶ lik⁶ *(translit.)*

Put physical strength to. (lit.)

Spare no effort.
Make an effort.
With one's strength.
Tooth and nail.

注 表示努力，認真，盡所能或賣力的意
思。

1940 落井下石

lok⁶ zeng² haa⁶ sek⁶ *(translit.)*

*Drop a stone on somebody that
has fallen into a well. (lit.)*

**Persecute somebody while he is
down.**

注 比喻趁別人遭遇麻煩或不幸時再加以
迫害。

1941 落手

lok⁶ sau² *(translit.)*

Place the hand. (lit.)

Put one's hand to the plough.
Set one's hand to...
Begin / Start.
Lay hands on somebody.

注 下手，着手開始或對……動武的意
思。

1942 落手打三更

lok⁶ sau² daa² saam¹ gaang¹ *(translit.)*

*Begin to beat the third interval on
the drum. (lit.)*

Begin with a wrong move.
**Put one's foot in one's own
mouth at the start.**

注 比喻一開始便出錯。

1943 落手落腳

lok⁶ sau² lok⁶ goek³ *(translit.)*

Put hands and feet. (lit.)

Do something oneself.

Do something with / by hands.

🈂️表示親自去做或用手去做（指有別於機器）的意思。

1944　落形

lok⁶ jing⁴ *(translit.)*

Put down the body. (lit.)

Become thin.

Bet emaciated.

🈂️表示嚴重消瘦以致變了樣兒。

1945　落住屎窟吊頸

lok⁶ zyu⁶ si² fat¹ diu³ geng² *(translit.)*

Hang oneself with one's hips supported by a net. (lit.)

Handle everything with great care.

Make two bites at a cherry.

🈂️參閱 "過夾吊頸" 條（1998）。

1946　落雨賣風爐——越擔越重

lok⁶ jyu⁵ maai⁶ fung¹ lou² — jyut⁶ daam¹ jyut⁶ cung⁵ *(translit.)*

Sell earthen stoves in the rain — the longer they are carried on a shoulder, the heavier they become. (lit.)

One's burden becomes heavier and heavier.

Be heavy-laden day by day.

🈂️意思是表示一個人所承擔的責任，一天重過一天。

1947　落雨擔遮——顧前唔顧後

lok⁶ jyu⁵ daam¹ ze¹ — gu³ cin⁴ m⁴ gu³ hau⁶ *(translit.)*

Raise an umbrella in the rain — care for the front not for the back (lit.)

Pay no regard to the future.

Be regardless of the consequence.

🈂️比喻不理將來或不顧後果。

1948　落狗屎

lok⁶ gau² si² *(translit.)*

Drop dog's manure. (lit.)

It rains dogs and cats.

🈂️形容滂沱大雨。

1949　落訂

lok⁶ deng⁶ *(translit.)*

Put a downpayment. (lit.)

Pay down.

Pay the deposit.

🈂️給訂金。

1950　落面

lok⁶ min² *(translit.)*

Put the face down. (lit.)

Lose face.

Be disgraced.

🈂️即丟臉。

1951　落……棚牙

lok¹... paang⁴ ngaa⁴ *(translit.)*

Pull down the jaws of teeth of somebody. (lit.)

Draw somebody's teeth.

Make somebody lose face.

Bring somebody down a peg or two.

Sheer off somebody's plume.

🈂️打掉（某人的）傲氣；殺（某人的）威風。

1952　落……（某人）嘅面

lok⁶ ... ge³ min² *(translit.)*

Put... (somebody's)... face down. (lit.)

Bring disgrace on somebody.

Make somebody lose face.

🈂️表示使某人丟臉。

1953　落膈

lok⁶ gaak³ *(translit.)*

Down the diaphragm. (lit.)

Stick to somebody's / one's fingers.

Line one's own pockets.

Misappropriate.

注 原指吃東西後休息片刻，讓食物在胃裏穩定下來的意思，此處引伸為侵吞款項的意思。

1954 落嘴頭

lok[6] zeoi[2] tau[4] *(translit.)*

Lay down mouth-head. (lit.)

Go about selling an idea.

Persuade somebody into doing something.

Fawn upon somebody.

注 表示遊説或奉承的意思。

1955 損手爛腳

syun[2] sau[2] laan[6] goek[3] *(translit.)*

Injure the hands and spoil the feet. (lit.)

Suffer heavy losses.

注 比喻遭受重大損失。

1956 鼓氣袋

gu[2] hei[3] doi[2/6] *(translit.)*

The bellows full of air. (lit.)

A man of few words.

A man of reticence.

Be uncommunicative.

注 比喻不愛交際而又沉默寡言的人。

1957 搗亂

dou[2] lyun[6] *(translit.)*

Beat a mess. (lit.)

Make trouble.

Cause a disturbance.

注 表示製造麻煩。

1958 搬弄是非

bun[1] lung[6] si[6] fei[1] *(translit.)*

Carry right and wrong about. (lit.)

Tell tales out school.

注 指蓄意挑撥雙方或在他人背後亂加評論，以引起紛爭。

1959 搶手

coeng[2] sau[2] *(translit.)*

Seize hands. (lit.)

Be most welcome to everybody.

Win popularity.

Be very popular with everybody.

Be sold like hot cakes.

注 比喻暢銷，受人歡迎。

1960 搶眼

coeng[2] ngaan[5] *(translit.)*

Snatch eyes. (lit.)

Dazzle the eyes.

Be dazzling and resplendent.

Offer attractions.

Attract attention.

注 表示顯眼；奪目或吸引人。

1961 撳 / 揿地游水

gam[6] dei[6] jau[4] seoi[2] *(translit.)*

Press on the ground to swim. (lit.)

Play safe.

Play for safety.

Go about steadily and surely.

注 表示不做冒險的事。

1962 撳 / 揿鷓鴣

gam[6] ze[3] gu[1] *(translit.)*

Press a partridge. (lit.)

Take somebody at advantage to practice extortion.

注 指乘人一時疏忽來進行敲詐的行為。

1963 勢利

sai[3] lei[6] *(translit.)*

Have blind faith in power and profits. (lit.)

Be snobbish.

注 表示諂上欺下的意思。

1964　塘水滾塘魚

tong⁴ seoi² gwan² tong⁴ jyu⁴ *(translit.)*

Pool water boils the fish in the same pool. (lit.)

Members of the same group gain profits from each other.

注 比喻自相謀取利益。

1965　塘底特

tong⁴ dai² dak⁶ *(translit.)*

The stick at the bottom of a pool. (lit.)

The person who shows himself while he is in low water or otherwise who covers his tracks.

注 水塘底的木杵，水乾時才見，以水喻錢，因此借喻沒有錢時便露面，否則便不易被人找到的人。

1966　塘邊鶴

tong⁴ bin¹ hok⁶ᐟ² *(translit.)*

The cane looking for food at the edge of a pool. (lit.)

The person who hastens to make away with his winnings / gains.

注 比喻一有所獲便立即離去的人，尤指在賭博方面。

1967　搓得圓撳得扁

co¹ dak¹ jyun⁴ gam⁶ dak¹ bin² *(translit.)*

Can be rolled into a ball and pressed flat. (lit.)

Be as mild as a dove.

Be amiable.

注 形容人性情溫和，和藹可親。

1968　搲爛塊面

we² / waa² laan⁶ faai³ min⁶ *(translit.)*

Scratch the face and make it become rotten. (lit.)

Fly in the face of dignity.

Have the cheek to do something.

Have no sense of shame.

注 抓破了臉皮或不顧羞恥的意思。

1969　靳度

gan³ dou⁶ *(translit.)*

Be miserly. (lit.)

Be grudging.

Be very calculating.

注 指斤斤計較。

Be scheming.

注 表示靳而不予，善為自己打算或工心計的意思。

1970　想話……

soeng² waa⁶… *(translit.)*

Want to… (lit.)

Be just going to...

Intend to...

注 即打算……或正要……（後接動詞）。

1971　碰啱

pung³ ngaam¹ *(translit.)*

Bump right against. (lit.)

Coincide with...

By a curious coincidence.

By chance.

As luck would have it.

注 意為“碰巧”，參閱“撞〔到〕正”（2159）及“撞啱”條（2162）。

1972　電燈膽——唔通氣

din⁶ dang¹ daam² — m⁴ tung¹ hei³ *(translit.)*

a lamp bulb — not ventilate. (lit.)

Not to stand to sense.

注 比喻人不通情達理或不知情識趣。

1973　零舍……

ling⁴ se³... *(translit.)*

Especially... (lit.)

Extraordinarily.

Particularly.

Especially.

注 即特別或分外。（通常後接形容詞或
副詞。）

1974　督背脊

duk¹ bui³ zek³ *(translit.)*

Pierce the back. (lit.)

Rip up the back of somebody.

**Speak ill of somebody behind his
back.**

注 即背後説人壞話，參閲"煮鬼"條
（1759）。

1975　督眼督鼻

duk¹ ngaan⁵ duk¹ bei⁶ *(translit.)*

Pierce eyes and nose. (lit.)

Irritate to the eyes.

Have a thorn in one's flesh.

**Detest to see
somebody / something.**

注 視作眼中釘的意思。

1976　當時得令

dong¹ si⁴ dak¹ ling⁶ *(translit.)*

Be seasonable. (lit.)

Be in season.

Be the main trend of today.

Win popularity.

注 表示合時令的，當時風行的或當紅的
意思。

1977　當堂

dong¹ tong⁴ *(translit.)*

All at once. (lit.)

On the spot.

Red-handed.

At once.

Right away.

Immediately.

注 表示當場，就地或馬上，立即的意思。

1978　當黑

dong¹ hak¹ *(translit.)*

Meet the black. (lit.)

Be down on one's luck.

Be out of luck.

注 比喻倒霉或倒運。

1979　賊公計，狀元才

caak⁶ gung¹ gai³, zong⁶ jyun⁴ coi⁴
(translit.)

*The trick of thieves and the talent
of 'zong jyun' (lit.)*

Know a trick worth two of that.

Each exercises his own wit.

注 比喻有更妙的方法或各顯才能。

*'Zong Jyun' — a title conferred on
the one who came first in the
highest imperial examination in
Ming and Tsing Dynasties.*

1980　賊亞爸

caak⁶ aa³ baa¹ *(translit.)*

Father of thieves. (lit.)

A thief of thieves.

**A person who extorts money
from rascals.**

注 指賊中之賊或專向發不義之財的人敲
詐的人。

1981　賊佬試砂煲

caak⁶ lou² si³ saa¹ bou¹ *(translit.)*

*A thief tries an earthen tea-pot.
(lit.)*

Put forth a feeler.

Pry about the reaction of others.

Make a trial beforehand.

注 表示試探別人的反應或先來一試的意思。

1982　賊眉賊眼

caak⁶ mei⁴ caak⁶ ngaan⁵ *(translit.)*

Thievish eyebrows and eyes. (lit.)

Thievish looking.

Look like a thief.

注 形容鬼鬼祟祟的樣子。

1983　賊過興兵

caak⁶ gwo³ hing¹ bing¹ *(translit.)*

Raise an army after the thief has gone. (lit.)

Lock the stable door after the horse is stolen.

注 表示事後才謀補救或防範的意思。

1984　盟塞

mang⁴ sak¹ *(translit.)*

Be unclever. (lit.)

Be as stupid as an owl.

Be poor at understanding.

注 指愚蠢或理解力弱。

1985　暗啞抵

am³ aa² dai² *(translit.)*

Bear without a word. (lit.)

Suffer in silence.

Swallow the leek.

注 表示被迫忍辱而説不出聲來的意思。

1986　暈得一陣

wan⁴ dak¹ jat¹ zan⁶ *(translit.)*

Faint away for a while. (lit.)

Be intoxicated by one's beauty.

Be enchanted with honey words.

注 被某人的美色或甜言蜜語所陶醉的意思。

1987　照板煮碗

ziu³ baan² zyu² wun² *(translit.)*

Cook for a bowl in accordance with the sample. (lit.)

Follow the beaten track.

Make one like the given sample.

Give an eye for an eye; a tooth for a tooth.

注 表示依樣畫葫蘆，要人按照所交出的樣板去做。又可引伸作以牙還牙。

1988　照單執藥

ziu³ daan¹ zap¹ joek⁶ *(translit.)*

Pick medicinal herbs according to the prescription. (lit.)

Follow the beaten track.

Act as listed above/below.

注 表示要人按照開列事項去做的意思。

1989　跣人

sin³ jan⁴ *(translit.)*

Slip somebody. (lit.)

'Professional informer or Professional clue informer'.

注 同 "俾蕉皮／西瓜皮人踩"。又 "跣人" 和 "線人" 同音異義。後者為供給警方線索的人。

1990　跳皮（調皮）

tiu³ pei²/⁴ *(translit.)*

Jumping-skinned. (lit.)

Mischievous.

Naughty.

注 即淘氣，頑皮或調皮。

1991　跪地餵／餵豬乸——睇錢份上

gwai⁶ dei⁶ hei³/wai³ zyu¹ naa² — tai² cin²/⁴ fan⁶ soeng⁶ *(translit.)*

Kneel down to feed a sow — for money's sake. (lit.)

Money makes the mare go.

For the sake of money.

Money talks.

📝 表示為了金錢，甚麼也做或為了金錢
甘於低三下四的意思。

1992　路數

lou⁶ sou³ *(translit.)*

The number of a road. (lit.)

Social connections.

The pull to find a job.

📝 即門路，參閱 "頭路" 條（2262）。

1993　過口癮

gwo³ hau² jan⁵ *(translit.)*

*Satisfy the addict of the mouth.
(lit.)*

Have snack to ease the mouth.

Talk at random.

Talk nonsense.

Cook up a tale.

📝 本意指吃零食，但引伸指瞎聊，胡謅。

1994　過水

gwo³ seoi² *(translit.)*

Pass over the water. (lit.)

Give somebody the money.

Pay somebody.

Grease somebody's hand.

📝 指付錢或向人行賄的行為。

1995　過水濕腳

gwo³ seoi² sap¹ goek³ *(translit.)*

*Wet one's feet as soon as one
wades across the water. (lit.)*

**Taste another's broth with one's
finger.**

Draw water to one's mill.

Nose a job in everything.

**Whatever one does, one plays for
one's own hand.**

📝 表示無論做甚麼也要佔點便宜的意
思。

1996　過分

gwo³ fan⁶ *(translit.)*

Over quantity. (lit.)

Overstep the bounds.

Go too far.

To excess.

📝 即出圈兒或超越……的意思。

1997　過火

gwo³ fo² *(translit.)*

Over fire. (lit.)

Overstep the bounds.

Go too far.

To excess.

📝 大致上和 "過分" 同，參閱該條
（1996）。

1998　過夾吊頸

gwo³ gaap³ diu³ geng² *(translit.)*

*Hang oneself with a rope round
one's armpits. (lit.)*

Handle everything with great care.

Make two bites at a cherry.

📝 比喻做事過分小心，參閱 "落住屎窟
吊頸" 條（1945）。

1999　過身

gwo³ san¹ *(translit.)*

Pass off the body. (lit.)

Pass out.

Pass away.

Pay one's debt to nature.

Meet one's death.

📝 死亡的委婉語。

2000　過咗海就神仙

gwo³ zo² hoi² zau⁶ san⁴ sin¹ *(translit.)*

*Crossing the sea, one becomes a
celestial being. (lit.)*

Sail under false colours.

Succeed in practising deception

十三畫

on somebody.

注表示瞞天過海的意思。

2001　過骨

gwo³ gwat¹ *(translit.)*

Pass through the bones. (lit.)

Get through/over...

Pass a test.

Slide through...

Scrape through/past...

注過關或通過的意思。

2002　過氣老倌

gwo³ hei³ lou⁵ gun¹ *(translit.)*

A behindhand actor. (lit.)

An actor who was once famous.

A used-to-be.

注本義為過去紅極一時的老藝人，但引伸作失去權勢地位或資財的人。

2003　過得去

gwo³ dak¹ heoi³ *(translit.)*

Just can pass. (lit.)

Be not too bad.

Be just passable.

So-so.

注還可以的意思。

2004　過橋抽板

gwo³ kiu⁴ cau¹ baan² *(translit.)*

Pull up the board after crossing the bridge. (lit.)

Kick down the ladder.

Once on shore, pray no more.

注比喻成功後便忘了幫忙的人，相當於"過河拆橋"。參閱"打完齋唔要和尚"條（0459）。

2005　嗰單嘢

go² daan¹ je⁵ *(translit.)*

That matter. (lit.)

The business between you, me

and the gatepost.

The matter of that.

注那檔事，指彼此心知的事情。

2006　嗰頭近

go² tau⁴ kan⁵/gan⁶ *(translit.)*

That end is near. (lit.)

Have one's foot in the grave.

Be at death's door.

注比喻接近死亡。

2007　嗲吊

de² diu³ *(translit.)*

Be laggard. (lit.)

Be sluggish and dilatory.

注形容人做事拖沓。

2008　嗌通街

aai³ tung¹ gaai¹ *(translit.)*

Scold the whole street. (lit.)

Bandy words with everyone.

注指到處都和人吵架。

2009　嗍氣

sok³ hei³ *(translit.)*

Suck air. (lit.)

Lose one's breath./Be out of breath.

Be tired out.

Be in straitened circumstances.

注表示喘不過氣來，呼吸困難或引伸作十分疲勞或處於貧困境地。

2010　筲箕打水——一場空

saau¹ gei¹ daa² seoi² — jat¹ coeng⁴ hung¹ *(translit.)*

Draw water with a sieve — vanish into the void. (lit.)

Draw water with a sieve.

注比喻希望成空。

2011　筲箕冚鬼一窩神

saau¹ gei¹ ham⁶ gwai² jat¹ wo¹ san⁴ *(translit.)*

Cover ghosts with a sieve to form a den of gods. (lit.)

Be hand and glove with each other.

Be in cahoots with each other.

Devils gang up with devils

注 表示同流合污的意思。

2012 僅僅夠（一）

gan² gan² gau³ *(translit.)*

Just enough. (Indicates small quantity) (lit.)

Be just sufficient.

注 指數量方面的足夠。

2013 僅僅夠……（二）

gan² gan² gau³... *(translit.)*

Just enough... (Indicates low degree). (lit.)

Be just...enough.

注 指程度方面的足夠。

2014 鼠入嚟

syu² jap⁶ lai⁴ *(translit.)*

Mouse in. (lit.)

Steal in / into...

注 表示溜進來的意思。

2015 鼠嘢

syu² je⁵ *(translit.)*

Mouse things. (lit.)

Steal things.

注 指偷東西。

2016 傾唔埋

king¹ m⁴ maai⁴ *(translit.)*

Cannot have a chat together. (lit.)

Be out of tune with somebody.

Do not speak the same language.

Do not get along well with somebody.

注 即話不投機。

2017 傾唔埋欄

king¹ m⁴ maai⁴ laan¹ *(translit.)*

Disagree with... (lit.)

Not to reach an agreement with somebody.

Fail to carry one's point.

Not to speak the same language.

Be out of tune with somebody.

注 表示未能達成協議，無法説服對方同意，或話不投機的意思，後義參閱 "傾唔埋"（2016）條。

2018 煲冇米粥

bou¹ mou⁵ mai⁵ zuk¹ *(translit.)*

Boil riceless congee. (lit.)

Be all talk.

Make an idle talk.

The business ends in talk.

注 指閒談（無目的），或商談沒有成果的生意。

2019 煲老藕

bou¹ lou⁵ ngau⁵ *(translit.)*

Stew old lotus-roots. (lit.)

Marry with an aged woman.

注 比喻娶老婦為妻的意思。

2020 鈴鈴鎈鎈都丟埋

ling¹ ling¹ caa⁴ caa² dou¹ diu¹ maai⁴ *(translit.)*

Throw away the bell and cymbals. (lit.)

Meet with a crushing defeat.

Be at the end of one's tether.

Be at one's wit's end.

注 廣東人稱銅鈸為 "鎈鎈"。鈴和鈸為道士作法的法寶，當道士作法時，如遇鬼魅法力較道士為強，則道士便要丟掉法寶而逃。所以這句話比喻遭到極大的失敗或 "智窮才盡"。

2021　會錯意

wui[6] co[3] ji[3] *(translit.)*

Get the wrong idea. (lit.)

Misunderstand somebody's intention.

Wrongly take a hint.

🈲誤會別人的意圖。

2022　亂晒坑

lyun[6] saai[3] haang[1] *(translit.)*

The pit gets confused. (lit.)

Be at sixes and sevens.

Be thrown into confusion.

Muddle things up.

🈲相當於亂了套。

2023　亂籠

lyun[6] lung[4] *(translit.)*

Disorderly cages. (lit.)

🈲同"亂晒坑"（2022）。

2024　飽死

baau[2] sei[2] *(translit.)*

Die of eating to fill. (lit.)

Be exasperated against somebody.

Be irritated by somebody's...

Be ruffled./Be annoyed for...

🈲這是輕蔑或挖苦別人的口頭語，意為"氣死"或"氣壞"，有時又可説成"飽死荷蘭豆"，參閲該條（2025）。

2025　飽死荷蘭豆

baau[2] sei[2] ho[4] laan[1] dau[2] *(translit.)*

Dutch pods die of being overfilled. (lit.)

Be irritated at somebody's...

Be ruffled.

Be annoyd for...

🈲和"飽死"同義，參閲該條（2024）。

2026　飽唔死餓唔親

baau[2] m[4] sei[2] ngo[6] m[4] can[1] *(translit.)*

Neither die of being full nor suffer from hunger. (lit.)

Earn no more than what one needs.

Have sufficient for one's needs.

Lead a passable life.

🈲表示過着僅夠溫飽或過得去的生活。

2027　腦囟／顋未生埋

nou[5] seon[2] mei[6] saang[1] maai[4] *(translit.)*

The forehead has not closed yet. (lit.)

One's mouth is full of pap.

🈲形容人年幼無知或乳臭未乾。

2028　斟盤

zam[1] pun[2] *(translit.)*

Talk about the plan. (lit.)

Hold talks with somebody.

Negotiate with somebody about something.

Enter into negotiation with somebody.

Talk about business with somebody.

🈲表示和人協商，談判或談生意的意思。

2029　話名係……

waa[6] meng[2] hai[6]... *(translit.)*

Say the name to be... (lit.)

In name only.

Nominally.

🈲即名義上，相當於"應名兒"。

2030　……（某人）話事偈

...waa[6] si[6] gai[2] *(translit.)*

As what is said by somebody. (lit.)

As what somebody says.

注即正如（某人）所説。

2031 話晒事

waa⁶ saai³ si⁶ *(translit.)*

Say all the things. (lit.)

Wield the sceptre.

注作主，説了算，掌握大權。

2032 話唔定……

waa⁶ m⁴ ding⁶... *(translit.)*

Not to fix the saying... (lit.)

Perhaps.

Maybe.

It is beyond expectation that...

注説不定，或難以預料的意思。

2033 話唔埋……

waa⁶ m⁴ maai⁴... *(translit.)*

Can hardly say... (lit.)

Perhaps.

Maybe.

It is beyond expectation that...

注説不定；難以預料。參閱"話唔定……"條（2032）。

2034 話極都……

waa⁶ gik⁶ dou¹... *(translit.)*

Say by every possible means but... (lit.)

Keep on advising somebody but...

注指不斷地勸告某人，但他……。例如 "我話極佢都唔肯做呢項工作"（我不斷地勸他，但他不肯做這項工作）。

2035 話落

waa⁶ lok⁶ *(translit.)*

Say down. (lit.)

Leave message.

Leave words.

Bid somebody to...at departure.

Say at / before one's departure.

注交代，留言或吩咐的意思。

2036 話實

waa⁶ sat⁶ *(translit.)*

Say firmly. (lit.)

Make sure that...

Be definite in saying that...

Surely.

注即説定或肯定地説。

2037 ……（某人）話齋

...waa⁶ zaai¹ *(translit.)*

As what is said by somebody. (lit.)

注同"……（某人）話事偈"（2030）。

2038 該死

goi¹ sei² *(translit.)*

Should die. (lit.)

Deserve it.

注相當於"該當"，但和普通話的"該死"有別。

2039 該釘就釘，該鐵就鐵

goi¹ deng¹ zau⁶ deng¹, goi¹ tit³ zau⁶ tit³ *(translit.)*

Nails should be nails and iron should be iron. (lit.)

Call a spade a spade.

注表示事情不能模棱兩可的意思。

2040 該煨咯！

goi¹ wui¹ lok³ *(translit.)*

It should be roasted in ashes! (lit.)

Just my luck!

What a bad luck!

Too bad!

注意為糟糕了（帶有可憐，心痛的感情）。

2041 稟神都冇句真

ban² san⁴ dou¹ mou⁵ geoi³ zan¹ *(translit.)*

Not a sentence is true even as praying down. (lit.)

Often tell the tale.

Lie in one's teeth.

Live a lie.

Lie like a gas meter.

注 強調（某人）講話沒一句真的，慣於說謊。

2042　遊車河

jau⁴ ce¹ ho² *(translit.)*

Stroll the car river. (lit.)

Go for a drive in a car.

注 坐車遊覽或兜風。

2043　新屎坑三日香

san¹ si² haang¹ saam¹ jat⁶ hoeng¹ *(translit.)*

A new lavatory smells of fragrance for three days. (lit.)

A new broom sweeps clean.

Prevail for a time.

Be all the rage for a while.

注 比喻成為一時時尚或風靡一時。

2044　道高一尺，魔高一丈

dou⁶ gou¹ jat¹ cek³, mo¹ gou¹ jat¹ zoeng⁶ *(translit.)*

The magical arts of Taoist grow one foot high but the glamour of the devil grows to ten feet. (lit.)

Offenders are a stroke above lawmakers.

Where there are laws, there are fierce offensives against them.

注 表示一法立，一弊生的意思。

2045　煙韌

jin¹ jan⁶ *(translit.)*

As tough as leather. (lit.)

Be heels over head in love with each other.

Enthuse each other over love.

注 形容男女間的熱火纏綿。

2046　爐起 / 着個火頭

laat³ hei² / zoek⁶ go³ fo² tau⁴ *(translit.)*

Light up the fire-head. (lit.)

Stir up the dust. / Stir up somebody to mischief.

Throw the situation into confusion.

Set the situation on fire.

Agitate for something to inflame popular feeling.

注 比喻煽動，煽動某人胡鬧，造成局面混亂或為……而進行鼓動來激動羣眾情緒等。

2047　滑頭

waat⁶ tau² *(translit.)*

A slippery head. (lit.)

Be shifty.

A sly fellow.

A slippery customer.

注 即狡猾或狡猾的傢伙。

2048　慌失失

fong¹ sat¹ sat¹ *(translit.)*

Get frightened. (lit.)

Be all in a fluster.

Be in a flurried manner.

注 慌手慌腳；慌慌張張，參閱 "失失慌" 條（0547）。

2049　塞古盟憎

sak¹ gu² mang⁴ zang¹ *(translit.)*

Suddenly. (lit.)

All of a sudden.

Before you could say Jack Robinson.

注 表示忽然間，轉眼之間。

2050　塞竇窿

sak¹ dau⁶ lung¹ *(translit.)*

Something to fill up the hole of the drain. (lit.)

A little child.

A kid.

🈁比喻小孩的諧趣語。

2051　裝假狗

zong¹ gaa² gau² *(translit.)*

Install a false dog. (lit.)

Be under the guise.

Make believe.

Camouflage something with...

🈁偽裝或弄虛作假。

2052　裝彈弓

zong¹ daan⁶ gung¹ *(translit.)*

Install a spring. (lit.)

Make an ambush.

Set a trap.

Drop a pinch of salt on the tail of a horse.

🈁即設圈套。

2053　媽媽聲

maa¹ maa¹ seng¹ *(translit.)*

With the sound 'maa maa'. (lit.)

Swear like a pirate / trooper.

🈁粗口罵人或破口大罵。

2054　嫌棄

jim⁴ hei³ *(translit.)*

Dislike. (lit.)

Be displeased at somebody / something.

Turn a cold shoulder to somebody.

🈁表示厭惡並疏遠。

2055　嫁雞隨雞，嫁狗隨狗

gaa³ gai¹ ceoi⁴ gai¹, gaa³ gau² ceoi⁴ gau² *(translit.)*

Follow a cock after marrying to a cock; follow a dog after marrying to a dog. (lit.)

Become a subordinate to one's husband once married.

🈁封建時代，婦女要三從四德，所謂三從，即未嫁從父，既嫁從夫，夫死從子，這句俗語是根據"既嫁從夫"演繹出來。

2056　隔山買牛

gaak³ saan¹ maai⁵ ngau⁴ *(translit.)*

Buy an ox at a separate mountain. (lit.)

Buy a pig in a poke.

🈁比喻未看過實物便買，瞎買。

2057　隔岸觀火

gaak³ ngon⁶ gun¹ fo² *(translit.)*

Watch a fire at other side of the bank. (lit.)

Show indifference towards somebody's trouble.

🈁指對別人的不幸等，毫不關心採取從旁看熱鬧的態度。

2058　隔夜油炸鬼

gaak³ je⁶ jau⁴ zaa³ gwai² *(translit.)*

The deep-fried dough-strip of last evening. (lit.)

A milk sop.

A person who never turns a hair.

A person who never gets angry.

A person of both unhurried and unperturbed dispositions.

🈁比喻懦弱的人，從不發怒的人或慢條斯理的人。

2059　隔夜素馨釐戥秤

gaak³ je⁶ sou³ hing¹ lei⁴ dang² cing³ *(translit.)*

The jasimine left over night is

weighed on beam and scales. *(lit.)*

The outmoded are sometimes outvalued.

注 表示過時的東西反而更貴，更有價值的意思。

2060　隔靴搔痕／癢

gaak³ hoe¹ ngaau¹ han⁴ / joeng⁵ *(translit.)*

Scratch an itch outside the boot. (lit.)

Work out no effective solution to the problem.

Hit beside the mark.

Not to keep to the point.

注 比喻説話做事沒有觸到要害，不解決問題。

2061　隔牆有耳

gaak³ coeng⁴ jau⁵ ji⁵ *(translit.)*

The separate wall has ears. (lit.)

Walls have ears.

Pitchers have ears.

注 表示牆外有人偷聽，秘密外洩。

2062　隔籬飯香

gaak³ lei⁴ faan⁶ hoeng¹ *(translit.)*

Neighbour's cooked-rice is fragrant. (lit.)

The grass at the other side of one's own fence looks greener.

注 和"本地薑唔辣"（0507）同義，但此語應用範圍較窄，多只用於表示孩子們多數喜歡吃鄰居的飯。

十四畫

2063　魂不守舍

wan⁴ bat¹ sau² se³ *(translit.)*

The soul does not stay in. (lit.)

Lose one's head.

Be distracted.

Be perplexed.

Be out of one's wits.

注 指人不知所措，迷迷惘惘或心不在焉的姿態。

2064　魂不附體

wan⁴ bat¹ fu⁶ tai² *(translit.)*

The soul does not attach to the body. (lit.)

Lose one's head.

Be distracted.

Be at a loss.

To be scared (almost) to death.

Be out of one's wits.

注 形容人受到極大的震驚，恐懼萬分。

2065　摸門釘

mo² mun⁴ deng¹ *(translit.)*

Touch the door-nail. (lit.)

Kiss the doorpost.

注 指到親友家找不到人。

2066　駁嘴

bok³ zeoi² *(translit.)*

Reverse the mouth. (lit.)

Answer back.

Talk back.

注 頂嘴。

2067　趕工

gon² gung¹ *(translit.)*

Rush into work. (lit.)

Work overtime.

注 即加班。

2068　趕住投胎

gon² zyu⁶ tau⁴ toi¹ *(translit.)*

Rush into reincarnation. (lit.)

Rush oneself off one's own feet.

Be in a hurry.

In a hot haste.

Make a hot haste.

🈯表示倉促行動，急急忙忙的意思。（多用於斥責別人行動太急。）

2069　趕到⋯⋯絕

gon² dou³...zyut⁶ *(translit.)*

Drive to the cliff. (lit.)

Drive somebody to the wall.

🈯令某人陷於絕境。

2070　趕狗入窮巷

gon² gau² jap⁶ kung⁴ hong⁶ *(translit.)*

Drive a dog into a blind alley. (lit.)

Compel somebody to strike back in self-defence.

Make somebody do whatever he can to defend himself.

🈯表示迫使人因自衛而反擊或使人做出可能做的事來自衛的意思。

2071　趕唔切

gon² m⁴ cit³ *(translit.)*

Fail to rush into action. (lit.)

Have not enough time to do something.

It is too late for somebody to do something.

🈯來不及的意思。

2072　墟冚

heoi¹ ham⁶ *(translit.)*

Bustle. (lit.)

Be as bustling as a market.

Be bustling with noise and excitement.

Be in a bustle.

Spread around.

Give publicity to something.

🈯形容人聲嘈雜，亂哄哄的像集市一

樣。但如作動詞時，則表示張揚的意思。

2073　摟蓆

lau¹ zek⁶ *(translit.)*

Put on a mat. (lit.)

Become a beggar.

🈯比喻做了乞丐。

2074　摟錯人皮

lau¹ co³ jan⁴ pei⁴ *(translit.)*

Wrongly put on a human skin. (lit.)

Behave oneself like a beast.

Be man and beast.

🈯指人行為不端或毫無人性。相當於"白披了張人皮"。

2075　蒸生瓜

zing¹ saang¹ gwaa¹ *(translit.)*

An under-steamed cucumber. (lit.)

Be half-idiotic.

A simpleton.

🈯比喻半癡的，不靈活，笨頭笨腦。蒸煮不熟的瓜必脊（音 san⁶）。脊即不夠綿軟的意思，但廣東人把"脊"又作"癡"或"傻"解。

2076　誓神劈願

sai⁶ san⁴ pek³ jyun⁶ *(translit.)*

Swear by God and trust forth a will (lit.)

Take an oath and call God to witness.

🈯起誓，發誓。

2077　誓願當食生菜

sai⁶ jyun⁶ dong³ sik⁶ saang¹ coi³ *(translit.)*

Swear like eating lettuce. (lit.)

Get used to making false oath.

Take an easy oath.

🈯比喻隨便起誓，但是從來不履行。

2078　壽仔

sau⁶ zai² *(translit.)*

A long-living guy. (lit.)

A fool.

A spoon.

注 指傻瓜，白癡。

2079　壽星公吊頸——嫌命長

sau⁶ sing¹ gung¹ diu³ geng² — jim⁴ meng⁶ coeng⁴ *(translit.)*

The god of longevity hangs himself — dislike long life. (lit.)

Tempt one's fate.

Do something at the risk of one's life.

Run risk of life.

注 歇後語。比喻人不顧危險幹某事，"玩命"。

2080　壽頭

sau⁶ tau⁴ *(translit.)*

A long-living head. (lit.)

A blockhead.

A spoon.

注 傻瓜，呆子。

2081　壽頭壽腦

sau⁶ tau⁴ sau⁶ nou⁵ *(translit.)*

A long-living head with longliving brains. (lit.)

Be foolish-looking.

Be muddled-headed.

注 形容人呆頭呆腦。

2082　輕佻

hing¹ tiu¹ *(translit.)*

Not serious. (lit.)

Be frivolous.

Be skittish.

注 表示輕浮，不莊重。

2083　輕枷重罪

heng¹ / hing¹ gaa¹ cung⁵ zeoi⁶ *(translit.)*

The wooden collar is light but the crime is serious. (lit.)

Be burdened with the work of a moment.

注 表示工作不多，但責任重大的意思。

2084　輕浮

hing¹ fau⁴ *(translit.)*

Light and floating. (lit.)

Be frivolous.

Have the indiscretion.

注 同 "輕佻"。

2085　監人食死貓

gaam¹ jan⁴ sik⁶ sei² maau¹ *(translit.)*

Force somebody to eat a dead cat. (lit.)

Lay the blame upon somebody for the fault.

Compel somebody to confess to having done something.

注 表示把過失歸咎某人或強迫某人承認曾經做過……的意思。

2086　監人賴厚

gaam¹ jan⁴ laai²⁄⁵ hau⁶ *(translit.)*

Force somebody to be intimate. (lit.)

Shamelessly take oneself for somebody's intimate.

注 諷刺人不知羞恥地把自己當作某人的知己。

2087　對牛彈琴

doei³ ngau⁴ taan⁴ kam⁴ *(translit.)*

Play the harp to a cow. (lit.)

Speak to the wrong audience.

Sing to a mule.

注 比喻對愚蠢的人講深刻的道理或用來譏笑說話的人不看對象。

2088　嘥

saai¹ *(translit.)*

Speak ironically. (lit.)

Play down somebody.

Depreciate somebody.

Give a dig at somebody.

Go to waste.

🈯表示貶低，挖苦，誹謗人或浪費糟蹋
東西。

2089　嘥心機

saai¹ sam¹ gei¹ *(translit.)*

Waste the mental labour. (lit.)

Flog a dead horse.

Plough the sand.

Shoe the goose.

**All the mental care expends to
no purpose.**

Bark up the wrong tree.

🈯白費勁。

2090　嘥鬼氣嘮

saai¹ gwai² hei³ laa¹ *(translit.)*

Waste air. (lit.)

It wastes energy / breath.

Waste one's words.

It is of no use.

🈯表示白費唇舌的意思。（2089 條指腦
力而這條則指唇舌方面。）

2091　嘥撻

saai¹ taat³ *(translit.)*

Waste. (lit.)

Go to waste.

Squander.

🈯浪費，糟蹋。

2092　嘥燈賣油

saai¹ dang¹ maai⁶ jau⁴ *(translit.)*

Waste the lamp and sell the oil. (lit.)

A game not worth a candle.

Let the gas go to waste.

🈯表示不值得花工夫去做的意思。

2093　嘥聲壞氣

saai¹ seng¹ waai⁶ hei³ *(translit.)*

*Waste the sound and spoil the air.
(lit.)*

🈯同 "嘥鬼氣嘮"（2090）。

2094　踂踂腳

ngan³ ngan²/³ goek³ *(translit.)*

Shake the legs up and down. (lit.)

Lead a rose-coloured life.

Lie in a bed of flowers.

Live well.

🈯"踂" 廣東話的意思是彈動。踂腳即
彈腿，比喻過着安逸的生活。

2095　踎墩

mau¹ dan¹ *(translit.)*

Squat on a mound. (lit.)

Out of work.

Be unemployed.

🈯比喻失業，相當於 "家蹲兒"。

2096　算死草

syun³ sei² cou² *(translit.)*

Calculate the grass to death. (lit.)

Pinch and scrape.

Pinch pennies.

Be misery.

A penny-pincher.

🈯比喻精打細算或吝嗇，有時亦比喻精
打細算的人。

2097　鼻屎好食，鼻囊挖穿

bei⁶ si² hou² sik⁶, bei⁶ nong⁴ waat³
cyun¹ *(translit.)*

*Since nasal muck is good to eat,
the nasal cavity is excavated
through. (lit.)*

Everybody strives for profitable

十四
畫

business.

Where there are profits, there
is a keen trade competition
between / among competitors.

A wide margin of profit has a
strong appeal to tradesmen.

注 比喻利之所在，人爭趨之或利潤大的
生意，競爭必大。

2098　銅銀買病豬——大家偷歡喜

tung⁴ ngan⁴ maai⁵ beng⁶ zyu¹ — daai⁶
gaa¹ tau¹ fun¹ hei² *(translit.)*

*Buy a sick pig with coppersilver
coins (false money) — both sides
feel happy on the sly. (lit.)*

Each of the two hugs himself on
having cheated the other.

Each of the two laughs in
his sleeve in spite of being
deceived by the other.

注 買方用偽幣，而賣方以次貨充好貨，
及至雙方交易成功，彼此認為自己詭
計得逞而暗自歡喜。因此這俚語便比
喻以為自己騙了別人，不知自己也是
受騙者。

2099　蝕底

sit⁶ dai² *(translit.)*

*Diminish the bottom by
encroachment. (lit.)*

Suffer losses.

Be in unfavourable situation.

Come to grief.

Get the worst of it.

注 遭受損失，處於不利地位或吃虧。

2100　領嘢

leng⁶ je⁵ *(translit.)*

Accept something. (lit.)

Rise to a bait.

Swallow the bait.

Be swindled.

Be caught with chaff.

注 相當於“上當”（即被騙）。

2101　疑心生暗鬼

ji⁴ sam¹ saang¹ am³ gwai² *(translit.)*

*Suspicion produces invisible
ghost. (lit.)*

Misgivings / Suspicions often
bring about imaginary fears.

2102　鳳凰無寶不落

fung⁶ wong⁴ mou⁴ bou² bat¹ lok⁶
(translit.)

*A male or a female phoenix does
not come to the place where
there is no treasure. (lit.)*

Draw water to one's mill.

Where there is profit, there is
one's trace.

注 比喻有利益的地方，便有某人的足
跡。

2103　認低威

jing⁶ dai¹ wai¹ *(translit.)*

Confess to be low-dignified. (lit.)

Say uncle.

Confess to be unworthy.

Admit to be inferior to somebody.

注 意指服輸，甘拜下風。

2104　認賬

jing⁶ zoeng³ *(translit.)*

Recognize the account. (lit.)

注 同“認數”（2105）。

2105　認數

jing⁶ sou³ *(translit.)*

Recognize the number. (lit.)

Acknowledge the debt / account.

Admit what one has said or done.

注 表示承認債項或承認自己所説或做過
的事。

2106 敲鼓邊
haau[1] gu[2] bin[1] *(translit.)*

Beat the rim of a drum. (lit.)

注 和“拗吓鼓邊”意思一樣。參閱該條（1176）。

2107 瘟瘟沌沌
wan[1] wan[1] dan[6] dan[6] *(translit.)*

Be dazzled. (lit.)

Lose one's consciousness.

Lapse into delirium.

Have a perplexed look.

Be at a loss.

注 指迷迷糊糊，頭腦不大清醒或惘然若失的樣子。

2108 瘦田冇人耕，耕親有人爭
sau[3] tin[4] mou[5] jan[4] gaang[1], gaang[1] can[1] jau[5] jan[4] zaang[1] *(translit.)*

No man ploughs a barren field, but if it is ploughed, others will fight for it. (lit.)

Once a wasteland is inhabited, a rush for an occupation is insisted.

注 暗喻一向沒人歡迎的東西，一旦有人垂注，便立即成為爭取的對象。

2109 塵埃落定
can[4] oi[1] lok[6] ding[6] *(translit.)*

The dust has come down. (lit.)

All is fixed.

Everything is decided.

The outcome has come to a conclusion.

注 表示一切已定或大局已定的意思。

2110 塵氣
can[4] hei[3] *(translit.)*

Dusty air. (lit.)

Put on airs.

Be arrogant.

注 形容神氣十足，擺架子或驕傲自大的神態。

2111 辣撻人有辣撻福
laat[6] taat[3] jan[4] jau[5] laat[6] taat[3] fuk[1] *(translit.)*

Dirty persons have dirty bliss. (lit.)

God tempers the wind to the shorn lamb.

Happiness often comes to mediocre persons.

注 表示庸人多厚福的意思，參閱“跛腳鷯哥自有飛來蜢”條（1812）。

2112 端端度度
dyun[1] dyun[1] dok[6] dok[6] *(translit.)*

Scrutinize and measure. (lit.)

Have evil intention.

Have ulterior motives.

Be calculating.

Have one's own calculation.

Be in quest of...

注 表示心懷鬼胎，老在打算着或心存謀取……的意思。

2113 精人出口，笨人出手
zeng[1] jan[4] ceot[1] hau[2], ban[6] jan[4] ceot[1] sau[2] *(translit.)*

A wise man give words but a foolish man takes action. (lit.)

Words are cleverer than action.

注 表示聰明人只動嘴說說，笨人才真的動手幹。

2114 精打細算
zing[1] daa[2] sai[3] syun[3] *(translit.)*

Reckon cleverly and calculate carefully. (lit.)

Pinch and scrape.

Pinch pennies.

注 指精細的謀劃打算。

十四畫

2115　精到出骨

zeng¹ dou³ ceot¹ gwat¹ *(translit.)*

Cleverness comes out of bones.
(lit.)

Act cleverly from selfish motives.

🈂形容人十分善於為自己打算，非常自私。

2116　精埋一便

zeng¹ maai⁴ jat¹ bin⁶ *(translit.)*

Be clever at one side. (lit.)

Be clever only at ill doings.

🈂指專把聰明用於做壞事，或為自己打算。

2117　精歸左

zeng¹ gwai¹ zo² *(translit.)*

Be clever at the left side. (lit.)

🈂同“精埋一便”（2116）。

2118　煽風點火

sin³ fung¹ dim² fo² *(translit.)*

Fan the wind and light up the fire.
(lit.)

Stir up troubles.

Whip up waves.

Incite trouble and create confusion.

🈂表示煽動或興風作浪的意思，參閱“攪風攪雨”條（2459）。

2119　滿肚密圈

mun⁵ tou⁵ mat⁶ hyun¹ *(translit.)*

The belly is full of close circles.
(lit.)

Be full of wrinkles.

Have full confidence to overcome the difficulties.

Be sure of the success.

🈂表示足智多謀，自信可克服困難或對成功有把握。

2120　滾友

gwan² jau² *(translit.)*

A boiling friend. (lit.)

A fast counter.

An imposter.

A swindler.

A person who talks nonsense.

An irresponsible person.

🈂即騙子，胡説八道的人或不負責的人。

2121　滾水淥腳

gwan² seoi² luk⁶ goek³ *(translit.)*

Dip the feet in boiling water. (lit.)

Hurry one's pace.

Hurry off.

🈂表示去得匆匆的意思。

2122　滾水淥豬腸 —— 兩頭縮

gwan² seoi² luk⁶ zyu¹
coeng² — loeng⁵ tau⁴ suk¹ *(translit.)*

Dip the pig's intestines in boiling water — both ends shrink. (lit.)

Lose out one both sides.

🈂表示兩頭損失的意思。

2123　滾紅滾綠

gwan² hung⁴ gwan² luk⁶ *(translit.)*

Boil red and green. (lit.)

Talk nonsense.

Make fast-talk.

Make irresponsible remarks.

🈂表示胡説八道，信口胡吹。

2124　漏口風

lau⁶ hau² fung¹ *(translit.)*

Let the wind of mouth leak. (lit.)

Be inadvertent to blurt out.

Blurt out a secret.

🈂表示無意中脱口而出或無意中泄漏秘密的意思。

2125　漏氣

lau⁶ hei³ *(translit.)*

Leak air. (lit.)

Be unhurried and unperturbed.

Be sluggish.

🈟形容人做事拖沓或慢吞吞的。

2126　漏罅

lau⁶ laa³ *(translit.)*

Leaking gap. (lit.)

A loophole.

A leak.

Slip over.

Miss out.

🈟作名詞用時，指漏洞或差錯，但作動
詞時，表示疏忽或遺漏的意思。

2127　滲氣

cam³ hei³ *(translit.)*

Talky-aired. (lit.)

Be long-winded.

Be wordy.

🈟表示絮絮叨叨的意思，參閱 "唥沉"
條（1825）。

2128　慢工出細貨

maan⁶ gung¹ ceot¹ sai³ fo³ *(translit.)*

*Slow work produces fine goods.
(lit.)*

Soft fire makes sweet malt.

🈟指精雕細刻才做成的精緻的作品。

2129　寡母婆死仔——冇晒希望

gwaa² mou⁵ po² sei² zai² — mou⁵
saai³ hei¹ mong⁶ *(translit.)*

*The sole son of a widow
died — have not any hope. (lit.)*

Be driven to despair.

Be in a desperate state.

Pin one's hope on nobody.

🈟表示沒了希望的意思。

2130　寡母婆咁多心

gwaa² mou⁵ po² gam³ do¹ sam¹
(translit.)

*Have as many minds as a widow.
(lit.)*

Hang in doubt.

Be in two minds.

Shilly-shally.

🈟參閱 "三心兩意"（0164），"心多多"
（0418）及 "十五個銅錢分兩份"
（0097）各條。

2131　寧犯天條，莫犯眾憎

ning⁴ faan⁶ tin¹ tiu⁴, mok⁶ faan⁶ zung³
zang¹ *(translit.)*

*Rather commit an offence against
heaven disciplines than cause
the hatred of the public monks.
(lit.)*

It is wise not to offend the public.

🈟勸人不要犯眾怒的警誡語。

2132　寧食開眉粥，莫食愁眉飯

ning⁴ sik⁶ hoi¹ mei⁴ zuk¹, mok⁶ sik⁶
sau⁴ mei⁴ faan⁶ *(translit.)*

*Prefer to eat congee of happiness
rather than cooked-rice of
sadness. (lit.)*

**Had rather be poor but happy
than become rich but
anxious.**

**Prefer to be under-paid for good
treatment rather than well-
paid for being ill-treated.**

🈟表達個人寧貧而樂，勝於富而憂或寧
受低薪而受良好待遇勝於高薪而受不
良待遇的心情。

2133　寧欺白鬚公，莫欺鼻涕蟲

ning⁴ hei¹ baak⁶ sou¹ gung¹, mok⁶
hei¹ bei⁶ tai³ cung⁴ *(translit.)*

Rather insult a white-bearded man

十
四
畫

than a snivel-worm (small boy).
(*lit.*)

A colt may make a good horse.
Kids are full of promise.

注 表示後生可畏，不容輕視。

2134　實牙實齒

sat⁶ ngaa⁴ sat⁶ ci² (*translit.*)

Say with solid teeth. (*lit.*)

Exhort again and again.
Clinch one's instruction.

注 表示千叮嚀萬囑咐的意思。

2135　實食冇黐牙

sat⁶ sik⁶ mou⁵ ci¹ ngaa⁴ (*translit.*)

Sure to eat without sticking to the
teeth. (*lit.*)

Be in the bag.
Be well in hand.
Be sure of the success.
Have the ball at one's feet.

注 表示完全有把握，十拿九穩。

2136　實鼓實鑿

sat⁶ gu² sat⁶ zok⁶ (*translit.*)

Real drums and real chisels. (*lit.*)

Be neither garish nor gaudy.
Be solid worth.

注 即並非花裏胡哨的，並無虛飾的或有
實際價值的。

2137　肇慶荷包──陀衰人

Siu⁶ Hing³ ho⁴ baau¹ — to⁴ seoi¹ jan⁴
(*translit.*)

The purse made in Siu Hing —
bring distress to people (*lit.*)

A person who involves somebody
in a disastrous state.
A person who causes somebody
to suffer a loss.

注 參閱 "陀衰家"（1156）及 "搭沉船"
（1926）條。肇慶除以 "端硯" 馳名

外；草蓆亦為名產，從前使用硬幣，
出外購物，因硬幣重，甚感不便，遂
有 "荷包" 出現，製造 "荷包" 材料，
有布或皮革等，但肇慶荷包為用水草
織成，因該地盛產水草，就地取材，
不過由於不夠耐用，配帶者常因荷包
破而招損失，遂有這俚語。

2138　聞見棺材香

man⁴ gin³ gun¹ coi⁴ hoeng¹ (*translit.*)

Smell the fragrance of the coffin.
(*lit.*)

Have one's foot in the grave.
Be at the death's door.
Live to a great age.

注 比喻離死不遠（用於對老年人的刻薄
話）。

十五　畫

2139　撒／殺手鐧

saat³ sau² gaan² (*translit.*)

A killer's mace. (*lit.*)

One's trump card.

注 即必勝的手段或最後的一着。

2140　撒賴

saat³ laai⁶ (*translit.*)

Scatter blames. (*lit.*)

Raise hell.
Make a scene with an intention
to shift the blame to other
shoulders.
Raise hell to lay the blame on the
wrong shoulder.

注 表示大吵大嚷企圖把責任推到別人身
上的意思。

2141　撩是鬥非

liu⁴ si⁶ dau³ fei¹ (*translit.*)

Tease right and provoke wrong.
  (lit.)
Stir up a quarrel.
Pick a quarrel.
Wake a sleeping dog.
📝 表示尋釁的意思。

2142 撲水

pok³ seoi² *(translit.)*
Catch water. (lit.)
Go for a loan of money.
Go for rush money.
📝 比喻到處去找錢或借錢。

2143 撇脱 / 撇撇脱脱

pit³ tyut³ / pit³ pit³ tyut³ tyut³ *(translit.)*
Cast way. (lit.)
Be prompt in action.
Fish or cut the bait.
Make a prompt decision.
Not to muddle away.
Bring to a quick decision.
📝 形容做事爽快，絕不拖泥帶水。

2144 撐 / 蹭枱腳

caang³ / jaang³ toi² goek³ *(translit.)*
Prop against the legs of a table.
  (lit.)
**Have a meal with one's
  wife / lover.**
📝 形容和妻子或愛人共同進餐的情形。

2145 賣大包

maai⁶ daai⁶ baau¹ *(translit.)*
Sell big steamed stuffed-buns. (lit.)
Bargain away.
Price-war.
Play up to somebody.
Curry favour with somebody.
📝 表示廉價出售的意思。從前廣州有所
謂"二釐館"者（下級茶館，茶價只
收二釐錢），光顧的人，多為貧苦大

眾，這些二釐館為了爭取顧客，特在
每日早晨推出一種大包，內有燒肉，
雞，叉燒，鹹蛋等物。而體積有碗大
飯碗，且售價僅為一分二釐（等於今
日一角的六分之一），普通人吃一個
足夠一餐。因這樣大包收到生意興隆
之效，不少茶館，甚至較高級的也爭
相效尤，遂又含有廉價出售，"減價
戰"的意思。進而引伸成為賣人情，
"迎合別人"，或"希望得人歡心"的
口頭語了。

2146 賣口乖

maai⁶ hau² gwaai¹ *(translit.)*
Sell the cleverness of the mouth.
  (lit.)
Oil one's tongue.
Say holiday words.
Talk glibly.
Boast somebody to the skies.
📝 表示用甜言蜜語或稱讚的話來取悅人
的意思。

2147 賣仔莫摸頭

maai⁶ zai² mok⁶ mo² tau⁴ *(translit.)*
*While selling a son, do not touch
  his head. (lit.)*
**Be very sorry to bargain away
  something that one loves most.**
**Be heart-struck to sell one's
  favourite at a bargain price.**
Sell one's hen on a rainy day.
**Express regret at being forced to
  sell one's favourite.**
📝 表示忍痛把自己的心愛東西賤價出售
的意思。

2148 賣花姑娘插竹葉

maai⁶ faa¹ gu¹ noeng⁴ caap³ zuk¹ jip⁶
  (translit.)
*The girl who sells flowers puts on
  bamboo leaves. (lit.)*

十五畫

A tailor makes the man but he clothes himself in rags.

注 表示自己捨不得用自己所賣的東西或薄於自奉的意思。

2149　賣花讚花香

maai⁶ faa¹ zaan³ faa¹ hoeng¹ *(translit.)*

Those who sell flowers praise their flowers for fragrance. (lit.)

There is nothing like leather.

Sing one's own praises.

Make a boast of oneself.

注 自己稱讚自己的意思，相當於 "老王賣瓜自賣自誇"。

2150　賣面光

maai⁶ min⁶ gwong¹ *(translit.)*

Sell the light of the face. (lit.)

Curry favour with somebody.

Ingratiate oneself into somebody's favour.

注 意指買好，拍馬屁或討好。

2151　賣剩蔗

maai⁶ zing⁶ / sing⁶ ze³ *(translit.)*

The sugar-cane left over unsold. (lit.)

A girl / daughter who remains unmarried off.

A person without a dancing partner in the ball.

The article(s) left over and unsold.

注 比喻剩下未嫁的女兒，舞會中沒有舞伴的人或剩下而賣不去的貨物。

2152　賣鹹酸菜——畀面

maai⁶ haam⁴ syun¹ coi³ — bei² min² *(translit.)*

Sell pickles — give face. (lit.)

Give face to somebody.

Show respect for somebody.

注 表示給某人面子的意思。鹹酸菜是一層一層疊在埕或缸內，賣時絕不能翻亂，必須從上層按次序賣出，所以有 "畀面（上層）" 的説法，這是語帶雙關的俚語。

2153　撬牆腳

giu⁶ coeng⁴ goek³ *(translit.)*

Prize off the foot of a wall. (lit.)

Carry off somebody's lover.

Snatch the business from one's competitor.

注 指把別人的情人佔為己有或奪去別人的生意的一種行為。

2154　熱氣飯

jit⁶ hei³ faan⁶ *(translit.)*

The cooked-rice causing fever. (lit.)

The devil to pay.

A difficult job.

注 比喻可怕的後果，未來的麻煩或不容易做的工作。

2155　熱煮不能熱食

jit⁶ zyu² bat¹ nang⁴ jit⁶ sik⁶ *(translit.)*

Cannot eat anything that is boiling hot. (lit.)

Fool's haste is no speed.

Be patient to wait.

注 比喻欲速則不達。

2156　撚化

nan² faa³ *(translit.)*

Twist. (lit.)

Play a trick on somebody.

Twist somebody around one's finger.

Trick somebody into doing something.

注 表示捉弄或愚弄的意思，參閱 "整蠱" 條（2257）。

2157 撞手神

zong^6 sau^2 san^4 *(translit.)*

Meet the luck with a hand. (lit.)

Try one's luck.

Take a chance.

🈲碰運氣的意思（一般用於與手的動作有關的活動，如賭博，抓鬮等）。參閱"撞彩"條（2163）。

2158 撞火

zong^6 fo^2 *(translit.)*

Knock against fire. (lit.)

Make one get angry.

Become furious.

🈲表示生氣，發火。

2159 撞〔到〕正

zong^6 [dou]^3 zeng^3 *(translit.)*

Bump right against. (lit.)

Coincide with...

By a curious coincidence.

By chance.

As luck would have it.

🈲意為碰巧，參閱"撞啱"（2162）及"碰啱"條（1971）。

2160 撞死馬

zong^6 sei^2 maa^5 *(translit.)*

Bump into a horse to death. (lit.)

A person who jostles his way in hot haste.

🈲比喻橫衝直撞的人。

2161 撞鬼

zong$^{2/6}$ gwai^2 *(translit.)*

Meet with a ghost. (lit.)

Have come up against fantasticality.

Be down on one's luck.

🈲即活見鬼或倒霉。

2162 撞啱

zong^6 ngaam^1 *(translit.)*

Bump right against. (lit.)

Coincide with...

By a curious coincidence

By chance

As luck would have it.

🈲意為碰巧，參閱"撞〔到〕正"（2159）及"碰啱"條（1971）。

2163 撞彩

zong^6 coi^2 *(translit.)*

Take a luck. (lit.)

Try one's luck.

Take a chance.

🈲指碰運氣的意思，而廣東人有時說成"碰吓彩數"（pung^3 haa^2 coi^2 sou^3）。參閱"撞手神"條（2157），不過"撞彩"又被引伸作"撞啱"用，參閱該條（2162）。

2164 撈

lou^1 *(translit.)*

Scoop up. (lit.)

Fish for dishonest money.

Engage in dishonest work.

🈲指從事不正當職業或謀取不正當的錢財。

2165 撈女

lou^1 neoi^2 *(translit.)*

Lady-scooper. (lit.)

Street-walker.

Unlicensed prostitute.

A hoodette.

Social butterfly.

A girl earning dishonest money.

🈲指妓女，暗娼，女流氓，交際花或賺取不正當錢財的女人的通稱。

2166 撈起

lou^1 hei^2 *(translit.)*

十五畫

Scoop up. (lit.)

Stick oil.

Earn good money.

Make a fortune.

Coin money.

Have a rise in life.

ⓘ表示發跡，高升或飛黃騰達的意思。

2167　撈家

lou¹ gaa¹ (translit.)

Scooper. (lit.)

A man engaging in dishonest work.

A man earning dishonest profits.

ⓘ指沒有正當職業，靠偷拐詐騙賺收不正當財物的人。

2168　撈家仔

lou¹ gaa¹ zai² (translit.)

Scooper Jr. (lit.)

ⓘ同“撈家”（2167）條。

2169　撈家婆

lou¹ gaa¹ po²/⁴/⁶ (translit.)

A woman scooper. (lit.)

A woman engaging in dishonest work.

A woman earning dishonest profits.

ⓘ指從事不正當職業或賺取不正當錢財的女人。

2170　撈過界

lou¹ gwo³ gaai³ (translit.)

Do business beyond the demarcarcation line. (lit.)

Have a foot in another's domain.

ⓘ表示串地盤，侵入別人的勢力範圍的意思。

2171　撈膥水

lou¹ zing⁶ seoi² (translit.)

Get the remnants (of the spails). (lit.)

Obtain an unnoticed advantage.

Gain the profit to which nobody pays attention.

Have all to oneself.

ⓘ比喻從別人不大注意的地方，或看不起的事物中，得到很大好處或利益。

2172　標青

biu¹ ceng¹ (translit.)

Shoot out the green. (lit.)

Be tip-top.

Be outstanding.

Have good looks.

ⓘ出眾，拔尖，亦表示美貌出眾。

2173　標松柴

biu¹ cung⁴ caai⁴ (translit.)

Shoot off pine wood. (lit.)

Embezzle somebody's money.

Line one's pockets with somebody's money.

Divert somebody's money to one's own pockets.

ⓘ表示侵吞，中飽或把別人的錢據為己有的意思。

2174　標參

biu¹ sam¹ (translit.)

Snatch the ginseng. (lit.)

Kidnap a person for a king's ransom.

Hold somebody to ransom.

ⓘ即綁票。

2175　磅水

bong⁶ seoi² (translit.)

Weigh the water. (lit.)

Give somebody the money.

Pay soembody.

Grease somebody's hand.

注 意和"過水"同，參閱該條（1994）。

2176 豬朋狗友

zyu[1] pang[4] gau[2] jau[5] *(translit.)*

Piggy and doggy friends. (lit.)

Friends of bad characters.

Bad companions.

注 即不三不四的朋友。

2177 豬嘜

zyu[1] maak[1]/mak[1] *(translit.)*

Pig mark. (lit.)

Be stupid.

Be as foolish as an ass.

An ass.

An idiot.

注 形容人像豬一樣蠢或逕意為極端愚蠢。

2178 豬頭骨

zyu[1] tau[4] gwat[1] *(translit.)*

A pig's skull. (lit.)

A job/workpiece without profit-margin.

A bad job.

注 "豬頭骨"無肉可食，即使吃之也費時，因此以此比喻無利可圖的工作或白費勁的工作。

2179 豬欄報數——又一隻

zyu[1] laan[1] bou[3] sou[3] — jau[6] jat[1] zek[3] *(translit.)*

A wholesaler of pigs reports the number — one more. (lit.)

One more has died.

注 比喻又多死了一人。

2180 豬籠入水

zyu[1] lung[4] jap[6] seoi[2] *(translit.)*

The water comes into a pig's bamboo cage. (lit.)

One's money comes from everywhere.

One's financial resources come from all directions.

注 比喻某人財源廣進。

2181 弊家伙

bai[6] gaa[1] fo[2] *(translit.)*

How bad! (lit.)

What a bad luck!

How terrible!

注 表示"糟糕了！"的意思。

2182 劏死牛

tong[1] sei[2] ngau[4] *(translit.)*

Slaughter a dead cow. (lit.)

Highjack.

注 即攔路搶劫。參閱"打腳骨"（0478）條。

2183 劏光豬

tong[1] gwong[1] zyu[1] *(translit.)*

Butcher naked pig. (lit.)

All the pieces (chessmen) have been taken by the opponent.

注 比喻下棋時，棋子全被對方吃光。

2184 暴富難睇

bou[6] fu[3] naan[4] tai[2] *(translit.)*

A parvenu is unpleasing to look at. (lit.)

Set a beggar on horse-back and he'll ride to the devil.

注 指暴發戶猖狂。

2185 賭氣

dou[2] hei[3] *(translit.)*

Make a bet with air. (lit.)

Do something in a fit of pique.

Do something rashly for being put in the wrong.

注 表示因不滿而做出……，或因受了委屈而草率地做出……的意思。

十五畫

2186　賤格

zin⁶ gaak³ *(translit.)*

Cheap style. (lit.)

Be bese-minded.

Make oneself cheap.

Be too mean to be favoured.

🈲 即下賤，做有損自己名譽的事或不識
抬舉的意思。

2187　嘩鬼

waa¹ gwai² *(translit.)*

Clamourous ghosts. (lit.)

Noise maker (s).

Clamour maker (s).

Bustling guy (s).

🈲 指狂叫的人或喧嘩者。

2188　數還數，路還路

sou³ waan⁴ sou³, lou⁶ waan⁴ lou⁶
(translit.)

A sum is a sum and a road is a road. (lit.)

Balance accounts with somebody in spite of intimates.

🈲 即人情是人情，數目要算清。

2189　踢竇

tek³ dau³ *(translit.)*

Kick the den. (lit.)

Gather together a bunch of women to create a disturbance in the house of one's husband's mistress / adulteress.

🈲 婦女發覺丈夫在外養了小老婆或情
婦，糾集一羣婦女去其住處搗亂泄
憤，這種舉動，廣東人稱之為 "踢
竇"。

2190　踏兩頭船

daap⁶ loeng⁵ tau⁴ syun⁴ *(translit.)*

Stand on two boats. (lit.)

Play both ends against the middle.

Attempt to profit oneself in two ways.

Fall between two stools.

Seek favour with opposing parties.

🈲 參閱 "一腳踏兩船" 條（0068）。

2191　踩死蟻

caai² sei² ngai⁵ *(translit.)*

Tread ants to death. (lit.)

Walk at a snail's pace.

Be snail-slow.

🈲 比喻慢吞吞的走路。

2192　踩着 / 倒芋荄都當蛇

caai² zoek⁶ / dou² wu⁶ gaap³ dou¹
dong³ se⁴ *(translit.)*

Stepping on a leaf-stalk of taro is thought as stepping on a snake. (lit.)

Take every bush for a bugbear.

🈲 表示杯弓蛇影的意思。

2193　踩親……條尾

caai² can¹...tiu⁴ mei⁵ *(translit.)*

Tread somebody's tail. (lit.)

Cause offence to somebody.

Touch somebody to his pain.

🈲 表示觸怒某人或觸犯了某人的忌諱。

2194　噠噠吃吃

gi⁶ gi¹ gat⁶ gat⁶ *(translit.)*

Stammer and obstruct. (lit.)

Stutter out.

Be troubled with stammer.

Be in the way.

Obstruct somebody from doing something.

Hinder somebody this way and that way.

Be a hind rance.

注 表示結結巴巴地説，阻撓人做……或（行動方面）礙手礙腳的意思（有時只説 "嘰㞢"）。

2195　幡竿燈籠——照遠唔照近

faan¹ gon¹ dang¹ lung⁴ — ziu³ jyun⁵ m⁴ ziu³ kan⁵ *(translit.)*

The lantern on the banner pole calling the soul home — It illuminates far, not near. (lit.)

Benefit any other persons than close ones.

Rather help outsiders than insiders.

注 表示寧關照外人而不關照自己人的意思。

2196　墨七

mak⁶ cat¹ *(translit.)*

Ink stick VII. (lit.)

A burglar.

注 即夜盜。

2197　靠呃

kaau³ ngak¹ *(translit.)*

Rely on deceiving. (lit.)

Live by getting something on the cross.

Double-cross somebody to earn one's living.

Sell somebody down the river.

注 表示以欺騙為生或欺騙。

2198　靠害

kaau³ hoi⁶ *(translit.)*

Do harm. (lit.)

Lead somebody into a trap.

Entrap somebody into a difficult situation.

注 誘使人陷入困境的意思，相當於 "坑人"。

2199　靠諦

kaau³ dai³ *(translit.)*

Make use of scathing satire. (lit.)

Talk at somebody.

Pout ridicule on somebody.

注 表示冷嘲熱諷的意思，參閱 "單單打打" 條（1819）。

2200　虢礫嘩嘞

gwik¹ lik¹ gwaak¹ laak¹ *(translit.)*

Kwick lick kwark lark. (lit.)

Odds and ends.

A gross medley of miscellaneous things.

Crackle / Rattle / Crackling / Rattling.

注 即雜七雜八的東西，但亦作象聲詞，表示物件相撞的聲音。（作象聲詞時，語音為 gik˚ lik˚ gwaak˚ laak˚）。

2201　餓死老婆燻臭屋

ngo⁶ sei² lou⁵ po⁴ fan¹ / wan¹ cau³ uk¹ *(translit.)*

Make a wife die of hunger and let her corpse vaporize the house to be foul. (lit.)

Cannot earn enough bread to get married.

One's income is too poor to have a wife.

Make one's wife suffer hunger due to insufficiency of income.

注 表示收入不足以養妻室。

2202　餓狗搶屎

ngo⁶ gau² coeng² si² *(translit.)*

Hungry dogs fight to seize manure. (lit.)

Compete against each other for something.

注 形容人搶奪東西時的醜態。

十五畫

2203　餓鬼投胎

ngo⁶ gwai² tau⁴ toi¹ *(translit.)*

A hungry ghost reincarated. (lit.)

Devour like a hungry tiger pouncing its prey.

Wolf down.

注 形容人的吃相醜，意為狼吞虎嚥的樣子。

2204　膝頭哥撟眼淚

sat¹ tau⁴ go¹ giu² ngaan⁵ leoi⁶ *(translit.)*

Wipe tears with a knee. (lit.)

Commit a gross error and shed sad tears.

注 表示"鑄成大錯而傷心流淚"的意思。

2205　劉備借荊州 —— 有借冇回頭

Lau⁴ Bei²/⁶ ze³ Ging¹ Zau¹ — jau⁵ ze³ mou⁵ wui⁴ tau⁴ *(translit.)*

Lau Bei borrowed Kingchow — borrowing it but never returning it (lit.)

Not to discharge / return the borrowing.

The loan once given never comes back.

Lau Bei — the emperor of the Minor Han (Hon) Dynasty in the period of The Three Kingdoms 221 A.D.

注 指借出的東西永沒有歸還或從不歸還借來的東西。

2206　諗鬼食豆腐

tam³ gwai² sik⁶ dau⁶ fu⁶ *(translit.)*

Deceive a ghost into eating beancurd. (lit.)

Cheat somebody into the belief.

注 表示用缺乏可信性的謊言，騙人相信的意思。

2207　諸事

zyu¹ si⁶ *(translit.)*

Like to interfere in all matters. (lit.)

Like to poke one's nose into...

Have an oar in every man's boat.

Poke and pry.

注 指好管閒事。("諸事"和"滋事"音義有別，"諸"為 zyu¹ 音，"滋"為 zi¹ 音，但南海順德及小欖等地人士，則"諸""滋"兩音一樣作 zyu¹ 音，"滋事"為無事生非的意思。參閱 1834 條)。

2208　諸事理

zyu¹ si⁶ lei¹ *(translit.)*

A meddler. (lit.)

A Nosy Parker.

A meddler.

注 指好管閒事的人。

2209　誰不知……

seoi⁴ bat¹ zi¹... *(translit.)*

Who does not know... (lit.)

Who would have thought that...

It turned out to be that...

注 這句口頭語用於發現了實情後説的，意為誰會料到……或原來是……。

2210　論盡

leon⁶ zeon⁶ *(translit.)*

Slow-moving. (lit.)

Be both doddery and obtuse.

Be not smart enough.

It is too bad.

Burdensome / cumbersome.

注 形容老年人遲鈍，老態龍鍾；年輕人舉止不靈活；物件累贅，笨重而不方便的意思。除此之外，還作感歎詞作糟糕意思用。

2211 諗縮數

nam² suk¹ sou³ *(translit.)*

Think of shrinking account. (lit.)

Be petty and scheming.

Pursue selfish interests.

注 為自己打如意算盤或謀私利的意思。

2212 諗爛心肝

nam² laan⁶ sam¹ gon¹ *(translit.)*

Deep thinking makes the heart and livers be rotten. (lit.)

Chew the cud.

Ponder deeply over...

Take counsel of one's pillow.

注 表示反覆思量或思考得不能入睡的意思。

2213 熟人買破鑊

suk⁶ jan⁴ maai⁵ po³ wok⁶ *(translit.)*

A familiar friend buys a broken frying-pan. (lit.)

Be sold a pup by one's friend.

Be imposed by one's friend.

注 指被熟人以次貨欺騙，上熟人的當。

2214 熟行

suk⁶ hong⁴ *(translit.)*

Familiar trading. (lit.)

Be adept in...

Be skilled.

注 內行；在行；熟練。

2215 熟性

suk⁶ sing³ *(translit.)*

Familiar-natured. (lit.)

Be reasonable.

Offer bribes to somebody.

Grease the palm of somebody.

注 表示通情達理或向人行賄。

2216 熟客仔

suk⁶ haak³ zai² *(translit.)*

A familiar vistor. (lit.)

A frequent caller / customer.

注 熟客，常客，熟主顧。

2217 熟能生巧

suk⁶ nang⁴ sang¹ / saang¹ haau² *(translit.)*

Proficiency can generate skills. (lit.)

Practice makes perfect.

2218 熟落

suk⁶ lok⁶ *(translit.)*

Ripe enough to come down. (lit.)

Be skilled in...

Know a lot about...

Be on familiar terms with somebody.

注 表示熟練，對⋯⋯很熟悉或和某人很稔熟的意思。

2219 熟檔

suk⁶ dong³ *(translit.)*

Familiar stall. (lit.)

Be adept in...

Know a lot about...

注 即內行；熟悉。

2220 熟讀唐詩三百首，唔會吟詩也會偷

suk⁶ duk⁶ tong⁴ si¹ saam¹ baak³ sau², m⁴ wui⁵ jam⁴ si¹ jaa⁵ wui⁵ tau¹ *(translit.)*

Having thoroughly read three hundred poems in the Tong Poetry, one can imitate the way how they were composed even though one cannot compose one. (lit.)

Practice makes perfect.

Skill comes from constant practice.

All genuine knowledge originates

十五畫

in direct experience.

📝 從經驗學得，從長久練習學成或熟能生巧的意思。

2221　摩囉差拜神 —— 睇天

mo¹ lo¹ caa¹ baai³ san⁴ — tai² tin¹ *(translit.)*

Indians worship their god — look at the sky. (lit.)

Be under the mercy of God.

Take notice of the change of weather.

It depends on the weather.

📝 表示一切望上蒼庇祐，（參閱 1679 "望天打卦" 條）或視天氣情況而定的意思。

2222　熠熟狗頭

saap⁶ suk⁶ gau² tau⁴ *(translit.)*

A well-boiled dog's head. (lit.)

Be on the broad grin.

Have a face beaming with smiles.

📝 形容人笑得齜牙咧嘴的樣子。

2223　潮州音樂 —— 自己顧自己

ciu⁴ zau¹ jam¹ ngok⁶ — zi⁶ gei¹ᐟ² gu³ zi⁶ gei¹ᐟ² *(translit.)*

Chiuchow music — one looks after oneself. (lit.)

Take care of oneself.

Near is my shirt, but nearest us my skin.

Pay one's bill for oneself.

Pay for something at one's own expense.

📝 自己照顧自己或各自付賬的意思，相當於 "老西兒拉胡琴 —— 自顧自"。

2224　潤

jeon⁶ *(translit.)*

Lubricate / Moisten. (lit.)

Give somebody ironical remarks.

It is meant to be a dig at somebody.

Hold somebody to ridicule.

Profit somebody.

📝 表示挖苦或諷刺別人或給人利益的意思。（前義和 2317 "㨃" 大致同義，不過 "㨃" 有激發而沒有給人利益的意思。）

2225　潑冷水

put³ laang⁵ seoi² *(translit.)*

Sprinkle cold water. (lit.)

Throw cold water on somebody.

Discourage somebody from doing something.

Throw a wet blanket over somebody.

📝 表示掃興，使人泄氣或打擊人（做某事）的熱情。

2226　潑辣

put³ laat⁶ *(translit.)*

Be shrewish-tempered. (lit.)

Be both shrewish and violent.

📝 形容人兇悍而不講理。

2227　窮到燶

kung⁴ dou³ lung¹ *(translit.)*

Being poor up to the degree of being scorched. (lit.)

Be as poor as a church mouse.

Have not a feather to fly with.

Have not a bean.

Be down on one's uppers.

📝 比喻一貧如洗。

2228　窮寇莫追

kung⁴ kau³ mok⁶ zeoi¹ *(translit.)*

Do not run after a foe too far. (lit.)

Not to try to run after the hardpressed enemy.

📝 原指圍殲敵人時要講究策略，對於陷

入絕境的敵人不可逼得太緊，否則敵
人會困獸猶鬥，造成己方不必要的損
失。後引伸為不追無路可走的敵人。

2229　褪軚

tan³ taai⁵ (translit.)

Turn back the steer. (lit.)

Beat a retreat.

Shrink back.

🈲 即放棄，退縮或"打退堂鼓"，參閱
該條（0469）。

2230　蝨乸都要擔枷

sat¹ naa² dou¹ jiu³ daam¹ gaa¹
(translit.)

*Even all the fleas have to put on
wooden collars. (lit.)*

**Deserve a very severe
punishment.**

**Even one's family are implicated
in a severe punishment.**

🈲 表示除個人應受極嚴厲的懲罰外，甚
至連家人也得受嚴厲的懲罰。

2231　劈炮

pek³ paau³ (translit.)

Chop a cannon. (lit.)

Quit from one's job.

🈲 意為辭職不幹。

2232　劈〔瓹〕撚鑿

pek³ nan² zok⁶ (translit.)

*In spite of being cloven, one
makes the chisel dirty. (lit.)*

**A person who swears black is
white.**

**A person who denies having
done something.**

🈲 比喻顛倒是非或否認幹過某事的人。
迷信者相信雷神會劈那些不忠不孝或
不義的人，對於那些顛倒是非或幹過
壞事也否認的人，即使受雷神劈了也

會弄污他的鑿。"撚"廣東人除作"玩
弄"意思外，還借音作"弄污"解。

2233　駕步

gaa³ bou⁶ (translit.)

The pace of cart. (lit.)

Haughty manner / airs.

Noble-postured.

Be arrogant.

🈲 駕勢或架子的意思，和"架步"同音
異義，參閱"架步"條（1319）。

2234　墮角

do⁶ gok³ (translit.)

Degenerate corner. (lit.)

Be out-of-the-way.

Be remote.

🈲 即偏僻。

十六　畫

2235　靜靜雞 / 靜雞雞

zing⁶ zing² gai¹ / zing⁶ gai¹ gai¹
(translit.)

Keep silence. (lit.)

Keep one's hair on.

**Keep one's countenance without
a word.**

Bite one's lips.

Act in silence.

🈲 指保持鎮靜，不露聲色或靜悄悄地行
事。

2236　蕩失路

dong⁶ sat¹ lou⁶ (translit.)

Lose the way while strolling. (lit.)

Lose one's way.

Be lost (somewhere).

🈲 即迷途。

十六畫

2237　擸／掹衫尾

mang¹ saam¹ mei⁵ *(translit.)*

Drag the tail of a coat. (lit.)

Ask gambling winners for money／tips outside the casino.

注 指在賭館門外向贏錢賭客乞取賞錢的行為（也有人説成拉衫尾）。

2238　擇使

zaak⁶ sai² *(translit.)*

Trouble with. (lit.)

Be troublesome.

Have some trouble in doing something.

It is a headache.

It embarrasses one.

Put one to inconvenience.

Have difficulty in dealing with...

注 表示麻煩，傷腦筋，難辦或不好使用，不方便。

2239　擒青／擒擒青

kam⁴ ceng¹／kam⁴ kam² ceng¹ *(translit.)*

In a hurry. (lit.)

Be in a tearing hurry.

Be short-tempered.

Be too impatient to wait.

Leap without thinking.

Be rash.

注 表示匆匆忙忙的樣子，魯莽，莽撞。

2240　擔屎都唔偷食

daam¹ si² dou¹ m⁴ tau¹ sik⁶ *(translit.)*

While carrying manure with a pole on a shoulder, one does not steal any of it to eat. (lit.)

Be very honest in deed.

注 形容人誠實可靠。

2241　擔戴

daam¹ daai³ *(translit.)*

Carry and bring something on the shoulder. (lit.)

Undertake responsibility.

注 表示擔待；承擔責任的意思。

2242　樹大有枯枝，族大有乞兒

syu⁶ daai⁶ jau⁵ fu¹ zi¹, zuk⁶ daai⁶ jau⁵ hat¹ ji¹/⁴ *(translit.)*

Big trees have decayed branches; big clans may have beggars. (lit.)

There is a black sheep in every fold.

注 意即十個指頭有長短；哪裏都有害羣之馬。

2243　樹大招風

syu⁶ daai⁶ ziu¹ fung¹ *(translit.)*

Big trees catch much wind. (lit.)

A person of reputation is liable to become the envy of others.

注 比喻名聲大或地位高的人在社會上特別顯眼，往往容易給自己招來麻煩或招人嫉妒。

2244　樹倒猢猻散

syu⁶ dou² wu⁴ syun¹ saan³ *(translit.)*

When a tree falls, all the monkeys scatter about. (lit.)

Rats leave a sinking ship.

As soon as an influential person falls from his position, all his hangers-on disperse.

注 比喻人一失勢，追隨者亦隨而分散。

2245　樹高千丈，落葉歸根

syu⁶ gou¹ cin¹ zoeng⁶, lok⁶ jip⁶ gwai¹ gan¹ *(translit.)*

Though a tree is ten thousand feet tall, the fallen leaves come back to its roots. (lit.)

No matter whether it is east or west, home is the best.

注 上了年紀的國人，鄉土觀念甚強，無論在何處謀生，到了一個時期，總是忘不了故里而作鳥倦知還之想。這就是 "樹高千丈，落葉歸根" 的道理。

2246 橫九咕十

waang⁴ gau² dim⁶ sap⁶ *(translit.)*

The breadth is nine and the length is ten. (lit.)

Such being the case.

In any case.

In for a penny, in for a pound.

注 這口頭語的意義是相當籠統的，既可表事實既然如此，又可表無論如何或橫豎，參閱 "橫咕" 條（2249），更可作 "一不做，二不休" 的意思。

2247 橫手

waang⁴ sau² *(translit.)*

Cross hand. (lit.)

The person who acts underhand for somebody.

注 指秘密代理某人的人。

2248 橫行霸道

waang⁴ hang⁴ / haang⁴ baa³ dou⁶ *(translit.)*

Walk on the cross and act in tyrannous manner. (lit.)

Play the bully.

注 仗勢欺人，做壞事；不講理。

2249 橫咕

waang⁴ dim⁶ *(translit.)*

Breadth and length. (lit.)

In any case.

Anyhow.

Anyway.

注 表示無論如何，反正或橫豎的意思。

2250 橫咕都係一樣

waang⁴ dim⁶ dou¹ hai⁶ jat¹ joeng⁶ *(translit.)*

Breadth and length are the same. (lit.)

It is all the same to somebody.

It is the very same thing whether...

注 表示 "對……而言，都是一樣" 或作強調來表示 "是否……也是完全一樣" 的意思。

2251 橫衝直撞

waang⁴ cung¹ zik⁶ zong⁶ *(translit.)*

Rush horizontally and knock straightly. (lit.)

Collide in every direction.

Jostle and elbow one's way through a crowd.

注 亂衝亂闖的意思。

2252 橫蠻無理

waang⁴ maan⁴ mou⁴ lei⁵ *(translit.)*

Be beastly and reasonless. (lit.)

Be savage like a beast.

注 表示非常不講道理。

2253 輸蝕

syu¹ sit⁶ *(translit.)*

Suffer losses. (lit.)

Be inferior to...

Be lower-graded than...

Be on a lower level.

Let another boat eat the wind out of one's own.

Let somebody gain the wind.

注 差；差勁；吃虧或讓人佔上風的意思。

2254 整古做怪

zing² gu² zou⁶ gwaai³ *(translit.)*

Make strangeness and do peculiarities. (lit.)

Make a face.

Make mystery of something.

Wrap something in mystery.

十六畫

注 表示做鬼臉故意出洋相或故弄玄虛的
意思。

2255　整色整水

zing² sik¹ zing² seoi² *(translit.)*

Make colours and water. (lit.)

Put on an act.

注 裝模作樣。

2256　整定

zing² ding⁶ *(translit.)*

Be determined. (lit.)

Be destined.

Destinies grasp one's fate.

注 即某種客觀規律決定，注定。

2257　整蠱

zing² gu² *(translit.)*

Make noxious worms. (lit.)

Play a trick on somebody.

Play pranks upon somebody.

**Trick somebody into doing
　something.**

Frame up somebody.

Catch somebody in a trap.

注 表示捉弄或惡作劇，參閱 "撳化" 條
（2156）或陷害的意思。

2258　賴貓

laai³ maau¹ *(translit.)*

A counterfeit cat. (lit.)

Make a denial / disavowal.

Disavow.

Play tricks.

注 抵賴，不承認或耍手段欺騙的意思。

2259　融洽

jung⁴ hap¹ *(translit.)*

On friendly terms. (lit.)

Get along well with each other.

Be harmonious with each other.

2260　頭先

tau⁴ sin¹ *(translit.)*

Just now. (lit.)

A moment ago.

Just now.

注 即剛才，和 "求先" 同。參閱該條
（0878），原因是有些廣州人帶些鄉
音，把 "頭" 音發成 "求" 音。

2261　頭痛醫頭，腳痛醫腳

tau⁴ tung³ ji¹ tau⁴, goek³ tung³ ji¹
goek³ *(translit.)*

*Cure the head when it aches; cure
the leg when it aches. (lit.)*

**Take only a stopgap measure,
　not a radical one.**

注 比喻治標不治本的方法。

2262　頭路

tau⁴ lou⁶ *(translit.)*

The heading road. (lit.)

A pull.

A way.

The ropes shown to somebody.

注 即門路，竅門或途徑的意思。參閱 "路
數" 條（1992）。

2263　頭髮尾浸浸涼

tau⁴ faat³ mei⁵ zam³ zam³ loeng⁴
(translit.)

*All the ends of hair become cool.
(lit.)*

**Gloat over somebody's / one's
　enemy's misfortune.**

注 參閱 "心都涼晒" 條（0428）及 "幸
災樂禍" 條（1006）。

2264　頭頭碰着黑

tau⁴ tau⁴ pung³ zoek⁶ hak¹ *(translit.)*

*Meet with black in every direction.
(lit.)*

Strike a snag everywhere.

Run into snags in all directions.
Meet with difficulties whatever
one does.

注 到處碰壁的意思。

2265　醒

sing[2] *(translit.)*
Awaking. (lit.)
Clever.
Smart.
Quick-witted.
Terrific.
Swell with pride.

注 大致和"醒目"同義，又有"了不起"，
"神氣"的意思。參閱該條（2267），
有時又説"醒神"（sing[2] san[4]）。

2266　醒水

sing[2] seoi[2] *(translit.)*
Wake the water. (lit.)
Come to realize...
Be awake to...

注 即醒覺的意思。

2267　醒目

sing[2] muk[6] *(translit.)*
Awaking-eyed. (lit.)
Clever.
Smart.
Be as smart as a steel trap.
Attractive.
Attract attention.

注 表示聰明伶俐，機警或形象明顯引人
注目。

2268　醒定啲

sing[2] ding[6] di[1] *(translit.)*
Be awaken. (lit.)
Take care.
Be careful.
Take yourself / himself...into
account.

注 表示當心（用於勸告）或提防……的
性命（用於警告或威嚇）的意思，參
閱 "因住"（2428）。

2269　霎眼嬌

saap[3] ngaan[5] giu[1] *(translit.)*
Instant beauty. (lit.)
Appear to be beautiful at a
glance.

注 乍看起來，似乎漂亮的意思。

2270　霎戇！

saap[3] ngong[6]! *(translit.)*
Scoundrel! (lit.)
(You) preposterous
Bastard!

注 即 "傻瓜"，"荒謬"或 "混脹"。

2271　頻倫

pan[4] lan[4] *(translit.)*
Hurry. (lit.)
Be in a tearing hurry.
Be hurry-scurry.
Hurry through something.

注 匆匆忙忙；手忙腳亂。

2272　頻倫唔得入城

pan[4] lan[4] m[4] dak[1] jap[6] seng[4] *(translit.)*
Too hasty to enter the city. (lit.)
More haste, less speed.
A watched pot never boils.

注 欲速則不達的意思。

2273　頻撲

pan[4] pok[3] *(translit.)*
Be busy running about. (lit.)
Have a run for one's money.
Shuttle back and forth for one's
living.

注 奔波或為生活東奔西走。

2274　蘸吓眼

zaam[2] haa[5] ngaan[5] *(translit.)*

十
六
畫

Wink the eyes. (lit.)

In a twinkle.

In a flash.

In an instant.

注 一眨眼功夫，轉瞬之間。

2275 跺蹄跺爪

dam⁶ tai⁴ dam⁶ zaau² *(translit.)*

Stamp both hoofs and paws. (lit.)

Stamp the floor in deep sorrow / in anger.

注 形容傷心或憤怒時捶胸頓足的神態。

2276 錯有錯着

co³ jau⁵ co³ zoek⁶ *(translit.)*

Take advantage of the mistake. (lit.)

Have a fault on the right side.

注 因禍得福的意思。

2277 錯蕩

co³ dong⁶ *(translit.)*

Have a wrong stroll. (lit.)

Be honoured by the undeserved visit / presence.

Be glad to have the undeserved visit / presence.

注 這是見到自己親朋忽然來訪時，一見面說的客套話，意為承蒙枉顧，實感榮幸，愧不敢當。

2278 錫住

sek³ zyu⁶ *(translit.)*

Give love to... (lit.)

Cherish a deep love for somebody.

Use something sparingly / cautiously.

Make the best use of something.

Stint the / one's money.

注 表示愛惜（人），善用（物）或吝惜（金錢）的意思。

2279 貓衣 / 兒毛 —— 順捏

maau¹ ji¹ mou⁴ — seon⁶ nip⁶ *(translit.)*

Kitten's hair — give it a smooth according to its natural tendency. (lit.)

Stroke the fur the right way.

Cater to somebody's tendency.

Beguile somebody with honeyed words.

注 指對吃軟不吃硬的人的哄騙手段。

2280 貓哭老鼠 —— 假慈悲

maau¹ huk¹ lou⁵ syu² — gaa² ci⁴ bei¹ *(translit.)*

A cat weeps for the rat — false mercy. (lit.)

Shed crocodile tears.

注 表示虛偽的仁慈。

2281 獨家村

duk⁶ gaa¹ cyun¹ *(translit.)*

One man's village. (lit.)

A person of uncommunicative and eccentric disposition.

An unsociable and eccentric person.

A lone wolf.

注 比喻不好交際離羣獨居或難與為友的人。

2282 親力親為

can¹ lik⁶ can¹ wai⁴ *(translit.)*

Do by oneself. (lit.)

Do the job all by oneself.

注 親自動手的意思。

2283 親生仔不如近身錢

can¹ saang¹ zai² bat¹ jyu⁴ gan⁶ san¹ cin⁴ *(translit.)*

A begotten son is not so good as the money in pocket. (lit.)

Money is the nearest relation.

注 表示靠自己的積蓄勝過依靠兒子的意思。

2284　親自出馬

can¹ zi⁶ ceot¹ maa⁵ *(translit.)*

Take out the horse personally. (lit.)

Act in one's capacity.

Take up the matter by oneself.

2285　龍牀唔似狗竇

lung⁴ cong⁴ m⁴ ci⁵ gau² dau³ *(translit.)*

A dragon bed (an imperial bed) is not like a dog's kennel. (lit.)

There is no place sweeter than home.

A man gets used to his own bed / kennel.

注 相當於 " 金窩銀窩，不及自己的草窩 " 。

2286　龍游淺水遭蝦戲

lung⁴ jau⁴ cin² seoi² zou¹ haa¹ hei³ *(translit.)*

A dragon swimming in shallow water is fooled by shrimps. (lit.)

No man is a hero to his valet.

Out of one's sphere of influence, out of one's power.

注 參閱 " 虎落平陽被犬欺 " 條〔1058〕。

2287　糖黐豆

tong⁴ ci¹ dau² *(translit.)*

Beans stuck with sugar. (lit.)

Form a close connexion with each other.

Hand and glove.

注 比喻彼此友好，關係密切。

2288　燒冷竈

siu¹ laang⁵ zou³ *(translit.)*

Burn a cold stove. (lit.)

Back the wrong horse.

注 比喻支持失勢的人，希望他重獲財勢

時，獲得好處。

2289　燒到⋯⋯喐疊

siu¹ dou³... go² daap⁶ *(translit.)*

The fire spreads to... (lit.)

The spearhead is directed to somebody.

Drag somebody in...

Transfer the subject of conversation to somebody.

注 表示矛頭指向⋯⋯身上，把某人拉進⋯⋯之內或把話題轉移到某人身上的意思。

2290　燒枱炮

siu¹ toi⁴ paau³ *(translit.)*

Fire the big gun on the table. (lit.)

Thump the table / desk and heap abuse on somebody.

注 拍桌子大罵。

2291　燒壞瓦

siu¹ waai⁶ ngaa⁵ *(translit.)*

An ill-burned tile. (lit.)

Cannot adjust oneself to others.

Cannot mate with others.

Not suit well with others.

注 比喻和人合不來的人。

2292　燈芯拎成鐵

dang¹ sam¹ ling¹ sing⁴ / seng⁴ tit³ *(translit.)*

Take a lamp wick for a long time and it will become iron. (lit.)

A straw shows its weight when it is carried a long way.

注 比喻最輕的東西，拿上一段時間，也會變重。

2293　閻羅王揸攤 —— 鬼買

jim⁴ lo⁴ wong⁴ zaa¹ taan¹ — gwai² maai⁵ *(translit.)*

The king of Jim Lo holds 'Fantan'
(The king of hell is the bank
of 'Fantan' — a form of
gambling) — ghosts bet. (lit.)

Nobody buys.

注 真意為無人購買。

2294　閻羅王嫁女 —— 鬼要

jim⁴ lo⁴ wong⁴ gaa³ neoi² — gwai² jiu³
(translit.)

The king of Jim Lo (The king
of hell) marries off his
daughters — ghosts want. (lit.)

Nobody wants (it).

注 表示沒有人要的意思。

2295　遲到好過冇到

ci⁴ dou³ hou² gwo³ mou⁵ dou³
(translit.)

Coming lately is better than not
coming. (lit.)

Rather late than never.

注 表示晚到比不到要好。

2296　遲嚟先上岸

ci⁴ lai⁴ sin¹ soeng⁵ ngon⁶ *(translit.)*

Come late but go ashore first. (lit.)

The last comer becomes the first
goer.

The person who comes first is not
like the one who comes all by a
happy coincidence.

注 相當於 "來得早不如來得巧"。

2297　隨便你 / 佢

ceoi⁴ bin² nei⁵ / keoi⁵ *(translit.)*

Follow your / his convenience.
　(lit.)

Do / Does what you want / he
wants to.

You / He can do what you / he can
at random.

注 表示任從你 / 他怎樣做便怎樣做的意
思，參閱 "隨得……" 條（2298）及
"你 / 佢想點就點" 條（0931）。

2298　隨得……

ceoi²ᐟ⁴ dak¹... *(translit.)*

Give rein to... (lit.)

As one / somebody likes.

As one / somebody sees fit.

At one's / somebody's
convenience.

注 表示隨便，或任便，參閱 "隨便
你 / 佢" 條（2297）。

2299　險過剃頭

him² gwo³ tai³ tau⁴ *(translit.)*

More dangerous than shaving a
head. (lit.)

Hang by a hair.

Be in great danger.

Be in the hour of peril.

注 表示千鈞一髮的意思。

十七　畫

2300　幫理不幫親

bong¹ lei⁵ bat¹ bong¹ can¹ *(translit.)*

Defend the reason, but defend on
relations. (lit.)

Be fair-minded.

See fair play.

注 表示公平。

2301　藉 / 借啲意 / 藉 / 借頭
藉 / 借路

ze³ di¹ ji² / ze³ tau⁴ ze³ lou⁶ *(translit.)*

Borrow some ideas / Borrow both
the head and the way. (lit.)

Jump at the chance.

Seize the opportunity.

Take advantage of the favourable situation.

Cook up a lame excuse.

🈯表示乘機，趁勢或製造假藉口。

2302　薄皮

bok[6] pei[2] *(translit.)*

Thin-skinned. (lit.)

Be apt to cry. (of person)

Be prone to blush. (of person)

🈯即臉皮薄，容易哭或容易臉紅。

2303　薄削

bok[6] soek[3] *(translit.)*

Thin and soft. (lit.)

Thin and soft (of cloth / paper...).

🈯指布料或紙張等很薄，稀疏。

2304　戴綠帽

daai[3] luk[6] mou[2] *(translit.)*

Wear a green hat. (lit.)

A cuckold.

A man whose wife commits adultery with another man.

Be cuckolded.

🈯即戴上綠頭巾。

2305　擤到骨罅都刺埋

sang[3] / san[3] dou[3] gwat[1] laa[3] dou[1] cek[3] maai[4] *(translit.)*

Utter moans until the articulations of the bones ache. (lit.)

Make a constant complaint for having paid so much for something.

🈯指因付出代價太多而發出怨言，參閱 "擤到樹葉都落埋"條（2306）。

2306　擤到樹葉都落埋

sang[3] / san[3] dou[3] syu[6] jip[6] dou[1] lok[6] maai[4] *(translit.)*

Utter moans until all the leaves

have fallen. (lit.)

Express one's repentance for having paid for something worthless.

Make a constant complaint for having paid so much for something.

Feel sorry for having missed a chance.

🈯大致和 "擤到骨罅都刺埋" 同義，但 這句更表示因花了錢購得無用的東 西而懊悔或因失去機會而難過的意 思。

2307　擤笨

sang[3] / san[3] ban[6] *(translit.)*

Utter moans for stupidity. (lit.)

Show repentance for having been stupid / fooled.

Feel sorry for having missed the opportunity.

🈯表示因自己過去愚昧，被騙或失去機 會而後悔的意思。

2308　擦鞋

caat[3] haai[4] *(translit.)*

Shine shoes. (lit.)

Flatter somebody.

Fawn upon somebody.

Toady somebody.

🈯表示奉承別人的意思。

2309　擦錯鞋

caat[3] co[3] haai[4] *(translit.)*

Brush the wrong shoe. (lit.)

Stroke the fur the wrong way.

🈯比喻本來想討好某人，但結果適得其 反。

2310　聲大夾冇準

seng[1] daai[6] gaap[3] mou[5] zeon[2] *(translit.)*

十七畫

The voice is loud but not correct. (lit.)

Much cry and little wool.

注 形容一個人說話很多，但沒一句是對的。

2311　聲大夾惡

seng¹ daai⁶ gaap³ ok³ *(translit.)*

Be big-voiced and ferocious. (lit.)

Come the bully over somebody.

注 沒道理還要大聲罵人。

2312　聰明一世，蠢鈍一時

cung¹ ming⁴ jat¹ sai³, ceon² deon⁶ jat¹ si⁴ *(translit.)*

Be clever all the life but foolish for once. (lit.)

A smartie is not always as smart as a steel trap.

Be clever all the time but become a fool this once.

注 表示一時糊塗的意思。

2313　韓信點兵——多多益善

Hon⁴ Seon³ dim² bing¹ — do¹ do¹ jik¹ sin⁶ *(translit.)*

Hon Seon called for soldiers — the greater the number the better. (lit.)

The more the better.

Han Sun was one of the three persons of great endowments in the Early Han Dynasty.

注 表示 "越多越好" 的意思。

2314　臨天光瀨尿

lam⁴ tin¹ gwong¹ laai⁶ niu⁶ *(translit.)*

Have an unvoluntary passage of urine at daybreak. (lit.)

There is many a slip 'between the cup and the lip.'

Suffer failure when success is within one's grasp.

注 表示功虧一簣的意思。

2315　臨老學吹打

lam⁴ lou⁵ hok⁶ ceoi¹ daa² *(translit.)*

Begin to learn blowing and beating when getting old. (lit.)

An old dog begins to learn new tricks.

注 比喻到年紀大時才學習。

2316　臨時臨急

lam⁴ si⁴ lam⁴ gap¹ *(translit.)*

When emergency comes. (lit.)

At the last moment.

Not...until an emergency.

注 表示到了最後時刻或非到緊急時刻不……的意思。

2317　嶖

ai³ *(translit.)*

Satirize. (lit.)

Hold somebody to ridicule.

Give somebody ironical remarks.

It is meant to be a dig at somebody.

Pour ridicule on somebody.

Prodding / Annoy / Enrage somebody with derision.

注 挖苦，以嘲笑來激發或激怒的意思。

2318　嬲到彈起

nau¹ dou³ daan⁶ hei² *(translit.)*

Spring up for anger. (lit.)

Hit the roof.

注 表示勃然大怒，發火。

2319　嬲爆爆

nau¹ baau³ baau³ *(translit.)*

Get angry. (lit.)

Be filled with anger.

Be hot with rage.

注 氣鼓鼓的。

十七畫

2320 點算好

dim² syun³ hou² *(translit.)*

How to reckon? (lit.)

What is to be done?

What shall we / I do?

How shall it be done?

注 即怎麼辦？

2321 簕竇

lak⁶ dau³ *(translit.)*

A thorny den. (lit.)

Be hard to make contact with...

Be hard to get along with.

Be hard to please.

Dirty work.

A hard job. / A profitless job.

Gain no profit from the job.

Work for a dead horse.

注 比喻難以打交道的（人）或無利可圖的（工作），這方面和"豬頭骨"大致相同。參閱（2178）條。

2322 簍休

lau¹ jau¹ *(translit.)*

Untidy (lit.)

Be in one's shirt sleeves.

Not to tidy oneself up.

Be slovenly.

注 表示不修邊幅的意思。

2323 臊臊都係羊肉，爛爛 / 舊舊都係絲綢

sou¹ sou¹ dou¹ hai⁶ joeng⁴ juk⁶, laan⁶ laan⁶ / gau⁶ gau⁶ dou¹ hai⁶ si¹ cau⁴ *(translit.)*

It is still mutton though it is rank-smelling; it is still silk though it is worn out / though it is very old. (lit.)

Gold is gold no matter whether it glitters or not.

注 比喻不論外表怎樣，價值始終是價值。

2324 膽大心細

daam² daai⁶ sam¹ sai³ *(translit.)*

The gall is big and the heart is small. (lit.)

Be bold but cautious.

Be courageous but attentive.

注 細心行事，勇於嘗試。

2325 膽正命平

daam² zeng³ meng⁶ peng⁴ / daam² zing³ ming⁶ peng⁴ *(translit.)*

The gall is upright and the life is cheap. (lit.)

Have too much spunk to care for one's own life.

注 勇氣十足，不顧生命危險。

2326 講心啫

gong² sam¹ ze¹ *(translit.)*

Talk about heart. (lit.)

Take each other to bosom.

Have a heart-to-heart talk.

注 推心置腹的意思。

2327 講多錯多

gong² do¹ co³ do¹ *(translit.)*

The more one speaks, the more mistakes one makes. (lit.)

The least said, the soonest mended.

注 即言多必失。

2328 講來 / 嚟講去都係三幅被

gong² loi⁴ / lai⁴ gong² heoi³ dou¹ hai⁶ saam¹ fuk¹ pei⁵ *(translit.)*

What one talks again and again is only but a three-sheet quilt. (lit.)

Sing the song of burden.

Repeat oneself.

注 表示不斷重複説。

十七畫

2329 講到話……

gong² dou³ waa⁶... *(translit.)*

Say to the words... (lit.)

As to / for...

🈯表示至於……或就……方面來説。

2330 講咗／過就算〔數〕

gong² zo² / gwo³ zau⁶ syun³ [sou³] *(translit.)*

What is said is in real earnest. (positive)

What is said is null and voil. (negative) (lit.)

One means what one says.

No sooner said than done.

Go back on one's words.

Only say without deeds.

🈯這口頭語有正反兩義，正義為説得出，做得到。反義為只是説説便算。

2331 講明就陳顯南

gong² ming⁴ zau⁶ can⁴ hin² naam² *(translit.)*

It is repetitious to say clearly. (lit.)

It is a tiresome repetition to make oneself clear.

There is no need to ask if a duck will swim.

It is understood without an explanation.

🈯指不言而喻或不必再加解釋也明白了。參閲"唔使問亞貴"條（1388）及"唔使畫公仔畫出腸"條（1389）。

2332 講起嚟一疋布咁長

gong² hei² lai⁴ jat¹ pat¹ bou³ gam³ coeng⁴ *(translit.)*

Telling in details is like as long as a bolt of cloth. (lit.)

It is like telling a long story.

🈯即説來話長。

2333 講倒話

gong² dou³ waa²ᐟ⁴ *(translit.)*

Say reversed words. (lit.)

Say to the contrary.

Speak an irony.

🈯説反話（用以譏諷人的反話）。

2334 講得出就講

gon² dak¹ ceot¹ zau⁶ gong² *(translit.)*

Say what one wants to say. (lit.)

Have a loose tongue.

🈯指説話沒有任何顧忌。

2335 講就易，做就難

gong² zau⁶ ji⁶, zou⁶ zau⁶ naan⁴ *(translit.)*

Saying is easy but doing is difficult. (lit.)

Easier said than done.

🈯説來容易，做起來困難。

2336 講開又講

gong² hoi¹ jau⁶ gong² *(translit.)*

Mention while speaking. (lit.)

By the way.

🈯意即順便説説。

2337 糟質

zou¹ zat¹ *(translit.)*

Spoil. (lit.)

Slander somebody.

Abuse / Ill treat somebody.

Play the fool of somebody.

Make fool of somebody.

Waste / Spoil something.

🈯表示虐待，作弄，誹謗人或糟踢東西的意思。

2338 濕水棉胎——冇得彈

sap¹ seoi² min⁴ toi¹ — mou⁵ dak¹ taan⁴ *(translit.)*

The cotton-padding soaked in

water — it cannot be fluffed (criticized). (lit.)

Be above criticism.

Be beyond reproach.

🈺 指無可指責或批評。本來 "彈" 字意為 "把棉花抖鬆" 的意思。但廣東人把 "指責或批評" 也叫做 "彈"，參閱 "蛋家婆打醮" 條 (1718)。

2339 濕水欖核 —— 兩頭標

sap¹ seoi² laam² wat⁶ — loeng⁵ tau⁴ biu¹ (translit.)

A wet kernel of olive — it slides this way and that way. (lit.)

Be fleet of foot.

Kick over the traces.

A person who leaves no trace.

🈺 比喻轉眼便不見人，不受約束或難以尋其行蹤的人。

2340 濕星

sap¹ sing¹ (translit.)

Petty things. (lit.)

Odds and ends.

Skin disease or the like.

🈺 零零碎碎的東西或皮膚病之類。

2341 濕滯

sap¹ zai⁶ (translit.)

Damp and impeded. (lit.)

Be impeded.

Meet with hinderance.

Meet with a hitch.

Be unfavourable.

Find it hard to deal with...

Troublesome

Knotty / Thorny

🈺 "濕滯" 本為中醫術語，意為腸胃不適，不好消化。廣東人藉以喻有梗阻，不順利，不好辦；難對付。

2342 濟軍

Zai³ gwan¹ (translit.)

Lung Zai Gwan soldiers. (lit.)

A regular mischief.

A person who runs wild.

🈺 "濟軍" 為 "龍濟光的軍隊" 的簡稱，龍濟光為民國早年的軍閥，他所率領的軍隊，軍紀全無，無惡不作，後來人便用 "濟軍" 這稱號來喻 "惡作劇" 或 "無法無天的人"。

2343 窿窿罅罅

lung¹ lung¹ laa³ laa³ (translit.)

Holes and gaps. (lit.)

Nook and corner.

Crannies.

🈺 即 "嘰里旮旯兒" 或 "旮旮旯旯兒"。

2344 擘網巾

maak³ mong⁵ gan¹ (translit.)

Tear up the silk kerchief. (lit.)

Break off friendly relation with somebody.

Sever connections with somebody.

🈺 表示和人絕交的意思。

2345 孻仔拉心肝，孻女拉內臟

laai¹ zai² laai¹ sam¹ gon¹, laai¹ neoi² laai¹ noi⁶ zong⁶ (translit.)

The youngest son pulls heart and liver; the youngest daughter pulls internal viscera. (lit.)

The youngest child often gains majority of parents' love.

🈺 指父母多數溺愛最小的子女。

2346 蝥

maau⁴ (translit.)

Pest-like. (lit.)

Malicious / Maliciously.

Unruly (unrulily).

🈺 "蝥" 的本義為害蟲之類的動物，但

粤人藉以喻人狠惡的或做事兇狠，同
時又喻在賭博或遊戲中不守規則。

2347　縮沙

suk¹ saa¹ *(translit.)*

Retreat. (lit.)

Beat a retreat.

Shrink back.

📝表示臨時反口，臨陣退縮。參閱〝打
退堂鼓〞條（0469）。

2348　縮骨

suk¹ gwat¹ *(translit.)*

Shrinkable bone. (lit.)

Be self-centred.

Act from selfish motives.

Be treacherous.

📝含有貶義，形容人自私自利或詭計多
端。

2349　縮數

suk¹ sou³ *(translit.)*

A shrinking sum. (lit.)

Be calculating.

Selfish calculations.

📝打小算盤或好為自己打算的意思。

2350　縮頭龜

suk¹ tau⁴ gwai¹ *(translit.)*

Shrinking-headed tortoise. (lit.)

A coward.

📝同作罵人語。比喻膽怯或懦弱的人。

十八畫

2351　鬆毛鬆翼

sung¹ mou⁴ sung¹ jik⁶ *(translit.)*

Slack both feathers and wings. (lit.)

Burst with joy.

Sing and dance for joy.

Be elated.

📝表示心花怒放，高興得載歌載舞或得
意洋洋的意思。

2352　騎牛搵馬

ke⁴ ngau⁴ wan² maa⁵ *(translit.)*

Ride a bull to look for a horse. (lit.)

**Seek for the better while holding
on to one.**

**Use one's present position as a
stepping stone.**

📝比喻保有目前手上的東西，另找一個
較好的或以目前的職位作基礎而另找
較高的職位。

2353　騎硫磺馬

ke⁴ lau⁴ wong⁴ maa⁵ *(translit.)*

Ride a sulphuric horse. (lit.)

**Divert somebody's money / public
funds to one's own purpose.**

📝把別人的錢財或公款據為己有的意
思。

2354　舊底

gau⁶ dai² *(translit.)*

Old bottom. (lit.)

Formerly.

In the past.

Once upon a time.

📝即從前，以前或過去的意思。

2355　舊時

gau⁶ si²⸍⁴ *(translit.)*

Old time. (lit.)

📝同〝舊底〞（2354）。

2356　擺到明

baai² dou³ ming⁴ *(translit.)*

Clearly display. (lit.)

Expose one's intention.

**Make a display of someone's
purpose.**

Show one's card on the table.
Wear one's heart on one's sleeve.

⓳ 指把意圖或目的開誠佈公地擺出來
或流露出來，參閱 "開心見誠" 條
（1894）。

2357　擺明車馬

baai² ming⁴ geoi¹ maa⁵ *(translit.)*
Openly set out the chariots and horses. (lit.)
Before somebody's very eyes.
Play fair and square.

⓳ 參閱 "明刀明槍" 條（1061）及 "開
明車馬" 條（1896）。

2358　擺烏龍

baai² wu¹ lung² *(translit.)*
Display a black dragon. (lit.)
Make a mistake.
Confuse A with B.
Confuse black and white.

⓳ 弄錯或搞誤會的意思。

2359　擺款

baai² fun² *(translit.)*
Put up the style. (lit.)
Put on airs.
Give oneself airs.

⓳ 擺架子。

2360　櫃桶底穿

gwai⁶ tung² dai² cyun¹ *(translit.)*
The bottom of the drawer is punctured. (lit.)
The funds of the shop / store / company...are embezzled / misappropriated.

⓳ 店舖／公司的款項被人侵吞或挪用，
參閱 "穿櫃桶底" 條（1295）。

2361　轉死性

zyun³ sei² sing³ *(translit.)*

Change the nature to death. (lit.)
Turn oneself into a person of different nature.
Suddenly change one's disposition.
Suddenly change one's tune.

⓳ 指性情改變或態度轉變（尤指在愛好
上忽然有較明顯的改變）。

2362　轉吓眼

zyun²ʹ³ haa⁵ ngaan⁵ *(translit.)*
Turn eyes for once. (lit.)
Like winking.
In a wink.

⓳ 即一轉眼，轉瞬之間的意思，和 "斬
吓眼" 同，參閱該條（2274）。

2363　轉軚

zyun³ taai⁵ *(translit.)*
Turn the steer. (lit.)
Change one's mind.
Make a change of heart.
Make a change in...

⓳ 改變主意。

2364　轉膊

zyun³ bok³ *(translit.)*
Change to another shoulder. (lit.)
Make an appropriate adaption.
Accommodate oneself to...
Be flexible.

⓳ 隨機應變的意思。

2365　躓直

gwaan³ zik⁶ *(translit.)*
Stumble flat. (lit.)
Be completely defeated.
Meet a lost cause.

⓳ 比喻已告失敗。

2366　歸根到底

gwai¹ gan¹ dou³ dai² *(translit.)*

Come back to the roots. (lit.)

In the last analysis.

In the end.

Reverting to the origin.

2367　翻抄

faan¹ caau¹ *(translit.)*

Re-copy. (lit.)

Reproduce.

注 再製，再生或複製的意思。

2368　翻炒

faan¹ caau² *(translit.)*

Fry again. (lit.)

Repeat.

Reproduce.

Reprint.

注 即重複，重影，重演或重印。

2369　翻渣茶葉 —— 冇釐味道

faan¹ zaa¹ caa⁴ jip⁶ — mou⁵ lei⁴ mei⁶ dou⁶ *(translit.)*

Infused tea leaves — they have not a bit of taste. (lit.)

Be as insipid as water.

注 比喻飲料淡而無味。

2370　翻閹

faan¹ jim¹ *(translit.)*

Be castrated again. (lit.)

Sing the same old tune.

Do the old job once again.

Stage a comeback.

注 比喻 "重操舊業"，"東山再起"。

2371　雞手鴨腳

gai¹ sau² aap³ goek³ *(translit.)*

Hen's hands and duck's legs. (lit.)

One's fingers are all thumbs.

Have two left feet.

注 笨手笨腳，或毛手毛腳的意思，參閱 "十指孖埋"（0101）條。

2372　雞仔媒人

gai¹ zai² mui⁴ jan⁴ *(translit.)*

A match-maker for chickens. (lit.)

A nosy intermediator.

注 指愛多管閒事的人。

2373　雞春咁密都褸出仔

gai¹ ceon¹ gam³ mat⁶ dou¹ bou⁶ ceot¹ zai² *(translit.)*

Though eggs are so dense, they can be hatched chickens. (lit.)

No secret can be kept.

The cat will at last be let out of the bag.

注 比喻秘密終會泄漏。

2374　雞春摸過都輕四兩

gai¹ ceon¹ mo¹ gwo³ dou¹ heng¹ sei³ loeng² *(translit.)*

The egg that is touched by somebody becomes four taels lighter. (lit.)

Do damage to whatever somebody handles.

Take some small gains out of whatever somebody deals with.

注 指責人用過的東西必受損害或無論經 手做甚麼也要佔點便宜。

2375　雞食放光蟲 —— 心知肚明

gai¹ sik⁶ fong³ gwong¹ cung⁴ — sam¹ zi¹ tou⁵ ming⁴ *(translit.)*

A hen eats the worm that glistens — its heart knows and belly understands. (lit.)

Have a clear mind.

Know what is what.

注 比喻心中知道得一清二楚。

2376　雞啄唔斷

gai¹ doeng¹ m⁴ tyun⁵ *(translit.)*

Cannot be cut off by the beak of a

hen. *(lit.)*

Talk somebody's ear off.

Rattle on without stopping.

注 不停地説話的意思。

2377 雞屙尿 —— 少有 / 少見

gai¹ o¹ niu⁶ — siu² jau⁵ / siu² gin³
(translit.)

Chickens pass urine — this doesn't exist / it is seldom seen. (lit.)

Seldom or never.

Rarely.

Be seldom seen. / Once in a blue moon.

注 表示少有或罕見的意思。

2378 雞噉腳

gai¹ gam² goek³ *(translit.)*

Be like hens' legs. (lit.)

Be fleet of foot.

Show leg.

Take to one's legs.

Walk at a good pace.

注 諷刺人聞風先逃或急急忙忙走路。

2379 雞髀打人牙骹軟

gai¹ bei² daa² jan⁴ ngaa⁴ gaau³ jyun⁵
(translit.)

A hen's leg beats a man's jaws soft. (lit.)

Beat a dog with a bone and it will not howl.

Serve him with nice food and the contention will cease.

Grease the palm of his and you will be able to make a convenience of him.

注 表示以利益相誘對方，行事無往而不利的意思。

2380 獵狗終須山上喪

lip⁶ gau² zung¹ seoi¹ saan¹ soeng⁶

song³ *(translit.)*

A hunting dog will at last die in the mountain. (lit.)

He who plays with fire will get burned at last.

A great swimmer is likely to meet his fate in the water.

注 表示善騎者死於馬的意思。

2381 雜崩嘸

zaap⁶ bang¹ nang¹ *(translit.)*

Assorted things. (lit.)

Odds and ends of miscellaneous things.

注 相當於 "雜八湊兒"。

2382 繞起

kiu² hei² *(translit.)*

Wind up. (lit.)

Beat somebody.

注 參閱 "臘起" 條（2394），意為 "難倒"。

2383 斷市

tyun⁵ si⁵ *(translit.)*

Break the market. (lit.)

Be out of stock.

Be sold out.

注 脱銷。

2384 斷估

dyun³ gu² *(translit.)*

Depend on an estimation. (lit.)

By guess and by gosh.

Make a wild guess.

注 表示瞎猜，瞎矇。

2385 斷尾

tyun⁵ mei⁵ *(translit.)*

Cut the tail. (lit.)

Effect a thoroughgoing cure.

Be thoroughly cured.

十八畫

注表示徹底醫好（疾病），不再復發。相當於"除根兒"。

2386　斷窮根

tyun⁵ kung⁴ gan¹ *(translit.)*

Break up the roots of poverty. (lit.)

Strike oil.

Not to live in poverty any more.

注表示一朝發達或生活不再窮困的意思。

十九　畫

2387　藤扔瓜，瓜扔藤

tang⁴ lang³ gwaa¹, gwaa¹ lang³ tang⁴ *(translit.)*

A melon hangs on the vine and the vine winds round and round the melon. (lit.)

Get entangled with each other.

An entangled affair.

注指互相糾纏不清或糾纏不清的事。

2388　難兄難弟

naan⁴ hing¹ naan⁴ dai⁶ *(translit.)*

Difficult elder brother and difficult younger brother. (lit.)

Be in the same boat.

Be in the same box.

Fellow sufferers.

Two of a kind.

注比喻處境相同或同患難，但亦比喻同流合污的人。

2389　蟻多摟死象

ngai⁵ do¹ lau¹ sei² zoeng⁶ *(translit.)*

Too many ants can swarm an elephant to death. (lit.)

Union gives strength.

The united efforts of the masses can fight for the accomplishment of the purpose.

注比喻團結就是力量。

2390　羅通掃北

Lo⁴ Tung¹ sou³ bak¹ *(translit.)*

Lo Tung (an ancient warrior's name) swept the north. (lit.)

Make a clean sweep of everything.

Finish all the dish on the table.

Sweep the board.

注以歷史人物的事件來比喻一掃而光或諧喻把桌上食物吃個精光。

2391　穩打穩紮

wan² daa² wan² zaat³ *(translit.)*

Be staid to fight and to take root. (lit.)

Go ahead steadily and strike sure blows.

Play safe.

Take no risk.

注指求穩或不冒險，參閱"揼/撳地游水"條（1961）。

2392　穩如鐵塔

wan² jyu⁴ tit³ taap³ *(translit.)*

As firm as an iron pagoda. (lit.)

Be as firm as it is founded on the rock.

Be secure against assult.

Be sure of success.

注比喻"固若金湯"，但亦喻"肯定成功"。

2393　穩陣

wan² zan⁶ *(translit.)*

Be firm enough. (lit.)

Steady.

Stable.

Safe / reliable.

Staid / Sede.

注 穩當，安全可靠的（物）或穩重的
（人）。

2394 臘起

laap[6] hei[2] *(translit.)*

Cure up. (lit.)

Beat somebody.

Baffle somebody.

注 參閱"繞起"條（2382）。

2395 識人眉頭眼額

sik[1] jan[4] mei[4] tau[4] ngaan[5] ngaak[6]
(translit.)

*Know somebody's brows, eyes
and forehead. (lit.)*

Be good at knowing somebody's
intentions.

Be quick at understanding what
somebody intends to do.

注 表示善解人意。

2396 懵盛盛

mung[2] sing[6] sing[6] *(translit.)*

Be muddled. (lit.)

Have a thick skull.

Be ignorant.

Sheer ignorance of something.

Have no inkling as to the real
cause.

注 懵懵懂懂；糊裏糊塗；對事實真相一
無所知。

2397 懵懵閉 / 懵閉閉

mung[2] mung[2] bai[3] / mung[2] bai[3] bai[3]
(translit.)

Be muddled. (lit.)

注 同"懵盛盛"（2396）。

2398 懶人多屎尿

laan[5] jan[4] do[1] si[2] niu[6] *(translit.)*

*A lazy person has more manure
and urine. (lit.)*

A lazybones cooks up more lame
excuses.

注 相當於"懶驢上磨屎尿多"，意指懶
人諸多藉口拒絕做事或拖拉。

2399 懶佬工夫

laan[5] lou[2] gung[1] fu[1] *(translit.)*

A lazy man's work. (lit.)

The work that saves labour.

注 容易做的工作；不費功夫的工作。

2400 關人

gwaan[1] jan[4] *(translit.)*

It doesn't concern me. (lit.)

None of my business.

There is nothing to do with me.

I won't concern myself with it.

I take no interest in it.

注 這為第一人稱説的口頭語，意為與我
無關或我不願過問此事。

2401 繡花枕頭

sau[3] faa[1] zam[2] tau[4] *(translit.)*

An embroidered pillow. (lit.)

All that glitters is not gold.

Ginger bread.

注 比喻華而不實的人或物。

廿 畫

2402 蘇州屎

sou[1] zau[1] si[2] *(translit.)*

Sou Zau manure. (lit.)

The trouble left behind.

注 比喻遺下的麻煩。

2403 蘇州過後冇艇搭

sou[1] zau[1] gwo[3] hau[6] mou[5] teng[5]

廿
畫

daap³ *(translit.)*

There is not a sampan to take beyond Sou Zau. (lit.)

The opportunity once missed will never come back.

🈯表示失去的機會，永不再來。

2404　鹹魚

haam⁴ jyu² *(translit.)*

Salted fish. (lit.)

Corpse.

🈯比喻死屍。

2405　鹹魚番生

haam⁴ jyu⁴ faan¹ saang¹ *(translit.)*

A salt-fish restored to life. (lit.)

The person falling into disgrace comes to fame again.

Rehabilitate oneself.

🈯比喻失去財勢的人重獲地位。

2406　鹹龍

haam⁴ lung² *(translit.)*

Salty dragon. (lit.)

Hongkong dollar / money.

Hongkong currency.

🈯指港幣。（民國初期未把白銀收歸國有前，市面的通貨，仍沿用前清鑄造的雙毫，面值為二毫，幣之一面，刻有龍紋，俗稱為龍毫。“龍”因此喻作貨幣，香港為鹹水地區，“鹹龍”因而得名。）

2407　鹹濕

haam⁴ sap¹ *(translit.)*

Salty and wet. (lit.)

Be salacious / bawdy.

🈯（指書，畫，言談等）誨淫的，猥褻的，下流的，黃色的；（指人）好色的。

2408　獻世

hin³ sai³ *(translit.)*

Offer oneself to bear hardship. (lit.)

Be penanced for one's ill deeds.

🈯表示因曾做壞事而被上蒼懲罰以捱苦行贖罪的意思。

2409　獻醜不如藏拙

hin³ cau² bat¹ jyu⁴ cong⁴ zeot³ *(translit.)*

Showing one's weak points is not so good as hiding one's ignorance. (lit.)

It is wiser to conceal one's stupidity than it is to show oneself up.

🈯寧願不讓人知道自己的無知，也不要將短處暴露人前。

2410　糯米屎窟

no⁶ mai⁵ si² fat¹ *(translit.)*

Glutinous rice hips. (lit.)

A visitor who sticks like a bur.

A visitor who overstays his welcome.

🈯謔喻賴着捨不得告辭的客人。

2411　瀟湘

siu¹ soeng¹ *(translit.)*

As delicate as a bamboo. (lit.)

Be slim.

Have a slim figure.

🈯比喻女性秀氣，身材苗條。

廿一畫

2412　趯更

dek³ gaang¹ *(translit.)*

Run away. (lit.)

Desert.

Show a clean pair of heels.

Take to one's legs.

廿一畫

Make away./Make away with...
Run away.

🈲開小差；逃跑；逃命。參閱"走路"
（0852）條。

2413 霸揸

baa³ ngaa⁶ *(translit.)*
Lord over. (lit.)
Be despotic.
Play the bully.
Seek hegemony.

🈲即霸道。

2414 露出馬腳

lou⁶ ceot¹ maa⁵ goek³ *(translit.)*
Expose a horse's leg. (lit.)
Give the show away.
Show the cloven foot.

🈲不留意暴露出弱點，秘密或罪行等等
的意思。

2415 鐵沙梨──咬唔入

tit³ saa¹ lei² ─ ngaau⁵ m⁴ jap⁶ *(translit.)*
*A russet pear made of iron ─ It
cannot be bitten. (lit.)*
**A person from whom nobody can
obtain any profit.**
A great miser.
Be very stingy.

🈲從歇後語"咬唔入"來解釋，意為"任
何人無法從他身上得到好處的人"，
但亦同時喻非常吝嗇的人。相當於
"鐵公雞──一毛不拔"。

2416 鐵杵磨成針

tit³ cyu⁵ mo⁴ sing⁴ zam¹ *(translit.)*
*An iron pillar can be ground into a
needle. (lit.)*
Little strokes fell great oaks.
Intestinal fortitude will prevail.

🈲表示堅穩終能成功的意思。

2417 鐵嘴雞

tit³ zeoi² gai¹ *(translit.)*
An iron-beaked hen. (lit.)
**A lady with a silver and bitter
tongue.**

🈲比喻口才流利，嘴很厲害的女人。

2418 鐸叔

dok⁶ suk¹ *(translit.)*
Uncle Dok. (lit.)
A niggard.
A miser.

🈲對"吝嗇鬼"的稱呼。

2419 爛口

laan⁶ hau² *(translit.)*
Rotten mouth. (lit.)
Obscene language.
Be foul-mouthed.

🈲下流話；愛講下流話。

2420 爛市

laan⁶ si⁵ *(translit.)*
Rotten market. (lit.)
Be unsalable.
Be dull of sale.

🈲表示賣不掉，滯銷。

2421 爛尾

laan⁶ mei⁵ *(translit.)*
Rotten tail. (lit.)
**Be irresponsible for what one
should do.**
Give up half-way.
Leave one's work unfinished.
**Not to go on with one's work to
the end.**

🈲相當於"拆爛污"或半途而廢。

2422 爛泥扶唔上壁

laan⁶ nai⁴ fu⁴ m⁴ soeng⁵ bik³ *(translit.)*
Thin mud cannot be put on to the

廿一畫

wall. *(lit.)*

Be good-for-nothing.

A silk purse cannot be made out of sow's ears.

Be not worthy to be favoured.

No pillars are made out of decayed timbers.

🈁形容人低能，不堪造就的意思。

2423　爛鬥爛

laan⁶ dau³ laan⁶ *(translit.)*

Being rotten for being rotten. (lit.)

Give tit for tat.

Give stick for stick and carrot for carrot.

🈁表示以打對打，以拉對拉，針鋒相對，一報還一報。

2424　爛笪笪

laan⁶ daat³ daat³ *(translit.)*

Rotten to the core. (lit.)

Be unbridled.

Make no scruple.

Throw all restraints to the wind.

🈁形容人放肆，無所顧忌，或稀巴爛的意思。

2425　爛船拆埋都有三斤釘

laan⁶ syun⁴ caak³ maai⁴ dou¹ jau⁵ saam¹ gan¹ deng¹ *(translit.)*

There are three catties of nails left when a ship is disassembled. (lit.)

Even the wrecks of a boat are still of some surplus value.

🈁比喻有錢人雖破產，但比窮人還是有錢（或有辦法）。相當於 "船破有底"。

2426　爛頭蟀

laan⁶ tau⁴ zeot¹ *(translit.)*

A broken-headed cricket. (lit.)

A person who cares for nothing.

A person who works for somebody without regard to his own life.

🈁比喻破罐破摔，無所顧忌的人或為人賣命的人。

2427　竈君上天——有嗰句講嗰句

zou³ gwan¹ soeng⁵ tin¹ — jau⁵ go² geoi³ gong² go² geoi³ *(translit.)*

Kitchen god goes up to heaven — he says the sentences he has in his mind. (lit.)

Say what one has to say.

🈁有甚麼說甚麼的意思。

2428　顧／因住

gu³／jan¹ zyu⁶ *(translit.)*

Be careful. (lit.)

Take care of oneself.

Restrain oneself.

Control one's emotion.

Not to exceed the limit.

Beware of one's life.

Take one's life into account.

🈁即留心，小心，抑制感情，作有限度的使用，或警告人當心⋯⋯性命。

2429　顧得頭嚟／來腳反筋

gu³ dak¹ tau⁴ lai⁴／loi⁴ goek³ faan² gan¹ *(translit.)*

While caring for the head, the leg becomes spastic. (lit.)

Attend to one thing and neglect another.

Aim at another bird in the bush and the one in hand is choked.

Cannot take care of so many things at the same time.

🈁顧此失彼的意思。

廿一畫

廿二 畫

2430 攤直
taan¹ zik⁶ *(translit.)*
Lie straight. (lit.)
Have met with one's death.
Have fallen flat.
注 已經死去的詼諧説法，參閱 "瓜直" 條（0567）。

2431 攤凍至嚟食
taan¹ dung³ zi³ lai⁴ sik⁶ *(translit.)*
Wait till it is cold and then eat it.
(lit.)
It is unnecessary to make haste to enjoy the prey.
Have taken a firm hold of something.
注 表示已掌握中，不必急於……的意思。

2432 攤攤腰
taan¹ taan¹ jiu¹ *(translit.)*
With a straightened backbone. (lit.)
To an unbearable degree.
To the state of fatigue.
To an extent of disability to stand up again.
In a situation of complete defeat.
注 這是用表達程度的口頭禪，例如説，"做嘢做到我～"，"佢俾人打到～"，"熱到我～" 或 "餓到我～" 等等。用處甚廣，意義不同，大致言之，不外到了難忍的程度，到了疲倦已極的地步，到了沒法站得住腳的地步或到了慘敗的地步等。

2433 攞豆
lo² dau² *(translit.)*

Get beans. (lit.)
Meet one's fate.
Go west.
Come to an untimely end.
注 比喻死亡。

2434 攞命
lo² meng⁶ *(translit.)*
Take away the life. (lit.)
Ride one to death.
注 即要命。

2435 攞便宜
lo² pin⁴ ji²/⁴ *(translit.)*
Make a joke. (lit.)
Jolly with somebody to amuse oneself.
Take somebody at advantage to make a pass at her.
Seek undue advantage.
注 表示跟人開玩笑以自娛；對婦女非禮，討便宜。

2436 攞朝唔得晚
lo² ziu¹ m⁴ dak¹ maan⁵ *(translit.)*
What is earned in the morning is not sufficient for the evening.
(lit.)
Live from hand to mouth.
Be unable to make both ends meet.
注 現掙現吃或收支不相抵的生活狀況。

2437 攞景
lo² ging² *(translit.)*
Angle a camera. (lit.)
Say / Do something to enrage somebody during his disappointment.
注 這本為攝影時找鏡頭的一種動作，後來轉義為趁人家失意，説或做一些事來氣他。

廿二畫

2438　攞景定贈興（慶）？

lo² ging² ding⁶ zang⁶ hing³ *(translit.)*

Do you give trouble or help in the fun? (lit.)

Do you make a mock or add trouble?

🈲當甲在失意或處於不幸時，而乙做些事或説些話觸怒了他，甲便會説，"你究竟攞景定贈慶？"意思即是説"你嘲笑抑或增加麻煩？"。

2439　攞膽

lo² daam² *(translit.)*

Take away the gall. (lit.)

Take away one's life.

Ride somebody to death.

🈲即"要命"的意思。參閱"攞命"條（2434）。

Awfully.

Extremely.

🈲作程度副詞用，例如"熱到～"，或"咳到～"，意為極，很，非常。

What a bad luck!

What a nuisance!

🈲用作感歎詞，但通常説成"真攞膽"，意為"真不幸！"或"多麼的討厭！"。

2440　攞嚟衰

lo² lai⁴ seoi¹ *(translit.)*

Make oneself decline. (lit.)

Bring disgrace on oneself.

Lay the blame on oneself.

🈲即自找麻煩；自討苦吃。

2441　攞嚟賤

lo² lai⁴ zin⁶ *(translit.)*

Make oneself cheap. (lit.)

Make a rod for one's back.

Work for one's destruction.

🈲表示自找麻煩或自暴自棄的意思。

2442　聽落有骨

teng¹ lok⁶ jau⁵ gwat¹ *(translit.)*

There is a bone in the hearing. (lit.)

More is meant than meets the ear.

🈲指某人的話，實在另有言外之意。

2443　聽話

teng¹ waa⁶ *(translit.)*

Listen to saying. (lit.)

Be obedient.

Be subordinate to...

🈲表示服從的意思。

2444　聽價唔聽斗

teng¹ gaa³ m⁴ teng¹ dau² *(translit.)*

Listen to the price but not to the unit of dry measure for grain. (lit.)

Care for whether the price is cheap or high but neglect the quality or quantity.

🈲意指只顧價錢貴賤，不理所購的東西的質量。

2445　聽講話……

teng¹ gong² waa⁶... *(translit.)*

Hear speaking. (lit.)

Be told that...

Hear that...

🈲即聽説……

2446　鑒粗

gaam³ cou¹ *(translit.)*

Act insistently. (lit.)

By force.

Make forcible demand for...

Do something with violence / by force.

Do something at one's insistence.

🈲參閱"鑒硬"條（2447）。

廿二畫

2447　鑒硬

gaam³ ngaang² *(translit.)*
Act by force. (lit.)

Make forcible demand for...
Force-feed somebody to...
Act blindly / recklessly.

注 "鑒粗" 和 "鑒硬" 同樣表示硬來，蠻幹。

2448　疊埋心水（緒）

dip⁶ maai⁴ sam¹ seoi² *(translit.)*
Fold up the mind. (lit.)

Not to think oneself into a
dilemma any more.

注 表示專心致志，集中精神，不胡思亂
想的意思。

2449　囉唆

lo¹ so¹ *(translit.)*
Speak too much. (lit.)

Be long-winded.
Be wordy.
Talk the hind leg off a donkey.

注 即嘮叨。

2450　囉囉攣

lo¹ lo¹ lyun¹ *(translit.)*
Be anxious about this and that. (lit.)

Be restless with anxiety.
Be anxiety-ridden.

注 表示焦躁不安或憂心忡忡的意思。

2451　籠裏雞作反

lung⁴ leoi⁵ gai¹ zok³ faan² *(translit.)*
The chickens in the same bamboo-
cage rebel against each other.
(lit.)

Have an internal dissension.

注 即內鬨。

2452　讀壞詩書包壞腳

duk⁶ waai⁶ si¹ syu¹ baau¹ waai⁶ goek³
(translit.)

Badly read poems and books and
badly wrapped the feet. (lit.)

Be not understanding and
considerate.
Be pedantic.
Be learned but
immoral / shameless.

注 諷刺人迂腐或不通情理。如果説時帶
有輕蔑語氣時，則指人文而無行了。

廿三　畫

2453　攬住一齊死

laam² zyu⁶ jat¹ cai⁴ sei² *(translit.)*
Embrace together to die. (lit.)

End in common ruin.

注 比喻同歸於盡。

2454　攬頭攬頸

laam² tau⁴ laam² geng² *(translit.)*
Embrace necks and heads. (lit.)

Be on intimate terms with each
other.
Be as close as lips to teeth.

注 比喻彼此相好。

2455　驚住會⋯⋯

geng¹ zyu⁶ wui⁵... *(translit.)*
Fear that... (lit.)

Feel anxious that...
Be afraid that...

注 即擔心會⋯⋯的意思。

2456　驚青

geng¹ ceng¹ *(translit.)*
Give oneself a scare. (lit.)

Be in a flurry manner.
Run scared.
Be flustered.
Be all in a fluster.

廿三畫

注 慌張，驚慌失措的意思。

2457 攪手

gaau² sau² *(translit.)*

A hand of stir. (lit.)

A sponsor.

注 即發起人或主辦者。

2458 攪出個大頭鬼 / 佛

gaau² ceot¹ go³ daai⁶ tau⁴ gwai² / fat⁶ *(translit.)*

Make out a big-headed ghost / Buddha. (lit.)

Put all the fat in the fire.

Scale something up.

注 比喻把事情搞糟或把事情擴大了。

2459 攪風攪雨

gaau² fung¹ gaau² jyu⁵ *(translit.)*

Give a stir to both wind and rain. (lit.)

Stir up troubles.

Make trouble.

注 製造紛亂或搗蛋的意思，前義參閱 "掘尾龍" 條（1581）及 "煽風點火" 條（2118）。

2460 攪屎棍

gaau² si² gwan³ *(translit.)*

A club for stirring up manure. (lit.)

The person who stirs up trouble / strife / hatred.

The person who fans the flame.

Play somebody off against one another.

Stir up the dirt.

Make a mountain out of a molehill.

注 比喻愛挑撥離間，搬弄是非的人，愛出壞主意搗亂的人或愛小題大做的行為。

2461 齙牙哵爪

ji¹ ngaa⁴ baang⁶ zaau² *(translit.)*

Show teeth and spread out arms. (lit.)

Be elated at something.

Laugh a hearty laugh.

注 指高興到咧嘴大笑，這話有人說成 "齙牙哵齒"（ji¹ ngaa⁴ baang⁶ ci²）或 "齙牙鬆肮"（ji¹ ngaa⁴ sung¹ gong⁶）。

2462 曬命

saai³ meng⁶ *(translit.)*

Dry one's own life in the sun. (lit.)

Cry up one's own fortune.

Crow over one's own life.

Sing one's own glorious song.

注 誇耀自己良好際遇的意思。

2463 變卦

bin³ gwaa³ *(translit.)*

Change trigrams. (lit.)

Change one's mind.

Retract one's promise.

Go back on one's words.

Break an agreement.

注 改變主意，毀約或不遵守諾言；已定的事忽然改變。

廿四畫

2464 鹽倉土地 —— 鹹夾濕

jim⁴ cong¹ tou² dei² — haam⁴ gaap³ sap¹ *(translit.)*

The local god of soil in a salt storehouse — He is salty and wet. (lit.)

Be salacious.

A luster.

A man of a bawdy disposition.

注 比喻好色之徒。

廿四畫

2465　靈神不用多致燭，好鼓不用多槌

ling⁴ san⁴ bat¹ jung⁶ do¹ zi³ zuk¹, hou²
gu² bat¹ jung⁶ do¹ ceoi⁴ *(translit.)*

*Neither put too many candlesticks
to offer an efficacious god nor
strike too many strokes on a
good drum. (lit.)*

**Put a word to the wise. / A word
is enough to the wise.**

注 表示智者一言已足的意思。

2466　蠶蟲師爺

caam⁴ cung² si¹ je⁴ *(translit.)*

A silkworm private adviser. (lit.)

**A person who is caught in his
own trap.**

**A person who gets enmeshed in
his own web.**

注 即作繭自縛的人。

2467　躝屍

laan¹ si¹ *(translit.)*

Let your corpse creep away! (lit.)

Scram!

Get out!

Beat it!

Get out of my sight!

注 相當於滾蛋。用於驅逐對方時的一種
喝令句，但通常又說成"躝屍趷路！"
或"趷路"。參閱該相關條目（2468）
及（1438）。

2468　躝屍趷路

laan¹ si¹ gat⁶ lou⁶ *(translit.)*

You corpse, crawl away! (lit.)

Scram!

Get out!

Beat it!

Get out of my sight!

注 斥責或罵人的話，即滾蛋。參閱
1438"趷路"及2467"躝屍"各條。

廿五　畫

2469　籮底橙

lo⁴ dai² caang² *(translit.)*

*The orange at the bottom of a
bamboo basket. (lit.)*

**The girl / article of nobody's
choice.**

A left-over.

A person of low level.

The article of poor quality.

注 比喻無人願娶的女子，無人要的東
西，剩下的人或物，水平低的人或質
量不好的東西等。

廿八　畫

2470　攍唔番

maang¹ m⁴ faan¹ *(translit.)*

Fail to drag back. (lit.)

Be incorrigible.

Be incurable.

Be beyond remedy.

注 無法糾正，無可救藥，或無可補救的
意思。

2471　攍攍緊

maang¹ maang¹ gan² *(translit.)*

Be tightly mounted. (lit.)

Be in straitened circumstances.

Scarcely make both ends meet.

Be out at elbows.

注 生活貧困，收支僅能相抵或甚至捉襟
見肘的情形。

2472　鑿大

zok[6] daai[6] *(translit.)*

Chisel big. (lit.)

Make an exaggerated report.

Make an overstatement.

Overstate something.

📖 誇大，言過其實的意思。

Stroke Index
筆畫索引

筆畫索引

筆畫索引

筆畫索引

筆畫索引

Jyutping Index
拼音索引

拼音索引

拼音索引

拼音索引

拼音索引

拼音索引

拼音索引

拼音索引

拼音索引

拼音索引

拼音索引

拼音索引

拼音索引

拼音索引